Merry Little Matchmas

Four Haunted Holiday Novellas

CHANEL SCHWARTZ

JESSICA KRUEGER

EMELIA STONEFIELD

CASSANDRA TREVELLE

Last Christmas

Chanel Schwartz

1

Nic

"WELL, IF IT isn't Saint Nic! Hope you haven't been here long, kiddo."

"Happy Thanksgiving, Eugene!" I gave the elderly funicular operator my warmest, definitely-not-freezing-my-butt-off smile. The night air had the sharp bite of coming frost, and I'd been waiting on the platform in Summer Springs far longer than I would ever admit. It was silly of me to assume the funicular would be running on its usual half-hour schedule on a holiday. I hadn't seen a single soul in the hour I'd spent waiting for the short trip up to the Bryson House Hotel.

"I was sitting up at Jo's Diner having a slice of pumpkin pie when this guy—" he nodded toward the passenger compartment "— came and told me you might be waiting."

I only knew one relentlessly over-protective person who would drag a sweet old man away from his pie on my behalf.

"You should have called, Nicola Louise Winters." The sound of the hotel manager's deep voice made my heart tip over like a snow globe and right itself in a chaotic swirl of sparkles.

West strode toward me, his long gait entirely unhurried. I put a fist on my hip in an attempt to look stern—a bold feat for a five-foot-two woman in glittery gold sneakers and matching nail polish. "*You* should have called, Westley Ross Schafer. I thought you were at your mom's and David's for the holiday. And I knew Eugene would make his way down here eventually."

West hummed in noncommittal acknowledgement and reached for the handle of my suitcase. I protested, but he rolled it out of reach. "I've got it, Princess."

I scowled at the old nickname. A teen girl refuses to pee in the woods *one* time. I had my period! There were bears, probably! "I can roll my own bag, West."

"You can," he said as he walked onto the funicular with my bag in tow.

I hmphed and followed. "Did you ride all the way down here just to get a jump start on being an overbearing jerk?"

West smiled at me over his shoulder. It was spiced cider. Mulled wine. A perfect Manhattan. His smile warmed me from the inside out. "No," he said simply, tone laced with decades of affection, and reached for me. "Come here."

Slipping into West's embrace was like slipping into a well-loved sweater. His arms tightened around my shoulders, and he rested his cheek on the crown of my head, relaxing into me on a long exhale. "Missed you."

I squeezed his middle and sighed inside, relieved we were apparently going to ignore the awkwardness of our last encounter. He smelled like fresh forest air, wood smoke, and something herbal. Sage, maybe? "Missed you, too," I mumbled into his warm wool coat. "How'd you know I was waiting down here?"

West's short laugh vibrated through me. "I'll give you one guess."

I smiled to myself. Ghosts.

A bell chimed twice inside the funicular, and the doors began to fold closed, the old hinges complaining about the effort. West and I let go of each other and settled on a wooden bench facing the village.

West reached down to the floor and turned back to me with two to-go cups from the diner. I perked up with a gasp of delight and enthusiastically reached for the hot drink. Jo made the best peppermint hot chocolate. "Jo sends her love. And she says you owe her a big hug as compensation."

"I'll visit her tomorrow." I took a sip and tried not to frown as the bitter taste of coffee slid across my tongue. It was too late for caffeine, and my holiday decorating was scheduled to start way too early for me to be up all night. But it was still an incredibly sweet gesture. I wrapped my hands appreciatively around the warm cup to thaw my frozen fingers.

West took a drink from his cup, hummed his disapproval, then passed it to me, easing the coffee out of my grip. "Wrong one. You don't need to be up all night," he said, echoing my thoughts. My eyes bounced between West's for a second too long, and he looked away, pushing a hand through his blond hair. It had been so long, I'd forgotten how nice it was to be around people who knew what you wanted before you even asked.

The train's speakers crackled, and Eugene's tinny voice filled the carriage. "Next—and only—stop, Edith's Landing and the Bryson House Hotel."

The interior lights dimmed, the brakes hissed, and the funicular started its five-minute ascent. West nudged my foot with his. "Why were you down here?"

The question shouldn't have caught me off guard. Normally, I'd drive to the hotel. "My car's in the shop." It wasn't a complete lie. My car was getting tuned up and detailed so I could sell it. I wouldn't need it where I was moving.

"You should have called. You know I would have picked you up."

"I know you would have. I didn't want to pull you away from family." Also, I wasn't ready to explain why my house was nearly empty. I'd spent the last week moving my things into storage so the flooring could be replaced before I put the place on the market. Because I obviously wouldn't need the house where I was moving either.

West didn't know any of that yet, and he wasn't going to take it well. He wasn't a fan of change. I'd have to tell him eventually, but it could wait a little longer. I didn't want to suffer through a whole week of his not-mad-just-disappointed face.

"Call next time, Nic."

"I will. Wait, why are *you* here?" He arched one indignant blond eyebrow, and I rolled my eyes. "You know what I mean. You should be at your mom's, not at work."

He scrubbed a hand over the pale end-of-day scruff along his jaw with an audible rasp. "I hired Hunter for the night shift. Entirely unrelated, I've been covering a lot of night shifts." He gestured to his coffee with a self-deprecating look before taking a sip.

His cousin Hunter was a good guy, but not someone you'd ever describe as dependable, especially in contrast to responsible, reliable West. My old friend was dependable to a fault.

I cringed playfully and sucked a breath through my teeth. "You do look pretty tired."

The corner of his stern mouth quirked up. "Gee, thanks."

I popped the lid off my drink to lick the whipped cream before it all melted, and West shot me a sidelong glance. His small grunt didn't necessarily sound like disapproval, so I carried on with my juvenile endeavor. Not that his disapproval would have stopped me.

The village shrank beyond the cold glass, all of the individual street and house lights merging into one unified glow. When I was a kid, my mom would bring my brother and me here to ride up for the annual Christmas tree lighting. She'd buy us hot chocolate at Jo's, then we'd join the crowd and sing carols in joyful anticipation while we awaited that magical moment when the towering pine would finally light up.

The same towering tree and joyful anticipation that I was now responsible for.

I still loved riding up the hill in the dark, even if the memories had become bittersweet in the half a lifetime since my mom died, and downright melancholic since my brother Thom died two years ago.

I glanced over at West, only to find him already looking at me. Serious. Assessing. West knew all of the emotional baggage that accompanied me onto the funicular. I squeezed his knee and gave him a reassuring smile before looking back out over the village.

That first Christmas without my mom, I was a fragile fifteen-year-old, and West's mom invited my brother and me to ride up to the tree lighting with the Schafer clan.

In hindsight, I'd never seen them there before. My West radar was well-honed by then—I would have known if the boy I was hopelessly in love with was nearby. It wasn't their family's tradition, and it wasn't by coincidence that they decided to join in the festivities that year. Looking back, it was easy to see all the ways Julia Schafer covertly shoehorned some normalcy into my life those first few years, from big things like the tree lighting to the way she regularly seemed to just be "in the area" for my field hockey games.

The year after my mom died, my brother joined the Marines, West went off to college, and Julia picked me up from the house I shouldn't have been living in alone every week for Sunday dinner. She always sent me home with enough leftovers to get me through to the next Sunday dinner.

The woman earned her *World's Best Mom* mug.

West absentmindedly ran his thumb back and forth across the vertical seam of his to-go cup. I took one last lick of whipped cream and turned to him. "Did you get to spend any time at your mom's today?"

His lips twitched when he looked at me. "You've got whipped cream," he said, reaching over to swipe his thumb across the tip of my nose. Heat flooded through me. "I was there most of the day. My mom had me hauling dusty folding tables out of storage before I'd even finished my coffee. She sends her love, by the way, along with some good-natured nagging about not seeing you since Sarah's bachelorette party. Everyone missed you at the wedding."

My smile faltered, and I pushed past the flash of guilt. West's sisters, Sarah and Kira, had become good friends over the years. Sarah had even asked me to be one of her bridesmaids in August. But I'd started a new job as a site coordinator for the design team at a boutique hotel chain at the beginning of the year, and I didn't get much say in where they sent me or when. It was pure luck that I was on a job in Vegas during Sarah's bachelorette party, and got to at least celebrate with her there. "I hated missing it. But the time I blocked out to be here already exceeded my PTO for the year."

"That's what Sarah said."

I tried not to frown at his insinuation. "Did David do the smoked turkey again?"

West's eyes narrowed on me, but he let my deflection slide. "Yeah. My mom sent a plate for you."

"Aw, really? She's the best." My insides felt warm. And hungry. Dinner at my dad's parents' had been brief, underwhelming, and, as usual, my dad hadn't even bothered to show up. I couldn't blame him. The food was probably better at whatever bar he was holed up in. "Wait, if you're here, does that mean Hunter's still cozy at your mom's, enjoying the tryptophan afterglow?"

"Probably. He cracked open his fourth beer before the turkey was on the table, and I knew then I wasn't destined for an evening on the couch."

Selfishly, I silently thanked the cosmos for Hunter's poor decisions. Less selfishly, I was upset on West's behalf that he wasn't the one kicked back on the couch full of beer and turkey. And he really did look tired. The man had a bad habit of stoically carrying more than his fair share of any load. It was both admirable and irritating. He made himself responsible for everyone else's well-being, but rarely considered his own.

Which was one of the reasons I hadn't called him when the funicular hadn't shown up. He would have dropped everything at his mom's, almost an hour away, just to speed over and drive me up the hill. I wasn't about to pull him away from his Thanksgiving dinner. He deserved to have that time at home with his family.

That, and I had been nervous about our reunion. I thought West would be gone for the evening, and I'd have until the morning to prep myself mentally, but he went and tore that Band-Aid off without preamble. And everything seemed mostly okay between us.

Which was a miracle since the last time we were together, I idiotically, drunkenly propositioned him.

Rumors had been circulating around the hotel that the Bryson estate was set to be sold to an international hotel chain, which would likely mean the end of my contract as a holiday decorator. It was a disappointment, to say the least, but it fueled my poorly calculated decision to shoot my shot with West while I still had the opportunity. My boozed-up brain figured, what the heck, we could at least enjoy a little naked fun time together.

My boozed-up brain was wrong. As boozed-up brains tend to be.

I'd sauntered up to him at the hotel Christmas party, hooked my fingers into his belt loops, and suggested he and I ditch the party. He stared down at me in appalled disbelief, like I'd just asked him to invest his life savings in a multi-level marketing scheme, before telling me it was time to lay off the eggnog and drink some water.

The next day, I pretended like nothing had happened and joked about what a blur the whole evening was.

Obviously, the hotel wasn't sold, and I survived to decorate another year. But the rumor had already forced me to think about what my life would be like without the Bryson House. The possibility hurt more than I could have imagined. The place was a part of me. It was home.

So, I decided that this—my tenth year—would be my last year at the Bryson House Hotel. I wouldn't risk the heartbreak of being forced out in the future for reasons beyond my control. It was time to step away while it was still on my own terms.

But first, I was going to wring every last bit of joy out of my time here.

2

West

FUN FACT: I put that fourth beer in Hunter's hand.

He probably would have made the irresponsible choice all by himself, but I was too anxious to leave it up to fate. I needed the excuse to be at the hotel when Nic arrived. It had been an entire year since I'd seen her, and I desperately needed physical proof of life.

But she was here now. Safe and smiling and *here*. Finally.

"I've got you set up in a suite for the next week," I said to Nic, biting back a smirk as I pulled her suitcase off the back of the hotel golf cart.

She looked at me with thinly veiled panic, lip verging on a pout. "West."

"What? It took a little maneuvering since we're booked solid through the New Year, but I know how much you love the North Tower Sweetheart Suite."

Nic scoffed and whacked my arm with an eyeroll. "Oh yeah, you know I can't resist those parking lot views."

I swiveled her bag away when she reached for it and started toward the front doors. "Don't forget the mauve heart-shaped tub in the living room."

"Not mauve. Puce," she said, trailing behind me. "One letter off from puke."

For all the love Nic had for the Bryson House Hotel, she definitely preferred the rich historical buildings from the 1880s over the North Tower addition built in the 1980s. The style hadn't aged well.

Nic insisted on staying in the original servants' quarters, which now functioned as seasonal employee housing. She said she liked the quiet and was too busy decorating to appreciate a guest room. But at least she'd agreed to stay on site, rather than driving the hour home on icy roads in the dark every day.

I pulled open the hotel door and watched Nic's shoulders relax as she walked into the warm, wood-paneled lobby. She took in a deep breath and smiled softly at her surroundings before her attention was drawn up to the flickering chandelier. The fire surged behind the grate of the lobby's stone hearth, and the soft classical music switched from Beethoven to Burl Ives.

Nic grinned up at the light. "Aw, thanks for the warm welcome. It's good to be back."

She wasn't talking to me.

I spotted two guests waiting by the front desk, one with bare feet and an agitated look. Tell-tale signs of ghostly antics. "Looks like your ghostly greeting committee has been busy this evening. I need to go see how I can help those poor, tortured guests. I'll grab you the key to the suite."

The last thing I wanted to do was hand Nic her keys and say goodnight. I was still coming down from the near panic attack I'd had when she hadn't shown up on time, and I would have preferred to keep her right where I could see her for a bit longer.

Or for forever. "Any chance I can convince you to stay in a guest room this year?"

Nic arched one auburn eyebrow and held out her palm.

"Keys to the servants' quarters, good sir."

The barefooted guest had been locked out of his room. I made a show of trying to get the door open, but I knew full well I wouldn't be able to do jack shit about it. The ghosts were working their matchmaking magic, and heaven forbid they make things easy for me for one night.

I went through the motions of customer service—offering the man a new room, adding meal vouchers to his account, and refunding his room charge when he (unsurprisingly) opted to take the second bed in his friend's room. Even from my layman's perspective, there were palpable sparks between the two men, and it was entirely possible they'd come to the hotel hoping for some ghostly intervention to nudge their relationship forward.

I wished I could relate. The ghosts had been utterly useless in advancing my relationship with Nic.

"Success?" I asked the empty lobby once the men were out of earshot. My desk lamp flickered in confirmation.

The Bryson House Hotel didn't publicly own up to its ghosts or their rumored matchmaking. The ghosts made it clear that they would not be exploited for profit, following an ill-fated attempt to market their services in the 1930s. They went on strike, so to speak, and didn't make a single match for fifteen years.

However, in the modern age of social media and review sites, the rumors were out of our control. A few years ago, #mistletoemanor trended as the happily and hopefully matched started tagging the hotel, and the Christmas season exploded for us. The ghosts didn't seem to take issue with the organic growth, but the hotel's official stance on the subject remained one of feigned ignorance, just in case.

"Thanks for letting me know where Nic was." The lamp flickered, and I slumped back into my chair. The echoes of anxiety still had a grip on my neck and shoulders.

I pulled a string cheese from my messenger bag and chomped through it in two bites. When Nic hadn't shown up around the time I'd expected her, the shadows of my anxiety had started to creep in. It was irrational, I knew that. There were a dozen entirely logical reasons for her to run late. But ever since Thom, my best friend and Nic's brother, died two and a half years ago, I'd struggled to keep the darkness at bay.

Logically, I knew Nic had probably just stayed later than usual at her grandparents. Or she'd gone to run an errand before heading to the hotel. Maybe she'd stopped at Jo's. There were plenty of reasons to assume she was fine. Still, the darkness had me convinced she was dying in a ditch somewhere while I just sat around and did nothing to help.

Logically, I knew how unlikely that was. But logic becomes a simpering fool in the presence of paranoia.

In a moment of pseudo-clarity, I asked the ghosts to see if Nic was at Jo's, then followed Adelia Bryson's trail of blinking lights to Edith's Landing. She'd flashed the lights on the funicular platform, and then I'd spotted Eugene through the window of Jo's, just sitting at the counter, eating pie. I'd almost lost my shit.

I'd stared into the void the whole ride down the hill, letting the darkness convince me Nic wouldn't actually be waiting at the bottom—that I was wasting precious time when I should have been out on the road trying to save her before it was too late.

Now, in a moment of actual clarity, why hadn't I just picked up the fucking phone?

The darkness is a real asshole.

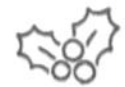

I took the narrow stairs up to the original servants' quarters two at a time. Soft light, quiet music, and warmth poured out of the open doorway. Too much warmth. The staircase got warmer as I neared the room, and was downright sweltering by the time I reached the top. The windows along the wall of the dorm-style room were all open, but the light breeze was doing very little to temper the heat.

I was about to knock on the door frame, but stopped short at the sight of Nic on the bottom bunk bed at the other end of the room, sprawled out on her stomach in red and green plaid sleep shorts and a tiny white top, her gaze intent on her laptop. I should have let her know I was there, but I stood in the doorway and watched her like an absolute fucking creeper instead.

Her suitcase was open on the unmade bed next to hers, with her shoes lined up neatly below the mattress and her iridescent puffy coat hanging from the corner of the top bunk. Her binders and clipboards and schedules were already neatly laid out on the small desk.

She looked like a dream in the warm glow of her bedside lamp. I could have stood there for hours, just watching her work. But then I started to think about some actual creeper leering at her from the doorway, and with a surge of protective anger, I knocked on the doorframe more aggressively than I'd meant to.

Nic yelped and quickly sat up on her knees, the lines of her muscles strung tight, ready to spring into action. Her quick response and defensive stance made me feel a little better, but some perv wouldn't have offered the courtesy of a knock to warn her he was there.

"You scared the crud out of me," she huffed, relaxing back onto her heels. My gaze followed her hand to her sternum, where she rubbed her palm over her heart, between her barely contained cleavage. And holy fuck did I desperately want to taste every inch of that creamy freckled skin.

My reptile brain chimed in to remind me that I had, to its continued disappointment, turned down the opportunity to get my mouth on those lovely breasts. I was so fucking tempted to say yes when Nic suggested we ditch the Christmas party last year, but, aside from the fact that she was drunk, it could have cost us our friendship—and that wasn't a price I was willing to pay for casual sex, regardless of how badly I wanted her.

It was only a drunken whim, anyway. Nic had never given me a single sober clue that she might be interested in something more with me. Not as an adult, at least. We had a briefly flirtatious relationship as teenagers, but her brother immediately gave her shit for it, and she shut it down quick. She was nothing but friendly after that. No more lingering glances or playful shoves or pink-cheeked teasing.

It didn't change the way I felt about her, though. Whether I liked it or not, she'd already built a cozy little home in my heart.

Nic leaned over to grab something from her suitcase and put her cleavage on full display. I belatedly realized I'd just been standing there flagrantly staring at her chest. I surreptitiously slid my gaze to the thermostat on the wall behind me. "It's a billion degrees in here." I fiddled with the dial for longer than necessary while she rustled around in her bag, probably looking for a giant turtleneck sweater to keep my eyes from crawling all over her skin. "The radiator was working fine when I came up to turn it on this morning."

"It's not that bad. I'm acclimating," she said, words muffled as she pulled an oversized t-shirt over her head. "I'll have maintenance take a look at it tomorrow."

"You can't stay in here with a broken radiator, Nic."

"Which is why I'll have maintenance look at it tomorrow. It's fine for tonight. The fresh air is really quite nice."

I shook my head. "It's not safe for you to be alone back here with the doors and windows open. There are a few rooms open in the North Tower."

"Ew, no. I'm fine here. Really. Any predator who feels compelled to climb three stories up the outside wall to come in through that window has my respect."

I shoved my hands into my pockets with a sigh. The chance of any real danger was admittedly low, and I could see her room from my cottage, but it was hard to turn that part of my brain off. "The North Tower isn't that bad, and it's only until we can fix the heat. Come on," I said, nodding toward the door. It was never going to be that easy, but it was worth a try.

She cocked her head and pretended to consider it, tapping a finger on her chin. "Let me ask you this: Are you going to throw me over your shoulder and haul me all the way to the North Tower while I flail and scream? Because unless the answer is yes, I'm staying right here."

I bit down on a grin. "No, I am not going to do that, because I value my job. But you will come with me, and quietly, because you value our friendship."

Nic scoffed and crossed her arms over her chest like a defiant teenager. "You won't stop being my friend. That's an empty threat."

"So's yours. You're not going to flail and scream."

Nic lifted an eyebrow with a smug little half smile. "Oh? Try me, Schafer."

I narrowed my gaze on her and rolled my shoulders, flexing my hands at my sides.

She scrambled to her feet and glared back at me through a smile. "You wouldn't."

I took a measured step toward her. "Wouldn't I?"

She held my gaze, her hazel eyes sparkling with mischief. After a beat, I lunged for her waist, and she tried to spin away with a shriek of laughter. I grabbed her from behind, pinning her arms to her sides, and tried to carry her toward the door. She flailed and kicked, and I was laughing too hard to get a good grip. She easily squirmed out of my arms in a peal of giggles and darted away with a yelp when I tried to grab her again.

I pulled my sweater off and tossed it on the bed as I stalked toward her.

"Not gonna happen, West," she sang, her chest heaving as she backed away. Her bravado was adorable.

"You could just come willingly," I said lightly.

Nic scoffed. "Yeah, right."

I shrugged casually. "Fine, we'll do this the hard way."

Nic's ass hit the wall, and her eyes went wide. Her gaze searched her periphery for an escape route. She was cornered. I was too close. My reach was too long. She had no way out.

"Okay, okay. You win." She held up her hands in supplication, but I kept prowling forward with a slow shake of my head.

I knew I was never actually going to win the battle for the North Tower, but the joke was on her because the real win was simply getting to be close to her. The woman had invited me to put my hands on her, and there wasn't a damn thing in the world that could make me walk away from that fleeting opportunity.

I narrowed my eyes at her. "Bull shit."

She shook her head. "I mean it! You win."

I took another step closer, crowding her into the corner. Nic would never give in so quickly.

Scratch that.

Nic would never give in, period. "What's your play, Princess?"

"No play." She looked up at me through her lashes, feigning innocence, and I knew I was definitely being played. I figured it out a second too late, though, and wasn't ready when her hands darted out and tickled my sides. I pulled back, choking on laughter, as she scurried to the back corner of her bed and brandished a pillow like a shield.

I leaned against the wall, panting through a smile. "It's too hot in here for this level of physical exertion."

Wary, she eyed me with caution for a moment before dropping the pillow back onto the bed with a scoff. "I was perfectly comfortable until you got me all worked up."

Same. "If this isn't fixed tomorrow, you're moving to a guest room, Nic."

"Fine. But it will still be under protest."

I swiped the hem of my undershirt across my sweaty forehead with a grin. "I would expect nothing less."

3

Nic

"TEAM LEADERS, DO you have any questions about your assignments?" I asked, addressing the three veteran volunteers who stood to the side of the group.

In my second season decorating at Bryson House, I realized I was going to need some extra hands. I didn't have the budget to pay anyone at the time, so I asked a friend who taught at the high school if he thought any of the student clubs would be willing to help. He did me one better and offered his history students extra credit if they helped for a day.

Every year after that, the kids showed up, and every year, I was endlessly grateful. The seed of community Adelia and Phinneas planted in the failing mining town of Summer Springs over a century ago continued to grow and flourish.

"I think you've covered everything," one of them said with a crooked grin, holding up the chunky binder I'd given her with all of the project details.

"Well, if I missed anything, my phone number is on the front page. Y'all know cell service is spotty around the estate, so just let West or whoever's at the front desk know if you can't reach me." At the mention of West, some of the girls elbowed each other. The hot hotel manager was undoubtedly a big motivator for some of the volunteers.

Not that I could blame them.

After last night, every thought of West was like that first sip of top-shelf bourbon, sending coils of smoky warmth through my core. I could still feel his hands on my body. His hot gaze on my exposed skin.

Any other man, and I would have taken it all as flirtation. But not West. I'd conditioned myself to stop looking for signs that he might be interested in me after my first three years at the hotel. If the ghosts hadn't matched us, then I had to accept that we weren't meant to be.

Not that I could ever give him up completely. First love is a hard drug to kick. Especially when the object of said love only got better with age. At thirty-three, the sharp features of his youth had softened, as had his physique overall. The man stayed in shape, but between a job that consumed his life and his ability to house a chunk of cheddar when stressed, he was no longer the chiseled specimen he was in his younger, more carefree days. I far preferred it. He was perfectly imperfect and beautifully human.

His golden blond hair had gone a little ashy around the temples, and laugh lines framed his mesmerizing ice-blue eyes. The tiny creases were utterly charming, but a bittersweet reminder of all the times my goof of a brother had us both in stitches over some entirely exaggerated story about his day, laughing until it hurt.

I missed that laughter. Both hearing it and feeling it.

And as much as I'd enjoyed West's physical proximity last night, indulging in that kind of laughter with him again had been the real treat. There hadn't been much mirth between us since my brother died.

But my plan was to stay under his radar for the day in case the radiator didn't get fixed. Out of sight, out of mind. The heat really wasn't that bad with the windows open, anyway. Staying in the servants' quarters was tradition, and I needed to soak up all the little joys at Bryson House while I still had the time.

I tugged my short ponytail tighter and forced myself to focus on the color-coded checklist clamped to my sparkly gold clipboard. Locally-farmed Christmas trees were being unloaded, the lighting crew was working in the front garden, and the teens were assembling fifty PVC arches for a canopy of icicle lights over the path from Edith's Landing to the hotel's courtyard, where the big tree would go up in a couple of hours. I needed to check in with Sadie, botanist extraordinaire, about the poinsettias, and then with Chef Angus to confirm lunch arrangements for the volunteers.

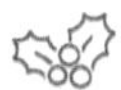

I rapped on one of the glass doors as I let myself into the greenhouse at the back of the property. "Hey, hot stuff."

Sadie's eyes briefly flitted up from the potting bench she was toiling over.

"Get it? Because this is a hot house? Not because I'm objectifying you." Sadie gave off a carefully cultivated go-away vibe. Box black hair, blunt bangs, sprawling tattoos, and combat boots that sent a lot of people packing. But I knew better.

She arched an artful eyebrow at the plant in front of her.

"Oh, hush. You're happy to see me."

She brushed off her dirty hands on the front of her black overalls. "Elated," she said flatly.

I beamed at her. "Right. Enough small talk. What have you got for me?"

Sadie turned to the bench behind her and reached into a crowded row of growers' pots. She turned to me with a plant held behind her back, eyes twinkling. I wiggled in place like a toddler waiting for a present.

This little tradition started five years ago. Sadie, whom I had been fairly sure despised me until then, greeted me with purple poinsettias. I was over-the-moon excited. The following year, the woman surprised me with stunning royal blue poinsettias. After that, it was a variegated green and fuchsia variety, then a shockingly black flower.

"Promise you're not going to get all weird." She cocked an eyebrow at me, but I could see a hint of nervousness in the set of her shoulders. For all the effort Sadie put into looking aloof, I'd come to recognize her softness over the years. I swear, sometimes the woman could see straight into my soul.

"Why would I get—" Sadie thrust the pot at me before I could finish asking. The plant had unusually petite poinsettia flowers, each crimson petal framed in gold. Beautiful, but surprisingly conventional.

Sadie looked impatient. "It's you."

I tilted my head and squinted at the plant, mildly confused. She gestured emphatically between my red hair and gold sneakers. When I finally grasped her meaning, my throat tightened and tears pricked my eyes.

"No, no, no. I told you not to get all weird." Sadie shuffled a step back and out of the hug zone.

I took a steadying breath and held up my hands. "Not weird. Promise," I said, accepting the plant from her. "I love it. How many are there?"

Sadie took another step back. "Just one. For you."

I swallowed thickly. "You know you're making it real hard not to get weird."

She waved me off. "Whatever. It's nothing." She started off toward another workbench, talking to me over her shoulder. "I have the traditional red flowers repotted and ready for placement. I'm still cleaning up the whites and pinks, but they should be done by Monday. Same with all your rainbow babies."

I hugged my tiny plant to my chest, nodding absently as Sadie rattled off numbers and plans and watering schedules. She pointed to a palette of flowers I could take whenever I was ready, and confirmed she would coordinate with housekeeping to place flowers in the guest rooms.

Sadie narrowed her eyes and gave me a wary once-over. "All good?"

"Perfect."

West

"You said January," I nearly growled into my phone.

"Change of plans. I know it's not ideal, considering the hotel is at capacity through the new year, but the company has assured us the process will be unobtrusive." Marsha Bryson, the current chair of the board of trustees that controls the family Bryson estate, offered the assurance in a placating tone that infuriated me. *Not ideal* was the under-fucking-statement of the year. "The cost reduction analyst who was scheduled to assess the property in January gave notice unexpectedly, but, fortunately for us, another one of their consultants is actually from Summer Springs and was open to taking the assignment during the holidays. Apparently, the little tree lighting thing on Monday is an annual tradition for his family, so he's already familiar with the property to some extent. Should make things easy for you."

My jaw was clenched so tight I could have given any wooden nutcracker a run for its money. This entire cost reduction business was a goddamn farce. When the board voted not to sell the estate last year, their concession to the few greedy stakeholders was that they would hire a consulting company to find ways to cut costs and increase profits. "There is no way we can be ready in three days. The checklist of documentation and preparations the consulting company sent over is exhaustive. I was already concerned about getting everything lined up for January."

"I trust you to figure it out, West. If I didn't know you could manage it, I would have told them no." Bull shit. Complete fucking bull shit. "Maybe Nicola can help you while she's there."

I pulled a pencil from my desk drawer purely to snap it in half. Marsha's unwarranted trivialization of Nic and her role at the hotel grated. "Nicola has enough on her plate."

"Oh, I'm sure she's got time between decorating Christmas trees," she replied, tone flippant. "It's not exactly a taxing job." My eyes shot to the three-inch binder sitting on the corner of my desk. Three inches of Nic's precisely timed schedules and detailed layouts and vendor contracts and passion and heart. Marsha could rot in fucking hell.

I needed to get off the phone before I said something I'd regret. "I'm needed at the front desk, Marsha," I said tightly. "I will do my best to prepare for the consultant by Wednesday."

"I know you will. I'll send an email introduction this afternoon."

"Sounds good."

"Oh, and West? He'll need a room while he's working on site."

Nic

With Baby Nic the Poinsettia snugged in the crook of my arm, I made my way to the kitchen to check on lunch for the volunteers. Chef Angus was braced over a notebook on the kitchen island, tugging at the front of his dark curls with one hand as he frenetically flipped through pages with the other.

"I don't suppose that's the menu for the volunteer lunch," I teased from the doorway.

Angus glanced up briefly, barely acknowledging my presence. "I am losing my goddamn mind trying to find the tomato confit recipe from the Autumn 2023 dinner menu."

"If I were that recipe, I'd be neatly indexed in a spreadsheet."

The evidently stressed chef finally looked up at me in earnest, huffing out a sigh with a half-smile. "That's my Christmas wish, Saint Nic. When you're done decorating, you can tackle the kitchen office and digitize Chef Sene's insane mess of old notes for me."

"I'll put in a good word with the big man, my friend."

"Speaking of the big man," Angus said, pivoting to flip down the lid on a to-go box on the counter behind him, "will you take this to West? We were going to have lunch together, but I need to find this recipe so Sene will stop breathing down my neck."

There was a lot to unpack in that seemingly innocuous statement, but my mind was fixed on the to-go box.

So much for avoiding West.

"And lunch for the kids?"

"Chef Mariane is on it. Sandwich platters and house-made kettle chips in the banquet room."

"Perfect. Thank you." I picked up the to-go box from the counter and peeked under the lid. "How's his cheese intake?"

Angus shot me a knowing look. "It's noticeably impacting my budget."

My brow furrowed. "Any idea what's got him bathing in brie?"

He shook his head. "It's been ten times worse this week, though, so I know where I'd put my money," he said, pointedly looking me up and down.

What the heck? "Me? You think it's my fault he's gulping down the gouda?"

"Could be something else. But you know how high-strung he gets when you're around."

"No, I do not know how high strung he gets when I'm around." Good to know I was making West miserable.

Angus clocked my reaction and quickly backpedaled. "Not in a bad way, Nic. I mean, it's bad how high-strung he gets, but it's not like he doesn't want you around. He definitely wants you around."

"Well, that's not confusing at all. Thanks."

Angus laughed. "You asked."

I did, indeed.

West

An hour later, and I was still absolutely seething.

The cost reduction nonsense was complete bull shit. The new timeline was untenable. And Marsha's attitude toward Nic was infuriating.

It did little to alleviate my gut-sinking fear that Nic's role would be the first thing they cut from the budget.

Bill Bryson, Marsha's late husband, had adored Nic. He was the one who enthusiastically approved the meager budget I requested ten years ago when I first approached him about hiring Nic for the holidays. She'd been decorating at the senior center where she worked, and I could see the amount of joy it gave her. Christmas was a big deal for her family when she was growing up.

There was an upbeat tappity-tap on my door, and it cracked open before I had a chance to yell at whoever it was to fuck off. An open to-go box floated through the gap. The sparkly gold nail polish peeking out under it eased some of the tension in my shoulders. So did the smell of cheese.

"I am going to be absolutely ecstatic if one of the ghosts has cultivated the power to deliver food."

Nic's face popped through the crack, frowning melodramatically. "Just me. Sorry to get your hopes up." *Just* you? I managed not to scoff.

I sighed in feigned exasperation. "What's one more disappointment?"

"Right?" Nic came into the office and bumped the door closed with her hip. I quickly slipped the folder of cost reduction paperwork into my desk drawer. "What's not disappointing is this grilled cheese that Angus asked me to deliver to you with his regrets. FYI, he might be losing his mind. You should probably check on him."

I nodded and scrawled *Angus = Crazy?* on a sticky note. "I'll add it to the list." I took the food box from Nic, then arched an eyebrow at her. "There's a bite missing from my sandwich."

"Well, that was unprofessional of him," she said, conspicuously brushing fake crumbs from the corners of her mouth with her sleeve. Nic plopped down in the chair on the other side of my desk and hugged the plant she was carrying to her chest.

I relaxed back into my own seat, contented for the moment that Nic didn't seem to be in a rush to run off back to work. I picked up the triangle of grilled cheese she'd taken a bite out of, and savored the imaginary taste of her lips on my lunch. "New plant?" I asked after swallowing.

Her whole face lit up. "It's Baby Nic."

When I asked, she excitedly explained, then beamed down at the small red and gold flowers. I had to have one of those plants. No fucking way there was only one.

"Will you babysit while I work? I can't carry her around all day, and I don't have time to fashion some sort of Poinsettia Bjorn to strap her in to."

"I'll keep a close eye on the Little Princess."

"Thank you," Nic said primly, nestling the flower pot into the space between my monitor and corkboard. She paused briefly, distracted by something on the board. The top left corner was full of family pictures. Her usual smile turned sad for a fraction of a second before she turned back to me, all traces of un-jolly emotion gone.

She picked up the uneaten half of grilled cheese from the to-go box, took a bite, then slumped back into her chair, eyes shuttering on a moan. "The tart apple is so darn good with the sharp white cheddar." She took another bite and put the sandwich back.

"You can have the rest. I had a late breakfast," I lied. I would gladly give up my lunch to listen to more of Nic's satisfied little moans, though.

"I'm going to go eat with the volunteers. Make sure the kids are all having fun doing free manual labor in near-freezing temperatures."

Nic stood, and tension immediately crept back into my muscles. The woman wasn't even gone, and I wanted to beg her to come back.

She pulled open the door and leaned in the frame. "You're working too hard, Schafe."

She wasn't wrong, but there wasn't much I could do about it. "Just the busy season. It'll be over soon enough."

Her eyes roved my face, looking too closely and seeing too much, before she nodded. "You need anything?"

Just more of you. "I'm okay."

Nic

There were ice crystals on the bedroom windows. On the inside.

I fiddled with the thermostat for the eighteenth time, shimmying my legs back and forth to keep warm, and for the eighteenth time, nothing happened.

I paced the length of the room, considering my options. Of which there was one: Lock the door, bundle up, turn my bottom bunk into an insulated little cave with the spare towels, and hope to fall deeply asleep before West showed up.

It wasn't a great option.

And there was no point going through all that and suffering in the cold when I knew exactly how things would play out when West inevitably showed up to check on the radiator. Even if I were sound asleep, he would just carry me like a baby to a warm guest room and tuck me into bed.

I hated to leave the old servants' quarters. The humble lodgings had been a part of my decorating tradition for so many years. But it was for the best. If I walked away now, at least I was doing it on my own terms.

I quickly packed up my things, collected my poinsettia from the desk, and gave the quaint room one last, longing look. It was the end of an era.

When West finished with the guest in line before me, I strode up and propped my elbows on the front desk. "Good evening, sir. I would like to secure a room in your fine establishment. A suite, if possible. Perhaps with a jetted tub."

He scowled at my suitcase. "Maintenance said they fixed the heat."

"In their defense, they did fix the heat. But now they need to fix the cold."

West didn't seem to think that was funny, and rather than laugh at my joke, he pushed my hair behind my ear. It was tender in a way I didn't know how to process. "I'm sorry, Princess. I know that was important to you."

I sloughed off his sincerity with a shrug. I'd made my choice, and I didn't want to dwell on it anymore. "It's just a bed and a place to stash my suitcase. It's really not a big deal. And,

look, I'm not even making you carry me kicking and screaming."

"Yeah, you know, I'm hearing all of these carefree words coming out of your mouth, but your face is making me feel an awful lot like the Grinch Who Stole Christmas."

"It's okay," I assured him, despite his probably apt descrip-tion of my traitorously emotive face. "The freezing tempera-tures weren't good for Baby Nic. And I'll survive the North Tower."

West dropped his gaze and shifted uncomfortably. "About that."

4

Nic

My jaw cracked on a massive yawn as I climbed the stairs to the hayloft.

Last night, West apologized profusely as we walked to his little cottage on the back of the property. I assured him it was fine, despite not feeling remotely fine about it, and tried to ease his conscience. It wasn't his fault a pipe had burst, and he had to move three guests to the only available rooms.

If anyone was to blame, it was probably the ghosts. Plumbing problems were solidly within their modus operandi, which hopefully meant some unsuspecting pair was having a better night than I was.

West made sure I was settled in, apologized for the situation, microwaved the Thanksgiving plate his mom had sent for me, ended up eating most of it himself, apologized even more, then went back to the hotel.

I tried to get some work done at his kitchen table, tried to watch an episode of *The Gilded Age*, then tried to sleep. But I spent most of the night tossing and turning.

Every little creak and groan of the old house made me think West had come home early. I fantasized about watching his silhouetted form undress in the dark, then quietly slipping between the sheets, trying not to wake me. He stayed on his side of the bed, but he couldn't fight the need for connection and found my foot with his before we both fell asleep with only our toes touching.

I'd never been more turned on by a less erotic fantasy.

Around five, West was still gone, and I gave up on sleep. I made the bed, made some coffee, then made the grievous mistake of using West's body wash in the shower while mine sat on the edge of the tub, mocking me. I let my hands linger on my body and imagined they were his for a few minutes before giving in a making use of his detachable shower head. I was deep in the fantasy, panting into the woodsy, citrusy steam, when the front door slammed and I dropped the shower handle with a yelp of surprise.

I'd subsequently been distracted all morning. It was hard to focus on wreaths and garland when I couldn't escape the masculine scent that got me keyed up earlier and continued to remind me of the release I missed out on.

At the top of the stairs, I turned to the empty space next to me. "Excited?" The overhead light blinked in response, and I grinned. "Me too."

My key slotted into the storage room lock. I'd found Adelia's antique ornaments crated up here the first year I decorated. She'd expressed enthusiasm when I pulled them out, but then followed me around the property, wildly flashing the lights any time she disapproved of my placement. It took a few tries before I realized she only wanted them in low-traffic areas. And fair enough, she didn't want them to get damaged. Neither did I.

Adelia approved when I put them on the trees in the library and the tea room, and that's where I put them every year after. That detail was prominently noted in the guide I'd prepared for whoever took over decorating next year, along with clear timelines, diagrams of the property, and vendor contracts. The hand-off would be seamless. Even if, at the moment, every thought of someone else's hands on Adelia's ornaments made me feel like I'd swallowed a pail of rusty nails.

Similar to the way every thought of someone else's hands on West made me feel, only those ones felt a little more like old razor blades and lemon juice. But moving on with my life was the right move. The healthy move. My sentimental attachments were holding me back. I'd get over them in time.

I propped my phone's flashlight on a closet shelf and started moving crates to the open hayloft. After several trips back and forth, I perched on the lowest closet shelf to catch my breath. The air was chilly, but pleasant on my heated cheeks.

I dragged myself up with a tired grumble and hauled out another crate, ditching my coat by the growing stack. Only four more to go, and then I'd just have to take each one carefully down the stairs. It was tiring work, but I reminded myself to soak up the little joys. Despite the care and effort required, Adelia's ornaments—and that deep connection to the Bryson Estate—were my favorite part of the job.

Resolve renewed, I went back for another crate. I nearly jumped out of my skin when the door slammed shut behind me.

The knob didn't budge when I twisted it. I jiggled it and tried it again. And then again. I gave the door a shove. I put my whole weight against it and then tried the knob one more time for good measure. I was locked in.

I dropped onto the lowest shelf with a huff. "Ghosts," I muttered. There was no cell service, and the keys were in my coat pocket. On the other side of the door.

"Ok, I don't know who's there or what exactly you're trying to accomplish by locking me in here, but I *really* don't have time today. The decorating schedule is already so tight. So, please let me out."

Nothing happened. "Seriously, guys, I have too much to do."

It could be hours before anyone realized I was missing, and even longer before they actually found me out here in the stables. After a few minutes, I fruitlessly tried some more polite pleading before shaking the doorknob again.

"I wonder if West has an exorcist on speed dial," I mused out loud, then immediately felt bad about it.

The dark, dank storage room wasn't one of the places on the property that I'd imagined spending a little extra time in for my last year on the property, but I figured it was as much a part of the place as the conservatory or hot springs. I should try to enjoy it. I settled on the floor, took a few deep breaths, and resigned myself to the wait.

West would find me.

West

I got home a little after six, completely wiped out from back-to-back shifts at the front desk and next to no sleep in the preceding thirty-six hours. It didn't stop me from taking a moment to appreciate the little signs that Nic was really in my home, and not just a deluded fantasy concocted by my over-tired brain. I felt bad about the situation, but not bad enough to not selfishly love coming home to the smell of coffee and her laptop open on my kitchen table.

And I didn't have to worry about her when she was here.

She was in the bathroom, so I flopped on the bed while I waited for my turn. The next thing I knew, I was being awoken by strobing lights. Half-asleep, I growled at the intrusion. But the alarm bells started clanging in my subconscious, and I shot up out of bed.

"What's wrong?" The lights continued to flash, which was as much of an answer as I was going to get.

Panic flared. "Is it Nic?"

The lights flashed once: Yes.

I was on the move, shoving my phone and keys into my pockets, then grabbing the nearest pair of shoes. "Can you take me to her?" One flash.

From my front porch, I spotted a flashing light on the path that led away from the hotel. I jogged in that direction with my clammy hands clenched into fists, looking for the next light. Why weren't there more fucking lights on the back of the property? My vision went hazy, my ears ringing, as numbness crept into my limbs.

When I spotted the flashing light on the outside of the stables, I broke into a sprint. My heart pumped hard and fast as my mind churned through worst-case scenarios. One of those damn crates fell on her. She fell from the hayloft. Or slipped down the stairs. There was a fire. Someone attacked her while she was isolated back there.

I burst through the doors and scanned the ground for Nic's body. That's when I heard her voice. Thank god, she was conscious. And yelling at the ghosts?

Disoriented, I struggled to track where her voice was coming from. I didn't have the breath to yell to her.

Adelia's ornaments were in the hayloft. That had to be where she was.

I took the stairs two at a time. "Nic?" I croaked.

"I'm in the closet!" she yelled in reply, and my knees felt like jelly. I rushed to the door, fumbled with the key that hung from the lock, and finally wrenched the door open.

Nic squinted as light flooded into the dark room. I yanked her into my arms, shaking.

She was saying something through the buzzing in my ears, but I couldn't make sense of it. She was safe. That was all that mattered.

Nic looped her arms around my waist and pulled me close, pressing her chest to mine. "I'm ok," she said softly. "I'm okay. Breathe, Schafe."

I fought the tightness in my chest to take a sharp, shallow breath and released it on a ragged exhale.

"Close your eyes. Focus on my breath." I felt Nic's slow, exaggerated breaths, her rib cage rising and falling against mine in a steady rhythm. "You've got me now. I'm safe. Everything's ok."

I folded around her and followed her breaths until I regained some control. The world slowly stopped spinning, and the tremors in my core started to subside. Sensation slowly crept back into my limbs, and I realized I was holding Nic with a death grip. "Shit, sorry," I muttered, mouth dry, and dropped my arms. She kept hers wrapped right around me, one hand anchoring me, the other rubbing soothing circles on my back.

She gazed up at me, soft and warm and reassuring. "Nothing to apologize for." With a crooked smile, she lifted my arms back over her shoulders. "You're not the only one who needs to be held. I was locked in a closet, you know."

I breathed a laugh and gladly snugged her close. "As you wish."

Nic

West slowly stroked the back of my hair, and I melted against him.

"Are you okay?" he asked.

I nodded against his chest. His grumble of approval vibrated through his ribs and into mine. His breath and heart rate were improving.

It had been over two years since I'd seen him have a panic attack. The first one I witnessed was the night my brother died. Thom had asked both of us to go night fishing on the lake. It had been a beautiful, hot summer—perfect for sitting on the dock with a cooler of beer and some fishing poles.

I already had plans to meet up with some guy for drinks and probably some sexy fun times. West was stuck at work. We both told Thom we'd try to join him when we were done. West was the first to get there. The first to find my brother in the shallows by the dock, unresponsive.

I can't even begin to imagine the trauma West experienced that night. He called me from the ambulance, but I sent him to voicemail. I was utterly oblivious to everything he was shouldering until he called again from the hospital. I raced to the hospital while West explained that the EMTs had administered compressions all the way to the hospital, but they weren't able to revive my brother.

Fortunately, I was nearby. I found West pacing outside the ER, still soaked from the lake. He fell apart as soon as he was in my arms.

We stood outside the hospital in this same position—West folded around me while I rubbed his back. That panic attack was far worse, but a nurse helped me get him to an exam room. They administered lorazepam, and I called his mom.

It was clear West had post-traumatic stress disorder after my brother died. The panic attacks weren't as severe, but they happened regularly. His mom finally talked him into seeing a therapist, and he started medication for his anxiety. Up until this moment, I thought he had it managed.

"Are you sure you're ok?" he asked again.

"Yeah. I got locked in the closet with no cell service, but I knew you'd find me before I froze or starved to death."

West leaned back to look at me. "I overreacted. I'm sorry."

"No apologies. I'm ok. Though I wish I could say the same for my poor, sad schedule." I pouted playfully. My schedule was off, but I always padded it in case things went awry. I probably still had enough buffer time to squeeze in a surprise for West later. He obviously wasn't taking care of himself, but I knew exactly how to force a little rest and relaxation on him. "I have no idea why the ghosts locked me in there."

West nodded toward my keys hanging from the lock on the outside of the door. "Adelia came to get me. I think this one was human error, Princess."

I gaped at the keys, aghast. I could feel my face flush, and I gave West a self-deprecating smile. "I hope none of the ghosts were around to hear me yell at them then. After twenty minutes, I got annoyed enough to threaten exorcism."

West chuckled, and I relaxed a little. "I know, from experience, that they do not take well to threats of exorcism. I had cold showers for days last time I threw out that empty threat."

I dropped my forehead against his chest and laughed. "I will mentally prepare myself for very short showers."

"Speaking of," West said, leaning into my neck, "my soap smells good on you."

Every inch of me blushed. I started to defend myself, but we were interrupted by a trill of feminine giggles from down in the stables.

A deep male voice drifted up to the loft. "*See? Empty.*" A stall door creaked open, and before I could holler down that the place was not, in fact, empty, the voice snapped, "*On your hands and knees, naughty little filly.*"

I gaped up at West, who looked at me wide-eyed.

"*Yes, sir,*" a coquettish voice answered.

"*You've been disobedient, haven't you? Touching yourself without my permission. You've left me with no choice but to punish you. I'm going to break you of your defiant ways.*"

The woman responded with something akin to a whinny, and I had to bite down on my lips not to laugh out loud.

The loud snap of skin on skin echoed through the stables several times, followed by a whimper and a moan. "*Have you learned your lesson?*" Another whinny. "*The next time I catch you making yourself come without my permission, the punishment will be far worse. Do you understand?*" She responded with a neigh that was not so much an actual neigh as it was just the word neigh. "*Good girl. Would you like a treat?*"

I pressed my palm to my mouth, eyes watering. West's shoulders were shaking with laughter.

"*I have a big, thick carrot for a pretty little pony.*" The chatter of a zipper echoed up to us. "*Good girl. Swallow that carrot. Yes, good girl. So good.*"

"Do you think it's an actual carrot?" I mouthed.

West raised his brow and shrugged.

"I wish I could see," I whispered.

West smirked. "Dirty."

"The carrot, you perv! I wish I could see if it's a carrot."

"Undress. Show me those pretty teats."

West shifted against me. "Ok, Schafe?"

"Just realizing that I am a terribly uncreative lover," West whispered.

Crunch.

"Oh my god, it was a real carrot!"

5

West

WHY HAVEN'T YOU matched me and West?

I'd spent the entire afternoon distractedly turning that over in my head. In the haze of panic, I wasn't sure I'd heard her correctly, but Nic had definitely been yelling at the ghosts for not matching us.

But did she want the ghosts to match us now, or was she just resentful they hadn't matched us in the past?

Despite the less-than-ideal state of my anxiety, I was cautiously optimistic.

Take that, darkness!

I rounded the greenhouse, where the path split from the public gardens of the hotel and back toward my cottage in the private housing area, and my breath caught in my chest. My usually dark porch was aglow with colored lights, a Christmas tree twinkled in the living room window, and wood smoke puffed from the chimney.

When I swung the door open, I found Nic hanging ornaments in polar bear pajama pants and bare feet, her haphazard ponytail bouncing to Christmas music. She grinned at me. "You're home!"

I had never been more *home* in my entire life.

I tried to swallow down the lump in my throat while I hung up my coat and toed off my boring dress shoes next to Nic's sparkly Chucks. "How did you find time for all this?"

Nic shrugged lightly. "It didn't take long. I cheated and had one of the tree guys help me steal this from the hotel. Don't tell the manager."

"I won't. I hear he's a real Scrooge."

She tapped her chin in consideration. "There might be some similarities. Works too much, forgets to enjoy stuff. But he also has that Michael Caine handsome old man thing going for him."

I choked on a laugh. "Of course, you went with *The Muppet Christmas Carol*."

"Is there another version?" Nic grabbed her phone off the coffee table, and after a few swipes, the soundtrack started to play on her Bluetooth speaker. "I'd put the movie on while we finish the tree, but dinner's almost ready."

"Dinner? Did you cook?"

She nodded excitedly. "Yep. And I'm starving, so if you would be so kind as to go hit broil on the oven, I would be ever so grateful."

I narrowed my eyes at her. "Nic?"

She fluttered her eyelashes. "Yes, West?"

"Did you make what I think you made?" She waggled her eyebrows, and I groaned. "You are a magical Christmas angel sent straight from the North Pole, Nicola Louise Winters."

"Of course, I am. Now, broil," she said, shooing me off with both hands.

I went to the kitchen and crouched down to look through the oven window. Macaroni and cheese. Nic's schedule for the day was jam-packed, and despite the hour she lost in the stables, my favorite woman had found time to make my favorite food and decorate my home. My heart felt so full it could burst.

I hit broil. "Do you want a glass of wine?" I asked over my shoulder.

"Yes, please." Nic padded into the kitchen and moved her laptop off the table before pulling down plates. How the hell was I ever going to go back to living without her?

"I'm seriously amazed you had time for all of this."

"I cheated a little on dinner, too." Nic grabbed plates while I picked a bottle of grenache off my small wine rack and popped the cork. "Your cheese drawer was, unsurprisingly, well stocked, but I stole par-cooked pasta, bacon bits, and fresh croutons from the hotel kitchen."

I got the wine glasses off the top shelf, and Nic pulled the mac and cheese out of the oven. My mouth watered. It had just the right amount of crunchy, nearly-burnt cheese around the edges.

Nic gave the still bubbling casserole a self-satisfied nod. "I did good."

I leaned over her to look, but it was just a flimsy excuse to get close. Was I imagining her leaning back into me, just the tiniest bit? She still smelled like my soap. "Indeed," I murmured low into Nic's ear. "Good girl."

She snorted and shoved me back with her shoulder. Her cheeks were bright pink when she faced me. "Oh, yeah? Do you have a treat for me?"

I gave her my most lascivious grin. "What kind of treat would you like, Princess?"

She rolled her eyes but flushed even pinker. "How about that wine?"

I put the glass in her hand, then went to change while the mac and cheese cooled to a less molten temperature. I threw on some sweats and slumped on the edge of the bed. I was bone-tired. My muscles ached from the adrenaline crash earlier. And I hadn't felt so content in literal years. The day had been a rollercoaster.

And it wasn't over yet.

I went back to the kitchen and we dished up. Nic's shoulders relaxed on a happy little sigh when her lips closed around the first bite.

I groaned around a mouthful. "This is so fucking good."

We ate quietly for a moment before she bumped her knee to mine under the table, lips tipped up in a soft smile, a knowing warmth in her gaze. "Felt like a mac and cheese kind of day."

My own smile faltered. "It's been a stressful couple of months," I offered in explanation. "But I'm okay. I promise."

Maybe I should have laid it all out on the table—the budget nonsense, the darkness, how hard it had been to have so much distance between us this year—but I didn't want her picking up the weight of my problems. She would pile them onto her own load with a smile if she thought it would make things easier for me. Plus, Nic was tolerating the move to my cottage and her break in tradition, but I didn't want to see her crushed face if she found out her traditions might be permanently broken once the cost-cutter rolled through here with his red pen.

But that wasn't a thought I could linger on.

"Mac and cheese makes everything better," I said, and speared the perfect bite of crunchy baked cheese and crisp bacon she'd been carefully eating around from her plate.

"Hey!" She watched in horror as I chewed.

I smirked at her, entirely unrepentant. "I'm no longer mad at Adelia and Phinneas for messing with the heat. This is a much better arrangement."

Her eyebrows lifted in surprise. "You think it was the ghosts?"

"You don't?"

She considered it with an adorable little frown, then shook her head. "No. I can't see any reason for them to chase me out of my room. It had to be human error."

It had to be the ghosts. I'd spent the afternoon thinking through the possibilities. Last night's plumbing problem hadn't led to any obvious matchmaking, so it was entirely possible they were trying to make sure there wouldn't be a room for Nic. I stared down at my plate, thoughtful, then shoved another bite in my mouth. Nic would be quick to call it matchmaking if these things were happening to anyone else.

"Disagree," I finally said, and downed the rest of my wine.

Nic took our empty plates to the sink while I wrapped up the mac and cheese and attempted to make space for it in the fridge amongst the Thanksgiving leftovers from my mom's.

"You know I would always rather have mac and cheese," I said offhand, balancing a container of green bean casserole on top of the Tupperware Jenga tower I'd built, "but we should probably eat the stuff from my mom's for dinner tomorrow. Before it goes bad."

Nic didn't respond, and I cringed at how stupid that must have sounded, like we were some old couple who had mundane conversations about things like leftovers. When I closed the fridge and turned to face Nic, she was at the sink, staring out the window. I wasn't sure she'd heard me at all. She threw me a smile over her shoulder. "It's snowing," she said quietly, as if anything louder would disrupt the weather. I could have stood there and admired the scene for hours.

Instead, I flipped off the kitchen light to kill the glare on the window and moved to stand next to her. She grinned up at me, eyes dancing with all of the life and joy I'd been missing for the last year.

No way in hell was I ever going that long without seeing her again.

Nic

Big, fluffy snowflakes drifted down in lazy whorls. The ground wasn't quite cold enough for them to stick, but the plants and trees looked like they'd been dusted with icing sugar. It was magical. And quiet. That was one of the things I loved most about snow—the way it muted the clatter and din of life.

West pushed up his sleeves and scooched me away from the sink. "I'll finish here. You go get some warm clothes and we'll go for a walk."

I considered him for a moment. He looked ready to crash, and it seemed frivolous to let him drag himself around the property on my behalf. "Nah. I've been on the move all day. Let's finish the tree and watch *The Muppet Christmas Carol*."

West scrutinized me before agreeing. I could see the warring factions in his face. He knew I'd love a snowy stroll, but he was smart enough to take the out I was offering. He plunged his hands into the dishwater and nodded toward the living room. "In case you didn't steal enough from the hotel, my Christmas decorations are in the green bin under my bed."

"I'm not going to find a bunch of porn down there, am I?"

His spine stiffened. "Oh, shit, the porn," he said dramatically, then smirked at me. "I'm a respectable gentleman, Nicola. The porn is strictly limited to incognito tabs on my phone."

I, thankfully, caught myself before asking about his porn habits. That was not the kind of information I needed floating around my head in perpetuity. "So gentlemanly," I said instead.

"There are also cookies from the hotel in my bag."

I beelined for his bag. "You're speaking my love language, Schafe. Decorations and cookies." I pulled out a slightly greasy paper bag containing four of the thick, chewy chocolate chip cookies the hotel put out at reception every evening.

"But not the porn. Noted."

I didn't mean to snoop, but under the cookie bag, a full prescription bottle caught my eye. I twisted it to read the label.

Antidepressants—good.

Expired—bad.

There could be a reasonable explanation. Maybe he was reusing the bottle. Or maybe he was on a new prescription and hadn't bothered tossing the old one. But if he'd stopped taking them, that would go a long way in explaining his anxiety. The thought of West trying to muscle through PTSD by sheer strength of will made my heart ache.

"Porn is more of a *self*-love language. Touch, however..." It obviously wasn't the right time to discuss mental health. I deposited the cookies in the kitchen and retreated to the bedroom before the conversation could get out of hand.

There was nothing gross under the bed, and I was delighted by the treasures when I pulled open the bin. It was a mishmash of holiday décor. Ornaments that looked like they were from his cousins' kids, who were really more like nieces and nephews in West's close-knit family. Things Julia had definitely passed along. A strand of old-fashioned bubble lights. A tree skirt that I would bet money his grandma crocheted. And—

"This one's my favorite," West said, startling me, as he reached for a gold star-shaped tree topper I made out of some garland and a wire coat hanger my first year at Bryson House.

"Oh, hush. It's on par with this paper plate snowman Aiden made."

"For the work of a four-year-old, that snowman is very well-crafted. And for the work of a highly capable twenty-year-old, this star is near perfection."

I followed West into the living room with the bin of decorations. He situated the star on the tree, then stepped back to admire it. "Yep. Perfection. What else have we got? Are those Adelia's ornaments?"

I reached into the box I'd brought from the hotel and pulled out an antique punched tin angel. "I got permission. From Adelia. Not from the hotel. Obviously."

"Hm, I hope she doesn't take that as an invitation to hang out here."

I looped the angel's red satin ribbon onto a tree branch. "You have a problem with her hanging around?"

"Not a problem, necessarily. When I moved onto the property, I politely asked the ghosts to respect my privacy. And I haven't really seen any sign of them in here, aside from the cold showers and Adelia's S.O.S. earlier."

"No ectoplasm?" I slapped a hand over my mouth as soon as the words were out.

West barked a laugh. "You'd better hope they're respecting our privacy, Princess. You know how they feel about *Ghostbusters* jokes."

My shoulders shook with laughter. "Remember my first year, when you helped me move that crate of old chains in the stables and I asked Adelia if she wanted to rattle them around like Marley's ghost?"

"Hell yeah. She blew every light in a fifty-foot radius." I could feel West's giant smile all the way down to my toes.

We finished hanging the ornaments, and West strung the old bubble lights across the mantel since they were probably a fire hazard.

"Flawless." I sighed happily when we stood back to admire our work. The falling snow was the perfect backdrop to our chaotic little tree full of mismatched mementos. There was nothing cohesive about it, and it was by far my favorite tree on the property. The thirty-foot pine in the courtyard couldn't hold a candle to it.

"Flawless," West agreed.

The microwave beeped, and West joined me on the couch a moment later with a plate of warm cookies. "Ready?" he asked.

"Always." I hit play on the movie and grabbed a cookie. "There should be more Muppet versions of classic stories. Like *Muppet Don Quixote*, or *Muppet Dorian Gray*."

"Or Muppet Treasure Island," West offered.

"Yeah! Oh. Right. But still." I shoved a chunk of cookie in my mouth.

West propped his ankles up on the coffee table and slung his arm over the back of the couch. He was more relaxed than I'd seen him in ages.

Angus was wrong. I wasn't the problem.

The space next to West was beckoning to me. Would it really be so terrible if I heeded its call? Would it be the end of the world if I soaked up these last little moments of connection with him while I still had the chance? I'd just be careful not to get carried away.

So, I scooched closer to West.

"Cold?" he asked, reaching for the blanket on the arm of the couch.

"No," I said simply. When I glanced up at him, his gaze was warm and welcoming, and that was all the invitation I needed. He grumbled his approval and wrapped his arm around my shoulders, snuggling me into his side. I tucked my feet under me and let my knees rest on his thigh. It was so easy and natural, like we'd already spent a lifetime of evenings together on this couch.

His fingers stroked absentmindedly up and down my arm as we watched the movie. "I know this story is set before their time, but the holiday party the Ghost of Christmas Past takes Scrooge back to is how I imagine Christmas Eve parties here at Bryson House in Adelia's and Phinneas' time. The trees trimmed to perfection, all of the men and women from Summer Springs in their finery, waltzing to Dr. Teeth and the Electric Mayhem. Probably with fewer rubber chickens, though."

West didn't laugh, and when I looked up at him, his brow was creased. "I don't think I've danced since Thom died."

The statement caught me off guard. I tried to remember if he'd danced at the last two Christmas parties. "What about your sister's wedding?" I'd seen pictures of West with a statuesque brunette. "You didn't dance with your date?"

West scoffed. "Date? Where would I find a date? I work seven days a week."

I stared up at him, incredulous. "Yeah, at a hotel with matchmaking ghosts. With a constant stream of single people hanging around looking for love. It's a veritable sex buffet."

He speared his fingers through his hair. "I guess I've never really been interested."

"You've never wanted the ghosts to match you?"

"I didn't say that. Of course, I've wanted that. Haven't you?"

The conversation was waltzing into dangerous territory. I needed to reel it back. I needed to tell him I was leaving. I needed to tell him about the house and the car and the job on the other side of the country. I needed to tell him I couldn't do this.

Instead, I shrugged dismissively. "Not really. That kind of thing isn't for people like me."

West wasn't buying it, and who could blame him? I was a terrible liar, and he knew I was a hopeless romantic. He knew I loved watching the ghosts make matches. "People like you?"

"Yeah. I'm a lone wolf. Out here, living by my own rules. Beholden to no one."

"Oh, really?" I could hear the smile in his voice.

I swallowed down a laugh. "Yep."

"Nic?"

"Yes, West?"

"Wolves live in packs."

"Well, not this wolf." *Not since my pack died off.* "And this wolf, who lives by her own rules, with wild and reckless abandon, beholden to no man, is quite sleepy and going to bed."

I started to disentangle myself from West, but my feet were so asleep I wobbled dangerously as soon as I tried to stand. He caught me around the waist with a burst of laughter. "Need a little help, lone wolf?"

"No, I'm perf—" In a flash, West scooped me up over his shoulder, and I scrabbled at his back, laughing hysterically. "What are you doing? You're going to hurt yourself."

"Putting you to bed," he huffed, and hauled me into the bedroom. He dropped me on the bed with a grin that made my heart flutter.

"I can't believe you did that."

"Can't you?" West reached over me to grab a pillow. "Sweet dreams, lone wolf."

"Oh, no." I sat bolt upright. "I don't think so."

"Don't think what?"

"You're not sleeping on the couch."

"Yes, I am."

I shook my head. "No. Look, I've already run through all of the scenarios in my head, and this argument ends with both of us sleeping on the floor. So, I vote we skip the debate over who sleeps where and just share the bed."

West stood next to the bed, pillow in hand, and stared at me like I had just revealed I was three elves in a trench coat.

I sighed in exasperation. "Okay, you insist I take the bed because I'm a guest, right? And you'll take the couch. But then I claim the couch because you're too tall to sleep on it, and I insist you take the bed. You get irritated that I won't take the bed, and lie down on the floor to prove how stubborn you are, but I won't be outdone in our race to the bottom, so I lie down on the floor, too. And then neither of us has anywhere to go from there. It's a stalemate. Neither of us can move unless both of us move. Which means we both move to the bed, or we both sleep on the floor. So, are we sleeping on the cold, hard floor? Or are we sleeping in the soft, warm bed?"

His shoulders were shaking with laughter by the time I was done. "I want to say you've lost your shit, but you're right. That is exactly how that argument would play out. I'm not sure what that says about us."

West flopped his pillow back down on the bed and started to pull back the covers, but I stopped him. "Nuh-uh. You didn't answer. Are we both sleeping in the bed? Because if you're being cagey because you think you found a workaround while I was explaining the situation—like, oh, say, waiting until you think I'm asleep, then moving to the couch—then you weren't listening to me. Race to the bottom, West."

He gave me a crooked smile. "Believe it or not, Princess, I'm not particularly desperate to get away from you. I will gladly share the bed."

"Oh."

I started to climb off the bed, but West hooked his fingers into the hood of my sweatshirt. "You're going to deliver that whole diatribe, then try to run off?"

"No," I said, unzipping my hoodie to slip away. "I need to brush my teeth, and someone needs to turn off the movie and the lights. And probably put another log on the fire."

"Oh. Right." West tossed my sweatshirt onto my suitcase. "I'll get the TV and the fire."

We went our separate ways to prepare for bed, moving through the house in synchronicity, like we'd done this song and dance a thousand times. The ease of it was almost jarring. I'd spent the last two and a half years alone at my house, racing through my bedtime routine, trying to outrun the metaphorical ghosts that refused to be exorcised.

When I finished brushing my teeth, West went into the bathroom, and I settled into bed with my notebook and reviewed my checklist for the next day.

"A little recreational reading?" West asked, pulling off his sweatshirt as he came into the room.

"I sleep better when I know exactly what the next day holds." I flipped down the covers on his side of the bed, then turned to put my notebook down. West had put a fresh glass of water on my nightstand while I was in the bathroom. The tiny gesture sent butterflies twirling through my stomach.

The bed dipped with West's weight. "Wouldn't that be nice?"

"Hm?" I asked, distracted.

"To really know exactly what the next day holds. Okay if I turn off the lamp?"

"Yeah," I said, snuggling down into the covers as the room went dark. "West?"

"Yes, Nic?"

"If I wake up and you're on the couch, I will get an armful of snow and shove it down your shirt." The mattress shook as West laughed. "I mean it."

"Ditto. G'night, Princess," he mumbled into his pillow. He was already half asleep.

I tossed around for a couple minutes before finding a comfy spot on my side of the bed. I was finally starting to drift off when West's foot brushed mine. Heat welled in my chest, and I pressed my foot to his. We fell asleep with only our toes touching.

6

Nic

WHEN I WOKE up, the sky was still dark, the room was cold, and our toes weren't touching.

But all our other parts seemed to be.

West had one arm stretched out under my pillow and the other cinched around my waist, where my fingers were twined with his. His front was pressed to my back from shoulder to thigh, our legs thoroughly entangled.

I felt warm and safe and cherished.

And I might have stopped to revel in that if I thought it was intentional. But the room was chilly, and we'd simply drifted together as the fire had died in the hearth.

"Go back to sleep," West grumbled into my hair.

Okay, maybe the cuddles weren't entirely unintentional. "Shh, I'm asleep," I whispered.

He pulled me impossibly closer. "You're thinking so loudly it woke me up."

"I can take my noisy thoughts to the couch."

I started to pull away, but West tugged me back with a little growl. "Don't make me get the snow, Nicola."

I breathed a laugh. "Can I at least go put another log on the coals before they die? It's freezing in here."

"I'll keep you warm." West's body shifted behind mine, unrelenting in his grasp, until his lips were brushing the sensitive skin beneath my ear, and I flushed with heat.

The sudden change in tone was unexpected but not at all unwelcome.

His teeth grazed down the slope of my neck. I shivered at the teasing sensation, and he did it again, up and back. "Is this ok?"

My body responded without thought, hips grinding back into his lap.

His huffed laugh tickled at my nape. "Was that a yes?"

"Yes." It came out as more of a gasp than a word as he trailed kisses along my neck and shoulder.

West licked and nipped and teased for long, drawn-out moments, as if high school-style necking was a pro sport. It was too much and not enough. Fingers still laced together, I slid our hands under the hem of my shirt. The heat of his palm was searing on my bare skin. West ground his hard length against my ass. "May I?" he asked.

"Yes." I wasn't sure what, exactly, I was agreeing to, but it didn't matter. The answer was yes to everything. Anything. Whatever he wanted, as long as he kept touching me.

He rested his hand on my sternum and urged me to my back. My eyes had adjusted enough to the dark to see his soft smile. "Hi," he murmured.

"Hi," I answered, feeling suddenly self-conscious about my hair and my breath. This was a different game, facing each other.

West kissed my jaw, and I was both relieved and disappointed that he hadn't kissed my lips. His fingers made quick work of the buttons on my pajama top until the loose fabric fell open. Even in the unlit room, my white lace bralette left little to the imagination.

He propped himself up on an elbow, his fingertips lightly tracing my ribs while he looked his fill. "There's a shortage of perfect breasts in this world."

I rolled my eyes, and he smirked. "Maybe quote movies later, Dread Pirate?"

"All right. Movie quotes aren't your kink." His knuckles grazed the lower curve of my breast. "How about horses?" He chuckled when I elbowed him. "No? Okay. Tell me what you do like."

You. "Use your mouth," I whispered, my pulse humming at the thought of his tongue on my body.

West dipped his head to my chest and slowly licked across the edge of the lace. "Good answer," he murmured against my skin before licking my nipple through the fabric. He teased both nipples with his hot mouth until the white bralette was nearly transparent. He hooked his fingers under the apex and slowly dragged it up, letting my breasts spill out, exposing them to the cold air and his hot gaze.

He hummed in approval and caught a peaked nipple between his knuckles, gently tugging and setting my core on fire. He closed his mouth around the other and sucked. I arched up into him with an unflattering whimper, and he sucked harder. He moved from breast to breast until I was restless with need.

"I have a confession to make, Princess," West said quietly, his warm breath ghosting over my wet nipple. He kissed across the swell of my breast, down to my sternum. "Yesterday morning," he went on, planting soft kisses up my chest, "I heard you in my shower. Moaning."

I shot up, pushing West's head away, wrapping my arms around myself, flushed with embarrassment. "Oh my god."

West grinned. "My sentiments exactly. I don't think I've ever been that hard, that fast in my entire life," he added, easing my arms away from my chest. He gave my shoulder a little shove to lie back down. "I'm not telling you to embarrass you. I'm telling you because I realized I did you a disservice this morning."

"By listening to me masturbate in the shower? Yes. Yes, you did." I was mostly teasing. I was too worked up to be anything other than turned on by the idea of making him hard.

"I didn't linger and listen. I'm not a complete creep. I went back and slammed the door and stomped around so you'd know I was home." His thumb brushed back and forth across my pebbled nipple. "I waited until you were gone to jerk off to the memory of your little moans. Like a gentleman."

"Was it good?"

"Explosive. And then when I smelled my soap on you later?" West eased my legs apart with his knee. "Fuck, Princess. I couldn't stop thinking about your beautiful hands spreading my scent all over your naked body, here—" he nuzzled his face against my breasts "—and here—" he rubbed his thigh between mine. "But that's not the point right now. After I got off—"

"Explosively," I interjected.

His lips twitched against my skin, and he looked up at me. "Yes, after that, when the blood flow finally returned to my brain, I realized you probably didn't get to finish yourself off before I slammed the door."

I shook my head with a pout.

"Which was not gentlemanly. I believe I owe you an orgasm, Princess." West moved to settle his whole body between my legs, holding himself several inches too far above me. "Is this okay?"

"Yeah." I slipped my hands under the back of his t-shirt. His skin was so warm and soft, I needed to feel it against my own. I tugged up at the hem, and West sat back to pull it over his head. His bare chest grazed mine. "Better," I said, running my fingers up his spine.

His head lolled forward in pleasure. "Perfect," he amended. West slowly rolled his hips between my legs, and I moaned. "Good?"

"So good." I pulled him closer, needing his weight to anchor me, and ran my tongue across his collarbone. He shivered and ground against me with a growl.

West rotated his hips in slow circles, rubbing his hard cock against my clit. I arched into him and hooked my legs around his thighs, drawing our bodies closer together.

I grew restless under him, skin flushed and sensitive. He kissed and licked my throat, and I felt like I could explode. But his pace was lazy. Teasing. Taunting.

"Can I make you come?"

I clung more tightly to him, fingertips digging into his back. "Yes. Please."

He braced a hand between us to toy with my nipple. "Is this enough? For you to come? Or do you need something else?"

Something else. I wanted to beg him to fuck me. I wanted him to fill me with his cock, and thrust into me hard and fast and punishing for the way I was about to leave him. It was a memory I was desperate to make with him. Something carnal to hold onto. To warm me when the world got too cold.

But I couldn't do that. West didn't know this was a one-night stand.

My mind was starting to reel, and I loosened my grip on West.

He pulled back and smoothed my hair with his warm palm. "Everything okay? Do you want to slow down?"

I nodded, not trusting my mouth to make the words sound right. West nodded back and ran his knuckles down my cheek. "I missed you so fucking much this year."

It was too much. A tear streaked back toward my ear, and I turned away.

West gently turned my face back to his and brushed at the tear with his thumb. "Hey, what's wrong?" he asked gently.

"I can't do this." I hated the quaver in my voice.

"That's okay. We don't have to do anything, Nic. I didn't mean to pressure you." West sat back on his heels, taking away the comforting shelter of his body.

I shuffled back to the headboard and wrapped my arms around myself to fight the sudden chill. "You didn't. I shouldn't have let things go so far. I got carried away."

He nodded like he understood. "We have all the time in the world, Nic. We don't have to rush. I'll never ask you to do something you're not ready to do."

There was no end to how deeply, desperately I wanted to escape this conversation. Even my body fought the words, clamping down around the breath I needed to force them out. "I'll never be ready, West."

His shoulders straightened. "What do you mean?" he asked apprehensively.

"I mean, I can't do this. You and me." I couldn't look at him. My heart was shattering. Those weren't words I could have ever imagined myself saying.

West looked confused. "But, today. You just yelled at the ghosts for not matching us."

"I know. It's just—it's too late now. They're too late. We're late. Maybe a couple years ago. But…"

West's fingers sliced through his hair. "Fuck, Nic, is there someone else?"

"No! No. Seriously, West, you know me better than that. I wouldn't have done those things—" I waved a hand between us "—if there was someone else."

"Then why?" He was growing desperate. "Is it because of today? Things have been stressful around here, but I'm okay, I promise."

"West, no, of course not. I know you're stressed. And it was a triggering situation. I know that. I know you." *But I also don't think you're okay.*

"Then tell me why it's too late. Tell me why this isn't right on fucking time."

I had no idea how to explain just how terrifying it was to feel so attached to him. To explain how loving him meant living under the crushing fear of losing him.

The phone in the kitchen rang, startling us both. "Goddammit," West breathed. On the third ring, he got up to answer it. "This conversation isn't over, Nicola."

I heard his low voice in the other room, but couldn't make out the words. I used the time to put myself back together, drying the tear tracks on my cheeks, buttoning my shirt, and running my fingers through my hair.

He came back into the room a moment later and started to get dressed with sharp, agitated movements.

"Everything ok?"

"Oh, just normal hotel shit. Some stupid fucking ghosts locked some people out of their rooms, but there hasn't been anyone at reception for who knows how long, and my stupid fucking cousin forwarded the front desk calls to my landline." He stopped and took a long breath, raking his fingers through his hair. "I'm sorry for venting. And I'm sorry I have to go deal with this. But I'll be back soon. We'll talk this through and figure it out, okay?"

What was I supposed to say? No amount of talking was going to change the outcome. "The sidewalks haven't been shoveled yet. Be careful."

"Always."

7

Nic

"Nic," Sadie snapped. I must have zoned out.

"Sorry!" I shook myself, beamed at her, and loaded another potted pine into my wagon. "I might need a little more coffee."

She stood there staring at me with her arms crossed over her chest, annoyance written all over her face. She shifted her weight from one foot to the other, then quickly back again. Sadie wasn't annoyed. Her gaze narrowed on me. "Stop looking at me like that."

"Can't help it. You look like I'm making you uncomfortable, and I don't know what to do with a Sadie who looks anything other than *over it*."

Pointing it out seemed to make her markedly less comfortable, and I couldn't help my spurt of laughter.

"Okay, yeah, fine, you're making me uncomfortable. You're acting like everything is sunshine and rainbows, but something is obviously wrong. And..." she trailed off, gesturing at me like I should know what she was trying to say.

I quirked an eyebrow. "And?"

She rolled her eyes with a huff. "And you're kind of my friend, okay? And a friend is supposed to ask when her annoyingly glowy friend is suddenly less than glowy."

"Aw, I am elated to be your kind-of-friend, Sadie."

"Great. Now tell me why you're weird today."

I shook my head, waving her off. "Just tired. It's no big deal. I'll get a good night's sleep after the tree lighting tomorrow and be right as rain."

She continued to stare at me expectantly, and I loaded another tree into my wagon. It was one of those times when I would swear she could literally see to the core of me. It was unnerving. I really wasn't being weird. Not in any way that a normal human would notice.

"Arguably, I'm not the one being weird," I said pointedly.

"Um, yeah, no kidding. But I can't go back to being *over it* until you tell me what's going on. Did West do something stupid?"

"No, why would you think it would have anything to do with West?"

She barked a laugh. "Why, indeed."

"I'm being serious."

"So am I. I really, truly hate to get involved in any of the hotel gossip, but you know it's obvious to literally everyone but the two of you just how sickeningly in love with each other you are, right?"

I gaped at her, stunned. "What the actual fuck, Sadie?"

Her eyes widened on a grin. "Holy shit, I made Saint Nic cuss."

"I cuss!"

"No, you do not. But let's not get derailed. The top's off the pot. Spill the tea."

I sat down hard on a stack of palettes, tired and defeated. "There's nothing to spill, really. We're friends, things got a little more than friendly, and they shouldn't have."

Sadie shook her head. "You're not friends. You both know it. I mean, fight it and make yourselves miserable all you want, but in the end, the two of you ride off into the sunset with all the rainbows and unicorns and happily ever after fairy tale bullshit. Trust me. I have a sixth sense for these things."

"It's not that simple."

"Isn't it?"

"I don't want that."

"Yes, you do."

"I don't want to want that."

"Ah. Now we're getting somewhere." She gave me an assessing once over. "You're scared?"

"Terrified." How'd she do that?

"You know, if there's one person *you* don't need to be scared of, it's West."

"I'm not scared of West. I'm scared of losing him. Or hurting him."

Sadie shrugged apologetically. "I hate to break it to you, but life is pain. There's not much you can do about that."

"I make him miserable every time I'm around. I *can* do something about that."

She waved me off. "The only thing making him miserable right now is not being with you. And probably the bull shit with the cost reduction analyst—but we're all rightfully pissed he's coming a whole month early."

Cost reduction analyst? Little alarm bells sounded in the back of my mind, but I nodded like I knew what she was talking about.

She looked at me wide-eyed. "Shit. Shit, shit, shit. You didn't know about that. Of course, you didn't," she said, clearly back-pedaling. "Because it's totally not a big deal."

"Right. So not-a-big-deal that West didn't even think to casually mention it." I tugged at my ponytail to tighten it. If they were bringing someone in to slash the budget, then West's stress levels were suddenly making a lot more sense. "Are there going to be staffing cuts?"

"We don't know yet," she said quietly.

My shoulders slumped at her tone. This wasn't just a West problem, it was an everyone problem. "I'm sorry you're all living in limbo," I said softly, then sighed. "That at least explains West's cheese intake. He's making himself miserable worrying about you guys. And himself. He could lose his job *and* his home. Why would he keep that from me?"

Sadie shook her head. "The board would never cut West. Even Marsha isn't that stupid. He takes on way too much around here. But, West knows she *is* stupid enough to cut the holiday budget."

Ah. "And Marsha hates me." The picture was starting to crystallize.

"No one hates you. It's literally impossible."

Sadie was trying to lighten things up, and I wished I could roll with it. I gave her as much of a smile as I could muster. "Thanks? So, West's worried I might lose my job."

"Bingo."

Given the chance, Marsha Bryson would cut the holiday budget just to be rid of me. No idea why. I'd always had an easy kinship with her husband, but petty jealousy *had* to be an oversimplification of whatever fueled her dislike for me. Bill Bryson and I had shared a love for the holiday season and the role it played in the Bryson family legacy.

But it was all irrelevant, wasn't it? I was leaving, and Marsha was about to get what she wanted without even needing to axe the budget. Merry fucking Christmas to her.

"Well," I stood up, puffing out a heavy breath. "I wish West would have told me. I could have spared him some of the stress."

"Spared me what stress?" West's deep voice crashed through my gut like an avalanche.

I turned to see him standing in the greenhouse doorway. He looked tired but sleep-rumpled, like he might have taken a nap, and it flooded me with memories from the night before. Heat joined the flurries of emotion inside me. We stared at each other for a long moment.

Sadie cleared her throat. "Sorry, West," she said, grabbing her coat off a bench. "I didn't know she didn't know about the cost reduction analyst."

West swallowed hard but didn't take his eyes off mine. "You don't need to apologize. I should have told her."

"Ok, well, I'm going to leave now. Before this powder keg blows." She beelined to the door, slipped behind West, and was gone.

West walked toward me. "Nic," he started, but I held up a hand to stop him.

"You don't need to explain. I get it. I don't like it, but I get it. I'm sorry you've been carrying all of that stress on your own."

His shoulders relaxed with a sad smile. "Of course, you are." He closed the distance between us and molded his broad palm to the line of my jaw. His thumb gently swept over my cheekbone. "I didn't want it to ruin your time here."

"I know. But you didn't need to keep it from me." I took his hand from my face, and he frowned, bemused. "West, I'm not coming back next year."

His ice blue gaze bounced around my face. "Nothing's been decided yet. The cost reduction analyst will be here the day after tomorrow, and there's every chance he'll recommend increasing the holiday budget once he sees all the magic you make around here."

He didn't understand. "Doesn't matter. Unrelated to possible budget cuts, I'm not coming back next year."

West's color blanched. "That doesn't make sense. You love it here."

He wasn't wrong. Bryson House had been more of a home to me than my house ever had. I couldn't stop the weighted sigh that blew out of me. "After the rumors about the hotel being sold last year, I spent a lot of time thinking about my own future. And I decided I need to focus on work. I'm moving to DC in January to work out of the corporate offices. I'll miss out on opportunities if I'm not there in person, demonstrating my value. Right now, I'm out of sight and out of mind."

West reared back. "Hold up. A second ago, you were just quitting decorating. Now you're fucking moving?"

I nodded once, and he started to pace. He needed a minute to process, so I waited, watching the kaleidoscope of emotions that contorted his face, and laboring to keep my own face composed while I fought the impulse to comfort him.

West stopped at a workbench and braced his hands on the plywood. He stared down for a moment, the lines of his shoulders taut with constrained emotion, before he finally broke the silence. "The house."

It was a statement. Like he'd found a flaw in my plan. I shook my head. "It goes up for sale next week. Most of my stuff is already in moving pods."

The tension rolled off of West and crashed into me in thick waves. "And this is the first I'm hearing about it."

"This is a good thing," I said softly. It was going to take West some time to join me in that feel-good place. I walked to the table and reached across the surface to put my hand on his, but he pulled away, his fingers curling into fists. I hung my head on a sigh. "The house was more than I could handle."

"Why didn't you tell me?"

Guilt churned in my stomach. "It wasn't worth bothering you about. You've got your hands full enough around here."

"Jesus, Nic, it was absolutely worth bothering me about. You're giving up your home!"

"I'm not giving it up. And I didn't need your permission." West's frustration was forcing my defenses up. "The house was making me miserable. The bad memories were crowding out the good ones. Upkeep was expensive. Thom hadn't paid the property taxes in two years. And did you know he took out a line of credit against the house at some point? His life insurance barely covered the debts he left me with. It was too much. I couldn't do it."

"You couldn't do it *alone*. If you'd just fucking told me what was going on, I would have helped, Nic. You know I would have."

"That's exactly why I didn't tell you. I'm not your responsibility."

West slammed his palm down on the table. "Like fuck you aren't."

"Seriously? You actually think that, don't you?"

"Of course, I do!" He threw his hands up in exasperation before going back to pacing. "Your mom is dead, your dad is a complete piece of shit, and I basically killed your brother. So, yeah, I think the very least I can do is keep my best friend's orphaned sister safe after letting him die."

I scrubbed my face with my palms. We'd avoided this conversation for a long time. "West, you didn't let him die."

"I was supposed to be there, Nic. If I'd been there..." he trailed off, pushing his hands through his hair.

"I was supposed to be there, too! But I can't—I won't—live the rest of my life dwelling on the massive what-if of whether or not the outcome would have been any different if I'd just gone fishing with him like he'd asked. Between the two of us, we can and *will* find and feel every possible way to blame ourselves before our days are up. But I will never blame you. Ever.

"What you went through that night? I can't even begin to imagine the trauma of finding him. Of trying to bring him back. I am so, so sorry you had to go through that. So sorry that you had to be the one to call me. You shouldered way too much of the burden that night."

"I wasn't there for you, Nic. Your brother was dead, and instead of holding you, I was having panic attacks. I fell apart and made you put me back together. I should have been stronger. I couldn't save Thom, and now you're telling me I can't save you, either." West dropped his head. "I should have known you needed help," he said, almost to himself. "I would have helped. If you'd just asked. We could have saved the house."

I couldn't stop the exasperated sigh that blew out of me. "I didn't *want* to save the house, West. I hate the house. Every corner is piled with reminders of everyone I've lost. And I thought, fuck it, why do I have to stay when no one else does? I don't have to keep letting a stupid house break my heart over and over and over again."

West speared his fingers through his hair in agitation. "We would have figured it out." The statement sounded more like a plea, as if I would stop the wheels I'd already set in motion.

"No, we wouldn't have. There is no *we*."

West flinched as if I'd taken a swing at him, hurt evident in the furrows of his brow, the downturned corners of his mouth.

"I was wrecked after you rejected me last year. I can't keep coming back here. I can't keep doing this to myself. I've wanted you for as long as I can remember, West, but it's so obvious I make you miserable when I'm around. You're better off with me gone."

"The fuck I am. You might be out of sight and out of mind at work, but you are out of sight and constantly on my mind. I never know where you are. Who you're with. If you're healthy. If you're happy. If you're safe. If you're alive. I don't go a single fucking day without panicking that if something happened, if you were in trouble, there wouldn't be a damn thing I could do about it. If something happened to you, who would even know to call me? The only time I'm not out of my mind with worry is when you're right here. Right where I can see you."

"Well, I can't be *here* the way you need me to be. I travel for work. I get waylaid by off-schedule funiculars. I get stuck in random closets. I can't change that. You can't change that."

West swiped at an angry tear, face pale and breaths shallow. "Please, Nic." His voice was full of gravel, and my heart cracked. "Please, don't give up on me. Not now. Not when we finally have a chance to be together."

"I'm not giving up. I'm letting go." I fought my own tears. "I'm so tired of hurting, West."

"And I'm part of the hurt."

"No," I admitted weakly. "But you will be. It's inevitable."

"Inevitable." The word fell out of his mouth like something bitter. "Tell me you don't love me, Nic."

I shook my head. "I can't. That's the point."

West nodded, but he was already a million miles away. He walked to the door, never looking back, and left me completely and utterly alone.

8

West

I OPENED THE real estate app, zoomed in on Nic's neighborhood, then tossed my phone onto the couch next to me with a growl of frustration. "I can't believe she's selling the house."

My mom hummed thoughtfully as she slid a plate of sliced cheddar with saltines and apples onto the coffee table in front of me. Someone might assume the snack plate was for a kindergartener if it wasn't sitting next to a half-drunk tumbler of whiskey. "It sounds like good news."

I gaped at my mom. "Good news? Nic's about to lose the only home she's ever known."

"Oh, sweet boy," she said on a sigh. "She's not *losing* the house. She's moving on."

"Only because she can't handle it by herself. But I can help. I want to help." Desperation pressed against my sternum.

"She doesn't like asking for help—you know that. Remember how hard it was to force even a little normal life on her after her mom died? I couldn't give the kid a ride to school without first convincing her I was already going that way. Our girl is obstinate. But that means if she wanted to keep the house, she would have made it work. Nicola can do any damn thing she sets her mind to. But this one is bigger than a detailed to-do list."

I sank back into the soft leather of my mom's sofa and tented my arms over my face. She wasn't wrong. Nic was one of the most capable people I'd ever known. She was scrappy and clever and insightful and optimistic and beautiful to her core and so goddamn perfect it made my ribs ache from how full she made my heart. She was always able to find her way out of even the muddiest, murkiest problems. So, why couldn't she find a way to save the house? Why *wouldn't* she find a way to save the house?

"I don't understand," I groaned, flopping my arms to the couch at my sides.

"What don't you understand?" my mom asked without judgment.

All of it, I wanted to shout. I took a deep breath and an even deeper drink of whiskey. Its warmth curled through me, easing a fraction of the tightness in my chest. "If I were in her shoes, and god forbid, something happened to you guys, I would do everything in my power to keep this house."

"Ah. You're comparing apples to oranges, sweetheart. I worked damn hard to make the house a home for you and the girls. It's full of love and warmth and happy memories. Not that everything's always been perfect here, or that we haven't had our own struggles, but they can't hold a candle to the things Nicola's survived. Her house is full of loss and insecurity and generational trauma."

I scrubbed a hand down my face. "I get that, it's just—it's all she has. I could have helped her make it a home. We could have filled it with new, happy memories together."

My mom's mouth twitched at the corners. In the haze of angst and alcohol, it took me longer than it should have to realize what I'd just admitted to her. I'd spent my whole adult life denying I had feelings for Nic.

I eyed her warily. "Can we save the gloating for later?"

"West, I've been watching you two circle each other for over a decade. It's been both entertaining and heartbreaking to see the lengths you've both gone to in an effort to hide your feelings. Especially this year. I don't know what happened between you guys. But you couldn't make it through a conversation with me or your sisters without *casually* fishing for updates about Nicola instead of just texting her yourself. While she basically disappeared into thin air anytime someone mentioned you at Sarah's bachelorette party. She was trying so hard not to love you."

"Why?"

"That's one of the many things the two of you are going to have to talk through. But my best guess? She knows how much it hurts to lose someone you love. And she thinks, from experience, she'll inevitably lose you, just like she lost Thom and her mom. Even her dad, in a way."

Inevitable. Fuck that. I leaned into my elbows on my knees, while my brain tried to pull together a plan of action. "I just have to convince her I'm not going anywhere."

"Oh, sweet boy," my mom said softly, rubbing a warm hand across my back. "You can't. None of us can give each other that guarantee."

"There is nothing in this world that would ever make me leave her."

My mom gave me a pointed look. "Maybe in a world where you can control everything. But you can't—as much as I know you'd like to. You don't have any control over illness or accidents. No one does. And, if you look at it from Nic's point of view, loving you poses the greatest potential for loss."

I scowled down at the floor between my knees. Was my mom implying there was something about me that was a danger to Nic? "You think loving *me* adds to the risk?"

"Not you. Romantic love, universally. The risk snowballs. In the beginning, it's just the two of you. But then it's the two of you and a home, and eventually it's the two of you, a home, and a baby." At my arched brow, she rolled her eyes and amended, "Or a pet."

I didn't want that to make as much sense as it did. I honestly hadn't thought about what all of that might mean for me, either. As bad as I got worrying about Nic's well-being, how much worse was the darkness going to get if we had kids? Panic started to build just thinking about how devastating it would be to lose a child. "How do you do it, Mom? How do you survive the fear of something happening to your kids without losing your mind?"

She gave me a soft smile and smoothed her thumb over the hair at my temple. My eyes fluttered closed, panic temporarily mollified. "It's never easy, West. Especially with you. When your dad died, you were still so tiny and fragile, and I had no idea how to cope. You were the last piece of him I had. I wanted to put you in a bubble. I felt like I had to protect you from the outside world at all costs, as if I could somehow protect both you and your dad that way.

"But I had to learn to loosen my grip on you when it was time to go back to work. I had to take baby steps. A couple hours a day at Grandma's, then a couple days a week at daycare, before I was willing to trust other people to share the job of caring for you. I also had to learn how to emotionally separate you from your dad. It wasn't fair or healthy for me to put the burden of his memory on you."

I swallowed hard against the lump in my throat, then finished off the whiskey. I might have been buzzed, but I didn't need my mom to spell out her implications. "You think I'm doing the same thing to Nic."

"I think you haven't processed your grief, West. It's going to eat you up if you let it."

I was hot from head to toe, flush with embarrassment and irritation and desperation and hopelessness.

At my protracted silence, my mom went on. "You might be thirty-three years old, but I'm still your mother, Westley Ross Schafer. I've been watching you struggle, and I've wanted to swoop in and fix it all for you. But I can't. Neither can Nicola," she added pointedly.

"You're going to use mom guilt to kick a grown man while he's down?" I asked with gravel in my voice.

She smirked at me, and my lips curved up despite the tears in my eyes. "You gave me no other choice."

I speared my fingers through my hair and slumped back into the couch cushions. "I've been having panic attacks again," I admitted. " I—I'm not okay."

Nic

THE FIRST GLINTS of daylight crept in through the living room blinds, and I turned to bury my face in the couch cushions. I'd only slept in fitful spurts, waking at every creak and groan in the old cottage.

West had not come home.

It was hard to convince myself that it wasn't because I'd hurt him irreparably and he never wanted to see me again. The thought shouldn't have felt like icicles between my ribs— I wanted him to let me go and forget about me.

But the frosty tendrils that had woven their way through my veins after our fight were pulling me away from simple hurt feelings and into darker and more insidious thoughts.

West had not come home.

He had not called. He had not texted.

Logically, I knew he most likely got stuck at the front desk, and it was so germane to his daily life that it didn't even occur to him that I might worry. And after our fight, he probably thought I wanted space. He probably thought he was doing the right thing by staying away.

I couldn't continue to cling to that logic when the sharp, silver lines of daylight began to stripe the room, though. Even on the night shift, West should have been home before sunrise.

I forced myself to get up and move quickly through my morning routine. I told myself West would be home when I got out of the shower. When he wasn't, I told myself he'd be home by the time I was dressed. Then by the time the coffee brewed. By the time the toast popped up. By the time my mug was empty.

My phone buzzed next to my nearly empty coffee cup, and I grabbed for it so hastily I knocked it off the counter. It clattered to the floor, and a picture of Julia Schafer smiled up at me. The icy tendrils tightened around my heart.

Something was wrong.

I could ignore the call and delay the inevitable. Like Schrödinger's Cat—whatever was wrong could both exist and not exist as long as I didn't take the call. When my brother died, I got an extra hour of normal life by ignoring my phone when

West called. But this wasn't the same. That night, I was blissfully ignorant of even the potential for the catastrophic hurt that awaited me. This time, I was all too aware of just how badly things could go and exactly how devastating it would be.

The phone continued to buzz through my philosophical crisis until the screen went black. I slid to the floor and sat next to it, waiting for it to ping with a voicemail or a text notification.

Nothing.

I picked up my phone and texted Julia with shaky fingers. *Is West ok?*

My phone rang immediately, and I swiped to answer. "Is he ok?" I asked quietly, skipping right past any semblance of phone manners.

"Yes! Oh, sweet pea, yes, he's ok. I didn't mean to scare you," she rushed to say. My lungs deflated on a heavy sigh of relief. "He fell asleep here last night. I wasn't sure if he let you know, and I didn't want you to worry. I should have just texted instead."

"Good. That's good. I was worried," I admitted, swallowing around the tightness in my throat.

"I don't think he meant to stay, but he was exhausted and a little drunk."

I nodded, as if she could see me. "He told you we had a fight?"

"He did. And he told me you're heading off on a big new adventure."

"Yeah, I, um—I think I'll have better opportunities for career growth if I'm in DC. Out here, I'm kind of out of sight, out of mind, you know?"

"Well, I'm excited for you. It's a huge step to take on your own. Just don't forget you always have a home here with us, no matter where you're living. You're *never* out of sight, out of mind for me."

"I know," I whispered, tears rolling down my cheeks.

"Good. You're an honorary Schafer, whether you like it or not, Nicola. There's no escaping us," Julia said brightly. "I've got to get to work, but I'll see you tonight at the tree lighting, sweet pea. And I will be claiming at least a few months' worth of hugs before you run away to the big city."

"I'll get my arms warmed up," I said with a weak smile. "See you tonight."

When I'd gotten off the phone with Julia, I'd cleared out of West's cottage, stashed my bag in the luggage room off the hotel lobby, and gotten to work on the final preparations for the tree lighting.

West had spent the night at his parents', and I'd lost my ever-loving mind worrying about him. It was a perfectly timed reminder of why I was moving across the country. We'd only spent a couple of days playing house, but it was enough to leave me exposed and vulnerable. My reaction was humiliating. I could have—should have—just called him to see where he was. It would have saved me hours of worry. But I froze. In the haze of fear, not knowing one way or the other was better than knowing something bad had happened. Now, in the crisp light of day, knowing he was safe and warm at home the whole time, my doom spiral looked completely unhinged.

The stress of the night—the sleepless hours of worry and fear—had sunk bone deep, and I was dragging. The end of the night couldn't come quickly enough. The carolers would lead the crowd in a spirited sing-along, I would flip the switch for the holiday lights, and then I would make my quiet goodbyes while everyone was happily distracted.

I kept a low profile for the rest of the day, working diligently to make sure the tree lighting would be perfect for the Bryson House and Summer Springs community. The vendors and volunteers had all done amazing work, and I was proud of what we'd accomplished.

Everything was perfect.

There was a small part of me that wanted something to go wrong, though. I needed the hotel to give me that same *see, this is why you're leaving* reminder I'd gotten from West. But there was nothing. And maybe that was the reminder, in and of itself. The ghosts were a bunch of nosy gossips, and there was no way they hadn't all heard that I wasn't coming back next year. Yet none of them were messing with me. Not a single soul tried to impede my progress.

I'd only spied glimpses of West throughout the afternoon, and we hadn't sought each other out. He'd texted when he'd woken up, just to let me know he'd stayed at his mom's and hoped I'd slept well. I'd responded with a thumbs-up and moved on with my day.

When the sun began to dip behind the mountain, I checked the tree one last time. I circled the courtyard with my freezing fingers balled in the pockets of my puffy coat, and made sure every last bow, ball, and bulb was perfect. Everything was in place, and people from the hotel and village were beginning to gather.

I headed to the lobby to get my things together so I'd be ready to go after the lighting. And, honestly, to hide from Julia and the rest of the Schafers. I wasn't ready to face them.

My stomach grumbled, and I realized I hadn't eaten any-thing all day. When I'd cut through the restaurant kitchen ear-lier in the day, Angus had been in a mood, so I definitely wasn't heading that way for food. And there wasn't time to sneak back to West's for leftovers. Plus, it was West's, which likely meant actually talking to West. And I wasn't ready for that. I might never be.

However, I felt confident I could get in and out of West's dark office without incident, and I knew for a fact there were Cheez-its in his bottom desk drawer.

I let myself in and plopped down in West's desk chair, spin-ning toward the snack drawer. It was a treasure trove of cheesy delights. Cheez-its, Pirate's Booty, Goldfish, those little snack packs with the cheese and the little red spatula. There were also a few satsumas and a bag of dark chocolate-covered pretzels—my favorites. The pretzels were unopened, and I fleetingly wondered if they were supposed to be for me.

After a moment, I realized not only that I hadn't eaten, but I also hadn't sat down all day. My body was sore and tired. Just a little longer until I could head back to my professionally staged house, rip the crisp loaner bedding off my mattress, and snuggle into my own old, worn-soft sheets. In the mean-time, I flipped on West's desk lamp, grabbed a satsuma and the pretzels, then slumped back into the chair with a groan and toed off my shoes. I had fifteen minutes until I needed to head back outside.

It was equally comforting and disquieting to be in West's personal space. His office didn't carry his smell the same way his cottage did, but it was still very obviously his. The snack drawer, the tidy scrawl of his handwriting on the sticky notes around his monitor, the corkboard dotted with pictures of his family. And friends. My brother. Me.

There was a picture of me with his sisters and mom at Sarah's bachelorette party that summer. And one of West, Thom, and me at the Bryson House holiday party the year before Thom died. It was partially obscured by what looked like a checklist of things to prepare for the cost reduction analyst, but I easily recognized it from the corner that was visible. I had the same photo on my fridge. The three of us had drunk too much and danced our asses off until most of the other party-goers had called it a night. I have no idea who took the picture, but Thom was in the middle of casting an imaginary fishing line, West was wiggling like a hooked trout, and I was between them, doubled over with laughter. It perfectly encapsulated our group dynamic.

A tear slid down my cheek. I swiped at it with my sleeve.

I missed my brother so much. But I also hated him for leaving me all alone. Sometimes it was nearly impossible to remember the good times with him because they were so obscured by the pain.

The picture from the party was a much-needed reminder that things hadn't always hurt. The happy memories were bittersweet, but they were still a balm to my wounded heart.

My relationship with my brother was complicated, especially after our mom died, but I was always going to love him, even when I hated him.

I was always going to love West. It was inescapable. Maybe someday, years from now, I'd find someone to be happy with, someone who I wouldn't be terrified to lose. Maybe West would meet someone else and get married and have the happy life I was too scared to share with him. And I would have to lose him all over again.

And it would hurt. It was inevitable.

So, if it was going to hurt either way, why would I choose to live with the endless dull ache of leaving him behind rather than stockpile all of the happiness I could wring out of a life with him? If the destination was the same, why was I forcing myself to take the most brutal path alone, when I could take the scenic route with my favorite person?

I'd been an idiot.

I'd found out the man I'd been in love with for more than half of my life had loved me the same way, that he wanted to build a life with me, and I'd shut him out.

He'd offered me the coast road, and I'd said, No thanks, I'll take the treacherous mountain pass.

Shit. I needed to try to make things right.

I popped out of the desk chair so quickly that it rolled back and hit the wall with a thunk. I cringed, apologized to the empty room, and headed to the luggage closet. My clothes were gross from working all day, and I hadn't bothered with makeup that morning. If I'd had my moment of very obvious clarity even an hour earlier, I would have gone back to the cottage to shower and get fixed up. I loved getting dressed up for the tree lighting.

My bag was buried behind a Minnie Mouse suitcase and an overstuffed hiking pack. I started to shuffle things around to get it out when I started at a loud bang behind me. I yelped and whipped around to see what had happened.

The door had slammed shut.

My shoulders slumped with a whimper. "Not again."

9

West

I TOOK A sick day. It was terrible timing, with everything I still needed to prep for the cost reduction analyst. But I was wiped out, hungover, and a coward. I wasn't ready to see Nic. There was so much to say, and I was still psyching myself up for the conversation that awaited us.

So, I slept until noon in my childhood bedroom, sat on the couch and ate leftovers out of my mom's fridge, and tried not to feel guilty for leaving Nic all alone.

When time was up, I got into my car and headed back to the hotel. I chewed my nails most of the way there. I knew I needed to let Nic go—it was what she said she wanted, and what I wanted was for her to be happy—but I also needed to explain that letting her go didn't mean I was giving up on her. That she would always have a place with me, in whatever capacity she was willing to fill it, though I needed to communicate that in a way that didn't create a sense of obligation. It was a minefield. And whether or not I avoided the explosives, it was going to hurt so damn much.

Nic had cleared out of the cottage when I got home. Of course, she had. I'd been an ass, and she was leaving. Didn't change the fact that my home felt hollow without her. I felt hollow without her. It was a feeling I'd have to get used to.

I sat in front of the Christmas tree and tried to figure out how the hell I was going to both fight for the woman I wanted to be with while simultaneously letting her go. Because that whole *if you love something, set it free* business was bull shit. Especially with Nic. If I didn't make it explicitly clear that I wanted her with me, she was going to write me off as pitying her. Like my mom said, she'd had to convince Nic that she was absolutely not going out of her way just to give the poor kid a ride to school after her mom died.

After a scorching hot shower that left my skin as raw as my heart and some leftover mac and cheese, I headed up to the hotel for the tree lighting. In the space of time it took me to walk from my front porch to the courtyard, I decided to change tack.

Fuck walking the line. I was going to fight for Nic. Anything else would feel like a manipulation. She didn't need my permission or approval or understanding or whatever to leave. She was going to leave regardless. What she *did* need was someone ready and willing to go to the mat for her.

There was already a large crowd gathered for the tree lighting, and the energy was electric. I prowled the perimeter, on the hunt for Nic. On my second lap, it was nearly time to turn on the lights, and there was still no sign of her.

She wouldn't have left without saying goodbye. Without finishing the job she started. Right? I tried not to panic, but the uncomfortable warmth of worry was starting to pool at the nape of my neck.

I spotted Sadie standing off to the side of the courtyard and jogged over to her. "Hey, have you seen Nic?"

She gave me an assessing once over, then shrugged. "She popped by the greenhouse about an hour ago. Haven't seen her since then."

I nodded, trying to think of where she might have gone between there and here. "Thanks," I said before trudging off.

A light on the footpath back to the hotel flashed as I walked passed, and I halted. It flashed again, and I walked toward it. Adelia knew where Nic was. I followed as the lights along the path blinked in sequence. My anxiety flared as we reached the fork in the path—the hotel to the left, the funicular down to the village to the right. A light to the left strobed, and I sighed in relief.

The darkness was trying its damnedest to break my focus. It wasn't like Nic to be late for something as important to her as the tree lighting. She had to be in trouble.

At the top of the hotel's front steps, I stopped and took a slow, steadying breath. If Nic was actually in trouble, I wouldn't be much help in the throes of a panic attack. If something was wrong, Adelia would have made that clear. The nerves were still crackling in my veins as I followed the flashing lights through the lobby.

My office door was open. But the relief was fleeting. She wasn't there. The lamp was on, her phone and a half-eaten bag of chocolate pretzels were on my desk, and her sneakers were on the floor.

She was barefoot. She had to be nearby. I stepped out of my office. "Nic?" I called loudly.

Her muffled voice called back. "I'm in the luggage closet."

I pulled open the closet door, and there was Nic. Sitting on her suitcase, entirely unpanicked. "Hey."

"Hi." She gave me a chagrined smile and pushed her hair behind her ears. "Told you I'd keep getting stuck in closets. Ghosts," she added with a shrug.

I nodded in acknowledgement. "Have you been stuck here long?"

"Maybe fifteen minutes? Not exactly sure. My phone's on your desk. But I've really only been here long enough to freshen up and change my clothes."

"May I?" I asked, gesturing to the red and white polka dot suitcase next to her. She nodded. I twisted the bag to face her and perched on it, my knees bracketing hers. I wasn't sure where to start. "I'm sorry—"

Nic stopped me with a raised hand, then reached over to swing the door shut for privacy. "You were right," she said, meeting my gaze. "Mostly. I've been building up walls and turrets and digging a moat around my heart to protect myself from even the potential for pain. The problem is, those defenses were mostly to keep you out, but you were already on the inside. Like a reverse Trojan horse. It was an exercise in futility. And I realized whether I hold you close or push you away, it's not going to change the hurt I'll feel if something happens to you. Which I know sounds a little nihilistic, but the realization made it seem pretty ridiculous to not enjoy the good parts with you, if the bad parts are going to suck either way. Because I love you. And I always will. As a friend, or as... more."

"As more would be my vote, if it's all the same to you."

"It's not all the same to me. West, I've been doodling Mrs. Nicola Schafer in my diary since I was thirteen years old. The first time you came over to our house, I fell rom-com level, slow motion, soft filter in love with you. And it's only gotten worse since then. Because you've only gotten better looking over time."

I nodded sagely. "Future GILF, for sure."

She bit back a laugh. "Right? And now that I know what you can do with your hands? Game over."

"Sorry to have ruined you for all other men."

"I think I'll survive," she said with a soft smile. "In all seriousness, though. You're my home, West. I trust you with my life. And my heart. But that doesn't mean I'm not still scared that forces outside our control could take you away from me. I'm still broken. We both are. And I don't want us to delude ourselves into thinking that being together will make us whole again. We both have work to do. We both need help."

"That's what I was trying to apologize for. Before you preempted my apology with your own entirely unnecessary apology because I was the one who was wrong. I was trying to use you as the glue to fix all of my broken pieces, and I'm so sorry I put that burden on you. It's my job to make me better, not yours. I made appointments with a therapist and with my doctor to talk about medication for my anxiety. But I know neither will be an instant fix, and this will take time, so I'll completely understand if you want to hit the pause button on us to work on ourselves."

Nic scrunched up her nose in offense. "Hell no. I'm happy and relieved you're taking meaningful steps to manage your mental health, and I think you should feel so proud of yourself, but now that I've accepted the fact that I can actually, really, *finally* be with you? There's no way in hell I'm going to give that up, even for a few months."

I sucked in a breath. "Oh, thank god. I would have understood if you'd wanted to work on ourselves first, but the idea of giving up the few weeks you're here before you move would have been a whole other thing that I'd need to talk to the therapist about."

Nic's brows pulled together. "You're okay with this being long distance?"

"I mean, it's not ideal, I'll admit that, but we can make it work. I have an unreasonable amount of unused vacation time. And you'll still be traveling for work, so, air miles? We'll figure it out."

She looked away and chewed on her lips for a moment. "What if I want to stay?"

I straightened. "Do you?"

She nodded sheepishly.

I slumped back in relief. "Then yes, please, let's definitely do that instead of long distance."

"I'm homeless."

I raised an incredulous eyebrow. "I thought I was your home."

"You are. But unless I can put a sleeper sofa inside you, I'm going to need a tangible housing solution." Nic's face shifted into thinking mode. I smiled to myself and gave my problem solver a moment to problem solve. "I guess I've got a few more weeks before I need to be out of the house. I can find something before then. Though winter isn't the best time to find a place, and I don't want to rush into something I'll regret later. Maybe my real estate agent will have some leads for temporary rentals. Or I'll get a vacation rental while I sort it out."

I reached over and smoothed the line between Nic's focused brows with my thumb and gave her a soft smile. "You'll figure it out. You always do."

"Right. Yeah." She shook her head like she was clearing her mental Etch-a-Sketch. "Those are problems for Future Nic."

"And, obviously, Future Nic is welcome to move in with me."

She looked surprised. "Really? You don't think that's too fast?"

"After all of the years we've spent moving way too slow? No. We've already wasted way too much time not being together. I have zero interest in ever again waking up alone, if waking up with you instead is an option." I could see the wheels starting to churn again behind her eyes. "But that's a consideration for Future Nic, not Present Nic."

Nic took a deep breath and gave me a chagrined smile. "Ok." She nodded once, definitively. "I'm present."

I slid my arms around her waist and pulled her toward me. "Me too."

Her hands settled on my shoulders, and her thumbs swept lightly up and down the sides of my neck. My eyes closed briefly on a contented sigh. She leaned her forehead against mine. "I love you," she whispered, her warm breath caressing my lips.

"I love you, too," I breathed, before the overhead light flashed wildly then went out, leaving us in pitch black. I pulled back with a startled laugh.

Nic reached to pull open the door, and the hallway light spilled in. She had a crooked grin on her face. "So much for matchmaking ghosts."

"If they try to un-match us, I will have them exor—" Nic slapped her hand over my mouth.

"Cold showers," she hissed, slightly panicked.

The closet light flickered again, then the hall lights flickered in succession. I stood abruptly and looked at Nic wide-eyed. "Oh shit. The tree lighting."

Nic

I dashed out of the closet and started to run to the courtyard.

"Nic." West caught up to me halfway through the lobby.

"Kiss later, West. Everyone's waiting," I half-shouted over my shoulder.

He pulled me to a halt, and I twisted to face him, exasperated. "Kiss later," he agreed with a smirk. "Shoes and coat now."

I stared down at my socked feet, then looked up at West. He was holding out my sneakers with my coat under his arm. "Right. Yes. Shoes are important."

He handed me my sneakers, and I plopped down in the nearest chair to put them on. When I stood, he held my coat out for me to slip into, and then we were off. As soon as West pulled open the front door, I could hear the carolers happily singing Rudolph the Red-Nosed Reindeer.

The courtyard was still dark, but the hundreds of people surrounding the tree were entirely unperturbed by the delay. We trotted around the outside of the crowd to the plug for the lights. West reached for the cord, and I put a hand on his arm to stop him. "Wait until the end of the song."

When the crowd reached the final line, West flipped up the weather cover on the outlet. "Let's hope they work this time," he muttered to me with a hesitant half smile. Around us, the singers stretched out the final note of *his-tor-y*, and the tree lit up, covering the courtyard and carolers in warm light.

The crowd cheered, the carolers started singing *Joy to the World*, and West smiled up at me from his crouched position, twinkle lights warming his cool blue eyes. "Perfect," he whispered. He took my hand, and we walked to find his family. His fingers twined with mine, and I swallowed down a lump in my throat. It was silly. The man had already had his hands all over my body. But simply holding hands with him in a crowd full of our friends and family flooded my heart with warmth.

"There you are!" Julia exclaimed as we approached. She looked down at our joined hands, gave me a watery smile, and pulled me into a tight hug. I squeezed her and fought back tears. She pulled away, but didn't let me go, keeping her grip on my upper arms. "Looks like you two talked."

A nod was all I could manage. She nodded back, satisfied, then hugged me again.

"Mom, you're going to suffocate her," West scolded affectionately.

Julia gave me one more squeeze and stepped away with her hands up. "She was warned she'd be subjected to extra hugs, Westley."

West looked to me for confirmation. I nodded in solemn assurance. "I was warned."

He quirked a curious eyebrow as he pulled me into his side. "We need to go finish up some tree stuff," he said to his mom.

"We do," I agreed, trying to keep the incredulity out of my voice. We didn't need to get back to do tree stuff. Tree stuff was done.

"Of course," Julia said. "The dinner reservation is in forty-five minutes. We'll see you inside."

West pulled me away and walked until he found a spot by the tree where the crowd had dispersed. He cupped my face in his hands and met my gaze with warm, smiling eyes. "Where were we?"

"We *were* in a luggage closet," I teased, as my stomach burst with butterflies.

His warm thumbs brushed lightly over my cheekbones. He leaned in and brushed the cold tip of his nose against mine. "But this is a better first kiss," he murmured, glancing toward the glowing tree, "right?"

I tilted my head up until my lips were less than an inch from his. "I can't confirm that until you actually kiss me."

He pulled back a fraction and frowned playfully. "We could probably do better, huh?"

As if on cue, a snowflake landed on West's brow, and we both looked up. The sky was swirling with big, fluffy flakes. I met his gaze. "I think this is about as good as it gets."

West's smiling lips met mine, soft and warm and perfect. I melted into him on a contented sigh, ready to take the kiss deeper when a flash of light strobed through my eyelids, and the small crowd to our left broke into applause and whoops. We both looked over at West's family, his mom holding up her phone to catch the moment with her camera.

"Who even uses the flash?" West groaned. His shoulders slumped, and he dropped his forehead to mine. "Sorry, Princess."

West's sister Sarah started to steer their mom toward the hotel. "We'll see you two in forty-five minutes," she said exaggeratedly over her shoulder. West gave her a defeated thumbs-up.

I tilted my face up and kissed him again. "No apologies. It was perfect."

West looked incredulous. "The kind of first kiss we can tell everyone about at our wedding reception?"

I quirked an eyebrow. "Our wedding reception?"

"You'd rather elope?"

I scoffed, but flushed with contented warmth. Yes, there was a very high likelihood I was going to marry this man in the near future—like he said, we'd spent too much time not being together—but that didn't mean I wasn't going to make him work for it. "I think you're putting the horse before the cart, Schafe."

West nuzzled into my ear. "What if I have a special treat for a very good horse?"

I laughed and gave him a little shove away, but he pulled me back, grinning.

"We have forty-five minutes." He waggled his eyebrows.

I pretended to consider it. "Stables?"

West gave a full-throated laugh. "I love you so fucking much."

All I Want for Christmas Is Sparks

Jessica Krueger

1

Sadie

"How is the rescue of your famous poinsettias going?" Nic asked, walking to the back of the greenhouse, her glittery clipboard raised to her face. The usually warm, gold base of her translucent aura swirled with anxious reds and excited greens that made her a Christmas display to anyone who could see emotions and personalities like me. Nic was a redheaded Christmas elf in jeans and a loose blouse, while I was the Ghost of Christmas Future in black overalls, elbow deep in dirt, black fringe bangs plastered to my sweaty forehead.

Just swimmingly. If by swimming...I mean drowning. I rubbed my forehead, feeling the grit I'd left there, but didn't bother wiping it off. I'd only make her aura worse if I mentioned this rescue would take me long into the night to accomplish.

A faster solution would have been to treat the plants chemically when I found the slow-developing fungal issue, but I opted for the more eco-conscious approach of replanting them in my custom sterile substrate mix. My hybrid-babies deserved the best.

I also needed to look extremely busy to make my job appear less expendable. Because at any moment, the cost reduction consultant the hotel hired to increase revenue would waltz in and decide a conservatory hybridization specialist—the lady who helped create fancy plants—wasn't worth the extra dollar amount compared to the other greenhouse workers. Ever since I heard the news, a nagging ball made my stomach feel heavier, and today another had joined to climb into my throat.

"I'll have the rest potted and ready to go back into the guest rooms tomorrow," I said, chewing the inside of my lip.

"Perfect." She smiled and touched the marbled pink and red leaf I'd slaved for years here to create. "These are truly beautiful. The staff can distribute them throughout the day."

She turned to talk to the greenhouse manager, my older, sweet-as-sin boss, about her other decorating plans. Though the clipboard weighed little, Nic had a lot on her plate. Christmas at the Bryson House Hotel was the event of all events. It was nicknamed Mistletoe Manor for a reason. This was the place to be for the holiday season, for visitors and locals alike. Even for someone like me, who had little love for the holidays—the decorations, music, and hot cocoa filled me with a Christmas tenderness I couldn't deny.

Sweat beaded and tickled a sensitive path behind my ear, reminding me of the lips that had been there last night. Clive. The impending doom of the cost reduction consultant's arrival led me to seek make-me-feel-good sex, and he hadn't disappointed.

He'd been attractive in the dark bar atmosphere, but damn, was he a Booktok girl's wish come true. His spiky blond hair may not have been my type, but he made it look sexy in a lawyer who always wins a lawsuit kind of way. His stern jawline gave him a resting bitch face that was all show as he had the warmest smile that made me melt. And when we'd returned to the hotel where he coincidentally was staying, he had known how to make me feel...worshipped.

He'd never once rushed me, and from the way he took his time, taking my pointers in stride, it seemed like he would not get off unless I did. At the memory of the multiple orgasms he gave me, my lower muscles pulsed. I squeezed my thighs together. Fuck. He was *definitely* the best decision I'd made in a while.

His foggy blue base aura had surrounded him, and the rippling white lines of relaxation had made it look like the deep ocean. Before I'd talked to him, his aura had told me he was an open and easy-flowing individual. Everything about him matched his aura as if he were authentically himself. I'd never met someone like him, but I'm sure there were hidden truths like sharks under his aura's blue depths. I'd just have to spill a little bit of my blood to find them. I shook my head, reminding myself that was for another woman to try. Not me.

I had ducked and bolted from that situation when he asked me out again. No one wanted to date someone like me who could read their emotions and expose their inner truths. He was probably already checking out of the hotel—and out of my life. But he'd definitely left such an impression on my body that I'd be thinking about him for a while.

Pouring dirt into the next five pots, I shushed my wayward thoughts and focused on the homework my therapist had given me. She'd challenged me to tell a complete stranger the truth about what I could see. I was learning to accept myself and be open with people after all the suppress-yourself bullshit my family put me through. I'd driven two hours to find a stranger because small towns were full of gossip. The older woman I'd settled on hadn't seemed convinced about my story, but she'd said in a granny way, "That's nice, dear," and walked away.

I'd told a few more people, and after a lengthy interrogation from a ten-year-old, I had gone home smiling. I'd felt like a superhero, but not everyone was as easy to tell as a kid. And my therapist wanted me to tell someone more personal to me. She also wanted me to stop having one-night stands, but I could only work on one challenge at a time, and Nic fit the bill for my prior mission.

She came to the hotel only during the Christmas season and was always kind to everyone. Hell, she understood that the red aura glancing over her shoulder was the ghost of Adelia—the original owner. And yes, even ghosts give off auras I can apparently see. I'd only known about Nic's understanding because I'd heard her muttering to Adelia from time to time. And if she could believe in ghosts, then surely, someone seeing auras wouldn't be too far-fetched?

"Hey Nic," I blurted when my manager walked off to do Nic's bidding. When Nic glanced up from her clipboard, my stomach gave an unsettling flop, but I continued. "I know this is super random, but my therapist wants me to open up to people, and I—can I tell you something personal?"

She smiled and a wave of yellow intrigue flashed over her aura. "Yeah. Sure. As long as it's not something about the stables."

"The stables?"

She wiped her forehead as a flare of fuchsia brightened her skin along with a bubbling orange, hinting that she was hiding a laugh. "Never mind. What did you want to tell me?"

That definitely seemed like an interesting story, but also a distraction from the task I needed to complete. I wetted my dry lips and tried to push away the heat rising up my back. This wasn't just telling someone I liked plants—this was telling someone my darkest shame. The part of me I had to keep hidden from everyone because they'd think I was delusional, or trying to take advantage of them, or worst of all—they'd fear me.

"I can—" My voice died as memories surfaced of all the times I told someone and a pop of silver symbolizing reflective thinking and caution would surface—skepticism followed by anxiety. Then I thought of the dark oil of hatred and resentment that built up around my parents. All those memories churned into a hand that squeezed my throat. "I uhh—" *Come on...come on. Think of anything else to say.*

"Nic," a voice called with ill-concealed delight. "I didn't expect to see you here."

West, the hotel manager, marched through the greenhouse. He always appeared put together despite the amount he worked, especially late hours, but today he was even more so. His shirt was pressed and his hair crisp. A golden happiness arced over his aura while tumultuous colors swirled underneath—a man under insurmountable stress but who was weathering it with honeymoon vibes.

A sigh whooshed out of me, welcoming the intrusion. That was a train wreck I'd gladly averted. And probably for the better, as I recalled why West was under stress. The consultant. And the last thing I needed was to let anyone I worked with believe I was delusional.

"I had a few things to check on with the upcoming garden events," Nic said. "What are you doing here?"

As soon as they were in proximity, sparks arced between their auras. My heart squeezed. Those sparks represented their chemistry—the I-will-be-with-you-forever kind. I grabbed at the roots of another poinsettia, wishing I could grab sparks for myself. As the only person who could love me would have to accept and believe in all my gifts, I assumed I'd be alone—albeit hopefully not horny, but alone.

Clive breezed into my mind like an unwarranted cologne ad, all dark, sultry, and smoky. He may have asked me out again before we'd passed out, but I'd never see him again. A part of me twisted inside. I should have gotten his number. Stuck around. But like a scaredy-cat, I ran.

West said, "I'm still showing the consultant around and introducing him to a few of the staff. A few things held us up."

My stomach lurched. He was here. *Shit. Shit. Shit.* Did I look busy? Was planting poinsettias working hard enough to pay for my salary? I couldn't lose my job. This place. I had nothing else. Only here was I given such freedom: living on site, creating beautiful flowers as I saw fit, and basking in the sparks flying around all the amazing couples.

But looking between the three of us, I was the odd one out. I always was. I was the strange, tattooed girl in dark clothing who kept to herself and her plants.

As pressure built in my chest, I sank my hands deeper into the soil, and on a breath out, pushed my emotions into the dirt like I was a grounding rod. A panic attack would not help me. I'd been working here for half a decade. I wouldn't let some man take my home away from me, even if I had to make his job hell. I imagined an array of equipment failures, doors staying locked for hours—

From behind one of the bushes, a familiar face with a charming grin walked toward us. My heart thundered in my throat. I froze as disbelief took the breath from my lungs. *It couldn't be...*

"Hey Clive," Nic said. "It's good to see you again. I hope everything has been going well so far."

"Just the usual hiccups as I'm paraded around like the villain." His eyes swiveled to me, and he gave me his stunning smile—straight teeth framed by full, bitable lips. I wanted to melt into the floor from both the heat of him and to escape this situation. Flashes of electrified orange surprise had surfaced across his aura, creating a distracting sunset over the rippling ocean. My breath caught as something dangerous fluttered in my chest.

"Sadie, this is Clive Doyle, the consultant I told you about. Clive, this is Sadie. She works here in the greenhouse, where all the magic for the conservatory happens behind the scenes. She's our prized botanist. She actually won an award from the American Orchid Society this year for a hybrid orchid she worked on here at the hotel. Ask her if you need access to anything."

"Hello, Sadie," he said, and from his twinkling eyes, I suspected he wasn't catching my "we're strangers" glare. "It's nice seeing you again as well."

Sweat dribbled down my back, and I longed to stuff myself into this planter like this poinsettia. He seriously went there? This man was honest to a fault—his aura shared as much, but—read the room!

"Again?" Nic asked.

Clive's eyes narrowed, as if coming to the reality of our very problematic situation. "We bumped into each other last night."

At the image of what bumping we actually did, heat scored up my neck. *Shit.* Of course, I fucked the cost reduction consultant. At that moment, I was glad dirt covered my hands. I had an excuse not to touch him, and I didn't want to as conflicting, well, everything rolled inside of me.

We hadn't had time to talk about our jobs between kisses. Why did the universe hate me? The man who might tell the hotel board to fire me also made my body catch fire.

"Anyway, as I've been saying to everyone, I will do everything in my power to stay out of your way this next week so we can both do our jobs," he said, sounding assertive and in his element. It was *not* sexy. "I have more of a data-driven approach than a hands-on one. Most costs come from energy efficiency, waste management, and supplier contracts, so I address those first. If you have any cost-reducing suggestions, feel free to share them. Did you have questions?"

How do you feel about sleeping with an employee of the place you're about to evaluate? Something diabolical inside me added, *and do you want to do it again*?

Good sex—no—amazzzing sex, the kind that puts you straight to sleep afterward and easy conversation alone didn't warrant a second hookup.

"Nope," I squeaked. "I'm good."

To chill my libido, I reminded myself why I had one-night stands with men. The fear and rejection in their auras when I accidentally dug too deep into their emotions. None of which I wanted to stomach again. I'd just do my job, keep my distance from him, and hope that despite my oddness, he considered me a valuable employee for the company.

Merry fucking Christmas to me.

2

Clive

"WHEN ARE YOU going to finish looking through old receipts and join Dad and me for hot cocoa and tree decorating?" Sid asked from my headphones tucked warmly under my stocking cap.

My breath puffed in front of me as I trudged across the barely visible path through the snow toward the small section of cottages next to the hotel. "How is it you still don't understand what I do? This isn't forensic digging into coffee-stained invoices. What I actually do is figure out where the money leaks are—inefficient staffing, overpriced vendor contracts, pointless amenities nobody uses. This week involves walkthroughs and interviews. Second week, I shake things up with recs. I should be home by the 20th, just in time for Mario Kart and Dad trying to set me up on another spectacular blind date. Again."

"It sounds like you're going to miss all the fun. You should stay here at Dad's with me instead."

"Why would I sleep on a creaky twin bed and share a bathroom with you when my company paid for quality accommodations here?"

"So you'd rather share your room with the dead?"

"Don't start that with me. You may believe in the paranormal and somehow make a career out of it, but I don't. And if you expect me to get done faster, I need to stay on the premises." The Bryson House Hotel was supposed to be a simple job. Well, as simple as evaluating any historical hotel, but this place seemed road-mapped to anything but saving money. I agreed to this job only to be close to family, but the regret of making a work commitment so close to the holidays sat heavily on my shoulders. I longed to sip melted chocolate and jest with my family. Instead, I was still busy giving myself a tour of the grounds.

"We only get to see you for Christmas, and now your job is encroaching on that time."

Sid's jab, though true, sent heat racing up my spine. "Some people have bills to pay."

"You'd have a lot fewer of them if you lived here instead of New York," he muttered.

He wasn't wrong, and lately I'd been wondering why I stayed in New York. I'd gone there for school and stayed for my job, but I had no real reason to stay, even if there was something in the pit of my stomach saying I needed to. I might have used money as an excuse, but I'd actually saved plenty— a nice sum that would afford a house. Being cost-reduction savvy had its perks.

"Isn't it about time you moved back here?" he asked. "I've heard nothing but you complaining about New York and your job ever since that new company took over."

That was another valid point from him. The new company had no ethics. "Screw green," they'd say. "Let's go gray, where the laws are a little murky." As Sid rambled on about the perks of moving back, I headed toward the overtaken and decrepit chapel in the center of the cottage village outside the hotel. This area, which housed some of the staff, was the last stop on my extensive tour. I slid the master key into the oak door, which appeared to be original wood and iron, and it opened with no resistance.

Warm air cradled my face, and the earthy scents of dirt and herbs filled my brain. I'd expected an abandoned termite-infested interior, but someone had turned the inside into a beautiful garden with the platform at the front as an office. Christmas lights twinkled warmly along the frame. Some pews sat in what I assumed was their original location while the others lined the walls. Plants acted as people on their wooden surfaces. Natural light bled through the large windows on either side, creating an ethereal glow. My breath stilled in my lungs.

This place was rustic. Functional. Beautiful. But I could imagine the hotel was paying a pretty penny to heat an old, uninsulated space like this. To save money, they could make room for the plants in the greenhouse. The thought conjured the image of the woman dressed in black, hands deep in a pot of soil—Sadie.

She'd been a gut punch at the bar last night—black hair, tattoos, and mystery. But in her element, she was a peeled-back truth—dangerous in ways charm only hinted at.

"Are you still there?" Sid's low voice pulled me from my awed stupor.

"Yeah, sorry. Got distracted."

"By a certain sexy woman again? What happened with her anyway?" I cursed myself, forgetting I'd kicked Sid out of the booth when I spotted Sadie. Since he was my wingman, he saluted and took off. She'd come over and asked if I had a significant other I was waiting for. I'd told her I was very much single. Her second question—asking if I enjoyed going down on women—had me so hard I nearly broke a zipper.

I'd never met a woman so direct with her needs, and it was such a relief compared to all the women I'd tried to date; I could have asked her to marry me. And with the way she fucked like her intuition came straight from cloud nine—

I rammed my knee into a pew, and pain shot up my leg. Just as well. I didn't need to finish that thought.

"It was one singular night of fun," I said.

"Dude, she was blunt as fuck. Yeah, yeah. I listened. Shoot me and get over it. She's the chick you need. Please tell me you asked her out again."

I hesitated too long.

"Oh, you did?" Sid sounded all too pleased with himself. "Does that mean your one-night stand funk is ending?"

I walked to the chapel's rear to work off the steam from him casually referring to my dating life as a "funk." "It doesn't matter. I liked her enough to go on another date, but she works here. That's a complication I don't need."

"That sounds like an excuse, especially when you really like her." As I sucked in a heated breath to deny it, he interrupted me. "Come on, don't let your job impede something good. It has been a year."

"And we were together for two, so I'm owed one more." For two years I thought we were fine, but like the others, she didn't voice her needs, and by the time I noticed, it was too late. I was doomed to never be able to read women or have them understand me. I mindlessly walked around the office and stopped at a bookshelf that held an assortment of interesting books.

"Fuck waiting another year," he said. "The wrinkles on your face are speaking."

"Shut up."

As Sid's laughter echoed in my ear, I found my eyes perusing the titles. Most of the texts were about botany—they were the large textbooks carried around by college students. On a lower shelf, the contents became a little less scientific and a little more woo-woo science. I grabbed a book that looked like the other textbooks but was titled *Aurascape: Reading Human Auras*.

"This place keeps getting weirder," I said, flipping through the pages with anatomy-book-worthy graphics. "Someone has an extensive collection of books about people's auras and different spirits hiding in a chapel turned greenhouse."

"I mean, Bryson House has a lot of lore. Even its own hashtag. The only reason I won't hunt there is because I don't poach where I live."

"You speak as if you actually catch ghosts."

"I'll have you know—"

"What are you doing in here?" a woman asked behind me. Stern. Surprised. Familiar. Maybe even malevolent.

Shit. As Sid droned on in my ear, I plastered on my charming smile. The only defense I had with this job...kindness. "Hello, I'm—"

"I know who you are, Clive Doyle." Damn, did that voice match the stance of the tall woman behind me. Sadie had her arms crossed over her breasts, and her neck tattoo bobbed as she swallowed.

I'd kissed that tattoo with both my lips and teeth. I swallowed. I hadn't expected to see her again, though I hoped I would. Like last night, she was attractive in that—I'm-a-reserved-girl-who-lives-and-breathes-darkness kind of way. My fucking type ever since the emo era of my youth. She'd never slept with a jock and had always wanted to, while I'd dreamed of sleeping with an emo chick. Dream fulfilled. But now—she was in this odd place, ready to skewer me.

"I have to go, Sid," I said, hanging up before he could utter a reply.

Before I could tell her I was glad to see her again and reassure her about last night, she snapped, "What are you doing in here?"

"My job. I was familiarizing myself with the area." I didn't know what had changed the woman I'd woken up to this morning, but she was tense—physically upset enough for even me to notice. Many people got upset around me. I mean, I even got upset around myself, but when my job was digging into people's finances and jobs, I could understand it felt like I was unearthing the skeletons in their closets. However, I wouldn't mind finding out what Sadie was hiding behind her piercing green eyes, tattoos, and black hair. Her hair was a straight bob with fringe bangs, making her a pale version of Cleopatra. And she was just as mysterious. Tempting.

"Even private residences without their tenants?" she shot back.

"This place doesn't look like a residence," I said. "And it's on my list of unoccupied buildings."

"What list?"

I pulled out my work phone and toggled through the apps until I brought up the list. When I held it out, she frowned over the screen. Straightening, she said, "It must have been a clerical error. This is my residence. I pay rent from my salary."

"This is *your* place?" No wonder she'd been so pissed off.

She glared on her way past me and took the book I'd been snooping through. Of course, she was the one reading about auras and spirits. It fit her vibe, but also further intrigued me. I was a skeptic on most subjects, but people's beliefs always tickled my curiosity.

She slammed the book shut, wafting her perfume over me and *fuck.* That spring sweetness, like the winter honeysuckle in the greenhouse, swirled intoxicatingly in my mind with a dark amber scent. The curve of her neck was tempting to my mouth; my tongue danced between my teeth, wanting to scrape across the phoenix tattoo. Once was not enough with this woman. I knew that the moment I woke. I wanted her in my bed again. This was terrible for business. Her daunting gaze told me she noticed I was looking at her. Okay, I was gawking.

"I apologize," I said. "Sometimes you stumble upon things, and you can't look away. But...come on. Auras? Spirits? Isn't that a bit..."

"Wicked? Dark? Odd?"

Was she describing herself? If so, I had a list of my own. "Tantalizing."

Her eyes narrowed.

I cleared my throat. "Like a mystery you want to figure out but never will."

"Some mysteries have answers if you believe," she muttered under her breath.

The window rattled, and a bout of cool air rushed in. I wrote it down as another draft. "This entire place seriously has insulation problems."

She laughed. "So, you're a full skeptic, huh?"

"I'm a black and white kind of guy." I shrugged. "Give me the proof to believe, but so far, ghosts and auras are figments of people's imaginations."

Her cheeks flushed red, and heat blossomed in my chest. I hadn't meant to rile her, but damn, did she look hot as hell. And that need to antagonize, mixed with my brutal honesty, was probably why I was still single.

"I'd appreciate it if you left now." Sadie crossed her arms in a stance no amount of talking would get past.

"No problem," I said, backing out of the room. "I didn't mean to step on your toes or invade your space."

As I went to leave, the door slammed in my face, nearly taking out my nose. *Stupid fucking drafts.* I wedged the door open and left.

3

Sadie

MY PEN DENTED into the supply list like I was Santa on a vendetta—less jolly, more justice—with Clive's eyeballs penciled in right between the cinnamon sticks and tape. Even after a night marathon of Christmas movies, I wasn't over what happened. He not only snooped in my residence, but he was also a judgmental prick about my books. Well, more brutally honest than judgmental, but still prickly.

His aura had been full of inquisitive yellow and teasing hues, but knowing he'd looked through my private book collection brought out my blinding rage—the one that masked the girl inside who feared rejection, and worse, getting fired. I was the odd employee who believed in auras and lived in the chapel.

I sighed and rubbed my pounding forehead.

An aura of calming and reassuring blues and violets brushed warmly across my shoulder. The smell of campfire smoke wafted past my nostrils. I turned back to the translucent aura, which was fading. I recognized the ghost as the witness to yesterday's confrontation with Clive, and I was glad I wasn't alone. Though I couldn't see them, I knew they were most likely wandering the room.

"Thank you for slamming the door in his face." The air grew colder as the aura shimmered in and out of sight, as if the ghost was offering a reply.

The door to the chapel slid open, letting in a burst of cold air.

"Knock. Knock." Celeste's familiar voice called into the chapel's interior.

"I'm over here."

She walked down the path between plants, stripping off her vintage flower print blazer that wasn't thick enough for the weather. My heart warmed at the sight of her. As my only real family—even if just a short-term foster sister when we were younger—I was so glad when she popped in from one of her runaway adventures to spend Christmas with me. Last year she'd vanished without a number to call, without a word—her typical MO. So when she showed up again, the tension I'd been holding finally let go.

With her cheery attitude on full blast, everything about her screamed confidence, from the blond fringe bangs she demanded I cut after she saw mine, to her overly patterned outfit with dazzling colors that somehow...worked even with her large, dangling gold earrings. She was the yang to my dark yin. And today her aura matched a kaleidoscope of color, but at the forefront, a green-spikey cloud of worry hung over her head.

"Hey, how are you doing?" Celeste asked. "According to the staff, you've been avoiding the greenhouse."

"By staff, you mean the nosy ghosts?"

"Maybe."

While I saw auras, Celeste saw ghosts as if they were real people; a problem I'd rather not have. It's what bonded us when we met.

"I'm trying to avoid a certain consultant," I said. "What about you? Has Angus been keeping you warm in the kitchen?"

"No one is keeping anyone warm. I'm just helping him with his ghost issue. That's it."

"Uh. Huh." She may have believed so, but the quick golden flashes like sparklers dancing around her head told a different tune. Sparks usually appeared when the auras of two destined people merged, but a strong bond could summon them with a thought. I had yet to tell my friend about her sparks, though I was sure they'd figure themselves out without my interference.

"When are you going to candy cane a guy?" she shot back. "Tis the season."

I hesitated too long.

"Wait," she said. "Have you hooked someone?"

I rubbed my hand across my forehead. "Ugh. Can you keep a secret?"

"Of course." She rushed to the chaise across from my desk and tucked her feet under her. "Tell me."

"I may have slept with the consultant. You know. Before I knew who he was."

"What?" She hopped in her seat. "Clive? He just got here, didn't he? West introduced him to Angus yesterday."

"Yes. That Clive."

"Wow. I mean...it's a good way to stay on his nice list...or would that be the naughty one?"

"Celeste! I didn't sleep with him for that reason. At least, I hope he knows I didn't. I did not know who he was."

"You should probably clear that up."

"Ugh!" I slammed my face into my palms. "I can't face him. I'm going to lose my job for sure."

"What happened?"

My stomach flip-flopped like I'd drunk bad eggnog. "The chapel ended up on his list of places to check. I mean, the house addition was only added recently, but he was snooping around my not-so-science books. And he's a hardcore skeptic. One ghost slammed a door in his face, and he acted as if it was normal."

"A few days here will make him question himself. But that doesn't matter. He can't judge you on your books. People have hobbies outside work. Did he still seem interested in you, even after knowing?"

Now that I thought about it, the fuchsia color of desire had wrapped around his skin. "Like it matters. I'm not dating him."

"He was interested, wasn't he? Oh. He's the perfect guy for you to go on another date with, you know, for your therapy homework."

"What's the point? He'll never accept me."

"Isn't that the whole thing your therapist said? Stop assuming the worst and give them a chance to get to know you first. Not everyone's your parents, Sadie."

I swallowed the lump in my throat. They'd discovered my truth when I asked them why they didn't love each other and used their lack of sparks as a reference. That led to church visits, doctors, anything to "cure" my gift for revealing their truths. And then when there was no cure, they'd shunned me, turning to fostering other kids because their daughter was a disappointment. I'd accepted that they'd never understand me or like me the way I was. I forgave them. But that didn't mean their actions didn't color my views of others, no matter how much my friend told me otherwise. It was best to keep my head down and my abilities to myself.

"At least date him and see what he's like. Maybe he'll be more accepting than you think. And it'll be better than sitting here worried about your job," she added. "Let him see the real you, so he'll know you're a good worker."

"I don't think going out with him will show him that."

"You're going to be dating on off hours, silly."

"Working hard isn't good enough. I'm a specialist, which means I also have a higher price tag."

"All the more reason to convince him of how important you are. Come on. Do it for therapy, or heck, science. You're so good at picking which two plants will go well together, so why don't you translate that to your own life?"

I rolled my eyes. Plants were so much easier than humans—I paired based on light needs, root depth, and soil chemistry. Science. But I couldn't splice away my fear that someone would see what I was and decide I was too strange.

Still, the idea of another date with Clive brought a hint of a smile. A guy who was that good in bed couldn't be all bad. And Celeste was right. I needed to keep pushing myself out of the protective shell of my seed to grow.

"But what about the whole consultant thing?" I said. "Isn't that a conflict of interest and a one-way ticket to getting fired?"

She shrugged. "Off hours. And as long as you don't get caught...it's no big deal. Now, let's see how Clive is holding up and if he needs any help. I'd like to get a good look at him."

"Right now?"

"Yes. Right now. I've got nothing better to do. Do you?"

"Actually, I have—"

My computer blinked off, and I pounded on the keys to wake it back up. The screen stayed obstinately black no matter what I did. A red aura shimmered beside me.

"Is this Adelia's doing?" I muttered.

"She wants to see you try."

"And if she doesn't knock it off, I'll take down her favorite ornaments."

Celeste winced. "Do you want cold showers?"

I sighed.

"Well, while you have nothing to do..." Celeste swept around my desk and tugged at my arm. "Let's put those Sadie customer service skills to work."

Although Celeste was stubborn in her own way, the ghosts were ten times worse. I grumbled the entire time I bundled up. Outside, the chilly air caressed my face as we made our way across the winding path to the hotel. The cloudy day was a billowing backdrop to the bare trees and white ground. Winter on the mountain was breathtaking. The view always looked amazing, no matter what the season.

A ball of dread thudded in my stomach as I thought about having to leave it behind. It wasn't just a job—it was the only place I felt accepted, even if no one knew the truth.

As we raced toward the hotel, we bumped into each other, hoping to knock each other into the snow. We were acting like bratty sisters, but I wouldn't have had it any other way. I always missed her when she wasn't around.

By the time we reached the conservatory, both of our clothes were soaked, but we were laughing too hard to care. The warmth was a pleasant reprieve, but soon I spotted a young woman hanging my arch-nemesis on a tree branch off the main trail: mistletoe.

"Oh, no you don't," I said, running over. "Stop vandalizing my plants with your absurd traditions."

"You're entitled to your opinions, but sometimes you should let people believe what they want." She stopped stretching and clapped her hands together in a job well done. "Otherwise, how do you expect to find love?"

"I expect to find a dead tree if you keep that parasite there. Now take it off."

"Parasite?"

"Yes, it'll burrow into the bark and steal food."

"Wow. I didn't know." The woman lifted and untied the twine.

"That's why I put a sign up," I grumbled to myself and sighed. "These tourists are going to be the death of me."

Celeste leaned over. "Don't say that. You'll be stuck with them, and you'll only have me to talk to."

"I feel like that's how it is now." I sighed. "Let's go find Clive."

"Cowgirl Cheyenne was already on the case." She lifted her eyebrows at me. "Come on."

"Wait...there were cowgirls here, and we have one as a ghost?" I asked, racing after her long strides.

"Yes and yes. She smells like campfire to me sometimes. Did I ever tell you about Henry, the ghost in the lobby? Poor old guy just wants to listen to the oldies."

As she told me about the myriads of ghosts, nerves danced in my stomach. At any moment we'd run into Clive. *Clive.* The man who rocked my bedroom socks off. The man who riled me with his comments yesterday. And the man I was going to...what was I going to do again?

Clearing the air I understood—but dating him? He'd ask too many questions about my book collection, and I couldn't tell him the truth. I wouldn't tell him the truth. But maybe Celeste was right. Maybe if he agreed to hang out with me, I could convince him not to put me on his layoff list.

Sparkling lights caught my eye, pulling me from my spiraling thoughts. Nic had really outdone herself this year. Garland and lights looped along the hallways, while different wreaths decorated the doors. Sweet and bitter coffee scents wafted by as we walked toward the lobby. The entire atmosphere filled me with a warmth I had never felt at my parents' house. This was why I couldn't leave this place.

We crammed into the space, bustling with guests either checking in or hiding from the cold. Auras flickered over each individual in rainbows I had long learned to tune out. Celeste slammed on the brakes with her hands on her hips. All I wanted to do was hide.

Her head cocked to the side. "I'm definitely going to need to hear that entire story because, and I hate to be shallow here, but on the surface you two don't appear to be each other's type."

I'd thought the same, but when I gazed across the room and caught sight of him, I swallowed the heat rising in me. Clive appeared upset about something on his tablet. He looked attractive in a Captain-America-faces-down-his-greatest-enemy kind of way—forceful and proud. And yes, he had the ass to match. My fingers flexed, remembering the feel of that firmness in my hands. *Get a grip, Sadie.* The diabolical part of me whispered back, *Of that ass? Yes, please.*

Someone squealed next to me. Their letter had probably crackled in the fire when they made a wish to the ghosts for love. Clive's gaze rose and caught on me. The fuchsia color against his skin grew until I could see it from where I stood.

His eyes swiveled to the dancing girls, and his eyebrow ticked up as he laughed to himself and returned to his tablet.

"Well, he's definitely still interested, and girl, I don't have to see auras to know you are crushing." Celeste pinched my warm cheeks. "You're flush and all."

"You mean from the chilly air outside? Sorry to break it to you but crushing on the guy meant to tell my boss to fire me isn't on my Christmas wish list."

"Well, pencil it in. I'm not the only one who wants to see how this ends."

A groan settled in my throat. If the notorious matchmaking ghosts were on her side, I was in a world of hurt.

4

Clive

I WAS LEAVING the distracting lobby, where Sadie stood next to a blond woman discussing something, when the lights on a Christmas tree died. I paused, and they twinkled back on. Bad wiring?

It was another upgrade I needed to add to my expense list. With the scent of natural pine tickling my nostrils, I circled around to unplug the tree before it started a fire, but the lights went berserk like a warning strobe light instead of a pro-grammed setting. Heart leaping into my chest, I jumped, nearly toppling the tree over.

"What the fuck?"

The lights sparkled in a way that took me back to a time when I was half my height. Sid had climbed onto my shoulders to put the star up, but we'd ended up under the tree, laughing. I could taste the nostalgia of that night on my tongue—choco-late and candy cane mint. Warmth bled through me, and an ache thudded in my heart.

"Fucking old wiring," I muttered. This place was a fire hazard waiting to happen—and the cost of that wasn't pretty. I spun on my heel to inform West and ran into someone. I jumped for the second time. "Shit."

"Sorry," Sadie said, arms out. "Didn't mean to scare you when you were reminiscing like that."

My back tingled. How did she know what I was thinking about?

"It's all right." I didn't expect Sadie to grace me with her presence after our interaction in the chapel, but I was glad she approached me.

She tilted away, suddenly shy—like we hadn't already seen each other naked. She said, "I feel like we got off on the wrong foot."

"We got off together, but feet weren't involved. Unless. Did you want feet involved?"

A small grin graced her lips, and I felt it hit my chest.

"After the getting-off part," she said. "I meant about the chapel."

"I am truly sorry that I invaded your space. I should have handled that better. You're into auras, spirits, and such. It's pretty on-brand." I lifted a piece of her silky dark hair, just to have an excuse to touch her. "Plenty of people have interesting hobbies."

"Hobbies...right." She cleared her throat and stepped back, putting some much-needed professional distance between us. "Besides that...I wanted to clear the air about that night. I had no idea who you were. If I had...that...wouldn't have happened."

Her rosy cheeks brought up the heated memory of exactly what she was talking about, and I had to remind myself that to her, I was the guy sent to her job to suggest lay-offs. And I had to remind myself: that was, in fact, my job. And sleeping with her definitely added complications. But being around her made me feel like a giddy high school boy around his crush—not an adult with responsibilities.

"Don't worry about it," I said. "We were two random people enjoying their off time together."

She sighed, and a small, relieved smile tilted her lips. "Anyway, I know this is probably the worst thing to ask after that, but I wanted to see if you'd—" Her face scrunched in a way I found adorable. "Are you settling in well?"

"If I'd what? I'm doing fine settling wise, but I'm more curious about your other question. I have a suspicion that despite the conflict of interest, you want to ask me out."

"Someone's arrogant."

"Like you didn't enjoy the chemistry between us. I know I sure as fuck did. And while I'm here, we could have fun in every room. On our off time, that is."

Her face turned a brazen red as if she were imagining it, and for a moment, I wanted to do just that.

"Do you want to get me fired? Or you fired, for that matter?" she asked.

"That's a possibility, but they'd have to catch us first."

She rolled her eyes. "Do you even date people?"

"Do you?"

She shrugged. "I've tried. It never lasts."

"Why not?"

"I guess I can be a lot to handle."

"I do like challenges." The words were out of my mouth before I could stop them.

Her chest lifted with a tight breath, and her lips curved upward in a flirtatious grin that won me over. "Maybe, but my so-called hobbies aren't everyone's cup of tea. Especially someone who's a skeptic."

"My being a skeptic should make this more fun." She could be crazy about her spirits, and I'd still want to peel those jeans from her round ass.

She seemed taken aback, lips parting as if she were searching for something to say. "I thought I'd stop by and check in on you."

"And so you have...thank you."

She tapped her foot, crossed her arms, and then glanced down. I couldn't hide the inner glee watching her struggle to say whatever she needed to next. This was the part where she would have walked away, but I couldn't tell from her expression what she wanted. I was about to shoot my shot in the dark and ask her to dinner when a squeal from a pair of middle-school-aged girls pierced my ears.

"What is it with that fireplace?" I asked.

"Oh, it's like a wishing well for the ghosts to help you with your romance. I think the squealing happens when crackles— showing the ghosts have heard you."

"Wow. The things people come up with."

"Yeah, it's cute as much as it's...ear-shattering. Too bad the ghosts have their own thoughts about matchmaking."

"I don't know why people are determined to bring the supernatural into things."

"Sorry to tell you but it's there whether you believe it or not. See that woman at the counter asking for a new room?"

I didn't know how she could pick that out so easily, but from the animation in the woman's features, and the employees' warm apologies, it seemed she was trying to get something.

Sadie continued, "The ghosts probably want her to share a room with—"

Like something out of a romcom, a man her age walked over and told her they could share a room.

"Case in point," Sadie said.

I laughed. "She probably sabotaged the room herself."

"Doubt it," she said. "He's going to be sleeping on the floor unless she cools down."

I had to admit the woman appeared not to give any shits about what the man was saying.

Sadie grabbed my arm, tight and firm. "Just watch."

As if the romcom production continued, the pair walked by another visitor, and he dropped his coffee. The woman slipped on the beverage, and as the man caught her, he also slipped, falling to his knees with her in his lap.

Their echoing laughter filled my ears, and my heart thundered in my chest. What the hell was that? "How did you know?"

Sadie shrugged and gave me a teasing look that shot fire through my veins. "Must have been a coincidence, right?"

"Right." Except that the hair on my arm was sticking up. That had been too on the nose.

"Trust me. If you watch enough, coincidences like that happen here all the time. This place comes alive, especially around the holidays. Bryson House would be nothing if it weren't for the ghosts."

"The ghosts. Right. Because they pay the bills."

"They kind of do…" she muttered under her breath.

"Then I guess I won't add them to my list of items to reduce."

She grinned. "I'm glad you're considering them."

I rolled my eyes playfully, and I felt myself growing curious. Curious about this place and even more interested in her.

5

Sadie

"ANYWAY, I'LL LET you get back to work," I said to Clive, stepping away to head back to the greenhouse. I'd failed in my mission—asking Clive on a date—but the risks were getting to me. Or that was another excuse. I could find someone else even if he had been the only one who'd interested me in the past few years. Surely someone could compete with his sexy banter and kindness.

"Actually, I could use your help to track down West," Clive said, stopping me short.

He had given me a lifeline: a second chance to ask him on a date. His base aura was the same blue—as open as the ocean—and inquisitive yellow weaved through the surface like solar flares. Mesmerizing. I shook my head. No. Not mesmerizing. Distracting. "Oh?"

"There are a few fire hazard concerns I need to discuss with him." His gaze flew up and down the beautifully decorated tree beside him. An aura of shimmering red stood in front of the Christmas tree like a nutcracker soldier standing guard.

Adelia, I'd imagine, was protecting her Christmas decorations again.

"We can hit up his office first, and if he's not there, we can ask Nic. She should be in the library preparing for the next Christmas event. The two of them have been inseparable since they got together." I stopped, feeling queasiness in my stomach. Why was he so easy to talk to? "I'm sorry. I shouldn't have told you that."

He laughed. "It's all right. Trust me, there's at least someone at every job that tells me their drama."

A weight settled over me. I'd never be able to tell him about my drama, but that didn't excuse my talking about other people's. I headed toward West's office, and Clive followed. "Do you like your job?" I asked.

"It's a paycheck, and I like numbers. Sometimes the locations are nice. What about you?"

"I love plants. So much easier than humans. Don't get me wrong, they are great...but they can be a bit much."

"You can say that. I sure feel daggers in my back from a few stares. Even though I'm not the bad guy. Just doing my job."

"I get that. I do my job to avoid stares like that."

"Why would people think you're the bad guy?"

"People judge things they don't understand or fear."

"I get the impression you aren't just talking about black hair and tattoos?"

"You saw my bookshelf."

"Your hobby?"

I crossed my arms over my chest, hating where this conversation was going. He knew I was into auras and spirits, but I'd have to curb the why. Usually, that wouldn't be a problem for me, but Clive's honesty made the idea of lying to him a dead weight in my stomach. "When people like me talk about spirits or auras, you know...others think you're into witchcraft or something heinous."

"Are you?"

"No. No. Not that witchcraft is wrong, but I find the occult stuff...fascinating."

"I find people's fascination with that stuff fascinating. My brother is a big believer. A ghost hunter, actually. I tease him all the time."

My foster siblings had teased me as well, but there was also bullying. I hoped Clive didn't do that to his brother. "So he's into it and you're not?"

"Don't ask me. I like firmly having my thoughts on paper while he has his in the clouds. Do you have any siblings?"

"Dozens?" It came out as a question to myself. "No blood siblings. But my parents fostered a lot of kids."

"That must have been difficult."

"It was *hell*." I twisted my hands in front of me. "The house was crowded and so loud. And with me being interested in the things that I am...most of the time, I was lucky not to be bullied. Even by my own parents. I never got told I was a good girl. Instead, they often gave me a mean stare. I also don't know why I'm telling you this. Let me uninvite you to my pity party before I spill too much tea."

"I don't mind. I've been told I'm easy to invite to parties."

"Has anyone invited you to any wedding receptions yet?"

He patted his jean pockets. "I think I have a bridesmaid's number around here somewhere."

"Ha. Ha. Funny."

We reached West's office to find his door open and no one inside.

"The library then?" he asked.

I chewed my lip. "Hopefully, we'll catch him on the way."

Walking side-by-side, his warmth was a sweater, smelling of spice and rum, that I wanted to wrap around myself. There was something so comforting about him and his aura. Like a safety net that wouldn't hide behind fake words.

"So, would you be interested in hanging out with me?" he asked. "Outside work, that is?"

My breath hitched as flutters filled my chest. I tried to tell myself they came from the idea that I was accomplishing my therapy homework, but I wasn't fooling myself. I had it bad if I reacted like this because he was asking me out. But it wasn't a bad thing as long as he didn't find out about my weirdness. "The whole occult fascination thing doesn't bother you?"

"The whole consultant thing doesn't bother you?" he shot back.

"It's not ideal, but...you're just doing your job."

He graced me with a small, satisfied grin. "And I am quite curious about you."

"Hanging out might get complicated, though. Conflict of interest in all."

"I can be your dirty little secret," he teased.

"You kind of already are."

"So that means we should sleep together again?"

"Ah. You're getting ahead of yourself."

"All right," he said. "But because this is risky, are there other private activities we could do together?"

I thought of all the secluded places I took advantage of for mini-adventures. "There are a few things we can do. But I'm not sure you'll be down for them."

"I'm down for anything...especially if it means going down on—"

He gave me a look, and my thighs quivered with the memory of how good he had felt between them. His fingers. His tongue. His cock. Heat dripped down my chest like melted wax. This was heading into dangerous territory. He might be open to learning about me, but that was a wide stretch to accepting me enough to stick around. But that didn't matter. This was about him getting to know me as a person, so I didn't make it on his chopping block—hopefully.

"Is this hanging out or a date?" I asked. "Because I feel you want this to be a date."

He sucked in a breath and—*fuck.* He gave me his full melt-worthy smile. "I want whatever is going to make you feel most comfortable. Besides, I thought emo people didn't like putting labels on things?"

"I never said I was emo," I said.

"I assumed you were emo because you didn't want a label."

"You are terrible. What attracted you to girls like that, anyway?"

He shrugged. "Other girls were boring, like they hadn't been through stuff. Well, other than trying to be liked for the wrong reasons. My mom left us when I was in middle school, so they felt more relatable."

"I'm sorry to hear that. I can't imagine going through that at such a young age."

"I'm just glad my family grew together instead of apart. We are pretty close." A passionate rouge flickered like a calm flame over his aura. He loved his family. A hollowness filled my chest. I didn't know what that felt like, but I imagined a family like that might patch the hole in my heart.

I cleared my throat. "I'm okay with spending time together, but I think we should keep sex and work off the table. It feels messy with our situation."

"I agree. No sex or work talk. But am I allowed to flirt?"

"Sure. Let me give you my number, and we can plan something." I licked my lips, feeling like this man was going to take flirting to a whole other level. What was I getting myself into?

6

Clive

I STUFFED MY shaking hands into my leather jacket pockets as I crossed the parking lot to the archway decked out with a dazzling display stating, "Christmas in the Park." Bryson House sat high in the mountains, a majestic backdrop to the park—far enough away that I didn't fear being caught for what I was about to do.

Despite the flurries in the air, my hands weren't shaking from the cold—they were shaking from nerves. After a few days of texting and horrible scheduling on both our parts, Sadie and I had finally agreed on our first date—not date—hangout? I'd let her call it whatever she wanted as long as I got to spend more time with her.

Was I out of my mind for seeing an employee of the company I was evaluating—yes. But as I saw her waiting under the glow of some icicle lights like we'd planned—none of that mattered.

Her black knee-high boots and deep burgundy long coat, tailored to her figure, made me wonder what she was wearing underneath. She caught my eye from under her jet-black fringe bangs and ducked into her dark scarf, staring down at her crossed boots. My heart skipped. Was she nervous, or did she not want to see me? I groaned internally, wishing I were better at reading people. I may have accepted that part of myself, but I still found it pestering. As I approached, it almost appeared as if she was trying to hide a smile. I let mine spread the muscles of my cheeks.

"Hello there, do you know this amazing woman named Sadie?" I asked, trying to play it cool when everything inside me was lit up with anticipation. "We were supposed to meet here tonight."

"You mean you don't remember what I look like?" Her smile broke loose, raising the redness of her cheeks to her green eyes. Man, she was…so beautiful. The flurries settled in her hair, a stark contrast to the darkness.

"I remember you were gorgeous." I sucked air through my teeth. "But I don't remember you being this gorgeous."

She shook her head, but she was beaming. "You're slick. But suddenly, I am even more excited."

"Truly?" I gave her my arm, and she twined her fingers loosely around my bicep. The temptation to bunch my muscles under her touch was too much to deny, and I held her closer to my side.

"I was a little nervous, but you've won me over. Just a little."

"I can work with that." Especially when she was willing to tell me how she felt so early on. We walked toward the tent, where workers huddled together serving warm beverages. I grabbed a steaming black coffee while she picked hot cocoa. Sadie pulled out her wallet, but I beat her to the punch.

"I'm only letting you pay because if I paid for yours…it might seem like bribery," she said.

"Right. Don't need to make this any more complicated."

We walked past giant Christmas lights shaped like mistletoe and into the gardens that local businesses had turned into a Christmas wonderland. Tension filled my chest. Spending time with her was nice and relaxing, but our texts had been bland, making me wonder if we'd have anything to talk about. We might have had amazing physical chemistry, but this would prove whether we should continue this affair. *Please let her be as direct in person as she is in the bedroom.*

"So how is Bryson House treating you?" she asked.

"The hot springs are wonderful, but the spotty Wi-Fi is somewhat of a pain."

"Ah, yeah, the hotel is quite...meddlesome."

"The hotel or the supposed occupants still haunting its premises?"

Before I worried if she knew I was only teasing, she gave me a secret smile. "I'm sure you'll figure it out."

Was she snapping back, referencing my tantalizing comment from the chapel? Oh, I knew I'd like her. "How does one become an award-winning botanist?"

She ducked her head into her scarf again and shrugged. "I have a way with plants, I guess. Some people design houses, and I design genetics to look a certain way."

"Are you responsible for the wicked awesome pink and red poinsettia I found in my room? I definitely had to sketch it when I first got here."

"Guilty. But wait...you sketch?"

I rubbed the back of my neck to stop the sudden itch there. "I dabble in art. It's always helped me relax."

"Huh...I'd love to see your sketch."

I smiled. "Of course. So...are you a plant mom? The kind that adopts all the browning plants from the stores?"

"And what if I am?" She cocked an eyebrow at me. Damn, I loved a feisty woman. Even if she was playing.

"No judgment. I find it endearing. I wish I could keep plants, but I travel too much."

"For your job?"

"I thought I'd love that part but coming home to an empty house can get lonely."

"I get that. How did you become a cost reduction consultant?"

"It kind of found me. I like numbers, and my internship turned into a well-paying job."

"Numbers are pretty black and white," she teased. "After I got my degree, I never believed I'd score a job where I could use it. I got really lucky with Bryson House. The conservatory has always been a draw for tourists because the original owner, Phinneas, brought in rare plants from around the world. After he passed, the subsequent owners maintained the rare plants, and they ended up hiring me for my hybridization specialty. It's been a dream come true."

"I'm so glad you found your dream job." The joy in her voice wrapped me in a warmth that gave me a whole new sense of purpose. I'd wanted to help Bryson House before—it was a staple in my family traditions—but now I wanted to do everything in my power to see it thrive. But I couldn't help the ball of guilt gathering in my stomach, knowing that to be the best at my job I had to be unbiased with numbers, which included her job.

"Shoot," she said. "I didn't mean to say that to make you feel a certain way. Forget I said all that. If anything happens, I'll figure out my next steps."

The smile she'd been giving me lost all its light, but her gaze swiveled to something behind me. "Oh!" She pulled me over to an enclosure where small white flowers sprouted from the snow. "These Christmas roses are blooming so early this year."

"Is that a good omen?"

She sent me a smirk. "Probably somewhere. I've been working on a deep purple variety, but with them outside, I don't know if anyone will venture out into the cold to see them."

"Maybe you could donate them to the park?"

"That's not a bad idea. I'd need the hotel's permission, but the colors against the snow would be breathtaking."

I never enjoyed plants or flowers, but with the way her face lit up, I was enamored. There was something magical about watching Sadie in her element.

"What do you think?" she asked.

"Huh?" I pulled myself out of my musings. "Oh, yes. I think more color is needed."

"Says the guy who likes black and white."

"Sometimes color can make things interesting. You're wearing burgundy tonight instead of black, for instance. It looks good on you."

"Thank you." She bit her lower lip, chasing fire right through me.

I cleared my throat. "Why don't you tell me about the other plants...at least the ones braving the cold?"

"You're interested in plants?"

"I'm interested in hearing *you* talk about plants."

Her chest lifted with a deep inhale. "All right."

As we continued walking, Sadie filled me in. Every once in a while, she'd send me a curveball question. Did I like watching sports? On occasion. What was my favorite music? Anything. Favorite TV genre? Action adventure.

The conversation never lulled, and each smirk she sent me or smile we shared felt like a win in my book. As we were heading back toward the arch, our totally-not-a-date ending, I held her hand in the crook of my arm.

"I have to admit," she said, stopping us under the icicle lights. "I was a little shaky coming out here. I thought we'd have nothing in common. But—this was really nice. I enjoy talking to you."

Her directness made me smile. "Same. A black and white guy isn't so boring after all?" I lifted my hand to tuck her hair behind her ear—slow and deliberate—drawing it out. Why was her skin such a magnet? I could touch her all day and not get enough.

"You're not boring at all." She wetted her lips. My body tensed with the need to kiss her. But I honored our agreement and stepped away from her.

"So, you want to meet up again?" I asked, heart rising into my throat. Risking my job and reputation didn't matter—I wanted more time with her. Besides, it wasn't like we were going to get caught.

Her nod sent me floating all the way back to my rental car.

7

Sadie

MY BREATH FOGGED in the chilly air as I pulled a sled from the toolshed and nearly ran into Clive. Nerves tingled in my chest. Spending time with him had been therapeutic. I felt like I was making a friend, someone to have fun with or enjoy silence together. I really didn't know why either of us kept tempting this affair, but something in me didn't want to stop. Especially when he'd been as enthusiastic about each of our clandestine meetings as I had been. This was date—ugh, not date—number three, or did the coffee he brought me this morning count?

"We're going sledding?" Clive asked, gloved hands stuffed into his pockets and his charming smile on his face.

"I feared you might think it too childish, so I brought an adult beverage." I patted the strap of the large thermos that slung over my shoulder. "Come on."

After flicking off the light to the shed, I illuminated the snow with my flashlight. The night was clear and beautiful as we walked the path. Mother Nature must have consulted with the ghosts tonight—the weather couldn't have been more perfect. A sharp wind cut into my coat, and I shivered. Perhaps it could be a bit warmer.

"How often do you come out here?" Clive asked.

"I'm embarrassed to say…a lot."

"You didn't really get a chance at childhood, did you?"

"No. My parents were very strict. Religious."

"I get that. After my mom left, I took on a lot of responsibilities concerning my brother. Driving him to football practice while I picked up a few jobs to help dad."

A peculiar darkness leaped across the surface of his aura, quickly drowned, as if he was hiding it from himself. Interesting. I might have found a shark, but it didn't feel like the time to pry. "So sledding was a good choice?" I asked.

"Yes. But give me that adult beverage."

I handed him the thermos, our gloved hands grazing in a way that shouldn't have shot through me, but it did. "It's hot chocolate and Kahlua."

"You have good taste." He unscrewed the lid, and steam wafted from the top. He took a tentative sip then a full swallow. "A little heavy-handed, but good."

He handed it over to me, and the sweet taste burned with liquor. I smacked my mouth a few times. "Jeeze, I'm usually not that bad at bartending."

"It's okay. You were probably nervous about our date."

I was, but I wasn't—wait, did he say date? "This is not a date. Remember? This is a hangout."

"It feels pretty romantic to me."

I swooped down to grab snow and shoved it down the back of his coat. He jumped with a curse.

Laughing, I said, "Is it romantic for you now?"

"You messed up, Sadie Anderson." He grabbed a wad of snow.

I had messed up, but I didn't let him off that easily. As we took turns sledding or riding together, he'd get me with a chilly snowball down my front, or I'd get him back with a face full of snow. We talked about silly shit for hours. The type of stuff normal people talked about, and his openness drew me to talk freely with him. Like any time we spent together, the honesty in his words made it feel like I didn't have to pay attention to his aura. I could see him—just him.

It was magical, and in the coldness, everything else seemed to fade away. There were no auras. No ghosts. He wasn't a consultant. We were just two people enjoying each other. And with every laugh we shared, tension loosened from my shoulders even as my mind warned I had to hold the truth back or I'd ruin the moment.

Hours later, Clive lay in the snow after having fallen off the sled from his shenanigans and I stumbled down next to him, the snow pillowing around me. We may have made a mockery of sledding with the amount of alcohol pumping through our veins, and I was tipsy enough that I blurted, "How are you so...yourself?"

"What do you mean?"

"I don't know...you're so authentic. Most people hide behind this mask, and you don't."

"Ahh. That's because my give-a-damn is busted."

"No...I mean seriously."

He sighed, breath fogging the air. "Not being myself is too much work. My dad expected me to be a pro football player like my brother, and all I wanted to do was make money. And I learned that being honest earned respect from people who truly matter. Why should I care what others think? I won't change who I am so they'll like me. Not that it doesn't have its drawbacks, like getting me into trouble at work sometimes or coming across as abrasive when I don't mean to be, especially in relationships. But people who aren't authentic don't seem happy. I guess that's why I like you so much."

"Me?" I squeaked.

"You know how people judge you, and yet you still rock this badass I-don't-give-a-fuck look."

"Yeah, I guess." I swallowed and buried my face in the flap of my collar. He had me all wrong, but I couldn't bring myself to correct him. I wore this look, hoping to ward people away because I gave all the fucks. If they knew who I really was, they'd hate me as much as my parents did. The attitudes of a couple of strangers I told wouldn't change that. "So other than being abrasive, what other problems have come up in your re-lationships?"

"I hate to be that woe-is-me guy, but some women expect men to read their minds, and I'm terrible at it. I don't pick up on certain cues like others, and so, if someone's upset or wants something, I completely miss it."

I couldn't imagine not seeing people's auras and under-standing them, let alone not being able to see those intricate signs that revealed someone's true feelings. I had to wonder if that's why he'd read me so wrong. "Have you communicated that with the women you've dated before?"

"In my most recent relationship, I did, but she still strug-gled with being direct." He sighed. "Okay, so tell me more about auras. Why is curiosity yellow?"

My back tingled, and I had to remind myself he was curious in a she-believes-in-auras kind of way, not the real, she-sees-auras way. I was surprised he'd remembered our previous brief discussion on the matter.

"I think of it as a lightbulb moment," I said. "A flash of yel-low."

"Doesn't a lightbulb mean you have an idea, not that you're looking for one?"

"Oh, give me a break." Heat pumped to my cheeks, and I blew out a breath. I stood to storm off, but his gloved hand wrapped around my ankle, stopping me.

"See? My honesty is abrasive, and—you know I love antagonizing you, right?"

"Let me guess. Your love language is confrontation and arguing."

"Feels like something I need to unpack. Is that one of the five?"

"It's not."

"Help me up."

As I grabbed his hand, I caught on to his trick too late, and before I knew it, I was on top of him. His laugh wafted over my lips with chocolate and liquor. My head was swimming.

"I think touching is a better one anyway," he said thickly.

I swallowed a lump in my throat. His large hands sprawled warmly across my back, and the tension in his arms meant he wouldn't let me get away. I settled into him, the fabric of our coats a safety net I clung onto as my heart galloped in my chest.

Clive's eyes bore into mine and dipped lower to my mouth. The heat arching between us was like a summer day. Lips tingling, breath quickening, I ached for him to kiss me. *Fuck.* The fuchsia in his aura was growing, bathing over me. Our physical chemistry hadn't been the problem between us, but it was fast becoming one when we couldn't act upon it. He made a deep, tantalizing sound at the back of his throat and dropped his gaze to my neck. "What's that tattoo mean?" he asked.

"It symbolizes rising from the ashes of my old life."

"Your old life?"

"My parents. They never really understood me. I don't think they ever loved me because of it. They doted on every child they fostered and left me with the scraps. I wasn't their daughter. I was an obligation, a job they had to finish. I blamed myself for their actions for a long time, though."

"Do you stay in contact?"

"No. I've forgiven them because they didn't know any better, but it's toxic for me to be around them." I imagined sitting in the same room with their snake auras of judgment and disappointment biting and injecting me with painful venom of doubt and despair.

"I'm sorry you had to go through that. A parent should love and accept their children, not push them aside because they don't understand. Maybe parents shouldn't always love their children's actions, but I'm pretty sure you were a good kid." The threads of genuine care and sorrow in his voice and aura twined around me.

Feeling suddenly naked, I rolled off him into the snow, and he let me. I shivered at the loss of his warmth.

"What about you?" I asked. "You have an Aquarius symbol over your heart, right? I thought you didn't believe in that stuff?"

He swallowed and rubbed his chest. "My brother Sid does, so we got matching tattoos. I have his birth sign, and he has mine."

"You two are pretty close, huh?"

"My dad too. He's just afraid of needles. I came back here for this consultation to be closer to them. Just wish this place wasn't such a money pit so that I could get home faster."

The flicker in his aura returned, the color too fleeting to catch. He felt something strongly around the idea of going home. Like a truth buried so deep it became real to him. I wanted to probe the oddity but clammed up at the thought of him figuring me out.

"We probably shouldn't talk about work on our off hours," I murmured.

"Ah, yeah, sorry." He rose to his feet, putting distance between us, but he reached out for me. "I don't want to worry you, though. This place has potential, especially if I get the ghosts on board."

He was teasing me again, but I didn't mind as it distracted me from my sinking heart. "Shhh...they'll hear you." I smiled and took his hand. He lifted me so I flew into him, and I had to catch myself against the solid wall of his chest. He wrapped his arm around me to keep me upright, his fingers dangerously close to my ass. And I wanted them lower. My body vibrated with need.

"The one perk of this place is I get to spend time with you," he said. "And I hope I get to again?"

I could feel myself melting into him. It would have been so easy to lean in and finally kiss him. From the fuchsia radiating from his skin, and the way he glanced at my lips, the thought crossed his mind, too. I pressed my fingers to his lips, regretting it the moment I did. "Fine. But no kissing. Only flirting."

"Oh?"

His hands at my sides turned into tickle machines, and I jerked, laughing. As we headed inside, I couldn't help the nagging feeling at the back of my mind that I was setting myself up for failure. Spending time with Clive only made goodbye harder. But I'd have to part ways with him because even if he was honest with me...I couldn't be fully honest with him.

8

Clive

I STROKED MY stylus over the artwork on my tablet, adding a dab of green to the sketch of Sadie. I'd originally started at lunch when Sadie had been working in the greenhouse. There'd been something about her, focused in her element, I had to capture. And now, as I sat on a bench, basking in the scent of honeysuckle and supposedly working while Sadie was actually busy, I filled the space around her image with colors—whatever my artistic brain wanted.

Spending all my extra time with Sadie this past week had been the highlight of each day, but I was ready to explode if we didn't drop this whole no-sex thing. My blood thundered around her. But it wasn't just that. She was an interesting person. Non-judgmental. Intuitive beyond anyone I've ever met. A steady rock when I needed space—like my art, always there.

I learned my first impression of her wasn't what really lurked under the surface. I may have had issues reading people, but Sadie's personality was glaringly obvious as she didn't tiptoe around her true feelings with the people she allowed close. Her dark persona was one she wore like a shield rather than a fuck you. If anything, it endeared me to her more, wanting her to feel comfortable enough to open up to me.

Though I wasn't the best at reading people, it felt like she was holding back. She was very intuitive, too much so. Even as a skeptic, I was thinking auras—the one I drew around her— weren't just fiction to her, but a reality. And if I wanted whatever this was to become a relationship, I needed her to open up to me about her abilities and trust me. But I had to try not to push her.

Still, I wanted to be around her, seeking her out for a morning coffee or making plans. Our nightly dates hadn't been enough, and I worked in the greenhouse more than I should, knowing my clock was ticking. Soon, I'd finish this project and return to New York. I felt hollow at the idea.

As if my tablet felt the same, it went dark. I pressed the power button, but nothing worked. It was dead. "Not again."

"I warned you about that, didn't I?" Sadie said as she pruned a flower bush by the bench where I sat. "And you thought it was…what again?"

"It's another faulty battery." Even if this was a new one.

Despite the break I'd taken to sketch her, I was on the last few sections of my report and on my last nerve. Everything but the woman behind me felt dysfunctional here. It was nearly impossible to send reports to my client.

"Uh. Huh," she said, still hammering on me about the paranormal presences that wanted to make themselves known. Something was killing my batteries, but I wouldn't call it paranormal. "We've switched over to paper and pens for a reason. And I'll say you've had a particular ghost following you around ever since you tried unplugging that Christmas tree."

"And how do you know that?"

She pursed her lips together, gave an exaggerated shrug, and said, "It's just a hunch."

She had a lot of those, and most, if not all, proved true. It was enough that I stopped questioning how she seemed to know things about people and accepted she had this sixth sense. Though anytime I pressed, she'd clam up, acting ashamed. Which only made me want to push her more. I wanted her to open up to me in a more intimate way than sex.

My phone vibrated in my back pocket, and something nagged my mind: this sense that I was forgetting to do something. It was a feeling of responsibility I couldn't shake when I was in town.

"What are you thinking about?" Sadie asked, plopping down beside me with a basket of clippings in her lap.

"Huh?"

"I don't know. It seemed like something was bothering you other than your tablet."

"Bothering me?" The back of my neck prickled with a sense of knowing. "I guess I was thinking about being back here. Close to home."

"Why did you move to New York?"

"It was where I wanted to go to school. Seemed like an adventure."

"Like somewhere you could escape the responsibility of caring for your brother?"

Something warm clawed at my back. "Where did you get that idea?" The edge in my voice surprised me. Why was I getting so mad?

"I'm sorry if I overstepped. Sometimes we keep things from ourselves so much so that they fester, even if we've forgotten them. Coming from someone who used to do it before I cut ties: you use work to avoid your family."

But that wasn't true, was it? I'd taken this job, hoping to spend more time with my family this Christmas. But…I could have been home, and instead I was here. Yes, I wanted to spend time with Sadie, but was I bullshitting myself? I couldn't deny that resentment had built up every time my father forced me to wait for Sid's football practice, or the way Sid kept me from a social life because I always had to be at his beck and call. "Family comes first," my father would say. But I could tell which family he meant. Sid over me.

"I guess I never thought about it," I said.

She shrugged. "I get it. It becomes second nature. But I'd think about why you left. I don't believe it's what you think."

She was probably right, but when I considered it, heavy guilt settled over me.

A meek voice called, "Sadie?"

One of the shy teen workers stared at her feet, like she normally did when wanting to get Sadie's attention.

"Oh, hun." Sadie's face fell. "Don't work yourself up. Whatever it is, I'm sure we can fix it."

I didn't realize the teen was upset until she wiped at her face, a sniffle escaping. My wonder at Sadie's intuition only grew. She seemed to be able to read anyone like a book—even me.

"Here," Sadie said, grabbing her by the arm. "Come on. We can go to the back."

My heart wobbled in my chest, melting. She was everything I felt I missed out on as soon as my mom walked out the door. Warm. Caring. A giver beyond compare. And it showed in the way she curved over the teen, sheltering her outburst. She wasn't the type of person to abandon people. Abandon her family.

Crushing guilt weighed on me as I thought back to what we'd talked about. A part of me wondered if I hadn't done that to my family. I'd wanted to go to New York to study accounting, but that might not have been the only reason—and the other reason was much more selfish than I cared to think about. Because it meant my mom had a bigger impact on me than I thought. I followed in her footsteps, walking away from my family, even if I visited them.

A few moments later, Sadie was rushing toward me, her face beautifully flushed as she held her hand over her mouth.

"Everything okay?" I asked.

"It's..." She let a giggle slip out. "Come see."

"Okay." I followed the hypnotizing sway of her hips to the rear of the greenhouse.

"But you have to put your consultant hat away for a second," she said.

"Why would I—"

Bright green water came out of a fountain tucked into an alcove of foliage. Droppings of neon paint left a trail to the ladder; a bucket sat on the edge. The teen must have knocked the paint into the fountain.

"It looks like Santa's elves had an orgy or something," she said, shaking her head.

I laughed, unable not to see it. "Or something. It looks kind of cool."

"I know."

"How's she doing?" I asked, understanding why the teen had gotten upset.

"I sent her home to calm down. The poor girl was a wreck. Anyway, now that you've seen the show." She leaned over the fountain, searching for something. I assumed the power, but her round ass ensnared my gaze until the ladder shifted. The paint bucket wobbled.

"Watch your—" I ran over as the tub fell. She ducked as I wrapped my hands above her head. Metal clanged against my fingers, bruising. Wet paint splattered over the two of us.

"You okay?" I asked.

She laughed, and it was a contagious sound, tickling my lips to rise. "I'm good."

I took my hands away, dripping paint onto the ground instead of her beautiful hair. Though the black strands hadn't gone unscathed. "I guess that ladder moving was the ghosts?" I teased.

"Nah, it was probably a draft."

We both laughed.

"Come on," she said. "There's a shower in the back."

I followed her through the garden, keeping as much of the paint on me as possible. She turned the faucet on at the shower station. I rinsed my arms off in the ice-cold water. The woman next to me was all heat. She arched to tilt her head back and fumbled for the nozzle in a way that made me wince.

"Let me." I grabbed the back of her neck, holding her, and something warm flowed through me. She gripped my arm.

"I got you," I said, enjoying her weight in my grasp.

She looked unsure but settled against my hand. Her hold on me was a tentative touch.

"That's a good girl," I murmured teasingly.

She grabbed me tighter, and the hitch in her breath raised her breasts toward my arm. I watched longer than I should have. *Oh. Fuck.* I should have figured that a girl who never received praise from her parents might find it stimulating.

"Stop that," she said half-heartedly.

To distract myself from the ember growing in my gut, I unhooked the nozzle from the wall and ran the spray over her hair, green paint sliding away from the black strands.

She closed her eyes, and my distraction soared out the window. "So you like praise?" I asked.

"I didn't think I did…"

Her breathy voice made me think that a 'but' came next, but she didn't finish. I moved the nozzle back to the hook, and she stood until only a damn breath lay between us. Like any time she'd gotten this close over the days we'd spent together, I sizzled and burned, wanting to shred our pact of not sleeping together. I could feel the way her breast would fill my palm, her sharp gasp against my ear, the silken channel between her thighs. My cock swelled in my pants, achy and full.

She swung her hair around to wring it out. Her face flushed like it would if I clasped her neck softly. The heat got the better of me. I crowded close to her, steam rising around her as the water had warmed.

I pressed my hand against the wall, caging her in as I bent to her ear. "And if I told you to be a good girl and straddle my face, you would—what?"

She shot me a glare, but a soft gasp parted her damn mesmerizing lips. Demanding desire volleyed through me. Hardened nipples beaded from her wet shirt, and my tongue salivated. I wish I had known she was into this kind of talk before our first time together. It was like I unlocked the door to my presents, and I couldn't wait to rip into them.

Hot water sprayed onto my chest, shocking me back to reality. I backed out of her aim. She released the nozzle and went to walk away. I should have let her, but I couldn't. The heat between us was too…well, damn hot.

I grabbed her wrist, tugging softly, and she came to me until I crammed her against the greenhouse's cold glass. I grasped her neck, covering her tattoo. Each full breath stretched my fingers, and her heartbeat thrummed under them. My cock pushed against my zipper. All the longing I'd been holding back came to a heady rush.

I bent slowly. This was a power move, but she could break free if she wanted to. She didn't. Instead, she met me halfway. Our lips crashed in blazing heat. The glass was blisteringly cold against my palm. I didn't care. She grabbed my hand, wrapped it around her neck, not to pull me away, to make me squeeze harder. I groaned. Damn, she was not afraid to ask for what she wanted.

I bit her lip and tugged. She grunted at the back of her throat, a warm sound that tantalized my mind, reminding me of when I plowed into her tight channel for the first time. *Fuck.* Chatter and footsteps on the path broke through the spell. People. We were bound to be caught if we kept acting like this.

She shoved me away. "We can't."

I hated those words as much as I understood them. "Right. I'll go." Fuck. I was stiff and cold as I walked away.

9

CLIVE BLEW ME out of the snow with that kiss. My body was still thrumming with need as I walked through the greenhouse, dripping wet, trying to put my head on straight. With the amount of chemistry between us, I wasn't surprised the inevitable happened. Seriously, we were like a tripwire waiting to blow. We were getting reckless.

Clive's tablet rested on the bench—forgotten. Not that I blamed him, my brain was still a heady haze. Glad someone didn't take it, I picked it up. The screen awoke as if only the backlight had malfunctioned. I jolted. *And I thought it was dead...*

The screen's image appeared to be a book cover until I took a closer look at it. It was a drawing of a woman bending over to smell one of the lavender and red bi-colored roses I'd created. It was so lifelike, the scent of the roses seemed to come right off the page.

A beautiful array of colors surrounded her—soothing greens mixed into warm golds and soft pinks. Whether they had meant to or not, the artist had somehow captured the aura of someone with warm, compassionate, and loving energy. But darkness surrounded the aura, a protective barrier to the inner layers. My breath stilled in my throat as recognition settled over me.

This wasn't just artwork of someone's aura—this was me. I'd never seen my aura before, but if I could, this was what I imagined I'd see. Magical. Breathtaking. I lifted my shaking hand to my lips as realization struck.

Clive drew this.

A sting erupted in my eyes. This was too much. Here I'd been hiding that part of myself from Clive, afraid of his rejection, and even if he was a skeptic, he'd drawn this. Maybe the books from my office gave him inspiration, but something inside me bloomed with warm hope, though I didn't know what to think. This was too intimate, too fast. We barely knew each other. Yet he'd depicted me so beautifully. It was a pleasant surprise, but I felt it only spelled the beginning of a beautiful end.

Someone cleared their throat. I drew my gaze up to find Clive standing across from me, his hands in his pockets, while his aura gave off blue and fuchsia colors. The fire from earlier couldn't burn the sudden nerves fluttering in my stomach.

I said, "What are you—"

"I came to get my tablet." He gazed downward.

The screen was black once again. "Oh, right. Here." I practically shoved the device at him. It didn't seem oblivious, and I was going to keep it that way. The red transparent aura standing over his shoulder made me grit my teeth. Adelia was playing her games again, but she'd gone too far in showing me that. "You should, uh…try plugging it in. It should work." I glared at Adelia.

"Thanks. I'll try that." He gave a smile and turned to leave. I felt my muscles relaxing until he froze and pivoted back to me. "Look, I—" He took a deep breath as if preparing himself. "Would you want to go to dinner with me and my family this weekend? They are doing this Christmas thing, and it'd be fun if you came."

Too fast. Too fast. He was going too fast for someone he'd never accept. No matter what that picture was—I couldn't meet his family just for us to what? Split up? Were we even together? "I—I don't know."

"Just think about it." His aura was the same calming blue, but a vibrant green stretched across the surface from his desire for me to come.

I barely felt my nod as he walked away.

10

Clive

THE MISTLETOE STARED at me from the desk in my hotel room, the red berries matching Sadie's flustered cheeks. "Stop thinking about it."

But it was impossible. I had nothing else to do. I had finished my work for the day. And now that kiss with Sadie in the greenhouse flew through my blood like Santa's sleigh.

My family dinner was tonight. We hadn't made plans since the day I asked her; it seemed as if she was pushing me away. Either to keep us from repeating what happened or because of the forwardness of meeting my family, I'd wanted to give her space. But I didn't want distance. I wanted her.

I couldn't tell if asking her had pushed her too far. I felt I was supposed to know if I'd fucked up, but she said she'd think about dinner. If this was going to work, we both needed to be direct.

"Fuck it." I grabbed the plant and headed out into the cold. The sun offered some warmth against my face. We had agreed that I wouldn't come to her residence since it might look suspicious, but I couldn't keep myself away. As I knocked on the back door of the chapel's house addition, I clenched the mistletoe to my chest. *Be cool*, I told myself.

The door swung open, and she hit me like a wave of warm air. She appeared delectably comfortable in her short crop top and baggy pajama bottoms. All the blood threatened to rush to my cock. Her wide eyes danced over my black pants and shirt before jumping to my eyes.

"Why are you bringing me mistletoe?" she asked, glancing around my shoulders, probably to check if anyone was outside to catch us.

"I found it on the apple tree in the conservatory. I didn't want the parasite to bother the tree, so...here."

She grabbed it from me, careful not to touch my fingers. "I feel like a guy only brings a girl a gift when he thinks he's done something wrong."

"I don't know. Have I? I'm sorry if asking you to dinner with my family crossed a line. I don't want to stop hanging out because of that or because we got carried away. Though seriously, I can't stop thinking about that kiss."

She licked her lips as if she too couldn't get it out of her mind. "Do you want to come in? It's freezing out here."

I was anything but cold. My blood rushed with the heat of needing to get things right with her, and the anticipation that she wasn't sending me away. "Are you sure? I just want to talk."

Her phoenix tattoo bobbed as she swallowed. "I know. Let's talk where it's warm."

She held the door open. I felt like I could breathe for the first time, even if a knot still sat in my chest. Her honeysuckle and amber scent wafted over me as she shut the door and walked to her kitchen island. On the television, it appeared she'd been watching A Christmas Story. She leaned back against the island. I stayed at the entrance, snow clinging to my shoes, knowing the closer I got to her, the harder this—and I—would become.

"Tell me the truth," I said. "Was the family dinner thing too much?"

"Kind of?" she said, voice shaky enough that I clocked she was as nervous as I felt. My muscles bunched with the need to take her into a hug until the nerves went away.

"Just kind of? Is there something else I'm missing?"

Her cheeks flushed. Was that a good or bad sign? She rubbed her hand over her face, and my body tensed. Then she sighed, arms crossed over her chest. "I saw your drawing."

"My drawing?"

"The one of me in the greenhouse. Your tablet worked for a second, and I think you'd been working on it before it died..."

"Oh." I hadn't meant for her to see it until maybe we were more established, but I wasn't bothered that she had. Only that it bothered her.

"It was beautiful, but also..."

"Creepy?"

She shook her head. "It felt too intimate. We've only known each other for a few weeks. We aren't even dating."

I closed the distance, butting up against those arms she kept stubbornly across her chest. "We aren't? I don't know about you, but this hasn't exactly felt platonic."

"Clive...I'm not as...open as you. Even if I'd like to be. You have this image of me, but I'm not her."

"You're right. I had an initial impression of you. But I've grown to know the real you, or I wouldn't have drawn you that way. I see you. The woman with such a deep empathetic side she keeps hidden by pushing people away. I want to learn more about her. Get her out of this dark shell."

Her arms loosened until one hand gently touched my chest. "I don't—"

"Come to dinner with me to meet my family as my date."

"What?"

"Sadie Anderson...will you go on a date with me? A real date. I'd rather it not be with my family, but it's probably the best way to see if we mesh. All of us. If there's nothing there, then we can—" I shrugged, jaw too tight. "—go our separate ways."

I felt analyzed under her gaze, like she saw too much of me. But damn, did I love the way she looked at me—completely, all-consuming.

"Are you sure you want to introduce me to your family, especially if we end up calling it quits?"

"I'm positive. So, yes or no?" I asked softly. I couldn't get over how much I wanted to ravish this woman, even as my heart hung on a wire.

"You're kind of pushy."

I closed what little gap there was between us, twined my arm through hers to reach the small of her back. As I pressed her closer, I whispered in her ear. "You have no idea how much I want to be. Are you in?"

She shivered against my body and nodded.

I felt the smile I gave her all the way to my fuzzy brain. "Now be a good girl and get into some warmer clothes. It's a drive to where we're going."

She swallowed thickly. "What if I wanted to ride you first?"

Fuck.

11

Sadie

I'D DECIDED TO step back from whatever this was with Clive—until he showed up, his aura radiating worry and determination. He blew all my plaguing thoughts away as if they didn't matter.

He wanted something real enough to take me out with his family. And I couldn't pretend this was platonic, not when he saw me so clearly, even without the truth. The aura he drew, his words—they unraveled me. I didn't care about my truth. I just wanted him.

And when he cornered me, my whole body tingled with need. His mahogany and whiskey scent overwhelmed me. I'd been unable to get him out of my head; Mr. Doyle with his hard yet soft lips, his spiked blond hair, and the heart-throbbing smile he gave me right before he robbed me of my sanity with that kiss in the greenhouse. If I could even call it that. It was a domination. A promise of so much more. And to know he'd been thinking about it too made me ache.

I wanted to go on our date, but I needed the edge off first because, damn. Being around him with this no-sex pact was torture.

"You are blunt," he murmured, leaning back to gaze deep into my eyes. "And not making this easy."

My libido had a mind of its own, and each breath was a fight past my growing desire. We danced around each other for weeks. All this pent-up sexual tension was clawing through me. "Good," I whispered, grabbing his shirt collar. "Because I want you ready to take me."

"Fuck," he said as I yanked him into my living room, not caring about the snow he dragged in. "Does someone want to be a good girl?" he asked in a purposefully low voice.

My body tingled. I don't know why that turned me on. Especially from him. "Shut up and fucking kiss me."

He laughed, and that hot, smiling mouth found mine.

His body pressing against me was all I needed to burn. His fingers scratched against the back of my scalp, and he yanked my hair down, baring my neck for him to splatter kisses and nip at my tattoo. *God, that feels so good.*

"I love this tattoo," he growled against my skin.

I was Frosty on a summer day, and Clive was the fucking sun, melting me into a wet puddle. I got him out of his warmer layers. In between long, greedy kisses, he removed my shirt. His rough hands rubbed against my bare breasts, eliciting tingles that shot straight to the apex between my thighs.

He groaned the same way he had the first time he saw the bars pierced through my nipples. "I also love these."

"And I love when you play with them."

He did just that, tugging them with his teeth and swirling them with his wet, rough tongue until I was quivering for him.

I tore off his shirt, kissed my way down his stomach, and set upon his pants with a vengeance.

His salty cock was long, hard, and thick in my mouth, throbbing, but he didn't give me time to play. He slung me on the couch, yanked my bottoms off, and showed me how much he understood the female body and how to make me so wet I was aching for release. His slippery, hot tongue was a force that had me panting, moaning out of control. He murmured praises over my body and tugged my nipple until I came with such vengeance, I saw shooting stars.

"Condoms?" he grated.

"Bedstand," I said in a daze, glad we'd already had this conversation. When he returned, my inner muscles were throbbing for his cock. "Sit," I said, noticing he sported a condom on his hardness.

His chest inflated, and he did as I commanded. I straddled him slowly, loving the way he watched me with rapt attention. He dragged me into a kiss with his hand wrapped around my neck. Our lips met, paused, and met again—each long stare between saying what words couldn't. This time was different. He might not have known the truth about me, but he looked at me as if he already knew—already accepted me. And I felt the quiver through my chest rising to my burning eyes. He stole me with a kiss that was slow and full of something warmer than desire.

When he was inside me, pounding the fuck out of me, hard and fast then deep and rhythmically slow, nothing existed except the pleasure that echoed in the beauty of his fuchsia aura. He came with a groan that rumbled through my body.

Breathing hard, I lay on top of him on the couch, our sweat mingling between our bodies. Awe grew over me, setting my skin alive with goosebumps. Unlike last time, when I only stayed because I'd passed out, I wanted to remain glued to him, relish in this cocoon of warmth and—

I definitely should not think about what this meant for us. I just wanted to enjoy being in his presence—naked and *utterly* satisfied.

"Now…" he grinned. "About that date."

"I can't convince you to stay in?"

"Nope." He gave my ass a quick tap that stung with pleasure. "We already know we have chemistry in the bedroom, and if we're going to complicate things, we should do it thoroughly."

"Is the restaurant far from town?" I asked with the fear of being caught still a lump in my throat.

He nodded. "I planned with the thought that you'd be joining us."

He was very determined. But as I walked to my bedroom to change, the negative thoughts swooped in to keep me company. I wasn't sure how this date would go. Coming clean seemed easy—until I remembered the therapy my parents put me through to make me "normal." The bullying. The rejection. Now that we were this close, I didn't know if I could go through with it.

Maybe I could hide it from him like I did my parents…until I couldn't be around them anymore because of how toxic it became. I groaned into my sweater as I threw it over my head. *Come on, Sadie.*

Today, I would enjoy being with Clive. There wasn't much time before he'd have to return to New York, anyway. As I ran my fingers through my hair, I tried to convince myself my heart didn't hurt over the idea.

12

Sadie

I FELT JITTERY and almost out of my body when Clive and I entered *Bigfoot Bites.* The restaurant was over an hour from Bryson House, but nerves still sat in my throat. I didn't want us to get caught. Not to mention, I was going to meet Clive's family.

"Tell me this was your dad's idea again?" I asked, trying not to fidget with my hands.

"More Sid's, but the food is worth it."

Clive held the door open, and I stepped into the restaurant, where the warm glow of lanterns cast light on the cabin walls adorned with vintage Bigfoot memorabilia, from newspaper clippings to rustic signs. The scents of pine, cedarwood, and grilled meat cradled me in an interesting experience. Clive brought me to the back, where two men sat.

The older gentleman I assumed was Clive's dad had a sturdy build, a testament to his years of hard work and dedication to raising two boys by himself. His time-lined face brightened, and his blue eyes sparked with vitality when he caught sight of us. The other man was a slimmer version of Clive with shoulder-length brown hair.

The two stood and hugged Clive and turned their attention toward me.

"So, she exists," Clive's brother murmured, sending his elbow into Clive's arm.

"Don't mind him," Clive's dad said. "I'm Richard, and the pesky one is Sid."

"It's nice to meet you both," I said. I wasn't much of a hugger, but the warmth in their auras had me opening my arms for them anyway.

After I removed all my layers, I sat across from Richard and tried to keep my attention from the Christmas bags at his feet. *Was I supposed to bring something?*

"Don't worry," Richard said, noticing my gaze. "It's for our sorry-I-forgot-Christmas gift exchange."

"What is that?" I asked.

Red crept into Clive's cheeks. "It's nothing—"

"Oh, no. You don't get off that easily." Sid leaned in to whisper. "For her sake, I hope you don't." Clearing his throat, he explained, "You see…when Clive was a teenager, working far too hard, he thought he had missed Christmas, so he threw gifts at us apologizing."

Richard added, "He was so adamant, we couldn't correct him, though it was still a week away. And he wouldn't even let me give him his gifts, saying he didn't deserve them."

Clive ran his fingers through his hair. "I felt silly and then mad that these two got their Christmas presents early."

"No…" I giggled.

"I'm afraid so," Dad said. "And now we open a few gifts early to celebrate."

"That's a nice tradition."

"What about you, Sadie?" Sid asked. "Do you have any traditions?"

"Not really," I said. "I'm not close to my family. I usually spend time with my coworkers at the hotel or my foster sister if she visits."

Richard gave a soft smile. "Work families can be the best kind."

Dinner with the Doyle family was not what I expected. Their loving banter was easy to fall into, and they never made me feel out of place. It was open, warm, and everything I imagined a family should feel like. They were inquisitive-yellow curious about me, not shying away from my occult subjects. I felt gooey around them like a chocolate warmed in a s'more, but I still watched what I said—playing the woman I was seventy-five percent of the time. While the part I kept hidden analyzed their auras.

Sid's base aura was mostly a growing, voracious yellow-green—like he was kind-hearted but also curious about the world. Richard's teal aura—a mixture of openness and curious nature—stayed steady. There was a depth to it that reminded me of reserved people. But occasionally, he'd bite his lip, and a spark would fly into the air. The guy had it bad for someone, and man, he could not stop thinking about them. But that wasn't something I'd bring to the table, as no one else brought up his love life.

Clive's aura fluctuated in its authentic and dynamic way, but a deep mossy slate lurked under the surface like algae. It had taken me a while to figure out what caused that guilt and resentment, but over time it became apparent that it centered on his family. It had taken me even longer to bring it up to him naturally in conversation before today, but it seemed like I'd planted the seeds as now that emotion was rising. I could only hope he'd talk to his family about it before the algae overgrew. Even now, he was into the occasion, but the root cause of that tradition spoke of a boy put under so much responsibility he hadn't known what day it was and had punished himself, thinking he'd forgotten Christmas.

"Oh, I wonder what this could be," Clive said with a flat tone as he tore into a wrapped gift. "Just what I needed. A new calendar."

"So you can keep track of Christmas next year," Sid said, as if this was a part of the tradition.

The image on the front was of a pack of adorable dachshund puppies in Santa hats. Their little faces were so cute. I squeezed the hem of my dress as I hovered over Clive's shoulder. "Aww," I said. "I didn't realize you were into dogs."

"I didn't know that either," he teased. "But they are cute."

"Okay. Last but not least," Sid said, bringing up a large red bag with gold wrapping paper sticking out the top. "This is for you, Sadie."

My heart dropped and flew around my stomach and into my chest. "Me? But I—I didn't get you guys anything."

Sid beamed. "That's the beauty of this exchange…it's before Christmas, so there's still time to get us something. And if you're making lists—"

Something rustled under the table, and from Sid's wincing face, Clive had kicked him. "Leave her alone, bro."

"Pay him no mind," Richard said. "Open it."

I licked my dry lips, part of me excited and the other part scared of what a group of men would get for me. Their vibrant green excitement surrounded me as I peeled the tissue paper back. A crinkled yellow leaf of a dying plant greeted me.

I bit my lip to keep from laughing as I gazed over at Clive. "You didn't."

"I saw it at the store and couldn't help but think of you."

"This is...great," I said, my voice shaky with the full and achy feeling in my chest. I pulled out the poinsettia that needed some tender love and care. "Thank you." As I lifted my head, a tear streaked down my cheek. "Gah. I'm such a sap. I've never really received any gifts. All my parents' money went to the foster children." I wiped at the waterworks, wishing they would stop. "I'm sorry."

"Nothing to be sorry about." Clive wrapped me in a side hug and pulled me in to nuzzle his chin into my hair playfully, easing the pressure of everyone seeing me cry. "Just glad we did good."

As I freed myself from him, there was a depth to his gaze that struck through me. Within his blue aura were little pops of gold, like sparklers flashing above water. Were Richard's sparks jumping across the table? No...that wouldn't happen. I froze.

Sparks? *We* had fucking sparks?

"Sparks?" Clive asked.

I slapped my hand over my mouth. *Shit.* Did I say that out loud? *Quick! Distract them.* "Sorry. I, uh...I was going to ask Richard about the sparks he has with a certain woman."

The table stilled.

"Or guy," I quickly added. "Whatever you're into."

I misread the tension, and the slow dawning of what I'd said crept over me like an uncomfortable chill. There I went, spouting out information I shouldn't have known. That ominous, shadowy gray, like a haunting specter I couldn't get rid of, appeared in Clive's aura. His curiosity had slowly turned into suspicion, and I felt it wouldn't be long before this thing between us was ruined—sparks or not.

"Dad has someone he's into?" Sid asked with a teasing grin.

Richard's eyes narrowed. "How did you know about that?"

It was my chance to come clean. Be honest with all of them. They'd gotten me this thoughtful gift, but that didn't tell me what they'd think if I told them the truth. How Clive would look at me. A heaviness fell over my chest. Sure, liking auras is one thing, but seeing them? I swallowed. "It was just a guess," I said, waving my hand a little too enthusiastically. "You seemed dreamy over there."

From their auras, no one believed me, and I wished my hair were a little longer. A little darker. Anything to hide me from them.

"Dreamy, huh?" Clive jumped in with a rescuing flare. "Let's hear about them."

Their attention may have swung to Richard, which had been my intention all along, but the ball in my gut swelled. I stayed pretty quiet for the rest of the dinner.

Soon, Clive and I were strolling past storefronts, admiring the tree decorations in the windows. I kept catching our sparks at the corner of my eye, and it would send a flutter through my chest. I'd wanted them ever since I understood what they meant, but I couldn't believe they were with Clive.

"Do you like living in the chapel?" he asked.

"Would you think me weird if I said I love my chapel garden?"

"You should love your home," he said, voice hoarse. "No matter the exterior. Or you're living in the wrong place."

"Do you love yours?"

"It's pretty nice. But if I'm honest, it doesn't really feel homey. I barely have any friends in the area, and it feels— lonely."

"I never bought that 'it's the people that make the home' thing, but it's kind of true."

"Who makes Bryson House feel like home for you?"

I covered my warm face. "You'll think me even weirder."

"For one, I don't think you're weird, and two, now you definitely have to tell me."

"It's the plants?"

"What?"

"I know. It sounds sad, but they are like my little children. And then there are the ghosts…"

"The ghosts? How are you friends with them?"

"Honestly? Coercion. On their part. They are lonely too. I think that's why they set people up sometimes."

His lips quirked upward.

"What?" I asked.

"You. You're so protective and loyal that I actually have to wonder if they are real."

"I can't imagine what it would be like if I had to leave."

Clive chuckled. "I'm sure you'd uproot the entire garden and take it with you. That is something I admire in you. Your loyalty."

Heat prickled at my cheeks, and the off-white of truth in his aura made me nearly dizzy with happiness.

"I wish my mom had half the heart you do," he murmured, staring off.

I squeezed his arm, feeling a similar sensation in my chest. "Have you tried reaching out to her? Maybe find out why she left?"

He shook his head. "She disappeared. Sid's the one who wants to find her, but…if she didn't want us in her life, then I don't want her in mine."

"I understand that. That's how I feel about my parents. If they don't agree with the life I'm living, then they don't deserve to be in it."

"What part do they not agree with?"

My throat locked, and I fiddled with my scarf, searching for any answer that wasn't the truth. But like Clive said…it was so tiring hiding from him. But was that tiredness worth the potential heartache from his rejection?

"My more occult fascinations," I said.

"I'm sorry. I find that particular side charming."

"Only because you get to tease me about it."

"Maybe." His grin made me feel light and airy. I didn't mind his teasing about the topic. If anything, it was fun. His skepticism felt open, like a flag waiting for the right wind to convince it to fly. But I still feared it'd point in the wrong direction.

"Clive Doyle?" a female voice called out, startling us. Where had I heard that sharp tone before?

Dressed in a long cashmere wrap coat, Marsha Bryson, one of Bryson House's board members, walked toward us. I recognized her from her no-nonsense updo and expensive boots because she'd spent time at the hotel, trying to boss people around—particularly me. She had a desire to tell me what flowers and colors I should create next. My heart leaped into my throat.

"I thought that was you," she said. "I don't know if you remember me, but I'm—"

"Marsha Bryson," he said, shaking her offered hand. "It's good to see you again."

Her shrewd eyes bounced from Clive to me with recognition, and her smile twisted into a condescending grimace. My stomach churned as the venom ebbed and flowed in her shadowy green aura, like a Grinch preparing to steal Christmas, and Clive and I were her targets.

Fuck.

We'd been caught. And out of all the board members, she was the only one who could recognize me. I tried to wrestle my hand free from Clive's arm, but his muscles tensed. He wasn't going to let me go.

This just got a lot messier.

13

Clive

I held onto Sadie. We were already caught. Though it may have appeared messy, I wanted to take the honest route. I'd only met Marsha Bryson once, but as a board member who hired my company, I put on a pleasant smile.

"Surprising to see you and Sadie here. Together," she said. The dig sent an uneasy tingle up my spine. "How's the report coming along?"

She'd asked me, but her stare remained on Sadie, who had stilled beside me. "I plan to give it to the board Monday morning."

"That's good. We were wondering if the holidays were getting to you, but I see it's an employee."

A wild heat climbed up my back. I understood this was messy, but pointing the finger at Sadie in such a way riled me. "Excuse me? What are you insinuating?" I stepped toward her and away from Sadie. The arm I'd been clinging to fell to Sadie's side.

Marsha didn't back down. "Can you really make unbiased decisions with this weirdo whispering in your ear? Does she want you to save the ghosts? Her job?"

I shook my head in disbelief. She didn't like Sadie but fuck if I'd allow her to talk to her like that. "I can do my job just fine. What I do with my time outside work is not your concern."

Marsha shrugged. "Maybe. But the board might not be happy if they learn you're delaying the report on purpose. And Barber Consulting doesn't seem the type of company to keep troublesome employees if they ruin a six-figure contract."

Shit. A chill raced down my spine. I'd known spending time with Sadie was risky, but I never expected it to snowstorm into my face and onto my career. This could get me fired. Barber, the owner, was a fair employer, but he also didn't like messes. If it were easier to fire me than lose this client, he would.

"Don't worry, Clive," Sadie said. "She's just trying to scare you."

Marsha scoffed, a plume of fog escaping her. "Oh really? You think you're all-knowing, huh?"

This situation put an itch of unease at the back of my throat, but I got the feeling Sadie was seeing more than I could. But without knowing *what* she could sense, I felt she was only stoking the fire, not putting it out.

I said, "Mrs. Bryson, I assure—"

"Just leave us alone," Sadie said, tugging on my arm as a heat started in my spine from her interruption. "Like Clive said. What he does on his off time is none of your damn business."

"This is my damn business, my company," Marsha said and turned toward me. "Turn in that report tomorrow night or go home without a job this Christmas." She whipped around and walked away as the snow fell in a thick layer. The chill couldn't combat the fire whipping through me. This was half my fault, but Sadie…

"I'm sorry about that," Sadie said and stopped when she looked at me. "Clive?"

When she took a step toward me, her hand lifted, and I stepped backward, needing space. The fear of losing my job and the sting of self-blame consumed me. Her green eyes scanned me, her brows sinking. She'd kept herself so guarded, and now I had to question who I was dating.

"Care to explain why you risked both our jobs on that hunch?" I asked.

"She has no pull, Clive. She was bluffing."

"And how do you know that?"

She bit her lip. "I just do."

An incredulous laugh seeped from my lips. "You expect me to trust your judgment when you can't tell me why? I thought we were getting to know each other, but there's something you keep between us, and even now, you won't tell me. At least tell me why you won't tell me?"

"Because—I—" She shook her head. "I knew this wouldn't work." Her obvious deflection plunged an icicle straight through me, leaving me numb and cold. "It'll be best for both our jobs if we walk away from this anyway, so I'll find my way back home."

"Sadie. Don't leave like this. Talk to me."

"Have a good night." Her breath hitched.

And just like that, she turned and left, walking out of my life.

14

Sadie

THE TV BLARED happy Christmas tunes I could barely stomach, just as I couldn't stomach sitting on my couch. The memories of my time together with Clive were too fresh. Instead, I bundled up on the floor in my warmest blankets. Light refracted off the amber of my whiskey, appearing like the sparks I'd been seeing in Clive's aura. We had sparks…and now. Nothing.

My throat stung, and I gulped back another smoky shot, feeling the burn all the way to my empty gut, a prickle of wooziness chasing soon after. The oily blackness that had engulfed him when I walked away from him was a thickness I'd never cross. I should have told him the truth, but…I couldn't. What I said was true. It was better for us to separate. My heart ached with each breath, but I kept telling myself this was easier than his rejection.

My door opened, startling me. Cold air burst through the room as a hunched figure in colorful attire shoved the door shut. Celeste shook snow from her blond hair onto her sweater and stomped her boots.

"Okay," Celeste said, staring off at a hazy red aura floating before her. "I'm here. Now wha—" Her eyes fell upon my blanket puddle, and a spike of nauseous green surfaced over her aura. "Oh, you're up. Sorry. Hi. What are you doing on the floor?"

"Adelia sent you after me, didn't she?"

"Uh…no?" She hopped around, trying to disentangle herself from her boots.

"Someone else is here."

"That's another ghost—" She waved her hand dismissively. "—Frank."

"Uh. Huh."

Free from her boots, she ran across the room. Before I could protest, she threw herself under my blankets, bringing in the chill with her.

"Hey! You're freezing," I said. "Ugh! You have snow all over your sweater."

"It's so c-c-cold," she said, adding a fake chatter to her teeth as she rose from the blankets like a puppy lost in a snow pile. She snuggled against my side and snatched the glass from my fingers. Giving it a sniff, her nose wrinkled. "Seriously? It's not even breakfast time."

I shrugged.

"So why are you on the floor?"

I shrugged again, not in the mood to kiss and tell.

"Oh, come on. Adelia said you went on a date with Clive and came back moping. Since it was off the premises, she doesn't know what happened."

I sent her a glare. "So, Adelia sent you after me?"

"That's beside the point. Tell me."

"We went on a date, but one of the board members showed up and threatened Clive's job. I told Clive she was bluffing, and that turned into this whole thing about what I've been hiding from him. He's been so suspicious of me for the past few days that I wasn't surprised, but I—"

"You couldn't tell him, huh?" she asked, resting back against the couch.

"Nope."

The TV turned on and off in rapid succession—Adelia's way of grabbing my attention. I knew Adelia brought Celeste to comfort me, not to hear my drama, but irritation still prickled at my neck. "I thought I told you I wanted to be left alone?" I said to Adelia.

The TV shut off. Stillness filled the room.

"Do you want to know what she's saying?" Celeste asked.

"Not particularly. She's probably telling me to rip off the band-aid, but I've only told five people in my life the truth," I said, resting my chin on my knees. "Well, eight if you count strangers. You're one of three people who didn't flat-out tell me I was crazy. And you're the only one not getting paid. I mean...I still don't feel like myself from those medicines my mom made me take."

"Your parents were terrible."

"Clive makes being honest look so simple, but I—I'd rather we weren't even together than see him look at me differently. I mean, he's a complete skeptic. He'll think I'm delusional. And that will surely get me on his chopping list."

"Maybe. But his suspicion didn't come from nowhere, Sadie. It's easy to tell you have a window into people's souls. I thought I had hidden it, but you kept asking why I was scared, and I knew you could see something no one else could."

"Why can't that be it? Why does he need the whole truth?"

"If I hadn't confessed to you about the ghosts, what kind of relationship would we have had?"

We wouldn't have had one. She would have passed through my parents' foster house like all the other kids.

She continued, "We became close when we opened up to each other. That's all Clive wants. And you shouldn't hold yourself back. You've been working so hard on yourself these past few years, like me, building self-acceptance and setting boundaries. Now it's time to build positive relationships. But you'll never find them unless you're willing to open up."

"Even if I wanted to...I already fucked it up. He no longer has sparks—"

"Sparks?" She stiffened, voice rising. "You have sparks, and you didn't tell me?"

"You don't have to yell."

She shook my shoulders in a non-gentle way. "You have fucking sparks?"

She continued shaking me until I burst out laughing. "Yes. Okay. We have—had—sparks. But that doesn't mean he'll accept me."

"Sadie. You've spent your whole life seeing those damn things between other people. Now you have them, and you're letting fear of rejection stop you?"

"No?"

"Damn straight, no. Sadie, if I can stay put this long, you can tell Clive the truth. And if he's dumb enough to get you fired, we'll weather that together. I just don't want you stuck with a 'what if.'"

I rubbed my forehead. "I don't either. Can you—Can you help me figure out how to tell him?"

15

Clive

"SERIOUSLY?" SID SAID, his irritation snapping across my headphones. "Christmas is in a few weeks."

"I'm aware," I said, throwing clothes back into my suitcase. "But Barber bumped our presentation up, so there's no time for the board to vote us out." I hadn't expected Mrs. Bryson to act rashly, but the moment my boss called, the anxiety that had been a sinking pit in my stomach came to a head. Mrs. Bryson had let it slip that she'd seen me with a Bryson House employee during non-working hours. With no way out, and with a heavy heart, I agreed to go back.

"But you did your part and turned in your report. I don't see why you have to return."

"Because I messed up." As I went back to the dresser, the scent of bonfire wafted over me. It was a common enough occurrence that I long stopped looking for the source. There wasn't one.

"But Barber is going to review the report with an unbiased opinion—problem solved."

I sighed. "It'll be better if I'm there to cover my ass." The sound of my coat zipper was loud in the following silence.

"You know you can visit sometime other than Christmas," Sid murmured.

The heat in his tone kicked an ember against my spine. "What is that supposed to mean?"

"You never come to see us."

"I came back in July last year."

"Because dad had heart surgery."

I'd stayed for nearly a month, but I understood that wasn't what he meant.

"I'm going to take a page out of Clive's book since honesty is the best policy," he said. "It feels like you abandoned us."

"I'm not mom."

"Aren't you? When will you be honest with yourself? I get that you needed space to find yourself, but you don't owe us anything. We're adults. So stop hiding behind your job."

Sadie had said something similar. And even if I hated thinking about it, they both were right. I'd gone to New York believing I'd help Dad pay for the bills, but it was really to get away from having to pick Sid up from school and take him to all his practices. Let him live his dreams while I felt—stuck. And maybe I was so concerned with believing I wasn't my mother that I lied to myself about it.

"I can tell you aren't happy in New York," he said. "Why don't you quit this blood-sucking job and let us take care of you for once?"

"You say that like it's easy."

"Isn't it? Sounds to me like they just want you there to cover their asses and be the scapegoat if it goes sideways. If they're ready to throw you under the bus, that's not a company I'd want to work for."

"All my stuff is in New York."

"I have a truck and trailer because I travel a lot, remember? We can do a family trip for all I care."

I'd be throwing my career away, tarnishing my name in the consultant circles, but I wasn't sure that mattered. I wouldn't hide behind my boss and try to defend my actions. I'd take responsibility and pull myself out of the contract. It was the ethical thing to do. Plus, it wasn't like I was sore for money. But there was a selfish part of me that felt I'd be stuck taking care of my family again.

"And what about Sadie?"

My heart felt like lead in my ribcage. "What about her? There's nothing I can do if she won't talk to me. It's time to move on."

"Fine. Just...Stay for Christmas?"

My phone buzzed, and a tightness squeezed my chest. "Listen, I have to go. My boss is calling me."

"Think about it, please," Sid said.

16

Sadie

"I SEE AURAS," I whispered under my breath, like forcing myself to say it aloud would make it easier. "I see auras?"

Each step closer to Clive's hotel room was a struggle. My heart was clawing its way out of my throat as if trying to escape the imminent pain. My shirt clung to my sweaty spine. Not even pulling my hair back cooled me from the heat of my body. I couldn't do this. I stopped in the hallway, poised to turn around.

But I had to.

Right?

A door creaked open, and there he was—Clive, trailing his blue aura like a bruise. My feet turned to run, but his suitcase froze me to the floor. He was leaving? The thought scuttled up my back like a spider. Was he going back to New York? Did he get fired? Was it all my fault?

"Sadie?" His low voice broke me from my thoughts—and *shit*. It was too late to run. "What are you doing here?"

"I uh—" My brain blanked, and it took my cheeks heating to remember why I'd come, and to dismiss the idea. He was walking out of my life. I couldn't tell him my truth when he was leaving, right? There would be no point. "I didn't realize you were leaving."

"Yeah. Did you come to see me?"

"No, I was…" The somber gray of a cloudy day washed over his aura with disappointment, pulling me under like an icy avalanche, and I couldn't finish that fake excuse. He wanted to see me. And that's why I was here—and I needed to stop hiding. Stop running.

"That's a lie," I said. "I did come to see you. I need to tell you something."

His eyes narrowed as too many distracting colors entered his aura. I remembered Celeste saying that if I was too scared to read his aura, I had to make myself look away. "I—umm…sorry," I mumbled, spinning around and awkwardly giving him my back, his presence now a heat against my already burning skin.

He asked, "Are you okay?"

"I know this is weird. Just—bear with me. If I walk away now, I probably won't ever tell you. And I want you to know before you leave. So—" I tried to say the words, but it dried in my throat. *God, I'm going to be sick.*

"What are you—?"

"Sorry." I stared up at the ceiling, hoping to find strength as the churning in my stomach became unbearable. "Give me a second." I closed my eyes and heard my therapist telling me to challenge my bad thoughts. I already assumed he would reject me, but that wasn't true. Clive could go either way; hell, he had drawn a picture of me with an aura. Like my therapist said: if he rejected me, it'd be an opportunity for growth. I'd learn what not to seek in a partner. Holding positivity in my mind, it all came out. I thought I was vomiting, but I realized I was only shouting words.

"I see auras. Like people's auras. Their emotions show up in colors, and that's how I know things, like your favorite color is blue...not because your aura is this amazing blue, but because it comes alive when you see the sky on a sunny day. That's how I knew Marsha was bluffing. I've only told a few people in my life and most of them shunned me: my parents thought I was delusional, my first crush became my biggest bully, and my therapist bobs her head because she's paid to, but she doesn't believe. It's easier not to say anything because I can see people's truths, and rejection is hard. I know you won't believe me, but I've been trying to tell people...well, failing. I mean, I'm facing this way because I don't want to read your aura."

Relief washed through me with every word. It felt nice to say it out loud. Really nice.

But doubt still whispered in my head. Even the slightest hint he might speak, I'd start talking—anything to avoid his judgment.

A warm hand grabbed my shoulder, and I startled.

"Sadie." It was just my name, so neutral and soft. My hands felt numb at my sides. "Look at me."

I shook my head. "I don't think I can."

His warmth pressed against my back as he stepped closer. "Then just listen."

I swallowed.

"I may be a skeptic, but I understand there are things in this world we don't understand. I apologize if that made it seem like I wouldn't believe you. I'm not one hundred percent sure, but I'm not stupid enough to think there isn't something special about you. I mean...you got my favorite color right...though it's sky blue specifically." His chuckle made me feel light until his tone turned somber. "I'm sorry you've had shitty people in your life that made you feel like you couldn't be yourself. That's no way to live. I'm so glad you had the courage to tell me the truth. I feel honored. And I understand your fear, so it's up to you if you want to turn around. Either way, I want you to know your secret is safe with me, but you shouldn't hide it. The truth makes you more...you."

My heart felt full in my chest. I meant to tell him and run, but my curiosity got the better of me. Clive was so honest I could practically see his aura in his words, but I still needed to know. I peeled my eyes apart. The bells attached to the wreath on the door in front of me glimmered, and I could just make out his face in their reflective gold surface. He looked calm, inviting. Taking a deep breath, I turned around.

His blue aura with white waves was the same openness that made me long to dip my toes in its depths. Green spikes of worry surfaced along with bright orange surprise, but his aura gave a feeling of being large and shield-like. Honor. I gasped softly. He accepted me. I didn't need to fear this open man all along.

But something was missing...and my stomach bottomed. He didn't have sparks. Under the surface, red-like dried blood mingled with lavender smoke. He was stressed and unsure, but also relieved, but I felt it had nothing to do with what I had told him. This was something he was burying deep.

"I hope it's not bad." He flinched, as if unsure himself.

"It's...you're..." I swallowed. "You're stressed about something."

He gave a disbelieving chuckle and raked his fingers through his blond spikes. "Always worried about other people.

Mrs. Bryson might have been bluffing yesterday, but she came back with an actual threat."

My back heated, and my insides shriveled. "Shit. I'm so sorry, Clive. I should have known better."

He shook his head. "We both knew what we were doing was risky. It would have come up whether or not you pushed her."

"Were you able to finish the report in time?"

"I did. My boss asked me to go back to New York to help out."

"Oh." Everything inside me felt like it was falling into a pit, dirt coming in after me like the roots I buried. I told him the truth, but it didn't matter. He was leaving. "Yeah. Okay. I shouldn't hold you then. Thank you for listening and being open."

"Anytime. I actually wanted to see you because…I know I shouldn't say anything, but I don't want you to worry. My report actually calls for additional staff. Though our situation has muddied it, my boss and I worked out that he would review it to keep it unbiased."

"Wow. So, no one is losing their job?"

He shrugged. "That's not my place to say. It'll be the board's decision, but that was my recommendation."

My heart fluttered. "Thank you for telling me. Though, I'm sure if the board finds out about us…your report won't save me."

"No, I'm sorry about that."

"I'm…actually not. I'm glad I met you. Even with the possibility of losing my job hanging over my head, I don't feel worried about it. I told you the truth, and your reaction makes me think that there are more open-minded people like you out there. I might be able to find another place that would accept me."

"I'm sure you would." His blue openness kept touching me, and something twinkled in my peripherals, but I couldn't imagine they'd be anything but Christmas lights. I closed my eyes against the sudden sting.

"I won't hold you any longer," I said. "No doubt you have a plane to catch."

"No plane. I'm staying here for Christmas."

"But don't you have to fix the situation?"

"I dealt with it already."

"What do you mean?"

"I quit."

My blood froze solid. "Why would you do that? If you needed me to say something, I would have…you didn't have to—"

He stepped into me, forcing me to stop and meet his gaze. "No, it's not that. You were right to question me about my family and why I left."

"I was?"

He nodded. "I was being so honest with everyone but myself. I've still got stuff to work out with them—I've been pretty shitty. But I chose to be here. With my family. And I was hoping…with you. If you're still interested in actually dating me?"

I swallowed the rising emotions threatening to consume me. Happiness. Excitement. Joy. "Knowing the truth, you're still interested in me?"

"Oh, now I'm definitely interested."

"It might not be the New Year yet, but new year, new me?" I held out my hand. His warm fingers clasped mine, and sparks went off around his head like fireworks. I'd never get used to them. Nor tire of them.

"New year, new me," he agreed.

"I'm Sadie Anderson, groundskeeper and an empath who can see people's emotions."

"I'm Clive Doyle. Most definitely a skeptic, but I can keep an open mind. And I really want to fucking kiss you."

"What's stopping you?"

"Not a damn thing."

Oops, I...

Married a Demon

Emelia Stonefield

1

Nia

MY BEST FRIEND was marrying my ex-fiancé's brother, and my plus one was a literal demon. I've lost my mind. Or maybe I was trapped in a very long and crazy nightmare? A nightmare where the postcard-perfect hotel Rose was getting married at had a temporary hot chocolate bar decorated with cute little marshmallow snowmen, holiday-themed cups, and chocolate-dipped spoons with sparkly snowflake sprinkles.

If this were a nightmare, I might actually be enjoying it.

Are you fantasizing about me again? Carwyn's deep voice sounded inside my brain. I jumped, and my just-poured cup of hot chocolate slipped from my hands. In slow-motion agony, the dark liquid splattered across the counter, spilled onto the floor of the Bryson House Hotel, and splashed down my red skirt and white knit tights. Heat hit my cheeks. I grabbed a stack of napkins off the hot chocolate bar and threw them onto the puddles.

My spine tingled as a dozen sets of eyes descended on me. Great. I was the idiot causing a scene. *Seriously, stop doing that,* I thought back, grabbing more napkins to blot helplessly at my now-stained tights. *I just ruined my tights. The hot chocolate is never going to come out.*

Are you taking them off right now? Never mind, don't answer that. It was a good thing Carwyn couldn't see me right now because the blush on my face was probably the same shade as Santa's suit. I tossed out the sopping napkins as someone from the staff appeared with a mop and bucket. Throwing them an apologetic smile, I made a hasty retreat to my corner table. All I had wanted was to stress eat complementary sugar cookies with a hot cup of cocoa after a day of long flights and sprinting between layovers. I was just going to have to settle for the cookie at this point.

I just got the fanciest text invite to a bridal brunch from Rose's mother, Carwyn said. I like her. She's the best sort of pretentious. Unbothered. Is the whole wedding going to be like that?

Pretentious? Very. I'm sure you'll fit right in, I said, gathering my things. My ex wasn't supposed to be here for another few hours, so I didn't have to worry about him lurking around the corner. Yet.

Because I'm handsome and witty and ruin your tights?

I rolled my eyes, hoping he couldn't tell I was actually fighting a grin. Flirtatious and charming, Carwyn had become the perfect distraction from the burnt remains of my life. *Because you're a literal demon bent on destroying my life?*

You summoned me, Nia dear, he teased.

On accident! Really, who would have thought the handwritten demon summoning spell on the back of their grandma's solstice cookie recipe was the real deal? Not me sober and definitely not me after two bottles of bottom-shelf sangria.

I can stay home if you'd rather attend solo? Despite his playful tone, my heart dropped. I'd rather drop dead than attend this wedding solo.

No, I very much need you for this wedding.

"Nia?"

I turned at the sound of my name to see Rose walking out of the elevator. Her long red hair hung in a single braid over her shoulder, and she wore a set of matching sweats that looked effortlessly chic in a way that only my best friend could pull off. I smiled wide and cried, "It's the bride!" We did a cheesy little run toward each other and hugged like long-lost sisters, something my ex would have said made me look childish. "I'm so happy for you," I said.

"I'm so happy you're here! Oh, no! What happened to your tights?! And where's Carwyn?" Rose asked, looking around.

"He had a work trip, so he's coming in on a different flight. And I spilled hot chocolate on myself." My stomach turned. It had become so easy to lie to her. It wasn't like I could tell her Carwyn was a demon. Or, that we'd been pretending to date all summer, so no one would know what a wreck I still was. I told her I'd met him through a dating app, which honestly seemed the most likely place to meet a demon.

Rose pouted her lower lip. "That stinks you didn't get to spend the whole day together. How was your flight?" she asked, walking with me toward the elevator.

"It was fine." I'd been too nervous to eat this morning, and then nauseous the entire flight, thinking about seeing Jake again tonight. Now, I was just starving and sick to my stomach. "How was your flight?"

"We took the red-eye this morning. Hawthorn is still sleeping, but I'm too excited." We stepped into the elevator, and I pressed the antique elevator button for the second floor. "How are you feeling about seeing Jake again?" Rose asked, watching me with a too-knowing look.

I made a dismissive sound and waved her off. "I'm not worried about him at all." Another lie. I was absolutely terrified. We'd been together for six years. Then he'd left me at the altar in front of everyone we knew. I had thought we were a perfect match, and I still didn't understand what I'd done to make him run away from our happily ever after.

Rose glared at me. "Uh-huh," she said in a tone that, after decades of friendship, could be translated as she was calling my bullshit but was going to let it slide for now.

"Really, I'm fine. I'm with Carwyn now. Jake is the furthest thing from my mind. I promise. Hawthorn and you are amazing together, and I promise there will be no Nia and Jake drama to ruin your wedding."

"I'm not worried about you causing any drama. I know you'd never ruin my wedding." The elevator dinged, and we stepped off. "But we both know Jake is an asshole, and I don't want him to ruin your glow again."

"My glow?"

"When Jake left...I mean, anyone would have been devastated. But I was really worried about you. You were drinking a lot, and it was like every smile was hollow. I knew you were trying to be happy for me, but I could see how much it hurt. These last few months, though, you're more you than you've been in a long time. I don't ever want to see you that sad again."

My room was about halfway down the hall. I stopped in front of the door and turned toward her. "Do you have time to hang for a bit?"

"I would love to, but I have to run and meet the wedding coordinator before the welcome dinner tonight. I just wanted to say hi." Her shoulders rose and fell, and her face scrunched up for a moment. I braced myself. I'd known Rose since elementary school, and she was worried about whatever she was about to say. "I completely understand not wanting to be on a wedding altar again, and that you think you're some kind of bad luck, but I wanted to make sure you knew you could still be a bridesmaid if you wanted." The pit of my stomach gnawed at me. I opened my mouth to apologize, but Rose shook her head. "Nope. Don't say anything. I'm not mad; I totally get it. I was just making sure you knew the possibility exists if you ever change your mind." I nodded, and we hugged. I didn't deserve Rose. She had been so supportive of me, and I couldn't ruin her day by having a panic attack behind her while she said her vows. Jake would be right behind Hawthorn. Rose's wedding had to be perfect, and I wouldn't risk a chance that I might ruin it. "Alright, I'm off. See you at dinner tonight," she said.

She walked quickly away, then disappeared around a corner. Rose deserved a perfect wedding day.

I cracked open the door to my hotel room. The room was beautiful, spotlessly clean, and beckoned me to relax and forget about all the tightening knots in my stomach. Old wooden floors, ornate rugs, and two queen beds that looked like clouds sat in a space that felt like a movie set. The bathroom was more modern, but still had a clawfoot tub with a shower combo.

I should have been Rose's maid of honor, but there was no way I could stand up in front of everyone. Half of her wedding guests had been guests at my wedding. Standing in front of everyone again, if I didn't have a panic attack, I'd probably vomit on the train of her wedding gown.

When Rose had invited me to her engagement party, I'd gotten really hammered. Drunk-Nia had thought it would be funny to do the spell Grandma had left on the recipe card. Trashed as I was, I hadn't clocked Carwyn's sudden appearance in my living room as abnormal. Instead, I'd told him he was hot and asked him to be my date to the engagement party. He'd accepted and then tucked me into bed. The next morning, I'd chalked it up to a wild dream until I found Carwyn making crepes in my kitchen.

I'd thought I'd actually lost my mind. But in the nicest way? Like, if I was going to have a complete mental breakdown, it might as well come with decadent chocolate crepes and fresh coffee served by my personal brand of seriously handsome man. By the time the engagement party came around, I'd already had a (few) full-on panic attacks that Carwyn was an actual demon and put myself back together again.

Are you thinking about me again? Carwyn asked. I'm going to have to start paying you rent for how much I live in your head.

I set my things down and fell face-first into one of the plush queen beds. This weekend had to be the last time I saw Carwyn. My heart was starting to get attached, and Carwyn was only pretending to be my boyfriend. The last thing I needed was to actually fall in love again. I wasn't sure I'd ever recover from the last time. And let's face it, I doubt I could truly trust a demon with my heart.

Can you go back to using your cell phone and pretending not to hear my thoughts?! This is so weird, I thought back.

What's our room number? My flight just landed, Carwyn asked. After an entire summer spent publicly fawning over each other, it wasn't like I could book us separate rooms. I picked up my phone and texted him the room number because it was the saner option. Then, I quietly screamed into the bed.

This was not how I was going to start my best friend's wedding. I peeled myself off the bed and went over to the mirror hanging above the dresser.

"You are going to survive this weekend. Rose and Hawthorn's wedding is going to be perfect. Jake is going to be there, and you are not going to break down anywhere he can see. No, in fact," I said, pointing at my own reflection. "You are going to be soooo happy for them. Your face is going to hurt from happiness. Then you can have a few drinks, and Carwyn will tuck you in."

I winced and leaned on the dresser. No. Carwyn could not tuck me in. His presence in my life had become too dependable, which meant I needed him out of my life before he broke what was left of my heart. The last thing I needed right now was to get into a serious relationship with someone. Once this wedding was over, I could go home and break things off with my demon.

2

Carwyn

I WAS COMPLETELY screwed.

A brass plaque engraved with 'Room 324' stared back at me with more authority than the actual gates of Hell. I adjusted my off-kilter Santa hat and straightened my jacket. The last thing I wanted was for Nia to see me disheveled after a long day of airplanes and layovers.

Something moved in my left peripheral, at the far end of the hall, but when I looked, the scene was still as a painting. Must have been a trick of my eye. As a rule, I didn't enjoy patronizing old hotels. The listless spirits of undead residents seemed to be a problem for older venues, and I loathed ghosts. While a lot of places claimed they were haunted, very few actually were. When I'd read about Bryson House having matchmaking ghosts, I hadn't believed the rumors.

Though at this moment, ghosts might be easier to deal with than the conversation I needed to have with Nia.

In a few hours.

After a couple of stiff drinks. Or a bottle of wine.

She might even laugh.

I knocked on the door, looking forward to seeing the way Nia lit up when she saw me. This wedding was a big deal for her, so I hoped that her ex-ass hadn't already stymied her smile. Jake would be here this weekend, and I was finally going to meet the world's biggest idiot.

The door opened, and a tense-looking Nia peered up at me. She was wearing a long tan sweater dress that gently hugged her body and set off the dark, wavy hair that framed her face. No tights. And no smile.

"We really need to talk about us." She reached up and pulled the Santa hat off my head.

Shit. With that, she'd thrown my plan, and a bit of my heart, out the window. I'd been daydreaming of Nia's smile, in between fretting, for days now. She wasn't wrong. We did need to have a conversation about us. But that conversation was going to be so much easier after a few glasses of wine, so we could laugh at the absurdity of that specific demonic bargain being casually, and frankly irresponsibly, scrawled across the back of a cookie recipe.

I smiled at her anyway because it was impossible for me not to. "Nice to see you too, Nia," I deadpanned.

She crossed her arms and stepped aside, her exasperation with me made obvious. I walked past her and into our room. One of the two queen beds had a Nia-sized rumple across the white quilted blanket, so I put my things down on the other bed. The sound of the door shutting was followed by the padding of her bare feet across the carpet toward me. She stopped beside the other bed, and I could feel her staring at my back, her unasked question hanging in the room like the scent of spoiled eggnog.

"Carwyn, I'm so grateful you've been there for me all summer, and especially for coming to this wedding with me. But at what point do you leave? Our bargain was only for the engagement party." Her tone had a note of worry in it. Understandably, as humans were inherently terrible at making bargains with demons, and the inevitable consequences that arose were steep.

"You're right," I started, keeping my voice light. "We do need to talk about us." I glanced around the room, spotting a pair of chairs with a coffee table that didn't quite fit the rest of the room's Victorian-themed decor. She was definitely going to need to be sitting down for this conversation, so I gestured over to the pair of plush chairs. Hell, I needed to sit for this conversation.

"Do you remember the night you summoned me?" I asked as we sat.

Nia's dark brown eyes narrowed at me. "I wasn't that drunk," she said somewhat defensively, her cheeks flushing. She had, in fact, been that drunk. That was part of the reason this entire mess had started.

I smiled, a somewhat nervous tic. "It's just...that spell is for something very particular, and I don't think you realize what it was actually meant for. Demonic spells don't really consider whether or not you are capable of consenting. Casting the spell, that's the consent part. Kind of. I'm getting off topic—" I forced myself to look at Nia then. She caught my gaze, panic widening her eyes as her skin paled.

I opened my mouth, getting ready to reassure her on instinct. But what could I say? There had to be something reassuring to say. If only my brain would work properly while she looked at me.

"Carwyn," she said, my name laced with a threat. "What actually happened that night?"

I did a shit job stopping the grimace that tightened my mouth because her panic became palpable. As much as I tried not to be in her head, her alarmed, *Oh fuck* lit up my brain like a Christmas tree catching fire.

"That summoning spell, when made on the summer solstice as you had—" I was so screwed. "It's the start of a demon courtship ritual, which ends after the winter solstice...with us being bound together forever."

She blinked at me as my words hung in the air. "What does that mean?"

"Well, it means we made a bargain to stay together forever. And demons, well, we derive our power from making bargains, and I'd been really low on power when you summoned me. I'm doing a shit job at explaining this. If we don't break our bargain before eleven fifty-nine PM on the solstice, we will essentially be in an unbreakable marriage. Marriages are much like a bargain, a deal to be with each other forever. There's some nuance lost in translation, but it's that. And if we break the bargain, I'll lose some, okay, a lot, of my power. Which I can stand to lose now, but couldn't before. And if we were forever bound together, I wouldn't stand in your way if you wanted to leave in the future, but I could never close the telepathic connection we have. And I could never be bound to anyone else."

Her thoughts sounded in my mind. *Holy Hell, what did I do?*

I cleared my throat. Why was this so hard? Oh, that's right. I actually liked her. Despite all my attempts this past summer to not have feelings for her, I'd failed miserably.

"Simply put, you asked me to marry you, and I said yes. If we don't renounce it before the end of the winter solstice, it becomes permanent. If we do renounce it, the magic will keep us apart, and we will never see each other again."

Nia blinked at me, her expression blank. Understanding bloomed across her features as she jumped to her feet, yelling, "What?!" She paced away from me toward the door, and my heart sank. Then she turned around and paced back. "No." She shook her head, as if this was a decision to be made and not a fact. She turned to me. "Wait, why would you accept a marriage proposal from a drunk woman you've never met before?"

I ran my hand through my hair, then gestured at her. "I'd had a really bad day and was nearly out of power. I needed a deal, any deal, to keep going. Then you rang, so to speak, and I jumped at the chance. I figured once I built myself back up, I'd renounce, and we'd go our separate ways."

"Why didn't you?"

"Because if we renounce the bargain, the magic will keep us apart. I wouldn't have been able to travel back to you and be your date to that engagement party."

"Wait, I'll never see you again?" My heart leaped at the fear in her eyes. She didn't want me to go. I didn't want to leave her either.

"That's just how demonic breakups work," I said, then added, "Demons tend to be a bit dramatic." Nia rolled her eyes at me, then turned away from me, pacing toward the door. I scrambled to my feet, pacing beside her. "Look, that night had been really shitty for me too, and when you summoned a demon and the magic picked me, it felt like fate offering the chance for something good for both of us." The admission was something I hadn't planned on telling her. "We spent all summer pretending to be in love, and at some point, I stopped pretending. You are so much fun, and brilliant, and I love talking with you and karaoke cleaning time with you. But, if you don't want me, I'll break our bargain tomorrow night during the reception and walk out of your life forever. Or now. If you want."

Please don't say now.

Nia stopped and faced me. She hadn't run out of the room, but the discordant change of expressions on her face was a marquee sign spelling out she wasn't eager to choose me. It didn't seem relevant at the moment, but I hadn't been entirely sober when I'd accepted her bargain, either. When I'd woken up the next morning bound to a human, I'd had a bit of a panic too. But then I went to talk to her, and it wasn't that I'd felt bad as much as I had felt a sense of solidarity. Nia had initially been too hungover to really question anything, and once she'd sobered up enough to start having a complete existential crisis, I left. I'd thought I'd keep the bargain long enough to regain some of my power and ignore her existence. But the mental connection had sent me all of her thoughts at first, and it wasn't long before I developed feelings. We'd both been madly in love with someone who hadn't loved us back.

Before she could shut me down on reflex, I added, "I don't want you to answer right now. Just think about it. And I know you don't feel the same way about me, but I just want a chance."

Nia stopped moving, her mouth hanging slightly ajar. All those nights over the summer, she really hadn't realized. Which I'd known from the thoughts that had made it to me. I was fun to flirt with. I was temporary, so she didn't feel the need to temper herself. She thought she was a mess, but all I could see was art.

"Why didn't you tell me about the bargain before you accepted?" she whispered, her voice cracking.

"Because once I'm presented with a bargain, I am bound by the magic to either accept or reject. I can't say anything else."

"You should have said no!" My heart cracked a little under the weight of those words, but I knew this was throwing a lot at her. I'd waited too long.

"I know. I'm sorry. I saw you were vulnerable, and I worried that if I said no, you would either summon another demon who would take advantage of you or do something else with worse consequences. I made what I thought was the best decision for both of us at the time."

Nia crumpled into the chair. I took the one across from her. For a long time, we stewed in silence, only occasionally looking at each other.

She blinked and then quickly wiped at her eyes. "I'm so stupid."

"You're not stupid," I said. "To be fair, a cookie recipe is a really ridiculous spot for that demonic bargain."

She rolled her eyes at me, her face and neck patchy and pink. "Does the bargain...does it influence my feelings for you? Or vice versa?"

Heart thumping, I reached out and took her hand. She didn't flinch away, but held my hand tightly. "No. Our feelings are our own." Hopefully, that truth would reassure her somewhat.

Her thoughts floated over to me. *Okay. I got drunk and married a demon.* Pause. *Shit. I have no idea what to do.* Her thoughts sounded clear as a bell in my head, and I had to work to push them out. I didn't need to be privy to her sorting out her feelings.

"You're not the only one putting your heart at stake," I said. "How about this? I pretended to be your boy toy all summer. You owe me this trip to be your man for real."

"Anyone can pretend to be perfect for a few days," Nia said.

I chewed my lip while I tried to think of a way to make this work in her favor. "How about we bargain on it? I will not, in any way, try to deceive you into thinking I'm someone I'm not, and if I do, a penny will appear."

"A penny?" she asked.

"Yes. They are inconspicuous. Easy to find on the floor. Or in a pocket. How many pennies do you have right now?"

"None, I don't have any cash with me."

"Perfect."

"What if you deceive yourself?" she asked.

"Hmmm. Fair enough. I will bargain with you, Nia, that anytime my actions betray my true intent toward you, you will find a penny—" I looked around. "You will find a penny in this drawer," I said, pulling open the nightstand drawer. "In return, you will give me one trial of being your proper boyfriend that will end at midnight on the solstice." I held out my hand.

Her throat worked as she watched my outstretched hand. "You're asking me to bargain with a demon?"

"It went well enough the first time, don't you think?" I asked.

"Being drunk helped with the scary part of this," she said, but reached a slightly trembling hand toward mine. "Only until the solstice? No soul damned to Hell?"

I looked her straight in her brown eyes. "No soul damned to Hell. It's exactly as stated. If I do something that might deceive you, or myself, about who I am, or my intentions toward you, there will be a penny in the drawer."

"I want to know immediately. I want the penny to be in my pocket."

"Are you going to be wearing pockets today? I was told women's clothing was seriously devoid in the pocket area."

"Yes, I will be wearing pockets today." She pulled back her hand. I remained steady.

Please, just trust me.

She let out a long breath and put her hand in mine. "Bargain accepted." The bargain's magic snapped on my skin like a hot rubber band.

Curling my fingers tighter around her hand, I pulled her in closer. "You're the ugliest woman I've ever seen," I said. Her eyes flared, but I quickly added, "You have one cute, tiny pocket on that flimsy pajama shirt." She looked down, then plucked a penny from her pocket.

Nia bit her lip as she tried to fight a smile. "Penny for proof, huh?" Her cheeks pinkened.

"I hope it will be the only one you find."

Her phone buzzed on the table beside her. Nia's face paled, and her eyes widened.

"What is it?" I asked.

"Jake wants to talk."

3

Nia

JAKE'S TEXT MESSAGE sat on read, the phone still lying on the bed behind me, haunting me. The stress from that stupid message pricked my chest, making breathing painful, just like it had during the weeks following our breakup. I needed to be digesting what Carwyn had just told me about the bargain and his feelings, and yet Jake was taking up all my brain space.

Now, after all this time, Jake wanted to talk? The last time he'd spoken to me had been on the altar. I'd walked down that flower-strewn aisle, my heart set ablaze when I saw the tears in his eyes. That moment had been exactly what I'd dreamed of; I'd felt completely seen, and absolutely in love. I knew in my heart I'd made the right decision in choosing Jake.

Then Jake had taken my hands in his and said loud enough for everyone in the church to hear, "You're just not the right woman to be my wife."

In the full-length mirror of our hotel room, Carwyn loomed over my shoulder, blocking my phone from view. I kept accidentally catching his gaze in the mirror as each of us scurried around the other while we got ready in silence for this first dinner.

A stifling, pregnant, choking, awkward silence.

Apart from the morning I'd been hungover while he made me breakfast, we'd never been awkward together. Pretending to be in love with Carwyn had been comfortable, like warm cookies and cold milk.

I desperately needed to talk to Rose, but this was her wedding. I couldn't go knock on her hotel door and say, "Hey, you know my boyfriend Carwyn? Yeah, I was so sad you got engaged to Jake's brother that I got trashed and summoned a demon to be my fake date to your engagement party. But I just found out that if we don't renounce our relationship before the end of your wedding, we're going to be bound together in some weird demon marriage forever. And if we do renounce, I'll never see him again, and I'm not sure I can deal with that. Oh, and Jake texted. He wants to talk."

Weddings were already stressful and exciting enough. Rose had already spent far more time than she should have holding my hand over the aftermath of my wedding. This weekend was about her and Hawthorn, not me. I was just going to have to handle this on my own.

Behind me, Carwyn put a gray tie around his neck and adjusted the collar of his button-up shirt. Carwyn looked like the handsome, alluring stranger in a hard-boiled noir, sitting at the end of the darkened bar, bent over his hard liquor like all the world was pressing down on his muscled shoulders. Which was really a false advertisement. Carwyn was all sunshine all the time. Except right now. A cloud was hanging over him.

"You look amazing," he said, the compliment splitting the silence.

"Thank you. You look amazing, too." The emerald green cocktail dress I wore had taken a damn miracle to zip up. There were only ten minutes left to finish my hair before I needed to walk out of this hotel room and downstairs to the welcome dinner and cocktails with my demon husband and avoid the man I was supposed to have married.

Husband. My stomach roiled.

I grabbed my hairbrush and started brushing loose the curls that had finally finished setting. My gaze caught again on Carwyn's reflection in the mirror. He looked ridiculously good in the black tailored suit he was wearing. Was being hot a demon thing, or just him? The suit accentuated his lean build and his broad shoulders. He turned toward me as he tucked an emerald green pocket square into his jacket that perfectly matched his—

"Did you change the color of your tie to match my dress?" I blurted.

Carwyn had the decency to look like he had no idea what I was talking about. "What if I told you I brought a range of colors so I could be sure to match you?"

I lifted onto my toes and leaned to the right to see past him and onto the bed, where he did, in fact, have at least ten ties of various colors. I took a hairpin from the table and started quickly pinning back some of my hair. "You could have asked me."

"And lost the opportunity to show off my glorious tie collection? No, thank you." He glanced toward the lone closet. "How many dresses did you bring?"

I'd brought six, but only this and one other had pockets. "Not everyone can look good in whatever they wear on any given day. I needed options."

He grinned, some of his usual sunshine lighting his eyes up like he had a secret. "You think I look good in whatever I wear?"

I wanted to deny it, but I couldn't actually think of an instance where he didn't look well dressed. He probably looked as good undressed. Nope. Wrong thought process. I rolled my eyes and grabbed my best stay-put red lipstick. "I'm not blind. You're very handsome. Don't let it get to your head."

In the mirror, his eyes locked with mine, and my heart skipped a beat as he leaned in until I felt his cheek brush my hair, and he whispered, "It went straight to my head," into my ear. He stepped back, preening his dark brown hair in the mirror.

His admission of feelings had caused me to question what I hadn't doubted before. I'd thought flirting with him had been an easy distraction, but now I was questioning every interaction. Despite my best efforts, the corner of my mouth twitched. I put my lipstick on with practiced speed. "You're a humble one."

"That's why you keep me around."

I hadn't meant to keep him around, and now I knew why he had kept showing up. He couldn't get rid of me either, needing whatever power our bargain gave him until we renounced our marriage before the end of the winter solstice. Or was this like an engagement period? I didn't care; it didn't matter. I had the rest of today, tomorrow, and until midnight the day after to spend with Carwyn before he would be gone forever.

Lips done, I picked up the setting spray and misted my face.

"Your zipper isn't all the way up," he said. I sighed and reached back, but it was in that spot right between my shoulder blades that was so hard to reach. "Do you mind?" he asked, gesturing to my back.

I lowered my arms. "Thank you."

Carwyn stepped close and pulled my zipper the last tiny bit up the track, closed the eye hook, and stepped back. I don't know what I expected. Some part of me thought he might take the opportunity to let his fingers graze across my skin or let himself linger close to me. Did I want that?

No. I didn't. So why did I feel slightly disappointed?

Because I was a mess.

"Are you ready?" he asked. "I hear the food here is amazing, and I'm starving."

"Just about." I slipped on the black kitten heels and leaned down to fasten the buckle at each ankle. I belatedly realized I was probably giving Carwyn a free show down the front of my dress. But when I looked up, his back was turned toward me. He was such a gentleman, it was sometimes hard to remember he was a demon.

I strode over to the door, where Carwyn was waiting, leaving my phone behind. When I reached him, he stepped in front of me, then took my hand in his. "You really are breathtaking, Nia." His eyes locked with mine as his lips pressed against my hand. Heat flushed up my neck. The way he was looking at me, I forgot how to speak as my heart decided to make itself known.

Carwyn only grinned and opened the door, holding it open for me. I forced my feet to move. I needed to get some more control of myself.

My pockets were still empty of any pennies as we stepped out of the elevator. I held Carwyn's hand as we entered the large, ornate lobby, which smelled of cinnamon and pine. We were to wait here for our dinner reservation in the hotel's upscale restaurant. In the December night, the warm lamplight made the lobby look like a painting so full of details an artist could spend days taking them all in. A small crowd of Rose and Hawthorn's families had gathered. Parents, grandparents, aunts, uncles, siblings, and a few close friends that had made the cut for the more intimate dinner tonight. The same crowd that had seen Carwyn and me pretending to be dating all summer. We couldn't drop the show now.

We hugged and grinned our way through hellos, and how are yous, and so great to see you toos, while we moved through the crowd to a quiet corner.

I didn't see Jake.

I half expected him to be waiting for me around every turn now that he was finally ready to talk, even though I hadn't agreed to talk to him. Avoiding me seemed to be the thing Jake was best at anyway. He was supposed to be at this dinner, though, Rose and Hawthorn had warned me of that weeks ago. Would Jake demand to talk in front of everyone, or would he want to hash things out in a quiet corner?

He'd left me, and I was completely preoccupied with him. I hated it.

Near the center of the room, Rose was wearing a white lace cocktail dress that hugged her curvy figure like it had been made just for her. Hawthorn was wearing a black suit that accentuated his broad figure. Hawthorn's hand casually rested on Rose's hip, his fingers sometimes tracing the details of the lace as they greeted their guests. Every couple of moments, they would glance at each other, like they were the only two people in the universe. They looked perfect together, their glowing smiles so big my cheeks empathized.

I found a space near the wall opposite the flickering fireplace and waited until the line to greet the happy couple died down. Carwyn stood quietly beside me, his arm around my waist just like it had been all summer. Carwyn always smelled like sandalwood and citrus, but I only ever smelled his cologne when I was close enough to feel the heat of his body. Could I live without this, or was I terrified of being single? Did I actually have feelings for Carwyn, or was I fooling myself? Worse, I'd thought Jake had loved me, and I'd been so mortifyingly wrong. I couldn't trust my own feelings. How could I trust Carwyn's?

Hawthorn and Jake's parents, Stella and Morgan, were gleefully introducing themselves to everyone. Stella caught my gaze from across the room, and her smile faltered. She had initially blamed me for her son fleeing, hurling public accusations of cheating at me while I was still crying on the altar. I wasn't holding my breath for an apology. Stella turned her back to me. I guess we still weren't on speaking terms. Which was fine. I'd never liked her, anyway. She'd insinuated I'd needed to lose weight while I'd been trying on wedding dresses.

"It's time," Carwyn said quietly to me.

"Hmm?"

"To greet Rose and Hawthorn."

Yeah. That. I swallowed and straightened. It was incredibly self-centered of me, but I was also terrified for Rose. I hadn't had a clue Jake was going to run away on our wedding day, so how could she be so sure of Hawthorn? Would he break my best friend's heart like his brother broke mine? Carwyn's fingers wrapped around my fingers, but I pulled away. I needed to wean myself off him.

We entered the sort of meandering line that had gathered to greet the happy couple and when it was our turn; I turned on the charm. Trying to radiate exuberant excitement, I grinned widely and said in my happiest-but-not-overdoing-it voice, "Rose! The festivities begin!" and I hugged her.

"I'm still so happy you are here. I couldn't imagine getting married without you!" she said.

I pulled back and looked at Hawthorn. "Of course, I'm excited for you as well," I said, and tried every bit to mean it. Rose had met Hawthorn at my engagement party. We'd joked that marrying brothers would finally make us officially sisters. It had been silly, and Jake had always been annoyed by it. Rose and I would always be family, even if it was only in our hearts. But it was another cut in the thousand Jake had given me. "Is Jake here yet?" I tried to sound neutral and uninterested because I didn't want them to know how I was really feeling.

Hawthorn gave me a knowing look. "He's somewhere around here." He glanced around, then turned back to me. "If you need anything, just let me or my dad know." He turned to Carwyn and reached out for a handshake, which Carwyn accepted. "Carwyn, it's great to see you again."

"Congratulations. It's great seeing you again as well," Carwyn said, then turned to Rose. "And you are absolutely stunning, as usual." He gave her a polite hug.

"Rose!" I heard someone call behind us.

"Come find me after dinner?" Rose asked, and I nodded. We awkwardly got out of the way so the line of greeters could continue. I kept walking until we found a quiet and unoccupied corner of the room.

"That wasn't so bad, was it?" Carwyn asked.

"No. Of course not. I love her and I'm so happy for her. I just—" I trailed off. Behind Carwyn, some of the Christmas lights flickered. Not the whole strand, only some of the lights, flickering on and off like they were programmable. It was a weird effect, as if Carwyn were the answer on a game show.

Weird. Everything else at Bryson House seemed as close to perfect as it could get.

What's the face for? Carwyn asked.

The lights behind you must be broken, I said.

Carwyn looked over his shoulder and jumped toward me. *Holy shit, it's a ghost!* He screeched into my mind.

"Nia, are you alright?" Rose's mother, Martha, glided over and wrapped me in a hug before I could react. Wearing one of those navy blue skirt suits that politicians, CEOs and old money housewives all seemed to own, along with a few strands of pearls, Martha always looked impeccable wherever she went. The bigger the event, the bigger her glow.

"I'm well. How are you?" I asked, pulling back. I glanced over to Carwyn, who was suddenly pale.

Are you okay? I asked him.

"I'm just so excited to see you! Thank you both so much for coming. This means the world to Rose." Martha leaned in conspiratorially and whispered, "Say the word, and I'll task Aunt Cynthia with keeping Jake away from you. She's on board, ready to help."

Over Martha's shoulder, Aunt Cynthia winked at me and raised a glass of red wine in my direction.

I snorted. "I don't think that will be necessary. I'm fine." I said, not feeling at all fine.

As always, Martha smiled, but it was thin because she saw right through me. That was part of the trouble with long-standing friends. Even their mothers knew when you were lying. "Carwyn, it's so great to see you again." She hugged him as well. That was new. I think they'd been on a handshake basis until now. She'd never hugged Jake. "Dear, are you alright? You're not both coming down with something, are you?"

"I'm fine, just some jet lag." He smiled wide, his typical sunshine radiating from him, though I could still see the subtle terror in his eyes. "You are stunning, as always, Mrs. Pran. I'm honored to be here."

"Please, call me Martha."

I must have given her a look, because she winked at me. Winked! Jake had never gotten to call her Martha.

"How is Dr. Pran doing? I don't think I've seen him yet this evening," Carwyn continued, and cleared his throat. Was that sweat on his temples?

"He finished emergency surgery this afternoon and is on his way now," she said. Dr. Pran was a prominent neurosurgeon who was always on call. When Rose and I were growing up, it was usual for him to be in surgery right until the moment she absolutely needed him. He'd probably walk into church at the same moment Hawthorn did. When it really, really counted, he had always been there for Rose.

"I wanted to make sure you got the note that we are all wearing the pink zip hoodies to the bridal brunch in the morning," Martha said, with a hand on my shoulder.

"Oh, I'm not a bridesmaid," I said awkwardly.

Martha gave me a knowing glare and stepped closer. "You can still wear pink tomorrow. Though if you change your mind, I may or may not have an extra bridesmaid's dress in your size." She squeezed my shoulder.

My chest tightened as guilt washed over me. Of course, she bought the dress, just in case I was brave enough to stand at an altar again. She and Rose had far more confidence in me than I had in myself. Martha smiled and made her exit, walking over to her trio of sisters.

"Did you say you think you saw a ghost?" I whispered to him.

I definitely saw a ghost. He ran his hand through his hair again. I stared at him for a moment. His entire body was tense. Carwyn was never tense.

Are you scared of ghosts? I asked. The terror in his blue-green eyes shocked me. *You're a demon!*

They're incorporeal! It's so gross, and my magic doesn't work on them. I hate them so much.

I blinked. My demon was scared of ghosts.

I bit back a laugh and took his hand. *Your human will protect you.* His fingers tightened around mine.

I'll be fine. He didn't sound convincing.

"They're ready for us to take our seats!" Martha announced to the crowd, and by the door I finally spotted my own ghost.

Jake was staring from the other side of the room, right at Carwyn.

4

Carwyn

THE GHOST I'D seen must not have liked the restaurant because I hadn't seen it again, and after a few minutes, I relaxed. I was here for Nia, and one unembodied frizzy-haired meddling woman would not ruin my time with her.

Despite Bryson House being in the middle of nowhere, the food here was as good as any five-star restaurant I'd been to. Six devilishly delicious courses helped me take my mind off the haunted hotel, but Nia hadn't been able to finish any of them. She sat beside me, stiffer than a nutcracker, still completely wrapped up in her thoughts as she'd been since I'd broken the news of the bargain. Her knee bounced, causing the hem of her dress to ride partly up her bare thigh. She fidgeted with the napkin on her lap as Rose's parents welcomed everyone to the wedding celebrations; which, as was becoming increasingly clear, they had happily paid for entirely. Nia smiled and beamed at her friend, but at no point did she stop fretting over her ex, who was sitting on the other end of the room to our right.

Nia leaned in close, putting her hand on my thigh. Her lips parted like she was going to say something, but then they sealed again, her eyes narrowing at me. *I'll be right back, going to the ladies' room.*

I kissed her cheek, mostly for me, but also in case the idiot was watching. "I'll be here." She smiled, though it wasn't her real smile, and left.

I took the last sip of my lukewarm beer and leaned back so I could get the clearest view of Jake. Throughout dinner, I'd been able to keep a discreet eye on him through a conveniently placed mirror on the wall across from me. I'd never seen a picture of the guy before. Nia's friends treated him like a damnatio memoriae, but I knew it was him the second I saw him. The giveaway had been the way his eyes had gone wide and his skin paled as he looked at Nia.

A coward to his core.

He really had a punchable face. He was probably the type who would bargain for no responsibilities and then would have no one find him competent enough to handle the smallest of tasks. He'd end up jobless, alone, and—

"These weddings have gotten so tame," said an older woman who dropped into Nia's empty seat. She sat so her knees nearly touched mine and rested her elbow on the table. Appearing around seventy, she was beautiful. Her long, salt-and-pepper hair was blown out, but her makeup was heavy-handed. Bright blue shadow with thick smoky eyes, and a form-fitting black dress with a slit nearly up to her hip. She might have been wearing a garter, but I wasn't about to confirm that suspicion.

"I'm Geminy." She held her hand out for me like this was some early Hollywood movie with her as the bombshell and me as the lucky bachelor. "Hawthorn's dearest Aunt. You are?"

she asked, batting her false eyelashes, the right one being slightly loose and hanging ajar.

"I'm Carwyn," I said, offering a handshake. "Nia's date." Geminy shook my hand, but didn't let it go. Instead, she held on tighter and leaned in.

"No official title then?" she asked.

"For what?"

"For you and Nia? You're not exclusive?"

Oh, I was being hit on by this woman. I patted her hand, encapsulating mine, and said, "We're very much exclusive," and retrieved my hand from hers.

Her face fell into an exaggerated pout, but she recovered quickly, leaning forward provocatively. "Well, if you change your mind, let me know. I'd love to ring your sleigh bells." Then she ran her tongue along her teeth and winked.

"I don't think he's available, Aunt Geminy," Hawthorn said, setting two beers on the table beside me.

Geminy stood. "I'm sowing my seeds. Some of these young men love an experienced woman. It's my community service." She hugged her nephew, kissing him on the cheek. Then she turned back to me. "Anytime, handsome."

I blinked at her, unsure of what to say, before she mercifully turned her back and sauntered away.

"Rose did not undersell the food," Hawthorn said, taking Nia's seat beside me and handing me a bottle of beer, which I accepted. It was cold, vapor curling out of the mouth of the dark glass bottle. "Her family has been coming to Bryson House every summer for decades."

"Is it the same kitchen for the wedding?" I asked. I guess we were ignoring his eccentric Aunt.

He smiled. "Yep. Everyone keeps telling me we won't have time to eat at the reception, but with food this good, I will be making time."

A beat of silence fell. I could tell he wanted to ask me something, but I didn't want to put him on the spot. So, I guessed. "That's your brother over there?"

Hawthorn gave a slow nod and leaned forward, putting his forearms on the table. "That's the biggest idiot on the planet."

I snorted.

Hawthorn took a swig from his bottle and gestured toward Jake with his chin. "I wish he hadn't come."

"You two aren't close?"

Hawthorn shrugged. "Not anymore. We were, right until he walked out on Nia and everyone else. He's always been his own person. Not going to lie, I thought he finally had his shit together with Nia." He shook his head. "He didn't just leave Nia. He quit his job, moved, and didn't talk to anyone but Mom for six months."

I wasn't sure why he was telling me all this, but I assumed there was going to be a point. "I wish Nia hadn't gone through that. But I'm glad they never married."

Across the room, Nia laughed at something, her face lighting up. That was Nia at her best. She'd forgotten all her worries and was just happily existing. I knew because when she was like this, it was easy to block out the thoughts she accidentally sent my way.

Hawthorn's shoulders rose and fell, and I braced myself. "I wanted to ask you for a favor," Hawthorn said, his gaze fixed on Rose.

"I guess it depends. What's the favor?" I asked.

"A few minutes ago, my brother dropped the bomb that he realizes he made a mistake and is planning on trying to win

Nia back while we are here. Over the last few months he's been trying to make amends to the family for shutting us out. He's only still my groomsman to keep my mother happy." We exchanged a glance, and I knew we were on the same page before he continued, "Jake doesn't deserve her. And between you and me, I think you two are way better than they ever were. But mostly this is my wedding, and I don't want his bullshit ruining a minute of it for Rose. If it weren't for my mother, I would kick him out."

"Does Rose know?" I asked.

"Not yet," he said, his eyes fixed on the beer bottle as he turned it with his fingers.

I took a not-so-subtle glance back at Jake. He was talking to his dad and probably an uncle in what appeared to be a tense conversation.

"We're going to do our best to keep him in line. But I wanted to know if I could count on you to help make sure that nothing uncouth happens here."

"You're worried I'm going to fight him or something?" I asked, not hiding my offense. If I wanted him gone, I'd pull a favor and have him possessed. Though that might ruin the fun of the wedding. Possessions were messy. Demon power came from making bargains, and that power kept me alive, healthy, and out of hell. Bargains themselves tended to be neutral, with the outcome determined by the intentions of the bargainee. Nia's bargain had been desperate, but she didn't intend anyone to get hurt, so no one would. In fact, she'd intended for me to have a choice and hadn't made a demand. Jake's the kind of person who would make a bargain with selfish and power-hungry intentions and blame everyone but himself when everything backfired.

"Not at all," Hawthorn amended. "I'm telling you all this because Nia means the world to Rose, and Rose means everything to me. If Jake puts Nia back into the same depressed state she was before she met you, then Rose isn't going to enjoy her own wedding. I'm just asking for your help in keeping our respective ladies happy."

That made sense. "That's not a favor. That's just doing what needs to be done," I said and raised my beer bottle.

"Thank you." He clinked his beer against mine. We each took a drink in a silent toast to our new alliance.

5

Nia

"AFTER BRUNCH IN the morning, we are going to the village to get manicures and pedicures," Molly said. She had been Rose's roommate in college freshman year and had stepped up as maid of honor when I had declined. Molly was still talking. I was still smiling. But my awareness lingered in the suffocating knowledge of him.

Jake was standing in the corner talking to his dad and uncle. After all this time, there he was. Existing. Living like he hadn't thrown me out in front of half of these people. Not the right woman for him.

"Did you see the wedding favors yet? They are so cute!" someone said.

He looked so...different. Older. More than the year we had been apart. His cheeks seemed slightly hollow, and his eyes were dark. Did I like that this last year looked like it had fed him through a wood chipper? Apparently, I was a horrible person because I loved the thought of him being miserable without me.

"Nia?" Rose said, shaking my shoulder. "Are you okay?"

I blinked and looked at her. "I'm so sorry. I guess I'm more tired than I realized. What did I miss?" I focused on Rose while forcing myself not to look at Jake. His text message asking to talk was still a weight in my chest despite my phone being two floors up. Did I want to talk to him? And if I did, what did that say about me?

"You are still getting ready with me, right? And going to brunch with us in the morning?" Rose asked. I'd managed to wiggle my way out of doing the pre-wedding activities with the bridal party, but I'd promised those two things. It had been with a heavy mix of guilt, embarrassment, and relief, but Rose understood why I wasn't up to taking part in the pre-wedding activities tomorrow when Hawthorn's mother had insisted it included Jake. But I'd promised Rose I would be there on her wedding day, and I meant it.

"Yes, Carwyn and I are looking forward to it," I said.

"Perfect," Rose said, her accompanying smile making my heart squeeze. I couldn't let her down.

Out of my peripheral, Hawthorn's Aunt Geminy sashayed toward me. She was wearing a black, form-hugging dress with a slit up to her thigh and a black garter. When she was a few strides away, she reached into the bust line of her dress, her hand disappearing into the neckline up to her wrist before withdrawing a small flask.

"This is for you," she said, shoving the slightly damp flask into my hands. She looked around, leaned in, and whispered, "It's a shot of Fireball. Just in case you need it."

"Ooh, thank you, Aunt Geminy," I said. Rose turned away, and I knew from the shake of her shoulders that she was holding back a laugh.

Geminy winked, her false eyelash sticking for a moment before it fell back into place. She was in vehement denial that her vision was waning, and if her makeup was an indication, she was going to need an intervention. Luckily, they'd gotten her a professional makeup artist for the wedding as a gift. Geminy beamed at me. "You are so welcome, dear. I also wanted to tell you your new man is very serious about you. He's got such an angelic face." Then she spun around and left before I could respond.

"Sooo. What are your plans for tomorrow?" Rose asked, squeezing my hand. My willpower failed, and I found myself glancing back toward Jake. Our gazes collided across the room. His lips pursed, and he raised his glass in acknowledgement of me. Heat burning my cheeks, I turned back to Rose.

"Probably just relaxing in the room." Despite looking at Rose, all of my attention was focused on where Jake was in the room. He was a bag of burned popcorn stinking up my house. "I think I'm going to have to retreat to bed now, though." I forced a yawn. "I'm so tired, but I can't wait to see you at brunch in the morning."

I hugged Rose and waved goodbye to the three bridesmaids, then headed back to my table, where Carwyn was already grabbing my purse. Sometimes it wasn't so bad that he could hear my thoughts.

"Thanks." I took my purse from him. "I'm going to bed, but you should stay and have fun."

"I'm tired too," he said, falling in step beside me. I wasn't going to argue; our time together was limited. We headed up to the room in silence. Why was I giving Jake this much control over me? This was my best friend's wedding, and I was leaving the family dinner to hide in my room like a coward. He'd left me, so why was I the one who had to remember what the murmurs in the church sounded like when the door had shut behind him?

"Hey, Nia?" Jake's voice was a hook, and I was the fish. My feet stopped, and I turned. He was standing just a few feet away, a small chagrined smile on his face. I swallowed over a lump in my throat as my heart felt like it stopped.

"Hi." The word fell out of me on reflex. We were still inside the restaurant, in full view of everyone. I had to keep it together or my drama would ruin Rose's night. Which was exactly why he was approaching me here. I couldn't make a scene.

You don't owe him anything. Not a conversation. Not forgiveness. Nothing. Do what you need to, for yourself. The sound of Carwyn's voice in my mind was reassuring, not demanding, or offended, or threatened. Carwyn didn't move an inch as Jake approached, rock steady as ever.

"You look great," Jake said, still managing to look ashamed while pointedly ignoring Carwyn. We'd dated for years, and he'd never been ashamed of anything. His brown eyes met mine. "Perfect, really." I used to melt when he looked at me like that. It hurt now.

"What do you want, Jake?" I asked, managing to keep my voice even and pleasant. I couldn't stand this. Once I'd pleaded with the universe to let me have closure with one last conversation, and now faced with him, I had nothing to say. Why did it have to be on his terms? Why now?

"I was hoping we could talk? Alone." Across the room, I spotted Hawthorn and Rose watching us. Damn it. I needed to get this over with so everyone could move on, and if I didn't talk to him now, he would keep trying. He was persistent like that.

"Of course," I said, and turned to Carwyn. "I'll be up in a few minutes."

Carwyn kissed me on the cheek. "I'll see you upstairs when you're done." There was something subtly seductive in the way he spoke. *I'm here if you need me*, he said as he left.

Jake stepped closer, and I was overwhelmed by the scent of his woodsy cologne. "Can we go for a walk? There is a really beautiful greenhouse here, I think you'd like," Jake said.

"You can walk with me to the elevator," I said.

"Don't be like that." Jake looked so unsure. Which was totally unlike him. Jake was the kind of guy who ran through life without consequences while everyone else balanced on a tightrope. "I've missed us. And I know you've missed me, too."

Hawthorn had started toward us. He was hindered by well-intentioned guests and dining tables, but I could tell he was heading this way. I couldn't let this turn into any kind of scene. This was his wedding, and he shouldn't have to deal with this. "Jake, it's just been a long day. Maybe we can talk more tomorrow, but for right now, how about just to the elevator?"

"To your room," he pushed.

"Fine." I turned toward the door. Jake hurried ahead and opened it for me. We both slipped out of the restaurant before Hawthorn arrived. "What do you want to talk about?" I asked.

"I want to apologize," he said.

We walked a few more paces before I realized he wasn't going to say anything else. "Then apologize," I prompted. A few hotel guests passed us, and then we were in the lobby. There were at least a dozen people standing about, all wearing ugly holiday sweaters and holding oversized candy canes. Probably part of some holiday event the Bryson House was hosting, no doubt. I'd always wanted to take a cheesy picture for a

Christmas card, but Jake had always insisted ugly sweaters were a stupid waste of money.

Jake's hand wrapped around the back of my arm, just above my elbow, pulling me to a halt. "I can't apologize if you won't look at me, Nia."

I tugged my arm free, but found myself staring at the wood floor. Then at the antique wallpaper and wood paneling. The lush evergreen wreaths and holiday decor. Literally, anywhere but him, while my heart felt like it was going to pound out of my chest.

"Nia," he admonished.

I finally looked at him, and I was back at that damn church, watching him turn his back on me again.

Jake reached out and stroked a hand down my cheek. "I'm sorry, Nia, for what happened. You are perfect, and I freaked out and thought I wasn't good enough for you, so I bailed. But you make my life complete, and I want to spend the rest of my life being the man you deserve."

I blinked at him.

His fingers brushed over my hand, and I folded my arms across my chest, his hand dropping to his side. He audibly sighed and put his hands in his pockets. "I got us a suite upstairs. I'll text you the room number, and you can bring your stuff over when you are ready. I know that dude isn't serious about you like I am."

My mind was hopelessly blank. I had dreamed he would realize he'd abandoned me for no reason and come begging for forgiveness. But it didn't feel like I had hoped it would. Instead of relief, it felt sour. A mix of emotions and thoughts tangled together faster than I could process them and formed a painful knot in my throat. No. I'd told myself he wasn't getting a tear from me, and he wasn't.

One resounding truth did come forward. I was never getting back with him. I couldn't tell him that now. Not here. He'd get upset, or he would double down, or do something else to draw attention to himself. Then I would feel guilty, and I was terrified I might actually cave just to keep the peace through the wedding. No, I wouldn't. This was my last few days with Carwyn, and I couldn't miss that either. Carwyn had never made me feel like I was walking on eggshells, trying to figure out the easiest choice to prevent him from having a temper tantrum like a self-centered brat.

"I just need some time," I said, then added, "and some space. Maybe we could talk more after the wedding?"

"Jake?" Hawthorn's voice cut off any response Jake was going to make. Hawthorn was looking at me as he said to Jake, "Family picture time."

Jake loosed a breath, his body taut. "Again? Fine. I'll be right there," he snapped.

"Aunt Geminy needs to get to bed, so you have to come now," Hawthorn pressed.

Jake turned toward me. "Want to come?" He held out his arm.

I shook my head. "No. I'll see you later." I turned on my heel and booked it for the elevator, and went up to my room. Damn it, why was I like this around him? I needed a long cry in a hot shower.

6

Carwyn

NIA WALKED INTO the room before I had finished taking off my shoes. She seemed deflated; her face was weary, and her eyes were dark. She set a flask on the table and crumpled into the chair before removing her shoes.

"What is that?" I asked.

She snorted. "Aunt Geminy gave it to me. She says it's a shot of Fireball."

"She seems like a wily one," I said.

"Once, at a late barbecue at Rose's house, she took her shirt off, lit a broom on fire, and ran circles in the driveway while singing." She sighed. "I wish I could be like that."

My eyebrows lifted. "Shirtless? I'm not stopping you."

"No. Just...free," she said, staring at the floor. Then she seemed to come back to herself, and threw me a sad smile. "I know I haven't told you, but I do appreciate everything you've done for me. I'm still processing, but I know I wouldn't have gotten through this summer without you."

Nia walked toward me, pausing for only a breath before she hugged me. She melted into me, her arms holding me tightly. I was terrified she was readying to tell me goodbye. There was so much I wanted to tell her about how much I'd needed her, too; how I hoped we had many more summers ahead of us. I didn't want to sound like her manipulative ex, or for her to mistake my hope for pressure. I swallowed it all back down to the pits of Hell.

"This summer with you was the best summer of my life," I admitted.

Her gaze held mine for a moment before she looked away. She let go and walked to her suitcase. I waited for her to say something back, any kind of acknowledgement that she had also enjoyed the summer with me. I wanted a clue as to what she was thinking about us. She unzipped the suitcase and started rifling through the neatly folded stacks of clothes. She had that look on her face, the one where she was dwelling on problems she didn't create. I knew how to fix that.

She said, "Tomorrow, besides brunch, I am planning on staying in the room all day, but you shouldn't feel compelled to stay here too."

"Staying in bed with you all day sounds fantastic."

She made a small noise of frustration. "That's not what I said, Carwyn."

"Are you planning on sitting in the chair all day? I could sit at your feet if that's better?" I stalked a few steps closer. She rolled her eyes at me. "Or maybe you'd like me kneeling between your thighs?"

"Carwyn," she said my name like a warning, but her face was turning pink and the corner of her mouth twitched up. "I don't want to flirt right now." One strike against me.

Alright, new approach. I ran my hands up her arms and began massaging her shoulders. At first, she tensed at my touch, but she relaxed into my kneading fingers. "How about tomorrow after brunch we go on a lunch date?" I asked.

She sighed, her shoulders relaxing a little bit further. "We're already married. Why not a date? And I'm sorry, I do like flirting with you, but it feels different now. I don't know what to do about us. I don't want you to leave, but I don't know how to trust my own feelings about you. I don't know what I want, and I...I wish we had more time."

My heart stopped beating. "It's a date," I said before she could take it back. Nia's entire body paused for half a second, then she pulled out what looked like pajamas. When she turned toward me, I got a sudden vision of a cheeseburger. I wasn't hungry. I'd eaten all my dinner and what Nia had abandoned. Demon appetite.

"Are you hungry?" I asked.

"No," she said, but her stomach disagreed loudly.

I leveled a look at her. "You're thinking of a cheeseburger."

"I don't think I like you hearing my thoughts. Why can't I dream of cheeseburgers without you knowing?" She paused as something lit in her eyes. "What if I want to fantasize about putting some *other* meat in my mouth?" The corners of her mouth twitched as she fought a smile. She was flirting with me like she had over the summer when we'd been pretending at parties and gatherings, and it caught me completely off guard. Her brilliant eyes danced with amusement. Was she distracting herself from her ridiculous ex? Or our impending deadline? I didn't care right now if this flirting wasn't real. It felt like she was picking me and I wanted to hold on to that feeling.

I brushed my hand down the side of her face. "One cheeseburger with fries coming up. If you think of anything else, let me know."

"You really don't have to. I can get my own," she said.

I pointedly looked at the pajamas she was clutching. "You'd better be in those pajamas and curled up in bed when I get back."

Thank you. You're the best.

We're best together.

Downstairs, the bar was comfortably full. The smell of peppermint and liquor hung in the background, a testament to the bar's drink specials for the holiday crowd. The bar itself was crushed with people, half of whom were in a drunken chorus of a naughty version of Jingle Bells. I plucked a menu off the hostess desk as I passed by and took a seat at an empty table to wait for a server.

Then Jake joined me.

"What are you doing?" I asked him, not bothering to hide the disdain from my voice. He could choke on it for all I cared.

"I thought we could have a conversation. You know, man-to-man," Jake said. His cheeks were a touch pink, and his beer was nearly empty. Drunk. He was wearing a grey fleece vest over the white button-up he'd worn to dinner in a strange take on outdoorsy trust fund asshole.

"Man-to-man might be difficult, as there is only one man sitting here," I said with a grin. Of course, that went right over his head. His features pinched together for a moment before he took a quick swig of his beer and set it on the table with a thump.

"I already talked to her. We're getting back together," Jake said, with all the confidence of a toddler reaching for a hot pan on a stove.

"Is that right?" I signaled a server delivering drinks a few tables down. She acknowledged me with a head dip. "Nia told you she forgives you?"

"Of course she does. You're a placeholder for me. And the faster you let go of her, the faster she can get back to me."

The server came, and I put in Nia's order to go.

Jake smirked. "She might not even be there when you get back. I already texted her my suite number. I bet she'll be there when I arrive."

I chuckled. "Really? I don't suppose you'd be up to bargain on that?" I asked. I leaned a little closer. "I have several suggestions we can negotiate on."

Jake went still. The hair on his arms rose as some buried primal instinct told him there was danger his eyes didn't see. My bargains kept me powerful, and he was a perfect candidate. A disrespectful, arrogant, and prideful prick. That was the trick. A bargain made from a place of selflessness had no ill repercussions. But this one was selfish to the core, and he'd keep coming back for more.

A ghost walked out of the wall and into the bar behind Jake. I took a steadying breath, then a second ghost stepped into the bar. The first looked a century or two out of place, but the second looked like they had stepped right out of a kitchen. I jumped out of my seat and onto my feet. The first ghost noticed me staring and said to the other, "I've got a treat for you tonight. We don't get a lot of people who both see us and fear us, but when we do, ohhh boy is it a blast! Watch this."

Oh, no. No. Not now.

Jake looked over his shoulder, right past the ghosts whispering to each other. Of course, the asshole couldn't see them. "You on drugs or something? You look like you're having a bad trip."

"I'm fine, just wanted to stand." I needed to look nonchalant. Calm. The first ghost came closer, and I braced myself. Fuck, its translucence turned my stomach. The air grew chilled as it came closer. *Stay away*, I thought at it, but it didn't acknowledge hearing me.

Jake's expression told me I looked like a crazed man. "Whatever. Don't make a scene when Nia tells you it's over," Jake said. "I don't need you tarnishing my reputation." The ghost was standing right next to Jake, its eyes completely fixed on me. "I don't appreciate it when people make me look bad."

The older ghost crept closer like some predator stalking its prey. The ghost chef watched, grinning like this was the most fun he'd had in years. And like a deer stuck in headlights, I couldn't bring myself to move. "Fuck off," I growled at it.

Jake scowled. "What did you say to me? You can't talk to me like that."

"Not you," I snapped. The ghost walked through the table, bringing his face close to mine. I leaned back on the stool, trying to avoid its icy touch. Maybe it would leave if I didn't move.

"Boo!" the ghost yelled at me.

I tumbled over the forgotten barstool behind me, sending me toppling feet over ass into the table behind me. Someone yelled. I hit the ground with a thunk. The sound of dishes crashing preceded cold liquid pouring onto my face and shirt.

"Oh my god, are you okay?" a blonde woman above me hollered. The bar had hushed. In front of me, both ghosts' belly laughed, wheezing with mirth.

"We'll be watching you," the older ghost said and they both vanished.

I stood up, bits of nachos falling off my custom shirt, now stained pink and red and smelling strongly of peppermint and tomatoes. "I apologize for the trouble," I said. "I must have slipped."

"You can fall into my lap next time, handsome," she said. My cheeks heated, and I picked up the stool. Slowly, the murmur rose to its pre-humiliation levels.

Jake took one long drag of his beer, then slammed the empty bottle on the table. "You're making Nia look bad. No way she picks you over me. Besides, I'm sure you'll find someone else. Lots of women like trash." He smirked and turned to walk away.

"So how is it you're still single, then?" I asked before he could get a step away. I picked off a tortilla chip wedged between two buttons of my shirt. He turned back toward me, the confused expression on his face almost worth the humiliation the ghosts had just put me through. I grinned, which probably wasn't as impactful with a shirt stained pink and nacho toppings stuck to me. "You know what I think happened last year? I think you blew up your life because you thought you were too good for it. You thought you were settling for Nia when she was the one settling for you. And now that you've failed to attain whatever it is you thought you were owed, you're crawling back to the life you still think you're too good for. But now everyone knows what a snake you are, and they aren't falling for your shit this time. Especially, Nia."

"We'll see about that," Jake said. "Later, asshole."

On his heels was the server with my to-go order already bagged up. I accepted it and had it charged to my card instead of Nia's room.

Watching Jake implode was going to be fun, but keeping Nia from getting harmed in his self-destruction was going to be exponentially more difficult.

A chill crept up my spine. I looked over my shoulder, but there were no ghosts. I could help Nia keep her heart together, as long as the ghosts left me alone.

7

LYING IN BED while waiting for Carwyn felt weird, so I moved to the chair. Over the summer, flirting with Carwyn had been fun without consequences. I didn't have to worry about him hating my weird sense of humor, finding me dancing while running the vacuum, or even singing along to the radio in the car while missing every note. He was temporary, and if he didn't like me, he could just stop showing up.

But he'd kept showing up. And he sang and danced with me. I had thrown myself into our fake relationship, loving the momentary vacation from my unexpected reality. And if I couldn't have fun with a demon, then there was no fun left to be had.

Tonight, though? I'd reverted to that silliness, and he'd looked at me like I was home. My lips had craved his kiss more than I wanted a cheeseburger. Did he know that? Part of me was terrified he wasn't coming back. Which was ridiculous. He'd gone to get a cheeseburger. He hadn't seen me in a wedding dress.

Was I really considering throwing caution to the wind and staying married to a demon? I mean, what would that actually be like? Or was I distracting myself from Jake? Jake had texted his suite number to me a few minutes after Carwyn had left. I didn't respond; instead, I'd silenced notifications from him. It was weird knowing he was upstairs waiting for me to walk back into his life as easily as he had walked out of mine. I wasn't sure exactly what I was feeling, but I knew for certain that none of my feelings were positive. Which was turning out to be somewhat of a relief. I didn't want to go back to him.

Carwyn came through the door, plastic takeout bag in hand. "I got you extra pickles."

"Us extra pickles?" I clarified. Carwyn set the bag on the table and started opening it.

A grin spread across his face that had me biting my lower lip. "I have all the pickle you'll ever need, dear," he said, waggling his eyebrows and drawing a chuckle out of me.

He set a takeout box in front of me, opened the lid, and inside was the most glorious cheeseburger I'd ever seen, with a side of golden fries and a stack of at least ten pickle spears. I immediately started on the fries as Carwyn sat down. Pink splattered his shirt. I hadn't noticed when he'd walked in because of the way he had been holding the takeout bag.

"What happened?" I asked, pointing to his chest.

"Oh, I had a minor mishap in the bar," he said, as if he'd just remembered he was a mess, and headed over to his suitcase. "Separately, I ran into Jake. He is completely convinced you're getting back together."

I took a huge bite out of my cheeseburger. It was juicy, cheesy heaven with some sauce that made it a divine momentary distraction from my idiot ex. I was probably hungrier than I realized. "We haven't—"

In the warm yellow lamplight, Carwyn started undoing his tie. I hated admitting it, but I loved the details of watching a man undress, and Carwyn was exactly my brand of handsome. His movements captivated me. The way he pulled the knot loose and then slid the tie free of his collar. The flick of his wrists as he removed each cufflink from its sleeve and the way his deft fingers moved over each button of his fitted shirt all the way down to the bottom.

My husband's deft fingers.

The thought had me reaching for the water bottle he'd brought. It wasn't cold enough. Carwyn removed not just his long-sleeve shirt, but the T-shirt beneath. I mean, I'd hugged the demon. I knew he took care of himself. I just—I didn't know I'd be able to see all his muscles moving as he took off his shirt.

"We haven't what?" he asked without a hint of anything but genuine curiosity. His gaze pinned mine, then something wicked sparked in his eyes. He stared into my eyes, grabbed his belt buckle, and pulled the black leather belt free of his pants in one smooth movement.

Damn it, I'd completely lost my train of thought. What had I been saying? Get it together, Nia. "We haven't gotten back to-gether," I finally said and turned my eyes back to my food. Crap, I couldn't just stare at it. I ate a French fry.

"Do you want to?" he asked, each word carefully spoken, his tone suggestive as all hell. Carwyn's voice pulled me right back to him. He folded his black belt in his hands as he stared at me, eyebrows raised expectantly, waiting for my answer.

I licked the salt from my lips. "Want to what?"

The slow, daring smile that lit his face could have melted the sun. Fuck. My brain went blank as he set the belt down on the bed, pulled out a pair of black sweats from his bag, and began slowly unbuttoning the top of his pants. "Do you want to get back with your ex?"

I whipped my face back to my food. "No," I said. The thought of Jake was a splash of cold water. I picked at my fries. I was hungry for something else entirely now. "When I saw him, I froze." Carwyn came into my side view as he slid a T-shirt on, then pulled the other chair so it was closer to me before sitting down and snagging a pickle. "He said he wants to apologize."

"Did he?" he asked.

"Yes."

"Do you forgive him?"

I shrugged. "I don't want to get back together with him. I just want to survive him, and if I forgive him, he'll leave me alone."

"No," he replied, as if I'd just said the most ridiculous thing.

"What do you mean, no?" I asked.

"You don't owe him your forgiveness. And whether he needs to leave you alone is up to you. Not him," Carwyn said, eating a French fry and pickle together.

"If I don't tell him I forgive him, he will cause a scene until I give in and ruin the wedding."

"What Jake does is Jake's fault," he said. "Rose and Hawthorn will support you. I'm fairly certain everyone at this wedding will support you."

I swallowed the painful lump in my throat. I wanted to believe what he was saying, but it felt untrue to my bones. Turning toward him, I was ready to tell him as much, but I found him watching me, and my words died on my tongue. He honestly believed what he was saying. I pushed my hands into my pockets. Empty.

That was the problem—and the allure—with Carwyn. He always believed in me.

Of course I do.

I frowned at him and playfully swatted at his hand when he tried to take some more of my fries. "You need to teach me to be better at keeping my own thoughts in my head and out of yours," I said.

A smile ticked at the corner of his mouth. *I enjoy hearing your thoughts.* He ran his fingers through my hair. *Especially when you are admiring me.*

I rolled my eyes at him. "You are so vain."

Guilty. I'm also lustful. And envious.

"Envious?" I asked. "What could you be envious of?" His blue-green eyes trailed along my face, while his own expression was open. Vulnerable.

"A lot of things." He again ran his hand through my hair, letting his fingertips drag along my scalp, causing my whole head to tingle. "Of everything you've ever called yours."

My head emptied as my heart beat in my chest. Was he really this stupid sexy, or was it some kind of demon magic? Did I care? He would be gone after tomorrow, right? I squeezed my thighs together. Damn it. His lips were parted, waiting, begging to be kissed.

Fuck it.

I leaned in and kissed him. This summer, all of our PDA had been socially acceptable smatterings of affection. But this was for us. I tasted the bits of salt on his lips as they rolled against mine and savored the way his tongue slid across mine. Carwyn's hand cradled my face as he kissed me like he was memorizing every feeling. Because it could be our last kiss. I didn't want it to be our last kiss. Shit.

I didn't want it to be.

All the passion and need that had been building soured into panic. My heart threatened to beat itself out of my chest and never come back. I pulled away with a sharp intake of air. I couldn't trust my heart to a literal demon. Not even Carwyn. Especially not Carwyn. If he left me, it would be even worse than Jake.

He pulled back, his hands flying up in surrender. "What's wrong?" he asked, worried and not frustrated. God, Jake would have been upset I'd ruined the moment.

"I'm sorry, I need to stop."

8

Carwyn

'SOS,' ROSE'S TEXt yelled at a tyrannical seven in the morning. I switched my phone to vibrate so it wouldn't wake Nia.

On her bed, Nia slept peacefully, wrapped in her cocoon of blankets, one foot hanging off the edge of the bed. Last night, things had gone terribly wrong, and she'd sobbed herself to sleep. She'd tried to be quiet about it, but I'd heard every sniffle and shuddered breath from my bed. And more than a few unguarded thoughts.

That was the part about being human that seemed the hardest. Convinced of their own downfalls and doom, they wrapped themselves in their pain until it was the only truth they knew. Nia had explained she didn't think she could trust her feelings because she hadn't seen Jake's betrayal coming. As if her absolute love and trust were her downfall and not Jake's selfishness and ego.

My phone buzzed again. 'Jake has a whole grand gesture planned for the morning brunch, followed by a proposal. Take

Nia anywhere but there,' Hawthorn's text read. Oh, it was a pre-dawn group text. Lovely.

Jake truly was an idiot.

'She's never going to miss it,' I texted back. 'Nia is determined not to be the drama.'

'Unfortunately, Jake is determined to be the drama, and I don't want Nia to be uncomfortable,' Rose wrote. Well, it was too late for that. Nia had clearly been very uncomfortable with me last night after kissing me.

'How do you expect me to tell her to stay away?'

Rose started typing. Then Hawthorn. Then Rose. There was entirely too much energy coming through the dimmed screen when the sun had barely clawed its way into existence. 'I'll tell her to stay away this morning, but you make sure she's not sad,' Rose said. Of all the plans hatched in the wee hours of dawn, this was terribly vague, and I was too groggy to argue.

Nia had spent half the night tossing and turning, and she deserved some damn rest. I started typing, 'Fine, but wait to text—' I didn't get a chance to finish before Nia's phone started ringing. Heart in my throat, I jumped up and leapt over to her bed. In my mind, I landed gracefully and silently beside her resting form, scooping up her phone and declining the call before she could stir.

In reality, in my still slightly sleepy state, I misjudged the landing. With all the grace of a cat high on catnip, I landed partly on the edge of her mattress. My weight was slowly falling more and more off kilter, so I grabbed for the bed, only to get a handful of covers. Nia's weight acted as a counter until it didn't. Her cocooned body slipped across the bed as I attempted to claw my way to safety. Then she woke, her body startling on reflex. "Carwyn!" she yelled. I let go of the blanket before she fell too, flailed about, and hit the floor. Hard.

"Hello?" Nia answered her phone. I blinked up at the ceiling. Was that a damn ghost laughing at me? I swear to the fires of hell— "What do you mean Jake is planning on proposing? To who?"

Nia was sitting up on her bed, hair gloriously rumpled, and pinching the bridge of her nose. She glanced over at me, eyes very alert. "No, I totally understand. I'll see you tonight sometime. Bye." She tapped the front of her phone, then fell back onto her pillow. "They don't want me to come to brunch because Jake is planning on proposing to me."

"They told me," I said, and peeled myself off the floor to sit on the side of my bed like a dignified demon. "I'm sure we can find something to keep ourselves occupied."

"I can't believe I'm her wedding drama. I'm a train wreck wherever I go," she grumbled.

I frowned at her. "You're not the drama. Rose is trying to protect you and prevent him from getting his way. No one thinks you are a train wreck, Nia." She picked up her phone and started texting. "Why don't we sleep in and order breakfast in bed? I think I saw a cookie decorating event happening after breakfast. You like cookies."

The glare she cut my way might have frozen hell. Then her face softened. Partially. "I don't like icing. I like the cookies with a sprinkle of sugar on top. Or the ones coated in powdered sugar."

"Ah, that's how it happened then," I said, as if some great mystery of the universe had just been solved.

"What happened?"

"You summoning me. I'm sugar-coated too." When her eyebrows knitted, I leaned forward, gave her my best sultry smile, and said in my sexiest voice, "You can give me a lick, if you'd like."

Nia burst out laughing. Watching her laugh was like watching joy enter the world. The light was brighter, the colors more vivid, and every minor ache a little duller. She rubbed her eyes and then looked back at me, and all of it was gone, replaced by the distance she'd put between us last night. "I can't believe I was dis-invited to the bridal brunch because of him."

"We could always still go," I suggested. "Let him make a fool of himself so we can all move on."

"That's the problem," Nia started while coming to sit beside me. "Jake is even worse to be around when he's embarrassed. For our entire relationship, I spent most of my time making sure things went his way so we wouldn't have a bad day or ruin a trip or a date. He would end up ruining the wedding instead of just brunch."

"He's not your problem," I reminded her. "If you want to go to brunch, I can keep Jake distracted."

"I'm not sending a demon after my ex," she said.

"I'm volunteering."

"It's the same thing."

I shrugged. "You should do what you want without taking him into consideration."

"It's not that simple."

"It is," I assured her.

She lay back on her bed, hands covering her face. "It isn't that simple for me. Look, I'm not going because Rose asked me not to, and that's final."

"Alright," I said.

She rolled over and wrapped the blankets around herself. "I'm going to sleep in." The wall she was putting up between us was growing bigger. I knew she wasn't entirely ready, but I had still held onto the hope that she trusted me enough to try. This whole summer, I'd fallen in love with the lie we'd paraded around for everyone else. If she hadn't kissed me last night, I would question whether she had feelings for me at all. But she had kissed me, and then everything shifted.

Did realizing how good we were together scare her off, or had that been the worst kiss of her life? Prideful as I was, objectively, I was a good kisser. At least, there had been no complaints before.

"I can't sleep when you are so loudly brooding," she said.

"I'm not brooding."

Nia sat up on the bed and turned toward me. "I can feel you brooding."

Could she? I needed to keep myself together. "Sorry. I'll keep the brooding on low."

She looked like she was about ready to say something before she turned away and then ran a hand through her hair. Looking back up at me, she said, "I'm sorry."

"About what?"

"Last night, I could have handled that better. I'm just...this whole thing is a lot. And I don't want to make the wrong decision for either of us. I'm scared I can't trust myself, or you're going to realize you made the wrong decision and be stuck with me forever.

"How about we only worry about today, how we make each other feel?" I asked.

Her throat worked, and she nodded. "Just today."

"Starting with breakfast."

9

Nia

Outside the town diner, fat flurries lazily drifted down and dusted the Christmas decorations on the town's street lamps.

"Do you ever celebrate Christmas?" I asked.

"Of course, all demons love presents," he said. "Actually, my favorite thing to do is go ice skating."

"Ice skating?" I repeated. "Why?"

"I've gotten pretty good at it. I enjoy flying around the ice, especially in the middle of the night when I'm alone. You should come with me sometime," he said, then looked down at his breakfast. Ice skating with Carwyn would be fun.

"What would you like to do today?" he asked.

I pressed my fork into my over-easy egg, letting the liquid yellow spill across my hash browns. If I had the option, I wanted to spend the entire day hiding in our room, so I didn't have to worry about running into Jake. But if we spent the day in the hotel room, there were only two chairs to sit on and they were only so comfortable, which meant we would probably spend the day in bed. His bed had the best view of the television, so I would probably climb into bed with him. We'd snuggle, Carwyn slowly running his fingers through my hair like he liked to do, while he admired the view down my low-cut silk cami—

My cheeks flamed as I cut off the thought. Where the hell did that come from? I didn't even own something remotely similar.

"Are you alright?" Carwyn asked, then took a sip of his coffee. "You look...scandalized." He didn't look at me while he spoke, just pecked at his scrambled eggs with his fork. Why did he look like he'd been caught red-handed?

"Carwyn," I hissed. "Did you just put a fantasy in my head?"

His dark eyebrows climbed his forehead. He pointed to his chest. "Me? No."

My hand flew to the pocket of my flannel jacket. I plucked out a single penny and slid it across the table to him.

He retrieved it, looking sheepish. "Damn. Alright. It snuck from me to you," he said. My pocket remained empty. "I was thinking of things to do today. With you. Preferably not in the hotel room all day."

"You were fine with the hotel room a minute ago."

Huh. Demons can blush.

He pressed on. "This town is a tourist destination. Do you want to go shopping?"

I shook my head. "No, I don't really want to be out and about. I think the front desk rents snowshoes. We could try that." The last thing I needed was to run into Jake in town.

"I thought you hated hiking?" Carwyn asked.

"No, I don't," I said, though it came out more like a question.

"Mmm hmm," he said. "And it would have nothing to do with the fact that the woods are the least likely place you'd run into Jake?"

"Correct."

"Nia," he said my name on an exhale. "You are not hiding from that toad."

My skin prickled. "I'm not," I stabbed a piece of potato with my fork, "hiding." Carwyn leaned forward slightly and stared at me. His gaze bore down on me with all the weight of eternal damnation, and I cracked like an egg. "Fine, yes. I really don't want to run into him again." Saying it out loud—suddenly I felt like a coward. Was I really going to throw roadblocks into my last day with Carwyn just because of Jake?

I was scared of Jake making Rose and Hawthorn's wedding all about him. And if I had the power to make their wedding better by changing my plans, I should. That's what good friends did, right?

"If it weren't Rose and Hawthorn's wedding—"

"—Today is not their wedding. We made a deal we would give each other a real chance, and I don't think you're holding up your end of the bargain by putting Jake above that," he said. Carwyn looked like a cat explaining to a mouse how it had been caught. Stuck between his claws, I knew he was right. I wasn't giving him a full chance because I was still managing Jake.

Huh. That's what I was doing. I was managing Jake.

"You look like you've stumbled on a thought," he said.

"Sort of. You're right. I just...I don't want to ruin any part of their wedding."

"You aren't."

"I hear you, but you don't know him. Let's snowshoe and then have lunch in our room?" I asked, taking a sip of my coffee.

Carwyn shook his head. "Boring. I think we should do an activity that requires far less clothing."

Coffee threatened to spray out of my nostrils. Carwyn chuckled while I grabbed for a napkin. The woman in the booth across from us raised her eyebrows at me. I flashed an apologetic smile.

"I was thinking of the hot springs at the hotel." He leaned across the table, his mouth curved into a wicked grin. "I didn't get to see what you were imagining, but please share, given how red your face is."

"Yes, the hot springs sound fine," I said. "The wedding party is supposed to be out all day, so that will be good." A nice long soak sounded really nice right now, and it had been the only thing Rose had mentioned about the hotel, so I had brought my bikini.

"And then our lunch date."

"What about after?" I asked.

He pinned me with his gaze, but instead of feeling the weight of him pressing upon me, he seemed to make up his mind. "Hot chocolate and cookies in the room with a holiday movie double feature?"

"It's a Wonderful Life is my pick." There was something about black and white movies I loved, especially at Christmas. His upper lip twitched like he was fighting a sneer. "What's wrong with that movie?" I asked.

"Nothing," he said. My eyebrows rose as I kept eye contact. *I don't believe you,* I thought toward him.

"Fine. The whole bell-ringing thing is not canon. They are angels. They always have wings."

"And what about demons? Do you have horns I can't see or a pointed tail?"

He barked out a laugh. "I am as you see me," he said. " It would be far too obvious if we had to hide such things from everyone."

"Fair. Though I do think you'd look cute with horns."

He smiled, his face lighting with mischief. "You think I'd look good horny? I can make that happen."

I couldn't stop the smile that pinched my cheeks.

There it is, he said.

What is where?

Your real smile. Not the one you wear for others.

"Refills?" The waitress asked. I almost startled, she'd appeared so fast. We both waved her off.

"I don't have a fake smile."

"I didn't say it was fake. It's practiced and perfect, but dull. Your real smile is a tad crooked, your eyes crinkle at the corners, and joy takes over your face."

"I think all my smiles are the same," I said, feeling defensive. I had a practiced smile? I suppose I had a go-to smile for photographs, but didn't everyone? Across the table, Carwyn shifted in his seat, then took a long drag of his coffee.

"Alright, I've said that wrong. I love all your smiles. I just have one that's my favorite."

"I love all your smiles, too." I was trying to accept his white flag, but realized at the same time I really meant that. I loved his smile. Once again, my heart thundered right into my throat, where it threatened to squeeze off any available air in this too-hot diner. How had I been stupid enough to summon a demon? My pocket was woefully devoid of pennies. He was being his honest self, and it was no different than being with him this past summer.

"Come on. Time to wear substantially less clothing," Carwyn said.

10

Carwyn

THE HOT SPRINGS were tucked away in a secluded area of the property. Multiple stone pools were interspersed across a rocky landscape, dotted with boulders, shrubs, and the occasional stone bench. Steam from the deep blue water created a thin fog over the area, making it feel completely remote from the rest of Bryson House.

"Which one?" Nia asked, her teeth nearly chattering. The supplied robes were not the sort of fabric meant to guard oneself from the bitterness of December, but were sufficient for a quick walk from the heated changing rooms to the pools.

There were only a few other people present, and one corner pool seemed to offer more secluded privacy. I pointed toward it. "There."

Nia bolted for it, leaving me to jog to catch up. Which was fine. I enjoyed watching the faint movement of her ass beneath the robe. She arrived at the edge of the water and toed her boots off before dipping her foot in. Then she dropped her robe and towel on the ground before sinking into the pool up to her neck, her eyes fluttering closed as she smiled.

"It's perfect," she said. "Wait, how does the penny thing work if I'm in a swimsuit?"

I held out her robe. "I never think of you when you're not around."

She rose out of the water enough to reach into the robe's pocket and pulled out a penny, then set it on one of the nearby rocks. "Good luck for someone else."

I set to work folding our robes and towels, placing them within arm's reach before slipping into the water. There were small stone benches carved into the sides of the pool. I sat, and the water slipped just below my shoulders. Nia sat across from me, neck-deep, humming as she sighed.

"Okay, this was a good idea," she said.

"I agree," I said, though I didn't like that she wasn't sitting next to me. I had one day to convince her not to end the bargain, and last night she all but decided. I'd heard her panicked thoughts when she realized she didn't want that to be our last kiss. Now Nia looked at me with sadness from behind the wall she was slowly building between us. I should have told her about the bargain sooner. Maybe it would have given her more time to see me as something worth keeping around? Or maybe she would have had an easier time walking away.

This was a damn mess.

I didn't want to lose her. And with the way she was looking at me, it had to mean she didn't want to lose me, too. Think, Carwyn. You have one chance at this, or she's gone forever.

"What are you doing after the wedding?" I asked. Ah, yes, immediately remind her of your impending absence. Dum-bass.

"I don't know. I took Monday off, but I might go into the office anyway. What about you?"

"I'm not sure yet." Segway into something else. I need a safe topic that leads to meaningful conversation. "If the deadline of the bargain wasn't looming, would you still want me to come around after the wedding?" I was an utter failure.

"Carwyn," she said, then sighed. "I was planning on telling you this needed to stop anyway."

"Why?"

"Because you…besides being a demon," she said demon in a barely audible whisper, "you were only ever supposed to be pretend." My heart stung on impact. That had been the intent of her original bargain. I knew that. I'd messed up waiting to tell her.

"But you kept calling."

She looked away, into the thin mist. "I know."

"Why?" I pressed.

She rested the back of her head against the rock. Her lips pressed into a fine line, and she shook her head. "You can't lie. It's not fair if I do," she said, more to herself than to me. Then she looked at me. "I was scared to be alone. Before you, everyone looked at me with pity and always told me I'd find someone else. There would be another chance. They meant well, but I couldn't move past what had happened. Once I showed up with you, people stopped pitying me, and I could just pretend everything was fine."

"Why were you planning on telling me we couldn't see each other after the wedding?"

Nia's throat worked, and she stared at the surface of the water. "I…I realized I was developing feelings for someone who was pretending to be with me."

My heart forgot how to beat for a moment. Hope twisted its way through me. Slowly, I moved to sit next to her in the pool. "So, it was a mutual development?"

She nodded and sniffed. "I can't do forever, though."

"Let's just worry about today." I slid my hand over hers beneath the water. She turned her hand over and curled her fingers with mine.

After a few minutes, another soft hum escaped Nia's throat, vibrating right through me. As she relaxed, more of her thoughts milled into my head like a little trickle of water. Easy to ignore until one caught my attention.

Really, he's my emotional support demon.

"Your what?" I asked, sitting up slightly.

Her eyes widened. "Ignore that," she said with a dismissive wave.

"Your emotional support demon?" I prompted. She thought of me as supportive. As hers. That was something I could work with.

"Why did you ask if you heard me?" She cried and sank into the water up to her eyes.

I pulled her up before she completely submerged. "I wanted to make sure I heard you right. I love being your emotional support demon." I leaned closer. "You are definitely my emotional support human."

"How am I yours? You've been in my life all summer, and I haven't been in yours. I'm a terrible girlfriend." Her eyes squeezed shut, and then she rubbed her face. "I mean support person."

"Nope, can't take it back," I said, raising our joined hands and kissing her fingers. "You make me feel included. I had been madly in love with my ex, Lamia, but she had never wanted me to be around her friends or even go out on dates frequently.

She hid it under the guise of wanting us to maintain our own identities," I said the last part with air quotes and shook my head. "She just didn't like me as much as I loved her, and when I caught her with my best friend, I realized our relationship had been her backup plan." I turned to her and smoothed a piece of hair away from her face with my free hand, then cupped her head. "But you've never made me feel like that. Even though you always thought this was temporary, you never made me feel hidden or just for show."

Her throat worked. "I guess we both had a low bar." I let my hand linger on the side of her face, my thumb sliding across her soft cheek.

Her eyes dipped toward my lips, and hers slightly parted, like she was waiting for me to kiss her. I wish I could have waited longer to tell her about the bargain, to give her time to heal and figure things out between us without a deadline.

The last time we'd kissed, she'd decided I needed to get out of her life. What was the right call?

"Nia!" Jake's obnoxious voice cut right between us. He waved from across the grotto. Exactly who I wanted to see right now. He beelined it straight for us. He didn't really have the audacity to sit with us? Did he?

Of course he did. That snake really had no sense of shame.

Jake slunk into our corner of the pool and sat down across from us. He'd dropped his towel on the edge of the pool behind him.

If you don't want him here, you can tell him to leave. Or if you want, I will. I thought to Nia. Her fingers curled tighter around mine as she sat up.

"Jake, you need to leave," she said with authority and confidence.

I'm so proud of you, I said to her.

Jake made a face that somehow read like he hadn't expected her to rebuke him, but he shook it off quickly.

"I know. I wanted to apologize to you," Jake said to Nia, outright ignoring me existing beside her. The wording pissed me off. He wanted to apologize. Not that he should, not that he owed her or whether Nia even wanted him to. It was about what he wanted.

"I don't want you to. And even if you ignore me and apologize anyway, I don't forgive you. I don't care. We are not getting back together."

He winced. "I'm not the only one who stopped believing in us." He gestured to Nia and me with his head.

Is he insinuating you cheated on him with me? I asked.

"That is offensive," she said to Jake. "Please, leave us alone."

"That's why you can't talk to me without him, right? You can't be apart from him for one minute so that we can have some closure, because you might remember how good we were together?" Jake pushed.

Maybe I could find an empty room on this sprawling estate and lock him in it until the end of the wedding. Or the end of time.

Nia turned to me and asked, "Carwyn, will you meet me back at our room? I should be no more than a minute behind you."

Logically, I knew this was about Nia getting closure, but my inner green-eyed monster bristled.

I kissed her cheek and rose from the pool. Did I put a little extra flex into my muscles as I stood? Yes. I also used some of my power to raise my body temperature, so the steam curling off of me was more intense. Jake's eyes narrowed at me, and I smiled brightly as I put the robe on.

"Take your time," I said. *Let me know if you need me to return.*

11

Nia

As soon as Carwyn was halfway to the locker rooms, Jake moved to sit beside me. I moved to the other side and crouched beneath the water.

"Don't come near me again, or I'm leaving," I snapped.

Jake put up his hands in mock surrender. "Fine. All I want to do is tell you I'm sorry for what happened at the church."

Not even a genuine apology. "Thank you," I said. "You can leave now."

Jake rolled his eyes. "I'm trying to give you a second chance."

"Me?!" I barked. I'd taken his bait, hook, line, and sinker and couldn't spit it back out.

"Yeah. It took me a year to get over what you did to me, and I am at a good place where I can forgive you and move on."

You alright? I'm not above punching him, Carwyn thought to me.

I've got this.

"What on earth could you need to forgive me for? You left me at the altar and then ghosted."

His towel hit him in the face. He pulled it off and glared at me. "You don't need to throw things at me like a child, Nia."

"I didn't," I said, not sure what happened myself.

"Sure. Anyway, like I was saying, before someone threw a towel at me, you were very demanding and belittling of me. Especially while we were planning the wedding."

I stared at him in open-mouthed shock. "You thought I was belittling you because I wanted you to participate in the planning of our wedding?"

"The details weren't important to me, and you knew that. I just wanted to show up. Yet, you kept insisting that I help pick things and call people. I'm not really a planner. I like to go where the wind takes me."

Had he always been this insufferable? I bit back an angry remark. If Jake didn't feel like he won this interaction, he was going to cause a bigger scene. I wouldn't be the wedding drama again, so I needed to make peace. They deserved to have a wedding where the worst thing someone would say was that the chicken was dry.

I swallowed my pride. "I understand you were hurt by my actions while we were planning our wedding. While it was sad, I'm glad you were empowered to stand up for yourself and leave. And I sincerely hope you've had a better life without me," I said. "I am going to go back to my hotel room, but maybe we can talk more after Rose and Hawthorn's wedding?" There, that had to be enough to get him off my back for a bit.

A few seconds flurried by, and something shifted in Jake's face. The tension in his shoulders dropped. Then he looked at me, really seeing me. "I would like that," he said, his voice soft. Wow, was this going to be that easy? It felt like closure.

I nodded, a labored smile tugging at my mouth. This felt not terrible. I started to stand.

"Wait. Nia?" Jake called.

"What is it?" I asked.

"I was wrong when I said you weren't the right woman for me. You are the only woman for me."

It was weird. He was looking at me like he used to, doe-eyed and full of love. But it felt hollow. Not his words or the soft tone of his voice. It was all an act. There was no closure here. He was just manipulating me into giving him what he wanted, and if I didn't react correctly, then he'd make me the villain. Again.

"I think we should continue this conversation another time. Maybe next week?" I asked.

"Come back to my suite," he pushed.

"I need some time to process, and I can't do that while I'm focused on the wedding."

"The wedding? You didn't even come to brunch this morning," he said.

I couldn't tell him why I didn't come. That would cause more friction between him and his brother. "I wasn't feeling well this morning, so I skipped."

"I'm glad you're feeling better. Are you coming to rehearsal tonight?"

"I promised Rose I would," I said and stood up. The heat of the water had sunk into my bones deep enough that I didn't feel the cold immediately. "I'm going to go now. I'll talk to you later."

"It's not surprising you don't realize he's going to leave you. I mean, you didn't realize you were driving me away until I left," Jake said, and my feet froze. "That dude?" Jake pointed toward the changing rooms. "He'll only hang around until he finds out who you really are. Then he will leave like I did, but he's never coming back." He huffed a laugh. "As soon as that guy sees who you really are, you're going to break his heart. Just like you broke Rose's."

"I didn't break Rose's heart," I said, my voice too shaky to hide.

Jake gave me a soft, sad smile. "Didn't you? You wouldn't be her maid of honor because you were too upset to stand at the altar. You've avoided spending any time alone with her since you pushed me away." Jake stood and walked over to me, my feet still cemented to the bottom of the hot pool. He stopped when he was close enough to touch, and I shirked away. Jake reached out, cradling my head in his hand so I couldn't move farther away. "You don't know how to be you without me."

"I love Carwyn. Not you. Leave me alone." I shrugged out of his grasp and climbed out of the pool.

"Only I know how to love someone like you," Jake called after me and sank back down onto the bench. "But I'll only wait for you so much longer." His towel slid off the edge and into the pool, sinking immediately to the bottom like it had been weighted down. He dove for it, cursing beneath his breath. "You're such a bitch."

"I was thinking the same about you." I put on my robe and picked up my dry towel and walked away.

What had I been thinking? Had he always thought so little of me? I was more mad than anything, especially at myself. Why had I been so blind? I put my hands in the robe's pockets and found them utterly devoid of pennies.

Nia!?

I stopped dead in my tracks. Carwyn sounded scared. *Where are you?* I asked in my head. *What's wrong?*

There's a ghost outside the locker rooms, and it won't let me in.

I'm on the way, I thought, and immediately spotted Carwyn pacing outside the line of changing rooms, attempting to dodge some invisible foe. And attracting a little attention from some bathers.

As I reached him, I took hold of his hand, and Carwyn jumped, dropping his bag. "You—" he started, but then tightened his grip on me and pulled me into one of the dressing rooms. The door slammed shut behind us. "It just charged at you," he said and pulled me against his bare, warm chest.

"Are you okay?" I asked him. His heart pounded beneath my cheek.

"Yes." He didn't sound okay.

I held him close for a few minutes. At first, it was because he clearly needed to be held after seeing a ghost. Then his heart slowed a bit, his body relaxed, and I found myself melding into him. I laid my head on his shoulder. It was so easy to relax with him.

"Did things go well with Jake?" Carwyn asked.

"Yes."

Liar, Carwyn thought.

I don't want to talk about it. I want to forget he exists for a while, I thought back.

Carwyn's hand slid up and down my back, leaving a trail of tingling skin in its wake. I wound my hand up the side of his neck into his damp hair. His eyes closed, and his forehead rested against mine. Falling into this feeling was dangerous. It was the type of quiet that soothed souls and calmed all the restless feelings Jake had stirred up. Jake had ruined everything, but I wasn't about to let him ruin my day with Carwyn.

Carwyn kissed my forehead and hugged me closer. I breathed in his smell of sandalwood and citrus. He was becoming precious to me, and it was terrifying. Not just because I wasn't sure I could trust myself, but because if he did have feelings for me, I would be the one to break his heart. He deserved happiness and to be loved.

His kiss lingered on my forehead, and I became aware of everywhere our skin touched, of his breath whispering across my hair, and of the way I felt perfectly safe. All my fears were suddenly intangible. He'd told me he was scared of me breaking his heart. It seemed so silly I could ever break a demon's heart, but I believed him. He had those same vulnerable eyes when he'd told me about the bargain. Jake had never been vulnerable; he'd always been a pillar in my life. A pillar I walked circles around, who gave me nothing back.

Carwyn always walked with me. We'd been a team all summer.

We felt inseparable right now.

My lips ached to kiss him. The last time we'd kissed, I'd panicked because I wasn't sure if I could trust my own judgement or his. But he hadn't lied once today. The pockets of my hotel robe had been penniless.

I pressed a small kiss against his shoulder, but it wasn't enough to quell the ache. I kissed the warm skin on his neck, stealing a quick taste of him with a stroke of my tongue. His chest pressed against mine as he took a deep breath in, then he melted beneath my touch as he exhaled my name. Of all the ways he's ever said my name, that soft moan would forever live in my mind. I needed him to make that sound again.

I continued kissing and tasting his neck, and then his ear. He shivered as I nibbled on his soft skin. The part of me that was always preoccupied with appearances nagged that someone might hear us in the private changing room. But there was hardly anyone in the hot springs, and I wasn't worried about Carwyn pushing for more than I was comfortable with here. Besides, if I stopped now, I might lose my nerve, and I didn't want to miss out on this moment with him. Not when it felt like our end was so close.

Carwyn's fingers wound into my hair, and he gently pulled my head back just far enough for his mouth to capture mine. His warm, soft lips moved slowly against mine. As if this were some dream and we would both snap out of it soon. I loved the way his body responded to my touch, the way his breath hitched with every slide of my tongue. Carwyn's hand stroked down my sides. His thumb and fingers brushed against the outer swell of my breasts, then down to the top of my ass.

Don't be a gentleman, I thought to him, hoping he would take the invite.

Another soft sound escaped him as his hands slid under my ass and squeezed. I could feel his grin while we kissed. *You have no idea how much I've enjoyed watching this ass,* he thought.

I didn't understand exactly why, but Carwyn made me feel powerful. He was a demon, and yet I felt like he saw me as his equal. Heat pooled low between my thighs, and feeling bold, I ran my hand down the front of his swim trunks. His semi-hard cock twitched in my hand as I palmed him from base to tip. I wanted to feel him, skin-to-skin.

Carwyn moaned into my mouth, which felt like a plea to keep exploring him. God, that sound had me squeezing my thighs. This demon was coming apart in my hands, and I loved it. I pulled his wet trunks down and took the hardening length of him in my hand. His kisses faltered on a sharp intake of air when I stroked the soft skin. He kissed my neck, then found the particularly sensitive spot on my ear that made my knees threaten to buckle. The way his lips moved over me felt reverent and meticulous. I worked him in my hand, wanting him to cum for me. His fingers hooked around the thin straps of my wet bikini and tugged them down my shoulders. For a moment, the air chilled my damp breasts, but his eager hands quickly warmed them.

Fuck, I heard him curse. His cock was fully hard now. Our kisses became more frantic as I worked him faster. For all his flirtations and innuendos, he'd never made me feel like he was owed this, or that this was his end goal. I'd picked this right now, and he'd let me lead.

Carwyn moaned, his hand grabbing mine as he came into his other hand. He wiped his hand off on a towel, then he held me tight against him. His heart thudded in his chest beneath my head, and I felt a smug satisfaction at its cadence and each of his panting breaths.

12

Carwyn

"THE MUPPETS CHRISTMAS Carol?" Nia asked. "That's your pick?"

Back in the hotel room, we'd taken a quick shower together to clean off after the soak and sweat from the hot springs and put on loungewear. It had been a very utilitarian shower, but one in which Nia had let me wash her hair.

I couldn't stop thinking about what had happened in the changing room. Nia hadn't meant to, but I'd heard all her thoughts loud and clear as she'd decided to explore me.

"It's my favorite Christmas movie," I confirmed and tossed the pillows from her bed onto mine, which had a slightly better view of the television. "You can't go wrong with any of the Muppets' movies."

None of my previous lovers had been so focused on me. They'd expected me to take the lead and be dominating. I liked that too, but Nia's intense study of me had been different. Nia had locked onto me like I was a mystery only she could solve, finding clues in every sound or breath or movement I made.

"I don't think I've seen it before," she said. "Or at least not in a very long time."

"Oh, you are in for a treat," I said.

The moment she was ready and comfortable enough for me to return the favor, I was going to pleasure her until she couldn't speak in complete sentences. Nia climbed onto the bed, fluffed the pillows to her liking, and pulled the tray full of our lunch into the middle of the bed. We'd secured a tray from the front desk and gotten some cookies and hot chocolate from the setup downstairs, then grabbed some finger foods from the bar as well. She'd finally have some hot chocolate without the ruined tights.

I set up my phone so I could cast to the room's TV. Nia's movie first, *It's a Wonderful Life*, came up on the big screen in all its black-and-white glory.

We ate in amicable silence for a bit. Then she started shaking with silent laughter when Clarence jumped in the river.

What's so funny? I asked.

It took her a few seconds to answer me. "Before I found that cookie recipe, I felt like George. But my angel is a demon," she giggled.

She reached out and stroked a hand down my face. "You know all about my ex and my life. Tell me about you."

"What do you want to know?"

"What was your life before me?"

"Not much," I said too quickly.

Nia gave me a disapproving look.

I shrugged. "You already know most of it. I'm a lawyer for private equity. I gain my power from making deals with humans, and that helps me stay out of Hell. It's alright there, but it's a lot like a small town. Everyone knows everyone, lots of gossip, and the scenery is always the same."

"But you had a girlfriend. Was it serious with her?"

I paused as my ex's face flashed in my mind. "Yes. Well, I had thought it was serious. Clearly, I had been mistaken."

"I'm sorry," she said. "No one deserves to be betrayed like that."

"I thought I knew her. I trusted her. Actually, the worst part of the situation was the betrayal of my best friend. He knew how serious I was about her more than anyone."

"How did you find out? If you don't mind me asking," she asked.

"I walked in on them. They were on my bed, in my apartment. I'd come home from a long, long day and they didn't hear me over their own noise."

Nia's nose wrinkled. "Oh no, that's horrible."

"It was absurd," I said, and a little chuckle followed. Talking about it now, it doesn't sting as much. It had been a horrible shock. Worse, even, in the moment. "They hadn't even finished…decoupling…when you summoned me."

"Wait, no—" Nia gasped. "I thought you'd had time between!"

I shook my head, a grin spreading across my face as her eyes widened. "No. I felt the summoning spell dance across my skin, and I took it so I could get out of there as fast as possible. I was probably the closest, or at least the first to answer. You felt like a lifeline."

Nia covered her face with both hands. "You went from one hot mess to another."

"Which is why I accepted the bargain. At that point, nothing mattered. And I'd recently lost a lot of magic to a deal I'd broken."

"What deal?"

"I'd dropped a deal with one of my clients when I found out the deal they were working on would have caused issues for my ex."

"Wait, why did you make us breakfast?" Nia asked.

I snorted. "You know how I put you to bed?"

She nodded.

"I slept on your couch because my ex had texted to say she and my former best friend were staying in my apartment that night, and they would be out in the morning. I probably should have gone back and kicked them both out right then, but I knew if I went back, I'd have to listen to their explanation, and I didn't even want to give them the chance. I didn't sleep well, so when the sun started rising, I walked to the store and picked up some breakfast items. My ex hated crepes and I love them, so it was a sort of celebration."

Nia covered her face with both hands. "I can't believe I was so drunk you slept on my couch and I never knew it." When she put her hands back down, her cheeks were tinged pink. But she looked at me. Really, truly looked at me in the way only she did. "I wish you hadn't gone through that, but I'm happy you're here." Then she snuggled up beside me, put her head on my chest, and laid an arm over my stomach.

I tried to hide the inhale I took to smell her hair. Some kind of coconut shampoo I'd loved the smell of in the shower.

"What do you think the lives of our exes would have been like without us?" she asked after a while.

"Without you, Jake would have drowned in a toilet trying to drink the lemonade."

Nia shook with quiet laughter. "No. He hates lemonade. He says since lemons are a man-made crossbreed, the saying about life and lemons makes little sense, which then destroyed any enjoyment of lemonade for him."

"He's the most pretentious prick."

"What about your ex? What would have happened to her without you?"

"She never would have met my best friend," I said.

"Boo. Try again," Nia jeered at me playfully.

"She would still think apples that grow on trees are inedible."

Nia sat up and gasped. "She did not."

"She did. City demon. Honestly, she was not bright. She was a socially manipulative creature, but lacked a lot of basic common sense and knowledge." Which made her a terrible conversationalist. Maybe I should try to introduce my ex to Jake. It seemed a fitting punishment for both of them.

Huh. I wasn't sure exactly when this topic had stopped being so bitter.

I ran my hand up her arm and back down before nestling my fingers in the crook of her waist. This quiet moment with her was all I ever wanted forever. I loved chatting with her. Even talking about our exes, it felt like a shared comfort. I didn't need lots of attention, or parties, or fame, or any of that. I liked this. Just us, a couple of old movies, snacks, and conversation.

Nia climbed on top of me. Her body weight settled comfortably across my hips, pressing down on my cock, which was quickly stirring to life. She toyed with the hem of my shirt, her fingers tickling across the skin of my stomach. I gave her space to work through whatever was moving behind her brown eyes. Her thoughts didn't echo in my head, so whatever she was thinking, she wasn't panicking.

I rubbed my palms partway up her thighs, trying to reassure her.

She leaned down, her hair falling across the side of my face as she kissed me like I was the only thing that mattered. When she pulled back, I knew that kiss had meant as much to her as it had to me. I took her in my arms and held her close. I breathed her in and memorized the shape of her. How she fit against my body. The cadence of her breathing.

I never wanted to let her go.

13

Nia

I'M NOT SURE during which musical number I dozed off, but when I woke, Carwyn was still asleep beside me. I carefully untangled myself from him and peeked at my phone. It was nearly time for the rehearsal dinner. I should've woken Carwyn up, but I found myself watching him sleep. He really had some long, dark eyelashes. The impulse to lay back down with him and go back to sleep was alluring. But I was here for Rose. Tonight was the rehearsal dinner, tomorrow the wedding. Carwyn and I had until eleven fifty-nine tomorrow night.

I checked the pockets of my sweats, but they weren't any new pennies. Not that I really thought there would be any.

Maybe staying with Carwyn wouldn't be so bad. I believed he genuinely cared about me. I liked being with him, his playfulness, and good God, he was an excellent kisser. He had a knack for being there for me without suffocating me or making me feel ridiculous for asking for help. Carwyn wasn't some gentleman with an umbrella shielding me from the storm. He was right beside me, laughing about the weather, holding my hand while the rain drenched us. Jake would have made sure he was dry and told me I should have planned better.

That was the difference between him and Jake.

I'd always been alone with Jake.

Jake had, unknowingly, taught me to live without him. He'd taught me to do the work alone, because it was faster and easier than asking him. If something was important to me but not to Jake, he would minimize my priorities and leave me to do it alone. Sure, Jake had listened to me when I was stressed, and he'd held me when I needed it, but that was it. I'd learned to expect less and less until I expected nothing at all. I hadn't even realized it had happened. I thought I'd been taking care of Jake, helping him, loving him, by doing all the things, but he hadn't appreciated or reciprocated any of it outside of check-the-box items he could hold over my head when I asked for help. Jake had stayed around because of what I provided for him, not because he ever cared about me.

I had been an idiot. And it had taken falling for a demon to figure that out.

I brushed a lock of his dark hair off his face. Carwyn's eyes fluttered open.

"We have another very fancy dinner to attend in two hours," I whispered.

He smiled, his arms weaving around me and pulling me on top of him for a full-body hug. The feel of his warm body beneath mine reignited the heat still smoldering from the hot springs. I swear I'd dreamed of his quiet moans during my nap.

How fancy? He asked.

I'm sure there will be some amount of math involved in using the correct utensils. I wiggled a bit, snuggling deeper into him, but also enjoying the subtle friction of my breasts against his chest.

Should we have watched Bridgerton instead of Christmas movies?

It probably would have been useful. I moved away enough to look at his face and to tease him about the Muppet movie, but the words dried in my mouth. There was something devastatingly intimate about his unkempt hair and the lines on his face from sleep. Soft afternoon light lit his expression in a gentle glow that highlighted his unearthliness in a way I had never noticed. Carwyn's blue-green eyes were locked on me, full of such heat that my toes curled.

Two hours is a long time. Carwyn leaned over and pressed his lips to my temple. My breath quickened at the whisper of his lips across my skin. My mind emptied of anything witty to say. His hand stroked my back, and though it was probably meant to be reassuring, it only ramped up my desire for him.

Do you want to sleep more? I asked.

No. He cradled my face in his hand and then kissed me. He moved slowly, his lips firmly pressing against mine in a kiss that had no right to be so electric. *I want to learn what sounds you make with me between your legs.* His voice in my head was a rumble down to my toes. I exhaled a breath, and he caught it with his mouth, his tongue brushing against mine in a searing kiss that had me reaching out to touch his face, his hair, any part of him I could get my fingers on. *Is that a yes?*

Was it? I wanted to be lost in the smell and taste of him again. But the voice of reason broke through the haze. I wasn't prepared to have sex with Carwyn.

"I didn't bring any condoms," I said, breathless.

He pushed back a lock of my hair, running his fingers through it. "I can't get you pregnant, and I'm not susceptible to human disease, so there are no worries there either." He nibbled on the very edge of my ear. *What do you want, Nia? Tell me.*

Part of me hesitated, wanting to stop this before I was too emotionally involved to walk away from Carwyn on the solstice. I also knew I was lying to myself if I thought I wasn't already head over heels for him.

I claimed his mouth in a kiss. *I want you to fuck me.*

Carwyn suddenly rolled, pinning me beneath him. His being enveloped me, his warmth, his smell, even the subtle quickening of his breath. I lifted my hips up, flush against him. His eyelids fluttered, and a tiny moan escaped his mouth as his head came to rest against mine.

I kissed him with an eagerness that had my heart fluttering. When was the last time I'd been this worked up? His hand worked down my shirt, his thumb stroking sweetly over my nipple. I groaned and could feel his answering smile against my mouth. *I like that sound,* he said. He pulled my shirt up, then sat up so he could finish pulling it over my head. I hadn't bothered to pack any sexy underwear, which I was now regretting. My well-loved nude bra was comfortable but as ratty as my favorite pair of sweats.

You would look glorious in a paper bag, Carwyn said.

I sat up and pulled Carwyn's shirt off, then kissed his neck. *You are so damn sexy*, I said. I pulled off his sweats. Mine were off next, followed quickly by any garments left until we were both naked. Carwyn grabbed me in his arms and set me on the bed. He braced himself over me, his eyes taking in every bit of my exposed body. *Like what you see?* I asked.

You have no fucking clue.

His hand ran up the center of my body, fitting between my breasts, up my neck, and to my hair. *Tell me if you change your mind.*

I nodded. Carwyn lowered himself onto me, kissing me again before his mouth enveloped each of my breasts, his tongue moving until my nipples were hardened and my hips were writhing beneath him. He was kissing and sucking every bit of me, finding every spot that made my body shiver and jolt. Being the object of such intense focus was almost overwhelming, but just when I thought I might be overstimulated, he found a new part of me to play with.

When his tongue finally slid over my clit, I couldn't stop my hips from bucking against his mouth. He licked and sucked me, working my body until my eyes were rolling in my head and my thighs were trembling against the sides of his head. This heady bliss was too much and not enough. I wanted this to last forever, even as I felt myself getting closer and closer to the peak. I clenched, not knowing if I was trying to stave it off or push myself over the edge. When his fingers pushed inside of me and began stroking my inner walls, there was nothing I could do to stop the throaty moan that he pulled out of me.

I've got you. Come for me, Carwyn said, his voice pushing me over. I came undone as his clever fingers and tongue coaxed every last wave of pleasure out of me.

It wasn't enough.

I got on top of him and slid myself down the length of his erection. The relief I felt as he filled me was only a tease to my insatiable ache. Rocking my hips, I moaned again. Beneath me, Carwyn's beautiful lips were parted as he breathed, his hands stroking up my thighs as I rode him. I had never felt so lost to pleasure as I was now. Moving faster, Carwyn pulled my face down to his, delivering long, slow, angled thrusts that had me whimpering for more. Pressure built low as my mind dissolved into desperate need.

Please don't stop, I begged. *Just like that.*

Carwyn would have made a goddamned metronome jealous. He moved exactly the way I needed him, patiently working with my body until I finally came hard on him. He kept moving as the waves of my orgasm subsided, and he finally moaned his own release.

He held me for a long time as I came down to reality. Part of me had worried the landing would be hard, but instead, I felt blissful contentment.

"Do you need anything?" he asked. "Water? Food?"

"Uh...um...I..." I apparently couldn't string together a sentence yet. "Water."

Carwyn grinned. I couldn't even be mad at the smug satisfaction on his face. He'd earned it.

14

Carwyn

NIA GLOWED THROUGH the rehearsal dinner, and my male ego took full responsibility for it. Alright, not full responsibility, but at least some. Every sound she'd made during and her stuttering sentences afterward still echoed in my mind. Nia laughed across the room at something Molly said, and she had listened with dewy eyes while Rose's parents gave a very heartwarming speech about welcoming Hawthorn into their family. She'd danced with Aunt Geminy and had eaten her entire dinner and some of my dessert. She seemed free, her real smile shining all night long.

Jake even kept his distance, occasionally stealing a sidelong glance at Nia, but otherwise ignored her. It seemed he'd finally gotten the message to keep away from Nia. Which was good because Nia didn't deserve to have to deal with him anymore. I think she was finally realizing she didn't have to punish herself because of what that jackass did. He was his own man, and she wasn't responsible for him.

At the end of the dinner, Rose and Hawthorn had gone their separate ways under the tradition of not seeing the bride before the wedding. Nia and I had spent some time in the bar laughing with their friends, and it was easy to forget I hadn't known them as long as she had. I fit easily into her life, so easily that it felt like a dream. Nia made me feel like I belonged with her, not in a possessive way, but in the same way the smell of freshly baked bread reminded me of home, filled me with warm memories, and lured me to the kitchen.

Back in our room, we found more ways to enjoy each other, then we talked until the deep part of the night, when Nia finally fell asleep, wrapped in my arms. Her steady sleeping breaths against my chest were a tiny sliver of perfection. For the first time since I realized I was falling in love with her over the summer, the fear of losing her felt distant. She seemed settled and self-assured, and I couldn't foresee a reality in which this wasn't how we would end every night. We hadn't said it yet, but I knew what this feeling was. I knew she did too. I saw it in her eyes every time she looked at me.

When I'd fallen asleep, it had been with a happy, full heart.

15

Nia

"I SWEAR I forget how stunning this wedding gown is every time I see it," I said to Rose. It was hanging artfully in front of a set of windows in the massive bridal suite, the photographer snapping away. It was an A-line gown with a soft sweetheart neckline with more rhinestones than the whole of Dollywood, and layers upon layers of soft tulle. Anyone else would have been swallowed up by it, but Rose wore the absolute hell out of it.

"Okay, I wasn't going to ask again, but I don't want either of us to have any regrets," Rose said. I turned toward her, my eyebrows knitting. "My mom bought you a bridesmaid dress, and it would make my day for you to be up there with me, but I totally understand—"

"I would love to," I interrupted her, feeling not an ounce of hesitation. Rose started nodding like I was rejecting her offer. I waited, and then her eyes widened as my words finally sank in.

"Tell me I heard that right?" Rose asked, her tone cautious, her hand pointing toward me.

I stepped forward, taking her hand in mine. "If you still want me as a bridesmaid after everything, I would love to be at the altar with you."

Rose started fanning her face with her hands, her eyes welling with tears threatening her freshly applied makeup. "I can't cry. I can't cry. Oh, shoot," Rose said. Tears burst from her eyes and streamed down her face. For a split second, I thought she was upset with me before realizing with heart-crushing shame it was relief on my best friend's face. Before I could say anything, she bear-hugged me.

"I'm so sorry it took me this long," I said, desperately trying to avoid smashing any of her perfect red curls. "I can't believe I thought I'd make your wedding better by staying away." I'd already faced my fear of seeing Jake again and proved to myself I could handle him. I wouldn't panic even if I had to walk down the aisle with him. He was completely irrelevant to my life now.

"I totally get it, though. What happened was awful, and I knew in your heart you thought you were looking out for me."

I nodded, then, cursing beneath my breath, pulled away. We both laughed as I fussed with a hairpin that had come loose. The makeup seemed like it was holding up fairly well, but the makeup artist swooped in for a last-minute fix.

"Finally!" Martha cried out from her chair. She strode over to the closet and pulled out a black garment bag. "It's not altered, but I'm sure it will fit you," she said.

"Thank you for believing in me." I accepted the dress from her. Martha gave me a warm smile and then an even warmer hug. I had learned long ago to never offend Martha with an offer of repayment for anything. I'd make a batch of her favorite cookies later.

Molly opened the door to the room she'd been changing in and stopped short in the doorway. "Yes!" Molly exclaimed when she saw me holding the dress. "This is going to be the best wedding ever! Wait!" She ran back into the bedroom she'd just come out of and emerged with another bouquet.

I laughed, my face heating. "You all had way more faith in me than I did."

I changed into the gold sequenced bridesmaid dress, feeling better than I had—maybe ever? Jake hadn't seemed to have looked in my direction at the rehearsal dinner, and he'd had plenty of time to talk to me. I think he'd finally realized this was his brother's wedding, and it wasn't the time or place for him to steal the show. Maybe he'd even finally understood things were dead between us and was moving on.

I didn't care what had happened with Jake. I was free.

Carwyn had ended up running errands for Rose and Martha all morning, helping with some last-minute setup in the reception hall. I hadn't needed him to be my emotional support demon during any part of getting ready with Rose.

I didn't need Carwyn, but I wanted him to share my life, my excitement, my everything.

I just agreed to be a bridesmaid! I told him.

Martha is going to gloat all night, you know, he said back, but there was approval, or maybe pride, in his voice that had my heart fluttering. *She was sure you'd be up there with Rose. We all were.*

After I was ready, we helped Rose into her dress while the photographer continued snapping candids. I nearly cried when Martha gifted Rose a pair of diamond studs that had once belonged to Martha's mother, who had passed away two years ago. Rose did cry. The makeup artist was a miracle worker because this time her makeup didn't budge.

There was a knock on the hotel room door, and the Bryson House wedding planner stepped in to announce that all the guests were seated. It was time for the wedding to begin. Rose was literally bouncing with happiness, the layers of her dress making it look like she was floating as we double-checked we had everything we needed. It was time for her to marry Hawthorn, who wasn't going to run out on her. My best friend was going to have the perfect wedding she deserved, and I was so happy for her.

We headed down the hallway, and Rose suddenly turned toward me. "Oh, the entrance! We're doing something different from the usual processional," Rose said quickly as we walked. "It's mostly the same, except no one is coming down the center aisle. Everyone is coming in from either side and meeting in the middle, in front of the wedding arch."

A little bit of nerves worked their way through my stomach, but I pushed them out. This was going to be perfect, and I wasn't letting my own issues ruin any part of this. "Okay, so when should I go? Molly is your maid of honor, so she would still go last, right?"

Rose nodded. "Molly will walk in at the same time as Jake on the other side. You'll have to go in after Aunt Geminy, who's a flower matron, alone. Is that alright?

"That's fine with me," I said. Joy was radiating off of Rose and I kicked myself for not agreeing to this sooner. I owed her so much. We arrived in the area outside the doors of the venue, where all the guests were waiting, and where Rose's Dad, Dr. Pran, was already waiting. He looked exhausted, but was beaming with pride and joy as he chatted with Aunt Cynthia. I stayed back while Rose talked to her parents off to the side.

"Oh! You missed the fittings! There are hidden pockets in our dresses," Molly said, and handed me a wad of tissues. I felt around at the seams and found the openings, depositing the tissues into the empty pockets.

"Thank you," I said to Molly.

You doing alright? Carwyn asked.

I'm a little nervous, I admitted. *But I can do this.*

I know you can, Carwyn said back. *I might miss the wedding ceremony.*

What? Why?

The wedding coordinator sent Aunt Cynthia off with her basket filled to the brim with red rose petals.

There was a slight mishap with the wedding cake, and while the cake has been saved, I'm covered in frosting.

The coordinator waved me forward.

Oh no. Alright, I'll see you after. I'm about to go in!

You got this. I'll see you soon.

"Okay, now," the wedding coordinator prompted me, and she opened the door. For a second, my wedding flashed in front of me, and my stomach dropped out. But this wasn't the church, and the setup wasn't the same. The altar, ahead and to my left, was empty. The audience was on my right, not ahead of me. Jake wasn't there, and he wouldn't walk out until Molly did after me. Aunt Gemini and Aunt Cynthia had laid down a thick carpet of flower petals in the aisles. I could do this.

I stepped onto the side aisle, heart feeling lighter with every step, and made my way slowly down in time to the music. When I got halfway down the aisle, Jake started walking down the aisle across from me. He probably just got the timing wrong, blowing in on his own wind, completely out of step with the music. Ignoring him, I did my best to take my place at the altar, leaving enough space for Molly and Rose ahead of me. Jake reached his mark shortly after. This was the moment I had been so terrified of? I almost wasn't a bridesmaid because of my fear? Living in this moment felt completely fine. Better than fine. I was so excited for my best friend.

Then Jake loudly cleared his throat. "Excuse me," he called out. "I'd like everyone's attention for a moment."

My heart dropped out of my body.

He wouldn't.

"Nia, in front of our family and friends, I wanted to apologize for what happened last year. I left you at the altar like a coward."

I couldn't speak. I couldn't move. This was a living nightmare. This literally could not be happening.

He continued, "I have spent the last year wandering the Earth, thinking I would never get a chance at true love ever again. Believing that I had blown my chance with the most beautiful woman on the planet."

There was some murmuring in the crowd, but I couldn't make out the words over my thundering heart. Breathe. I needed to breathe. Fuck. I was going to pass out.

"Nia, there is no one else in the world for me. And I know you've been just as miserable this last year without me. I know you miss us, too." Jake stepped forward, as if this moment was meant for his dreams and his desires. Reality slowed into heart-thumping agony as he reached into his pocket and pulled out a tiny square black box. I bit my cheek so hard I tasted blood. When he opened it, a diamond engagement ring sparkled back at me. The processional music had stopped. The crowd was deathly silent as the judgment of over two hundred people lay down on me.

This was not the perfect wedding Rose and Hawthorn deserved!

This was my train wreck coming back to haunt me.

What was I supposed to do?!

How did I fix this for Rose?

He knelt in the middle of Rose and Hawthorn's wedding altar, looking up with the same doe eyes he'd worn when he'd proposed the first time. "I want to spend the rest of my life with you. Nia, love, will you marry me today?"

I gaped at him. I scanned the crowd, but half of them were either clutching their hearts or covering their mouths in horror. Everyone seemed frozen, trying to figure out the best way to handle this. The quietest way. The solution that caused the least harm.

This was exactly what had happened at my wedding when Jake had walked out. The murmurs would start soon. The accusations against me would follow, as people tried to figure out what I did to cause Jake's behavior. It was my fault. This was all my fault.

Maybe I could fix it. Please, please. I needed to fix this for her.

The seconds were ticking away. I just had to get him to stand up and be quiet long enough for this wedding to happen. I could do that. I could handle him.

When I looked back down at him on his knee, that stupid, completely self-assured smile on his face—I completely lost my mind.

"You selfish, narcissistic, self-absorbed brat!" I shrieked at him. "You're here at your brother's wedding, making it about you! It's always about YOU! I wasted YEARS of my life with you, loving you, only for you to manipulate me at every opportunity. Even now, you are asking me this in front of everyone because you don't think I will make a scene!" I flailed my arms as I spoke, loose petals from my bouquet falling to the ground between us. "You can go straight to HELL for all I care, you coward. I will never be with you again!"

Jake turned white, his jaw hanging open.

The silence turned to murmurs and then chuckles, dragging me back to reality. Back to the room filled with over two hundred guests waiting to witness my best friend's wedding.

I had just ruined my best friend's wedding.

I was the wedding drama.

At the entrance, the wedding coordinator looked horrified. The pastor was talking to Jake, trying to gently pull him up by the elbow. I looked behind me to the side where Rose was supposed to enter and saw Martha with both hands over her mouth, her face pale.

My face burned, then my neck. I was going to puke.

"You really do ruin everything." Jake spat beneath his breath. "Rose won't forgive you either."

"You need to leave," someone said. They were right. The only way Rose could get married was if I left. The only thing I could do to fix this was leave. Tears streaming down my face, I whispered, "I'm so sorry," to the crowd. Then I ran down the center aisle and right out of the room.

16

Carwyn

AFTER CHANGING OUT of my frosting-covered shirt, I snuck into the back of the venue, where Rose and Hawthorn were in the middle of exchanging rings. It was surprising I'd made it at all, given how long ago Nia said they'd been starting. I'd even made a wrong turn on the way here and gotten held up by some costumed Christmas carolers. It was hard to see from the back, but when I peeked around the back row of guests, I couldn't find Nia at the front of the room. Only Rose and Molly. Maybe she had sat down in the first row?

Actually, Jake wasn't here either. That nitwit better not—

"Looking for your girl?" Aunt Geminy whispered, causing me to jump.

"You are quiet as a cougar," I whispered back, holding my hand on my heart for emphasis.

She grinned but then became more serious. "My idiot nephew tried to ruin the wedding by proposing to Nia in front of everyone. She found her backbone and finally gave him a piece of her mind; she said everything we were all thinking.

But then she took off before anyone could stop her. Jake's been removed from the property. Nia really should come back. No one blames her. In fact, I think it was some good pre-event entertainment. Been waiting a long time for someone to teach that boy a lesson."

Jake was going to see some wrath later.

"Which way did she go?" I asked. I'd just come from the room, so I knew she wasn't there.

Aunt Geminy pointed out the back door I'd just snuck in through. With more self-control than I thought I possessed, I walked out of the ceremony and made sure the door shut completely silently behind me.

Nia, where are you? I asked, and for once I hit a wall. She'd blocked me out. I was proud that she'd finally figured out how to do it, and irritated that it had happened now. *Come on, Nia, where are you? We don't have to talk about it.* I tried, even knowing she'd shut me out.

I jogged through Bryson House, looking everywhere I went, and asking everyone I came across if they'd seen a bridesmaid running through. But no one had seen her. I headed back up to our room. Maybe she had sought refuge there, and I'd missed her when I'd gone down to the ceremony.

Stepping off the elevator onto the carpeted floor, I headed down the corridor. A chill swept across my neck, and I whirled around. No one was there. The hallway was empty. It was just like the incorporeal ass-hats to start harassing me now when Nia needed me the most.

"Not now, you idiots," I growled and turned back around.

A ghost was inches from my face. I screeched like a child. The ghost chuckled.

"You need to follow me if you want to find Nia," the ghost said. It was the same jerk from the bar.

"You've delighted in scaring the actual devil out of me, and now you want me to trust you?" I asked.

The ghost shrugged. "You really need to learn to take a joke. You're too serious. Besides, my wife is insistent that you go talk to Nia."

"Your wife? Did you not get the memo about until death do us part?" I was getting off track. The ghost was offering me help, and I had no other leads. After what Jake had pulled, it was time for me to be the emotional support demon. As much as I loathed this— "You know what? Never mind. If you can show me to Nia, I would be in your debt," I ground out.

The ghost grinned. "Follow me." I trailed behind the ghost as it led me right back to my room.

"I could have gotten here alone," I said.

"We wanted you to take the most expeditious route," it said and then disappeared. I unlocked the door. Inside, Nia was shoving things into her suitcase, her face red and puffy. The door clicked shut behind me, her head snapping in my direction.

We stared at each other. It was like being back in her living room that first night, but without the smell of sangria. Desperation and hopelessness hung off her, along with an unhealthy bit of panic.

"What are you doing?" I asked.

Tears rolled down her red cheeks.

"I can't do this. I ruin everything. I just ruined my best friend's wedding. I ruined my wedding. I'm going to ruin—" she let out a noise of frustration and wiped the tears from her face. She'd thrown a sweater over her bridesmaid dress, washed her makeup off, and put her hair up into a haphazard bun.

"You didn't ruin anything," I said. "Rose is downstairs getting married right now. They tossed Jake out. Aunt Geminy sent me to find you and bring you back."

She shook her head. "I don't trust myself to know what's right. I loved him once. I didn't see what a self-absorbed dick he was. I didn't even dream he'd hijack the wedding to propose to me. I screamed at him in front of everyone before Rose even made it down the aisle. I ruined everything because I'm an idiot who doesn't know what the right answer is."

"No one thinks you ruined anything. He deserved what you said and more." I walked closer to her. "His family kicked him out, and they are asking you to come back." I took a few more steps toward her, but she stiffened.

"No," she said, her voice cracking. "I can't do us."

I blinked at her.

"What?" I asked.

"I need to end our bargain. I'm not in a good place right now. I wish we had more time, but we don't." Tears streamed down her face. "The best thing I can do for you is let you go. You can't be tethered to me."

My chest felt like it was filled with lead. "Nia, please. Let's take a breath first—"

"No. I need you to leave. Go find someone else who is not a train wreck."

"Nia, you are not a train wreck."

"Carwyn! Please. I'm begging you. End this," she said, and the desperation in her face to be rid of me—it broke me.

I grabbed a receipt off of the dresser and wrote the words to break our bargain on it. "If you want this to be over, then you read these words, and that will be it. I won't say them, but here they are when you're ready." I put the receipt on top of the suitcase she was packing. She reached into the pockets of her bridesmaid dress and turned them out while pulling out a tissue. She blew her nose and threw it away, seeming to make a point not to look at me.

I tried to speak, but it took me a few seconds to get myself together. This was the worst I'd ever seen her. I wanted to hug her and hold her, but she didn't want me right now. Maybe if things were different, I would have been enough for her. But we were out of time; we only had a few hours left. I had to respect it even if I didn't understand it.

"I'm sorry I can't stay," she said, her voice breaking.

I swallowed and forced myself to clear the growing ache in my throat. "I understand," I said as my heart broke.

She nodded, then sniffed and wiped at her tears with the sleeves of her sweater. "I can't stay here any longer. I just need to be alone," she said, as if she was justifying something.

"I'll go for a walk so you can be alone. When you read those words, I'll be back home." I pulled out my phone and started ordering a car. "I got you a car. It will be here in about an hour. Is that enough time?"

Nia only nodded.

It took everything I had not to ask her for one last hug.

She was done with me. Holding on to hope with her in this state risked too much. I was a selfish creature, but I couldn't be selfish with her. Not with the deadline so close. She had to pick me without ever feeling like I guilted her into it.

"I hope you find someone who loves you right." She picked up the receipt.

My throat ached as I swallowed down everything. I nodded back because there was nothing left to say. She sniffed and kept her eyes off me. That was my cue to leave. I left my heart with her and walked out the door.

17

Nia

THE DOOR SHUT behind Carwyn. I set the receipt aside and went back to packing my bag. I would read it when I could see through my tears. There was no way I was going back to the wedding. I could never show my face here again. Rose must hate me. God damn it, where was my cell phone?

With a sickening twist of my stomach, I knew exactly where I had left it. The damn bridal suite. Part of me wanted to leave it and buy a new one, but I'd also left my purse filled with my makeup and wallet in there. I could make it without a phone, but not without my wallet.

Especially if I wanted to get on a flight.

I had no choice but to face Martha and plead for the room key so I could retrieve my things. She had to hate me right now. She and Dr. Pran had spent so much money on the perfect wedding, and I messed it up by being there.

In the bathroom, I took one of the face cloths, ran it under the coldest water, and started patting my face. I looked awful. My entire face was puffy, especially my eyes. There was no hiding that I'd run crying from that room, and had been crying ever since. "Alright, Nia, the worst has already happened. It sucks. We'll find a therapist on Monday." I cry-laughed, blotting the next few tears away with my cold washcloth.

After a few more minutes, I accepted my face was as good as it was going to get and snuck out of my hotel room. Part of me had apparently been hoping Carwyn would be waiting right outside the door, but he was nowhere to be seen. He really had left. I shouldn't be surprised. Carwyn had said he'd understood why we couldn't be together. He'd understood. Maybe after seeing me come apart, he'd been happy to leave. Happy to avoid the disaster that was me and my life. I couldn't blame him. I wasn't perfect like he deserved.

I'm glad he left before I could ruin his life, too. He deserved so much more than me.

I took the elevator down and crept toward the reception hall. Guests were lingering around with cocktails and appetizers, the buzzy murmur of the crowd loud enough that I didn't worry about anyone hearing me coming. I did my best to hide my face as I passed through the crowd. I'd forgotten Rose and Hawthorn had already taken their wedding portraits a few weeks ago because they hadn't wanted to take a bunch of pictures on their wedding day. They were smiling and laughing with Molly and a few other friends, sharing a plate of appetizers.

Sticking as close to the wall as possible so they wouldn't see me, I found Martha chatting with one of the waitstaff in the corner.

"Mrs. Pran?" I asked, trying to keep my voice as low as possible while still gaining her attention.

She glanced over at me, then back at the waitstaff. Then her eyes went wide as she looked back at me. "Nia! There you are!" she cried.

"I'm so sorry to be back here. I'm sorry for ruining literally everything," I said as my voice cracked. "I left my phone and wallet in the suite, and I just need them back, and I promise I'll leave. Immediately."

Martha cocked her head at me. "What in the hell are you talking about?"

I blinked at her. She never spoke like that.

"Nia!" Rose called out my name. I winced.

The crinkling of layers of fabric came my way. I braced for my best friend's ire.

"Why did you run out like that?" she asked.

"I promise I'll leave as soon as I get my wallet and phone back from the suite."

"No, I didn't ask when are you leaving. I asked why?" Rose asked. "Have you been crying this whole time? I never should have pressured you into being a bridesmaid. I'm so sorry."

"You didn't pressure me. I wanted to. I've always wanted to. I'd just been scared of him," I said. "But I ruined everything for you because I couldn't keep it together for your wedding."

Rose shook her head. "I was so proud of you when I saw the video of you yelling at him. You didn't ruin anything. In fact, that was the best damn wedding gift anyone could give me."

"What? But he's Hawthorn's brother. His family hates me."

"Oh no," Rose said. "The family is so pissed at Jake. Literally, everyone was so embarrassed that he even thought that was appropriate. Everyone thinks he had it coming, and that you were awesome."

"But your wedding—"

Rose put her hands on my shoulders. "It's wonderful. But it will be perfect with you here, where you belong."

I hugged her, feeling all the weight and dread melting off. I hadn't actually ruined her wedding, my ignorant ex had. God, he was so awful, I'd actually truly believed it was my fault he'd done something stupid.

"Thank the heavens you found a better man," Martha said, and handed me a couple of folded-up tissues. "Put them in your pocket for later. Dr. Pran has another fantastic speech for later."

I stuffed them in my pocket only to find something small and solid within. I pulled it out and then stared at the perfect, bright penny in my hand.

"Is that a penny?" Martha asked. "I wonder how it got in there."

What had he lied about? The cake?

"Where is Carwyn, dear?" Martha asked. "I was told he was a miracle worker with the cake earlier. I still need to thank him for handling that for us." What else? What could he have lied about? The car? I saw him open the app and order it. And he literally left the room after he said he was going for a walk so I could be alone. I knew it wasn't the words he'd written to break the bargain, because I'd gotten tissues out of my pockets immediately after he gave me the instructions.

His words floated back to me. *"I understand,"* Carwyn had said. He'd lied. I closed my fingers around the penny. He hadn't understood. That's why he hadn't broken our bargain. It's why he left the words on the dresser. I still had time to apologize to him. I'd spent so long trying to make my relationship with Jake work that I was pushing away someone because he was easy to love.

"I'll tell him you're looking for him. I'm going to run back upstairs and fix my makeup," I said. "I really thought I'd screwed everything up," I admitted. This time, Martha and Rose both hugged me, murmuring assurances. "Okay, okay, this is not how you are supposed to be spending your wedding."

"It's my wedding, and I can celebrate my best friend dressing down the biggest dick in the world if I want to," she said, grinning. "Go fix yourself up and get your ass back down here for food and party time!"

I headed back to my room, walking as fast as I could to the elevator, then sprinting down the hallways. I had to apologize to Carwyn, tell him how stupid I'd been about everything, and hope he'd forgive me. I pushed open the door to our room, but it was empty.

Carwyn's suitcase was gone.

18

Carwyn

I WASN'T SURE how this day could get any worse.

Nia had asked me to leave, which was pretty much as rock bottom as things could get for me. Or so I thought. Now, I was being held hostage in an elevator by multiple ghosts bent on terrorizing me. They had me backed into a corner so that I couldn't even reach the emergency button to let the operator know I was trapped between floors.

Even worse, they seemed to be bickering among themselves about how long they could keep me trapped.

"I have a driver waiting for me!" I seethed. I didn't even have enough service to let the gentleman know I was stuck.

"There's no horse and carriage out there," one of them said.

"Not a carriage driver, a car, you nitwit," another one answered.

"I thought they ran on horses."

"Horse power," multiple ghosts responded at once, as if they'd been through this multiple times. I was just trying not to vomit at this point.

It was extremely difficult to tell how many there were, given that they were all see-through and layered upon each other like the plastic sheets in an old schoolhouse projector. Why were they such disgusting entities?

"We're here to ensure your stay was a delight. Please let the concierge know if you need anything," a ghost said, then cackled.

I closed my eyes. I wasn't even that scared at this point. Grossed out with goosebumps? Yes. But mostly heartbroken.

"Just let me leave. Please."

"Aww, he said please. You gotta let the hell-born demon loose in time for Christmas!"

"That's really a hateful stereotype," I said.

This time, they all laughed. I squeezed my carry-on against my chest a little harder. They would eventually get bored and leave me be. Right?

Something in the elevator dinged, and it finally started to descend again. Thank fuck. Even if I only made it to the next floor, I should be able to take the stairs the rest of the way down and hopefully still meet my driver.

The ghosts seemed to be disappointed by the development and dissipated into wherever they went when I couldn't see them.

The elevator leveled out, paused, and the doors opened. Nia was standing there, panting.

"Thank God you didn't leave yet," she said and pulled me out of the elevator and into the main lobby. Then she pushed a penny into my hand. "You lied."

I frowned at it. When had I lied to her? I opened my mouth to defend myself, but I realized when it had happened, and I wouldn't deny it.

"You said you understood why we couldn't be together. But you lied, because you don't. And you know what? I don't either." She peered around the lobby, then she inhaled and exhaled while locking her gaze with mine. "I freaked out and pushed you away when you have always been there for me. You have given me patience and respect and space whenever I have needed it. You have asked for so little in return. I do not deserve you, Carwyn. You are considerate and kind. I love the way you flirt and make me laugh, and most of all I love our long conversations. I love who I am when I am with you. I fell in love with you, too, and I don't want you to leave." Hotel guests were walking around, and some were even staring, but Nia didn't seem to notice. The only thing she was focused on was me.

"Nia," I tried to cut in, the lump in my throat cutting off my words for a moment. She'd come back for me, and my heart was so full I couldn't speak.

"I want you to know: I choose you forever if you are still willing to be with me," she said.

I held her head in my hands and brushed away two tears with my thumbs. Finally, I stammered, "I was terrified I'd lost you." I pulled her up and into me, feeling like I could finally breathe again as her arms wrapped around me tightly.

"I love you," she breathed in my ear.

"I love you, too," I told her. "I love how considerate you are toward those you love. You are selfless to a fault, and you have always made me feel like I was a part of your life. And tonight you faced your worst fears and conquered them before they conquered you. I admire your strength and bravery so much."

The ghosts from the elevator popped out of the wall and yelled, "Kiss her already!"

So I did.

Nia

I dropped my oversized sparkler into the bucket of water. A soft fizz sounded as it hit the water. Rose and Hawthorn's limo was just a pair of vanishing red lights in the distance. Carwyn took my hand, and we walked away from the slowly dispersing crowd and onto a walkway which overlooked the small town twinkling below Bryson House. I shivered, and Carwyn gave me his jacket, which was warm as if it had just come out of the dryer.

We walked until we found a bench between two small streetlights decked out with sparkling garlands with red ribbons. The night was frosty, and the sky clear, letting through a few more stars than usual. Carwyn pulled me close on the bench, and I was more than happy to be snuggled up against him again. We'd danced together all night. My feet were an aching mess, but I wouldn't trade any of it.

Carwyn's phone screen flashed on. "We're down to the last two minutes. It's okay if forever is too much," he said. My chest squeezed, not at the thought of keeping him, but of losing him. I didn't need to check my pockets for any pennies; I trusted him completely.

"You know, with anyone else, I might still be worried. But you have always respected my boundaries. And if we don't work out, I know you'd give me space. Really, it's you who should be worried. The stakes are much higher for you," I said.

He shook his head. "I can't imagine someone better to take that risk with than you," he said. Carwyn picked up my hand and brushed a kiss against my knuckles. Already, I was thinking of all the ways and positions I wanted to show my love to him. Carwyn unbuckled his watch and held it up for both of us to see the seconds ticking down. "It's when the second hand reaches fifty seconds past the minute."

"Why not exactly midnight?"

"It's the time you summoned me. So just before."

"You mean if I had waited a minute that night, this all would have been moot?"

"That summoning wouldn't have worked at all," he confirmed.

"Demon magic is very specific," I said.

"You have no idea," he replied. The second hand reached twelve and started around for the last minute. My heart didn't pound. I didn't feel a wave of panic. I felt completely and blissfully at ease. I put my hand over the watch and pushed it down.

Then I kissed my demon husband.

A Medium Rare Romance

Cassandra Trevelle

1

Celeste

THE FUNICULAR SCREECHED into the station like a banshee getting a wedgie.

A family of five rushed past me from the platform into the carriage, tossing their bags across all the seats before crowding around the front window, covering the best views of the ride up.

"Ce-ce-de!" Terrance stood to greet me, dressed in his usual old-timey conductor uniform.

I paused midstride into the carriage. "You talking to me?"

The father in the family threw me a curt, "No."

"That's the new nickname I've come up with for you," Terrance explained. "Ce-ce short for Celeste. And De is short for death."

I grimaced. "Thanks, I hate it." It better not have caught on with anyone else at the hotel.

The mother in the family shepherded their bags closer to them, leaving a space on the bench clear for me and my well-worn duffel. I sighed contentedly as I sat. My long gold earrings chimed pleasantly with my descent.

"Don't get too comfy," Terrance said. "I need your help with Eugene."

I blew a loose strand of platinum blond hair from my face. "About the screeching?"

"You heard it, right?"

"Yeah, I'm not deaf." If anything, I'm the opposite.

"They've been oiling up all the wrong things trying to get it to stop." Terrance approached the closed door to the conductor's cabin. "Come on."

I heaved myself up, earrings jangling in protest, and opened the narrow door, ignoring the family's is-the-crazy-lady-hijacking-the-vehicle looks.

"Celeste!" Eugene, the funicular conductor, greeted me. "Thank goodness you're back."

"Terrance told me about the screeching issues."

"It started a couple of days ago. We've checked the gearbox, brakes, and even replaced the wheels. Nothing's working, and this evening is our busiest with everyone coming up for the Tree Lighting Ceremony."

"They've got to check the hydrostatic auxiliary," Terrance said.

"It's the hydrostatic auxiliary," I repeated.

Eugene pulled out a notepad and a pencil from his pocket. Terrance continued, "There's an internal seal failure in a hydraulic cylinder. After removing and disassembling it, you need to look closely at the cylinder bore and the rod for any damage."

A knock interrupted me in the middle of relaying the information. The father squeaked the door open and peered through. "Is everything all right in there?"

Eugene's friendly face morphed into no-nonsense sternness. "Guests can't be back here. Kindly return to your seat, sir."

The man threw a confused glance my way. "But—"

"Please," Eugene repeated. "Return to your seat."

I flashed the man a full-toothed smile, and he hesitantly backed up and closed the door.

"You were saying?" Eugene asked.

"I lost my place," I admitted. "Where was I?"

Terrance ran through the instructions again, and I followed right behind as Eugene scribbled every word.

"We'll look into this right away," he said, closing his notepad. "Thanks, Celeste. You're a lifesaver."

"Yes, I was about to go crazy before you arrived," Terrance said. "I thought you'd be back by Thanksgiving. I lost to Adelia on that bet."

I smirked and gave Eugene a friendly warning. "Our friend Terrance here owes Adelia a favor. You know what that means."

"Oh, how lovely." Eugene clasped the pad over his chest. "It warms my heart witnessing the matchmaking ghosts in action."

"I'm not a matchmaking ghost," Terrance grumbled. "I get roped into things."

"Well, it serves you right for betting against me," I responded.

Eugene chuckled. "I take it our friend is not happy about this."

"He's fine," I said, ignoring the sour pout on Terrance's face. All he'd have to do was jerk the carriage one day when Adelia wanted someone to bump into another. Then he'd be debt-free once again.

"I hope you are staying longer this time," Eugene said.

I swallowed back the lump in my throat. I'd cut my stay short last year.

"That's the plan," I told the conductor. "There's an open storefront down on Main Street that I'm looking into."

"Opening up a psychic shop?"

I cringed internally. "More like a paranormal-themed book and gift shop." I helped the dead with their messages to the living. I wasn't interested in making shit up for people who didn't have a ghost haunting them.

"That sounds wonderful. Oh, give me a moment. We're about to arrive." Eugene focused on the controls, and the funicular screeched to a stop at the top station. Walking me back to the passenger carriage, he said, "Thanks again for all your help. Truly, we're glad to have you back."

The tourist family continued to regard me warily as they disembarked. I continued to ignore them. Merely another group of people I'd never seen before and would never see again. I awarded them the appropriate number of shits: none at all.

"Say hi to Sadie for me." Eugene patted me warmly on the shoulder before returning to his conductor station.

"You told me about your paranormal store idea last year," Terrance said. "What happened?"

"Nothing," I lied. "Last year wasn't the right time."

I disembarked before the nosy ghost could ask any more questions.

The crisp air bloomed with the scents of pine and cinnamon. The holiday season had barely started, but you couldn't tell walking down the path from the station to Bryson House, already decked out with arches of lights. Nic and her crew prepared everything beautifully for the Christmas tree lighting ceremony tonight.

Only at the front door of Sadie's dark chapel did it hit me how early it was. Way too soon for her to be up. As a worker for the conservatory, one of the things she relished about the off-season was that it didn't require nearly the same rise with the dawn schedule as spring and summer.

I dug into my bag and pulled out my bus ticket to Summer Springs and a pen, then scrawled, "Guess who's back bitch! I got a new number. Call me when you're up," on the back along with my number, and pushed it under the door.

My ex-foster sister was the closest thing I had to a family. She loved this place, which brought it to the top of the list of places I could make into my home.

I walked around the hotel grounds. I could chat with a hotel ghost or a friendly guest while I waited for Sadie to wake up. My stomach growled for breakfast, and my feet started moving without me actively choosing my destination. There was only one place to go.

It's fine. I'm sure Angus doesn't even work here anymore. He told me last year he was going to start his own restaurant. And even if he is here, it's fine.

So what if we shared one incredible night the last time I was in town? Who cares that no one has satisfied me as thoroughly, in both the kitchen and bedroom? Not me!

Okay, so I may have freaked out and bolted when it started feeling like we were getting too close for comfort. But that was last-year-Celeste. This-year-Celeste was cool as a cucumber. And hungry as a bear coming out of hibernation.

"Celeste? Is that you?"

My blood pulsed at a man's sudden voice, but its familiar baritone wasn't Angus's.

"Chef Sené!" I greeted the head chef of Savoir, the five-star restaurant that served out of the Bryson House.

"Look who's crawled back with her tail between her legs."

Excuse me? I don't have a tail, obviously. But if I did, it would be tall and proud. Maybe flickering in annoyance. But this was a typical Sené greeting. "Nice to see you too, Sené," I responded sarcastically.

But it was also genuinely good to see him. If he still worked here, running Savoir as usual, Angus must have moved on. He was ready to be in charge of his own kitchen a while ago.

The only reason for Angus to still work here would be if Sené retired, and Angus took over as Head Chef.

"How's the restaurant?" I asked.

"Terrible."

"I'm sorry to hear that."

"The crew can't do anything right."

I rolled my eyes. Sené's complaining about being unable to find good help was a tale as old as time. "Well, it sounds like it's been going as well as ever. And it smells amazing too!"

We stood near the back entrance to the restaurant, where employees entered the kitchen. Breakfast wafted like crazy. The buttery aroma of fresh, flaky croissants, mixed with the savory smokiness of crisp bacon, was buffeted by an undercurrent of freshly brewed coffee.

"You carrying?" he asked, momentarily distracting me from my growling stomach.

I smirked and pulled a case of joints from my pocket. Last year, Sené and I bonded over a smoke or two. Weed was pretty pedestrian for him, but I didn't go harder. And this small, Christmas-y town wasn't flush with friends to imbibe with. "You want to split one?"

He sighed heavily. "I wish. But I can't. I'm six months sober."

"Oh my god! Congratulations! I'm so proud of you."

"Don't be. It's not up to me."

"What do you mean? Is it court-enforced?" I sounded surprised, but it was only a matter of time until Sené ass-holed too hard in front of the wrong authority figure.

"Not exactly."

"Why are you being so vague? What's going on?"

"Celeste?" A new voice sounded from behind me. I recognized that timbre immediately. Before I even turned around, I caught a whiff of him on the cross breeze. An intermingling of coffee, peppercorn, and underneath, the faintest musk of tobacco. Not like someone who had finished smoking. More like how the inside of a vintage cigar box smelled. "You're back," he said.

And you're here. You're still here.

I turned to face my old fling. "Hey, Angus."

He wore the same black Canada Goose winter jacket as last year, zipped most of the way up, still exposing his thick neck and prominent Adam's apple. The short dark brown beard was new. I liked it. It accentuated his cut jawline and full, pale lips.

His dark blue eyes held something like hurt. But that couldn't be right. It's not like I ghosted a full-blown relationship with him. In fact, he was probably in a relationship and a bit uncomfortable with my sudden reappearance.

"Yeah, I'm back. Right on time for the tree lighting," I filled my voice with a cheeriness that I hoped radiated no-big-deal-it's-all-good energy. "How have you been?"

"I'm sensing some tension here," Sené cut in, unhelpfully. We both ignored him.

"I've been managing," Angus said.

Sené scoffed. "Hardly."

Last year, Angus would've reacted to his boss undercutting his efforts like this. But this year, Angus didn't even flinch. Didn't even glance his way.

I smiled, proud of the growth of this man who'd always taken things so personally. "I think you're doing better than that."

A rosy red tinged his cheeks. Blushing? Or from the cold.

Sharp wind blew my earrings against my cheeks and hair into my mouth. I tucked the strands behind my ears.

"You're cold. Your ears are red." He took his hat off and slid it over my head before I could protest. That faint tobacco musk enveloped me, and it was all I could do not to fall back into it, like falling back into a feather bed. "Still can't dress appropriately for the cold."

I liked the cold. The brisk air kept me quick and sharp. Now, warmth spread from my head down to my feet, and all I could think of was a soft, pillowy mattress and strong arms wrapped around me.

"Ugh, get a room already." Sené's words splashed the cold water I needed to wake up.

My head turned to the chef. "Don't you have to get to work?"

"If only."

Angus looked from me to Sené. "Ghost?"

"No, it's Sené—" Oh. My. God.

That's why Sené's been sober. That's why Angus hasn't moved on to his own restaurant.

I whirled, whole body pivoting to face him. "You're dead!"

Sené shrugged.

"And you didn't think to tell me?" I continued, incensed.

"You didn't ask."

What the hell? I'm a medium who can speak to ghosts. So how am I always the last person to know?

2

Angus

I KNEW CELESTE had returned the moment I pulled into the employee parking lot and spotted that multi-colored, multi-patterned maxi dress under a too-thin coat.

I braced myself on the walk up, but nothing could prepare me for those pale grey eyes. Her blasé laugh and attitude made it seem as though we were nothing more than passing acquaintances. Like we hadn't seen each other naked. Felt each other's shuddering climaxes. Like she hadn't been the first and only person I shared my dreams with.

She left abruptly after yelling at Sené, muttering under her breath about the goddamn dead that can pass as living.

And just like that, I was alone again. Or I guess not fully.

"Can you go easy on me today?" I asked the space she had been talking to.

A piercing wind nipped at my exposed ears, and I speed-walked the last steps to the back kitchen door.

It had never been easy working under Chef Sené. He had very particular opinions about every aspect of his kitchen.

However, it had taught me a lot, both about what I wanted and didn't want to do with my own kitchen. That was when he was alive.

The last six months since his death, however, have been hell. Like a never-ending exam where every time you don't do something perfectly, the burners on the stovetop flare up and ruin your dish, or the flames go out and the delicate sauce you were simmering congeals. It has been nearly impossible to keep things running smoothly and keep the customers unaware of the constant chaos in the kitchen.

My pastry chef, Marianne, ran the kitchen for breakfast as usual, but I had taken to coming in early to catch up on the administrative tasks in the office and then get a head start on lunch prep.

I caught my saucier, Daniel's, attention. "Are you free right now?"

"For a bit. Do you need my help?"

"Could you do me a favor and run two breakfast plates out to Sadie's cottage?"

Daniel's eyebrows rose. "Two?"

"Yeah. Thanks so much." I retreated to my office before he could ask me any more specific questions, relieved to get a "Yes, Chef," from him as I departed the main kitchen.

My office hung off the empty old kitchen, but I paused before passing through. I bowed my head in front of the gas burner stovetop and whispered a tiny prayer, "Today's going to be a good day." Flicking the knob, I held my breath at the faint clicking of the pilot lighter and let it out in a whoosh when the flame caught. "Okay." I smiled at the circular blue fire.

Then it went out.

I turned the knob back off and let out a defeated, "Okay," before dragging my feet to my office and slumping down into my chair.

The tree-lighting evening was one of our busiest dinner services. The crowds started rushing in early. There would be a brief lull during the actual ceremony, and then the post-lighting crowds would run us ragged until closing time.

If we even made it to closing time.

I got Sené's message loud and clear. He didn't care how busy we were or how stressed I was. He would let us know the moment something wasn't to his exacting specifications, and he wouldn't let us continue until we fixed it.

After all those years working together, I thought I could do a better job at this. My crew tried to tell me these incidents weren't my fault, but I was the head chef. The buck stopped with me. And god, I really hoped I'd kept my temper in front of them. The lid I'd placed over my seething anger had been popping for days.

The only break I had from the feverish rage was Celeste. Running into her was like licking an ice cream cone on a hot summer day. Maybe I should be more upset with her for leaving last year in the way that she did.

Last Christmas, I gave her my heart, etc, etc.

But I was happy to see her again. Those dangly gold earrings that she always had on, even when she wore nothing else. The mischievous curve of her mouth was identical to the one on her face when I caught her and Sené high as kites in the kitchen. Sené tried and failed to cook up her wild requests. He didn't like that I could create the perfect things to fulfill her cravings. He left in a huff, but that left us alone so that I could meet her other physical needs in privacy.

The feverish heat returned. Lower this time. Less angry. More distracting.

Daniel knocked on my door, and I pretended to be immersed in the inventory order forms in front of me. "Come in."

"So, Celeste is back in town."

"Yep." I scribbled a note with my pen. Something very important, cause I'm very busy.

"That's pretty good timing, right?"

"What do you mean?"

"The tree lighting ceremony is today." He stared at me meaningfully. I blinked back at him. "She can tell us what Sené is saying. We can fix whatever issues he has without him sabotaging us on our busiest day."

Celeste. In the kitchen. Watching me work. Hearing Sené call out every single way I failed.

"No. We can't ask her for that."

"Why not?"

"She's busy."

"She's just hanging out with Sadie."

"They have a lot of catching up to do. And I'm sure she wants to see the tree lighting." I was running out of excuses and very aware of how lame I sounded.

Truth was, I would be ten times more distracted with Celeste here. But I couldn't tell Daniel that.

"It's an idea," I relented. "Let's keep it in the back pocket if we really need it."

3

Celeste

I SAT ON Sadie's chaise, contentedly observing her as she hung up twinkle lights. They were the extent of her holiday decorations in the renovated chapel – an unorthodox living arrangement, but she made it work. Would it only take a string of lights to make a home I loved as much?

"The studio I found is small, but it came furnished, which is pretty sweet," I said.

"When can I come see it?"

"Anytime. I've already unpacked and everything."

"Unpacked? But you always live out of your duffel."

"Not this time." I showed her the picture proof on my phone. My new apartment, with a pile of stuff I dumped out right in the middle of the floor. My stuffed hippo, Hippy, perched on top like a mountaineer.

"It's progress." She blinked at it a couple of times and smiled at me. "I'm proud of you."

I pocketed my phone, grinning. Sadie's always been my support person. We met as kids under her asshole parents' roof and bonded over our abilities to see things others couldn't; me with ghosts and her with auras.

Someone rapped on the chapel door.

"Celeste! We need your help!"

That sounded like Daniel, the lovely man who brought us breakfast this morning. I hid my disappointment at his empty hands when I let him in.

"The incidents in the kitchen are escalating, and Angus keeps blaming himself. Sené is being even more unreasonable in death than he was alive. Can you come and talk to him for us? Maybe if you tell us exactly what his problem is, we can fix it, and he'll be satisfied."

An overly optimistic idea.

"I don't know that Sené has ever been satisfied. In life or death," I answered.

"Please, only for today. We are swamped with the tree lighting crowds."

"Celeste will help you," Sadie volunteered for me.

"But what about our plans to see the tree lighting?"

"I have to check on the conservatory first anyway. You go with Daniel, and I'll meet you in front of the hotel before the ceremony."

Daniel led me to the restaurant kitchen, and I dawdled behind, stopping for quick chats with the ghosts who greeted me.

"Henry, great tunes. That's right. They're called the golden oldies for a reason. You keep that radio at the right station."

"Cheyenne! Nice hat, cowgirl! Is it new? Naw, I'm just playing with ya!"

Daniel's energy grew more and more like a boyfriend eager to go home from a party. But his girlfriend wouldn't stop making the rounds, saying goodbye to everyone.

Was I stalling? Maybe. Sené was never a reasonable man in life; in death, he would be even more stubborn. I could hear ghosts, but I was no more capable than anyone else at convincing them to do something they didn't want to do.

"Celeste!" An older, usually jolly ghost stopped me as we passed the library.

"Hey, George. Are you okay?"

"My granddaughter is visiting. She's about to make a horrible decision, and she needs to know the truth about her brother."

"Where is she? In the library?"

"Yes, she's sitting by the fireplace."

I turned to Daniel. "I'm going to need a quick minute to deliver a ghost message."

His are-you-kidding-me expression notwithstanding, he didn't stop my detour.

"What's her name?" I asked George.

"Olivia."

The young woman slouched dejectedly in the wingback chair, her hands working along the edges of the folded white paper in her lap.

"Hi, Olivia."

She straightened, startled at my sudden approach. "Um, hello?"

"I have a message for you, from your grandfather, George."

Turning to the ghost to prompt him, he began speaking, and I repeated his words to the dumbstruck woman staring at me. "Don't give in to Michael. The letter from the lawyer is all bluster. You are the rightful heir to the lake house, and I want you to decide what happens with it. Not your brother."

I didn't know the context of any of this, but I didn't have to.

"I chose you because I trust you. I want you to trust your-self. You have always been there for me. I know you will make the right decision."

"But what is the right decision?" Olivia whispered.

"That's not up to me," George said. "Keep the lake house or sell it. Whatever you need. I know either way, you will take care of it or ensure it ends up in the right hands. I love you, Olivia. I wish you could have even half the trust in yourself that I have in you. I wish I could stop Michael from trying to tear you down. But know that anytime you come to Bryson House, I'm here for you." George's eyes misted.

Olivia's expression mirrored his as I recounted his mes-sage.

Daniel poked an anxious head into the library, and I nodded quickly at him. "I've got to go. But remember, your grandfather loves you so much, Olivia."

She nodded, tears streaming down her cheeks. "Thank you."

"You good?" I asked George.

He wiped at his eyes but nodded. "I owe you, Celeste."

I'd collect on that later. But not all ghosts were positioned to help me out monetarily. I'd have to find out what kind of favor George can do for me. I glanced back before I left the li-brary to see the girl throw the letter into the hearth.

"Okay, I'm ready," I told Daniel.

He shook his head. "I hope the kitchen hasn't burnt down by now."

"Was it on fire when you left?"

"No."

"Well, then don't be so dramatic."

He rolled his eyes but upped his pace to speed walking. I had to trot behind him to keep up.

I spotted Lady Adelia directing a trio of ghosts to hold a door closed. I slowed, making out a faint "Again? Are you kidding me?" from the other side of the door. Was that Nic the decorator?

Adelia tilted her head in acknowledgement of me. We're on good terms, though she never needed me during my previous visits. Her matchmaking plots were more about nudging people rather than telling them directly they belonged together. But trapping someone in a room was a bit more than a nudge. Was Nic okay?

Adelia gestured for me to follow Daniel. Move along, nothing to see here.

I considered the door one more time, then continued to the kitchen, running to catch up to the anxious cook. Adelia wasn't mean-spirited. And whatever matchmaking plans she had going on with her party of ghosts were not my monkeys, not my circus.

4

Angus

WE HAD four orders of risotto on the board, and our four burners were down to one. My soul died a little each time the burner flames went out. We were trying to maintain the proper stirring technique on the rice. I could practically hear Sené yelling at me, "Always in the same direction. The same speed. No, not like that! You're not a cement mixer, you brêle."

I told myself it would be okay with the one burner. While we usually cook every order separately, since all four plates need to go out at the same time, we could cook all four portions in this one pot on this one remaining burner.

A trickle of sweat dripped down the back of my neck. I prayed that the final pilot light would remain lit a little longer. My nervous hand adjusted the knob, but the flame defied orders, getting progressively smaller.

"Sené, you need to calm down!" Like a choir of angels, Celeste's voice rang through the kitchen.

Daniel stood behind her, panting as if he had to carry her on his back the whole way.

The beautiful medium put a hand against one of her dangling gold earrings. "I've been here five seconds, and my ears are ringing. How do you guys stand it? Or I guess how did you stand it when he was alive?"

My relief at her presence mixed with dread at her insulting our resident ghost chef. I defended my old mentor. "I think he feels he has to be louder as a ghost, since we can't hear him."

"That's dumb. It doesn't matter how loud he yells. If you can't hear the dead, you can't hear him."

I glanced fervently at the flickering flame under the risotto, my hand never straying from its consistent, clockwise motion. "Celeste, I've figured that his interventions with the kitchen appliances happen when he sees us doing something incorrectly. What is the issue? What are we doing wrong now?"

"Okay, slow down," Celeste said to the space next to me. "I can't pronounce that." After a heavy sigh, she stumbled over her syllables. "So, for the lang—langrousteen,"

"The langoustine risotto with a bisque espuma," I filled in.

"Yes. That. He said it. Can we move on, please?" She paused a moment before continuing, "You need to be mixing it with a wooden spoon."

"I am!" I didn't raise it from the risotto to show her, but the wood handle was clearly visible in the grasp of my stirring hand.

"Not that one. Sené's looking for uh, Madame Bouillonne?"

Oh no.

"Is that a type of spoon?" she asked.

It wasn't a type of spoon. It was a very specific spoon. I thought the issues we were having last week were punishment for what happened to her. But he appeared to have missed that.

"So, about the Madame. Something happened." I only needed a few more seconds of stirring.

"You've got his attention," Celeste prompted.

I took the cooked risotto off the stove and began plating while I confessed, "She was washed. In the industrial washer."

Celeste jerked back, her hand returning to her ear. "Oh my god. Sené, that's a bit much. If she were murdered, then her ghost would be with you, and you could be happy together forever." She ducked, then blushed at me. "I don't know why I did that. Ghosts can't touch the living."

The pink in her cheeks nearly distracted me from the delicate work of placing the grilled scampi. I grabbed the whipping siphon, already loaded with the bisque, and topped each dish with its own cloud of shellfish essence.

"Nope. Can't feel that either," Celeste said, no doubt egging on the murderous Sené.

The servers took the dishes from the kitchen, and my body sagged in relief. The board cleared up. The gap in orders lined up with the impending start of the tree lighting ceremony. But the reprieve would be brief. And now Sené was in a vengeful mood.

"Chef," I addressed my mentor directly. "I take full responsibility for what happened to Madame Bouillonne." A newer server thought they could help with scooping the kitchen utensils in with the dining ones. But I wasn't going to say that. Everything that went wrong in this kitchen was my responsibility. It was true when I was sous chef under Sené, but it was even truer once I became head chef. "I promise I will find the perfect replacement for her. It won't be the same. We will never have a Madame Bouillonne again. But I promise, I'll make sure to get an olive wood spoon with a flat edge, exactly like the one you praised her for. And she can be the Madame's daughter. Mademoiselle Bouillonne."

"He says you can't serve the risotto anymore tonight without her replacement." Celeste flinched back. "Wait, what? It's not risotto?"

"It's langoustine risotto with a bisque espuma," I corrected with the air of a beaten donkey. "That's very important." Sené would scream at anyone who used the shortened name. *Risotto is an overdone dish from Italian amateurs. What we do is elevated. We are creating art.*

"But to not serve it anymore tonight would be complicated. The langoustine prawns are expensive. And that dish has been so popular."

Celeste rolled her eyes. "Stop being such a pretentious dick and let the people cook." Before she finished her sentence, I may have tightened, thinking she was insulting me. But no, she was talking to Sené. Then I tightened all the same. Sené took his wounded ego out on his staff.

"Chef, please," I said. "I want to do things right. Like you taught me. I'm asking for a little bit of grace. Only for tonight."

All four burners flared up in an undeniable expression of his rage. I slouched, the fight draining from my body.

"Sené, I'm going," Celeste said. "I'm meeting Sadie for the tree lighting ceremony. If you leave the kitchen alone, then I will come back tomorrow. I will spend as long as we need so you can tell everyone every single thing that isn't to your particular standards." Celeste spoke calmly, ignoring the flaming burners. Then the fire reflecting in her gray eyes took on a life of its own. "If I hear that you got in the way of the crew at all tonight, then I'm never coming back. I'm never going to help you deliver a single message to anyone. I will leave you here in the hell of your own making."

No, Celeste, you'll be leaving us all in that hell. We can't go on like this. I was in denial this morning, but I had to face the facts. If she couldn't help us with Sené, we would have to close the kitchen. Close Savoir. I would have failed the staff, the restaurant, the hotel.

But the flames lowered. Sené was listening to Celeste. She saved us at least for tonight.

Her eyes narrowed. "I'll come back tomorrow, and that's it. I have a life too, you know." She threw up her hands. "Fine, I'll come back the next day to wrap up any loose ends, but that's it."

"Thank you, Celeste." I knew Sené wouldn't be offering even that much appreciation for her help.

She gave me a tight smile. "I'll see you tomorrow." Her multipattern skirts swooshed around her legs as she turned on her heels and walked out of the kitchen.

There were only a few tickets left on the board, mostly desserts.

"We can handle the queue, Chef," Daniel said quietly by my side.

"We're almost done. I can—"

"Chef, we need you to rest before leading us through the next rush. Go take a rest for an hour." His words propped up my broken-down body like a crutch.

I gave him a grateful nod and retreated to my office. The chair squeaked as I collapsed into it.

I had to pull myself together. Falling apart had been a slow, constant process ever since Sené died. Life under his rule wasn't easy, but I knew how to handle it. I didn't know how to handle this. I wasn't ready to step up to the position when he passed. I had learned so much from him, but I still needed more time under him to become truly proficient.

His actions beyond the grave flashed a bright red light on all my incompetencies.

Aside from my frustration, it was good to see Celeste again. Her quirky confidence always lightened even my darkest days.

A few years ago, around this time, Sené yelled at me in front of everyone and ultimately banished me from the kitchen for the rest of dinner service. I stopped for a much-needed drink at the bar and ended up in a conversation with Celeste, Sadie, and the bartender. Servers joined us as they finished their shifts, and soon a rambunctious conversation grew between all of us about our favorite Christmas carols. Celeste's stool had moved close to mine to make room for the others, and the hair on my arm tingled with electricity at her proximity.

When she shared her favorite carol, I was tipsy enough to let loose a teasing admonition.

'I Want a Hippopotamus for Christmas'? That's almost as bad as saying your favorite Christmas carol is 'The Chipmunk Song'.

Her perfect Gayla Peevey impression, really hitting on the child-like pronunciations of "rhinoceroseses" and "hippopotamuseses", nearly made me spill my drink from laughing.

She had turned one of my worst days into the most fun evening I had with my co-workers in a long time. And Sené had cooled down enough to join us after the service. He treated me like the banishment never happened. He had always been hot and cold like that.

After his death, I went to several months of group grief counselling, hoping it would help. It didn't really. In one session, they kept talking about how growth sometimes required letting things go. That was the last session I attended. I figured letting go of counselling would lead to growth. Seemed more plausible than letting go of Sené. He wasn't moving on anytime soon. And I couldn't even be mad at him. I owed him for teaching me everything I knew about running a restaurant.

He may be dead. He may be haunting me from the other side. But goddamnit, I still needed him.

On the bright side, that meant I still needed Celeste's help, too.

5

Celeste

ONE DAY IN the kitchen, acting as a ghost interpreter, turned into three, turned into five, and before I knew it, a whole week had passed. I wasn't spending the entire day at Savoir anymore like I needed to at first. But Sené kept insisting I come back.

I stood with him, observing the crew hard at work during dinner service. He wasn't yelling. Wasn't hyper-fixating, hovering over someone's shoulder, watching every move they made to prepare a dish. But he emanated a cloud of malaise.

"What's wrong?" I asked.

"Something."

"Something?"

"Something's not right."

I was so tired of this nonsense. "Well, if you tell me what it is, we can fix it." The crew listened to every word I said and adjusted immediately to Sené's feedback. Yet nothing satisfied him.

"The kitchen, it is missing a—je n'sais quoi."

I scoffed. "Well, you're gonna have to sais quoi. I can hear ghosts, not read their minds."

Sené didn't answer me. Whatever. I was his interpreter, not his therapist. I brought my attention back to Angus, stationed in the middle of the kitchen, at what they called the chef deck.

He moved the chits in front of him with the deftness of a blackjack dealer, calling out orders to his crew, keeping track of exactly how long everything took. Every dish got his approval before it went out the door. He commanded the team with clarity but also kindness, recognizing everyone's strengths and contributions each night.

"He's pretty good at that, you know," I said to Sené. Understatement of the year. He looked downright sexy with his sleeves rolled up, those biceps flexing with each movement—that deep voice, confident and commanding.

"Yes, well. After ten years under my tutelage, I suppose something has worn off."

I rolled my eyes. "I'm not coming back tomorrow."

"What?" He whirled on me. "But you have to."

"You barely had any feedback for me to communicate today. The kitchen is fine. Everything is going great. Maybe you should also take a break tomorrow. Go for a walk around the grounds. Chat with the other ghosts."

"That's preposterous. I belong here."

"Sené. You can have the best trained crew in the world. They could do everything exactly like you did. But this isn't your kitchen anymore. And it never will be."

His brow furrowed with genuine hurt at my words. He stomped to the other side of the room and then through the doorway to the old kitchen. I followed him into Angus's office.

Once alone with him, Sené rounded on me. "How could you say that? And out loud, where any of them could hear? This is my kitchen. My restaurant. I built it from the ground up."

"And now you're dead. You can't run a kitchen if no one can hear you."

"That's why you need to come back."

"I don't work for you! I'm not your sous chef. I'm not your assistant. Frankly, you owe me majorly for all the time I've given you already."

"What do you want?"

I shrugged. "Have any gold buried somewhere?"

He sneered. "Do I look like a pirate to you?"

I had ghosts pay me actual fortunes back for my interpretation services before. You gotta love libertarian ghosts. They always had a stash of valuable goods hidden somewhere.

"I put everything into this place," Sené continued. "So how can you say it's not mine?"

I shook my head. I initially thought Angus stayed here instead of starting his own restaurant because Sené's passing left him in charge of Savoir. But Savoir didn't belong to Angus. I don't know why he was still here.

"So, you're pulling an If I can't have it, no one can? Then burn the place down and be done with it. Set the crew free to find jobs with decent, or at the very least, living executive chefs. Let Angus go and start his own restaurant like he's always wanted."

Sené gaped at me. "Always wanted?"

"He was so close last year. He had name ideas, menu drafts, and interested investors."

At that moment, Angus entered the office. "Celeste, is everything okay?"

"Are you telling me," Sené started, rage building, "that Angus has been plotting to become my competitor this whole time? Taking my knowledge to stab me in the back?"

"Angus, I'm sorry," I confessed to him. "I didn't know your career aspirations were a secret from Sené. I didn't think he'd react so unreasonably. But, of course, he would. He reacts unreasonably to everything."

Angus cringed. "He's really mad?"

"When was he going to tell me this?" Sené shouted. "Or was he planning on simply not showing up one day? Trotting off to his new kitchen and leaving me high and dry!" He tried to sweep the papers from the desk, but his incorporeal form had no impact on them. In fact, without any burners in the office, he couldn't do much to convey his anger to Angus. Unless I told him.

"Actually," I began, "he's come around to the idea pretty well."

Sené glared at me in complete betrayal.

I continued, "In fact, he says it's a great idea."

"Stop lying!" Sené charged me, passing harmlessly through my body and then through the wall on the other side.

I turned back to Angus, who gave me a knowing look. "He didn't really come around, did he?"

I couldn't lie to him directly, especially without the fun of it riling up Sené. It wouldn't do any good, anyway. Angus knew his mentor too well to believe me.

"Can you tell him—"

"He left," I cut Angus off. "Sorry."

His broad, strong shoulder leaned against the doorframe of the office in a moment of defeat. Then he pulled himself back upright. "Well, at least we're done with dinner service for today. That'll give him the rest of tonight to cool off." As if reading my mind, he said, "I'm hungry. Want something?"

"Yes," I said immediately.

"You weren't there for the family meal before dinner, and I made a pretty good chicken wild rice soup. There are leftovers in the pantry. I'll heat it."

"How good can it be if there were leftovers?" I teased.

"Fine. No soup for you." He turned his back toward me.

"No! I was kidding!" I ran to him and flung my arms around him without thinking. "Please feed me."

He stiffened beneath my touch. I should have let him go, but I was too deep now. And his muscles felt so good. Hard and warm and sturdy.

"I'll make you a bowl," he said after a pause. "If you let me go."

"Deal." I released him.

He disappeared into the walk-in fridge and came out with a medium-sized pot. As he warmed it up on the stove in the old kitchen, we heard the last of the crew finishing cleanup in the main kitchen and heading out. By the time steam rose from the soup, we were alone. The last people in Savoir.

I took a deep inhale. "Smells comforting." Like getting a hug from someone who isn't bothered by the fact that you're sick and germy.

He unwrapped a crusty loaf of bread. "Cut us a couple of slices of this. I'll get the final touches added to the soup."

As he returned to the fridge, I took the loaf in one hand and the knife in the other. I don't usually handle this kind of artisanal bread. I was more of a Wonder Bread kinda girl. The crust was harder than I expected. I pressed down more firmly on the knife, refusing to be bested by a baked good.

"What are you doing?" Angus returned, hands full of fresh ingredients. He dumped them on the counter and rushed over with the urgency of a lifeguard coming to halt improper use of CPR.

"You asked me to cut the bread."

"I asked you to slice it, not crush it!" He took the, admittedly slightly mangled, loaf from me and cradled it gently in his large hands.

"Is that bread or a baby?" I teased. Then I offered my own placating shushing noises. "Shhhh. Daddy's here. Daddy's got you."

Angus's face turned beet red. His stern tone failed to hide his embarrassment. "You nearly squished all her beautiful air pockets."

"But you rescued her in time. A true hero."

For some reason, my joking didn't put him at ease. Weird. Everyone loved my jokes.

Angus put the bread back on the cutting board. His hand held the loaf gently but firmly. Fingers wrapped over the rounded corners. What would they look like wrapped around something rounder? Softer? He sawed the knife in a few strong motions. The blade jutted back and forth, slicing cleanly through the bread that remained standing tall, supported in his grip, instead of crushed like in mine.

What else could he do better than I could?

My mind wandered to dirty things as Angus grated that nutmeg in smooth, regular strokes. Pulled the parsley leaves from their stems. Drizzled cream into the soup in easy circles. He could drizzle that cream over my chest. Smaller circles around my nipples.

He looked up when a moan escaped me. I stood a little straighter and blinked innocently until his attention returned to the soup.

Usually, I was a one-and-done kind of girl, but we were going to need to sleep together again. I mean, after all the time I spent in the kitchen helping out with Sené, it was the least Angus could do.

Time to settle your debts, Chef.

Okay, I needed to reel horny Celeste back. If we had sex, it would be as two consenting adults, both wanting some fun. Not a weird payment plan. Even though that idea was kinda hot.

"And voila!" Angus interrupted my thoughts, presenting two bowls of perfectly plated chicken soup.

We pulled up stools at the counter. Our spoons clinked against the ceramic dishes, and I let out an appreciative "Mmmmm" at the first bite. The chicken was so tender and moist that it practically melted on my tongue. I crunched down on the crusty bread after drenching it in the creamy, savory broth, and the change in texture was perfection. "Oh my god."

"Are you alright?"

"I'm having a moment. Don't interrupt." I slurped down another bite. The wild rice had the most delightful chew and burst with more flavor. Despite the richness, there was this hint of lemon that made each bite almost refreshing. I don't know what it was, but I had to keep going back for more. Another moan escaped me.

"Should I leave you alone with the bowl?"

"Don't leave. I'm having an out-of-body experience. I might fall off my stool." My eyes rolled back. "I don't know who I am anymore. All I know is this soup is my new god."

He chuckled. "Do you want more?"

"Please." I eagerly held out the already empty bowl.

I relished the second serving more slowly. All my muscles relaxed as much as they could while still keeping me upright. Any tension in my body got washed away by the warm broth. I knew chicken soup was healing, but this was crazy. I felt like I'd just had a full-body massage.

"You look satisfied," Angus said with more than a hint of pride in his voice.

Not completely. Not yet.

"I bet this is your special soup you make all the girls," I accused.

Here we were. Alone, at night, in the kitchen, exactly like last year. Our simmering energy when we hung out with the other hotel employees erupted in a naked frenzy the first time we found ourselves alone.

"No, it's based on a soup my mom made when I was sick. It was one of the first things I learned how to make by myself. I cooked it for my little brother when we got his cancer diagnosis. Though chicken soup isn't exactly as effective as chemotherapy."

That splashed a bucket of ice water over me. "I'm so sorry."

"Don't be. He's been in remission for years." Despite his grin, his eyes stayed cold. "Chemotherapy was really effective. And he got to be the miracle, golden boy of the family for the rest of time, so it all worked out for him."

"That sounds like it was hard for you."

"It's fine. It taught me not to expect a gold star for existing. My parents are there when it matters. Like when I graduated from culinary school, or when I was interning at Smyth in Chicago. They made a whole trip out of it."

"Do they visit you here?"

"They're coming this Christmas. They're excited to see me and my work as an executive chef." He deflated a bit.

"What?"

"Nothing."

"What are you thinking? I know it's not nothing."

"I imagined their first meal from me as an executive chef would be different."

"You mean something other than Sené's menu."

"He wouldn't allow it."

"Angus. Sené is dead. Both of you need to realize that."

"He may be dead, but he's still here. He still has his particular ways things need to be done and can make things impossible if we don't step in line."

"Are you really the executive chef then?"

"I guess not."

"Not yet. Not until you get your own place."

He laughed. "I can't leave them high and dry."

"Sené doesn't deserve your loyalty."

"Not Sené. West would have to deal with the fallout of my leaving."

Fair enough, the poor hotel manager had enough on his plate with the extra holiday crowds.

"I will start my own restaurant eventually," Angus continued, "but I need to find my replacement first. Ideally, a chef who could hear Sené's instructions." He grinned at me. "Looking for a job?"

I laughed. "I'm not a chef, and even if I were, I would never work under Sené full-time. This week has been more than enough for me, thank you. Time to focus on my real job."

"The paranormal bookshop you want to open?"

"Yes," I said with a smile. "You remembered."

"Of course." Those midnight eyes pinned me. "Is that why you're back? Cause this town would be a good place for your shop?"

"It's fifty percent about the town being a great market for a paranormal bookshop. The people here are hungry for ghost stories, and even the tourists seem to have spirits on the mind."

"And the other fifty percent?"

"Sadie." I shrugged. "She's my best friend. I can't imagine calling a place home without her."

"Makes sense." He raised his eyebrows at me. "What percent did I factor in?"

I laughed and answered honestly. "Like negative ten percent."

"Ouch. Well, no need to sugarcoat it."

"It's not my job to make things tasty. I just tell it like it is."

"I like that about you." His lips quirked back up. "Even if the truth is you are here despite me."

I shrugged. I had convinced myself that Angus had moved on from last year, and that it didn't matter anyway, cause our one-night fling hadn't meant anything. We were essentially strangers to each other.

But we weren't strangers. Over the years, during each of my visits to Sadie, Angus and I circled each other's orbits. At first, trading glances across the room, then joining the same group conversations. Eventually, we broke off for one-on-one chats during hangouts. Now, we knew too much about each other, both under our clothes and deeper too.

Best stay focused on what's beneath the clothes, though. It was easier that way.

"The soup is really good," I said unnecessarily, the empty bowl speaking loud enough. "But it would be better if you added something new. Something wild and fresh that's never been done before."

I smiled at the intrigued lean of Angus' body. Last year, our foreplay was him listening to my wild food combination suggestions. His perplexed responses always made me laugh.

"Like what?" he asked.

"Like pineapple."

He gave me exactly what I wanted, responding like my words had physically hit him in the face. "Pineapple? In chicken soup? That's the craziest thing I've ever heard."

"It'd add a bit of brightness and sweetness to it," I continued, hiding my glee at his incredulity.

"It would overwhelm the whole flavor profile."

"I've always been partial to a sweet and a meat."

"It makes no sense to throw a tropical fruit into a European soup."

"Well, I think it would be fun."

"Well, you have the palate of an alien."

That was true. And since I couldn't retort, I went with a non sequitur. "That's ridiculous. Pineapples don't grow in space."

He laughed and shook his head. "No one else can surprise me quite like you."

I took that as a compliment. "Maybe that's what you need. Maybe the recipes Sené taught you are too basic. You need to embrace the element of surprise."

"The element of surprise?"

I didn't recognize the gleam in his eyes. Skepticism perhaps.

"Yeah. You're really good at giving people exactly what they want." My eyebrows twitched up with the innuendo, and I moved a step forward. "You might surprise them with how good you can make something that seems simple, like with the chicken soup."

He nodded and matched my step.

"But surprising them with something that they didn't expect could bring you up to that next level."

Still that indecipherable expression.

"I'm sure you can do it," I said. "You just got to be spontaneous."

"Okay," he said with a small smile. His gaze was like the glow of a roaring fire on a cold winter's night: warm, intense, and inviting me to give in to the irresistible pull and close the gap between us.

Yes! Kiss me.

My eyelids fluttered closed, and I tilted my chin up.

For a kiss that never came.

I opened my eyes when he cleared his throat.

"Speaking of chicken soup, would you like the leftovers?" He gestured to the pot.

"Only if I can have all of it." And more.

Missing my tone, he shrugged. "There's like six servings left. Way too little to serve the crew again. It freezes well if you start to get tired of it."

"I won't."

He poured the soup into a large takeaway container. Our hands brushed as he passed it to me. I had a hold of it, but he didn't let go.

"I got it," I said.

One of his hands tilted my chin up. "To being spontaneous."

Finally!

Immediately, I leaned into his warmth, into his gravity. Nothing about his lips was hard or forceful. They guided mine, like the lead in a dance. My mouth opened and let him in. He held me, and I clutched his chef's jacket. Where'd the soup go? Distantly, I figured he must have put the container back on the counter, but it didn't matter if it had splattered over the floor. I was free-falling. I was floating. Somehow, both were true, like a snowflake taking its lazy, long journey from the sky to the ground. One of his hands reached for mine, and I held on for dear life, like it was the only thing keeping me from blowing away.

Oh my god, I think I like you.

Wait a second. That wasn't horny Celeste. This wasn't feeling like the start of a spontaneous sex-a-pade.

It was feeling like something more. Like something way too much more.

My racing heart veered completely off the course, and I broke away before everything crashed and went up in flames.

"I—" I had to run. Now. Every instinct screamed at me to leave.

I grabbed the container of soup with my right hand, but he still held onto my left even after I tugged at it.

His grip gave up when I wrenched away.

"I have to go."

The words had barely left my mouth before my feet shot me toward the back exit. I almost forgot my jacket in my haste to get out of there.

I couldn't process anything other than that relentless, Go, go, GO! Pushing me forward.

It was the same shouting in my head that urged me to leave last year. The all-consuming run impulse lessened by the time the funicular reached the bottom of the mountain.

When I got to my apartment, the adrenaline had faded. I put the soup in the fridge, grabbed Hippy the hippo, and stumbled into bed, exhausted.

What happened?

How did I switch from horny as hell to running for my life?

What the fuck kinda kiss was that, Angus?

It wasn't a bad kiss. A bad kiss wouldn't give me heart palpitations. It wasn't that I didn't like it. I liked it a lot. Too much.

I sighed into Hippy's soft belly.

This was last-year-Celeste's problem; fleeing the second things felt out of control. This-year-Celeste was always in control. I spent the time away talking with the therapist about it and everything. Sure, that therapist was a ghost who studied under Freud. But Dr. Waltz took my health insurance (he gave me free sessions in exchange for the occasional message to the living). At our last session, he even told me that I had achieved a greater integration of the ego.

Your id no longer runs rampant. Your superego no longer tyrannizes, and your ego now mediates with balance. You are no longer at the mercy of your neuroses.

That's what he said. So, what the hell?

I set Hippy next to me and settled down against my pillow.

It's fine. My id was balanced. My heart rate was back to normal. That was a freak incident, all because a teeny, tiny remnant of my past fear resurfaced.

Past fear.

I wasn't afraid of liking Angus.

I liked lots of things. I liked my hippo stuffie. I liked Sadie. I liked this town.

I liked Angus. Why not? Could I really imagine staying here long-term and never talking to him? Never joke with him? Never eat his cooking again?

My stomach rumbled in protest.

I could stand to have more corporal friends. Someone for Sadie to talk to at my birthday party.

I'd never had a party celebrating me before, but it was a funny image, a room full of ghosts and those two. To any outsider, it would appear that Sadie and Angus were my only guests.

Angus could make the birthday cake.

Okay, it was decided. I wasn't afraid to like Angus, because I liked my friends, and Angus was my friend.

I hugged Hippy to my chest and drifted off to sleep, where my dreams replayed the kiss with my friend. I tried to push it to the next step, but each time I did, the kiss reinforced itself, and I ended up kissing Angus all night long.

6

Angus

I SHOULDN'T HAVE kissed her.

That's all that ran through my head for five days straight. She said to be spontaneous. Clearly, that only referred to my cooking. And now I couldn't even cook. Celeste took up every corner of my mind. Her soft lips on mine. Her chest pressed against me. I hated every article of clothing between us.

But that alarm in her grey eyes when she pulled away haunted me. I saw that same panic before she left last year. I thought I'd never see her again.

At least this time, I knew she hadn't left town. I overheard Sadie say she'd had dinner at Celeste's place last night.

Did they talk about me? Did Celeste tell Sadie I practically assaulted her? What did they have for dinner? Was it the soup? Did it reheat okay?

I was obsessed and unable to focus on what really mattered: the crew and Savoir.

At least Sené had been giving us a break. We were all a little terrified when Celeste didn't come back to continue interpreting. Of course, she didn't want to come back after the stunt I pulled. Even after several days with no incidents, it felt like we had been collectively holding our breaths, waiting for the other shoe to drop.

Right before lunch service today, the pilot light flickered for ten long seconds before I brought the knob back to its home position and freaked out internally. I reviewed every action I took, trying to identify the issue Sené was calling out. I couldn't think of anything. It could be something someone in the crew did. Before I began asking the staff awkward questions, I tried the knob again, and after two clicks, the stovetop ignited.

That lunch service was particularly stressful. I didn't want to let the crew on to my inner meltdown, but they could tell something was wrong. Afterward, they insisted I take the rest of the day off.

"There are no large reservations or anything out of the ordinary for dinner," Daniel said. "Let us take care of it. We've got you, Chef."

They were the best kitchen team a man could ask for. And I'd been giving them a sub-par head chef in return.

"Thank you, Daniel." It came out a bit gruffly, but only because I was this close to unravelling entirely.

"Also, we wanted to give you this." He held out a gift bag.

"Early Christmas present?"

"Sort of."

It didn't have any tissue covering the contents: a box of chocolates next to a small bottle of whiskey.

"We know how stressed you've been, so we wanted to give you some things that might help take the edge off."

Neither chocolate nor alcohol was really my vice of choice. I used to smoke, a habit I picked up in culinary school. I tried more intense substances shortly after joining Sené's kitchen. After too many out-of-control benders, I decided to cut out everything other than the occasional drink. It had been five years since my last cigarette, and I really liked the idea of keeping that streak.

What would help take the edge off?

Sex? Piped up the baser part of me.

I quickly hid my cynical smirk with a genuine smile.

"Thank you, Daniel. This means a lot." Yet another sign of how much my crew cared about me. I needed to get them something to show my appreciation.

Before I left, I grabbed some extra ingredients they wouldn't need for dinner. Sex was off the table, so I might as well try to experiment with recipes at home. My apartment kitchen didn't have everything the professional kitchen had, but it didn't have a ghost haunting me either. And maybe a bit of cooking, away from Sené's watchful eyes and without the high pressure of a five-star kitchen's clientele, might help me de-stress.

As I drove home, I considered what dish I could try to make. I had already experimented a bit with the chicken soup. Celeste's pineapple idea was ludicrous, but it made me think of adding apples in the end to give it a sweet crunch. There were still tweaks to be made, but I liked the direction it was taking.

I did end up buying a pineapple. Not for soup, but it certainly would be a surprising ingredient in most dishes. I just needed to find the right home for it. It might not work at first, but if I tried multiple different ways, I'm sure it would click together.

Would Celeste find a way to click here with this town? A medium was the perfect addition to Summer Springs, a place infamous in certain internet circles for ghost sightings.

As if I conjured her out of the falling snow, she appeared, stepping out of the Crystal Shop.

She wore a silk slip dress under a thin jacket. No hood. No gloves. Snowflakes immediately clung to her blond hair.

The street was empty behind me, so I pulled closer to the side of the road.

"Get in!" I yelled through the open window.

She jolted at my sudden voice, then peered in and cracked a smile that washed over me from the tip of my head down to my boots.

"I only get in cars with strangers if I'm offered candy first," she said.

"Let me give you a ride."

"It's fine."

"It's snowing, and you dressed inappropriately for the weather as usual."

Her lips pursed into a thin line.

"Get in the car."

She surprised me by getting in without further argument.

"You are going to get frostbite if you keep going out like this." I pulled back onto the road and continued driving slowly. "At the very least, you'll catch a cold."

"This is me."

"What?"

"This is where I live. You're passing it."

There was still no one behind my car, so I stopped abruptly. We were two doors down from where I picked her up.

"There's a spot there if you want to get off the road." Celeste pointed to an open space.

I sheepishly pulled into it.

Celeste turned her whole body to grin at me. "Thanks for the lift."

"I was out of line," I admitted.

"Little bit."

"Sorry."

"It's okay. I really do appreciate the ride. Come up, and I'll make you hot chocolate as thanks."

She's inviting you up to her place, my horny inner voice chimed.

I'm sure she's only being nice.

But I wasn't going to miss out on the chance to see where she was staying.

She lived in a spacious studio with a good amount of light coming through south-facing windows. And best of all, it had a massive island counter in the kitchen.

The place had good bones.

But those bones hid under a complete mess. I wasn't sure how someone with so few possessions could make a place look like a tornado had run through.

"Shoes off, please," she said, kicking off her Dr. Martens.

I placed my black boots in the corner next to the door. She tossed her jacket, maybe intending it to land on her bed, but it missed by a good margin.

Her silk slip dress was sleeveless with spaghetti straps. No bra. I swallowed as I took off my own coat. There were no hangers in the closet, so I draped it over the back of the chair nearest the door.

"I got this cocoa mix as a Christmas treat for myself. You're lucky they were having a buy-1-get-1-free sale." She pulled two plastic pouches out from under the bed—powdered chocolate topped with a fat square marshmallow. The chocolate resembled dust from the world's driest garden.

I tried not to be a pompous dick about it and failed.

"Lucky me." The words came out sarcastically, and my grin was probably more of a grimace.

I caught the pouch she threw at my head. "Hey! This could have exploded, and then we'd both asphyxiated on cocoa powder dust."

"Death by chocolate. That's how I want to go."

"This chocolate?"

Celeste pulled two mugs out of two different places. A "World's Best Grandma" mug from the top shelf of her desk. A "Fuck Mondays" mug out of the oven.

I opened the fridge to find her milk. Surely, she still kept her perishables there.

"What are you looking for?"

"Milk?"

"Don't need it. This pouch has powdered milk. All we need is water."

"Oh." It sounded more like a strangled no.

I bit my lip as she poured water directly from the tap into the mugs. It was okay. The town's water came from the mountain springs, so a filter like the one I had at home wasn't entirely necessary.

Then she put the mugs into the microwave, and I couldn't contain myself.

"No kettle?"

"No need," she chirped. In a minute, the mugs came out steaming. She slid the best grandma one over to me, along with a spoon.

I gave in to my pompousness. "Two radioactive waters, hot and fresh."

"Like you've never used a microwave before."

"I do my best not to."

"Hurry up." She poured her chocolate mix into her mug and gestured for me to do the same. "Melt it in before the water cools."

I followed suit but corrected her verbiage. "Chocolate melts. This is called disintegrating."

"Tomato, potato."

"Those are different things," I muttered. "Just like melting and disintegrating."

She clinked her mug against mine, and we took our first sips together.

"Mmm," she said. But the difference between this and the sounds she made eating my soup was night and day.

"Mmm," I echoed, matching her enthusiasm. "Gritty." I gave her a full-toothed smile, chock-full of brown bits. Celeste laughed and coughed on her second sip.

"It is a little more watery than I expected for seven dollars."

I choked. "Seven dollars! You were had."

"It was for two."

"And they called it a sale. I call it highway robbery."

She gave the mugs a small smile. "Hot cocoa was always the thing that made it feel like Christmas. Most of the people I stayed with made it at least once during the season."

"Was it gritty like this?"

"Almost always. But some people had their own twists. My foster mom, when I was twelve, made cocoa with cinnamon and a hint of chili. When I was fourteen, I was staying with my uncle, and he added some adult fun to the pot for me and my cousins." She laughed. "We were way too young for that amount of whiskey."

"How many different people have you lived with?"

"They ping ponged me around to so many distant family members, I stopped counting. The foster families I stayed with were usually okay. At least if it didn't work out with them, I got moved to another family in the area, so I could stay in the same school. But then they'd find some second-cousin-twice-removed and convince them to take me in. And off I'd go across the country again."

No wonder it was such a struggle for her to stay put in one place. She never had that opportunity as a child. But she was trying now. That meant it was something she really wanted.

"Wait! We didn't put our marshmallows in," she said. "That'll make all the difference."

I rescued the fluffy squares from a watery grave. "These marshmallows are the one thing the producers splurged on making these mixes." Their delicate bounce gave away their origin. "I bet they sourced these from the confectioner in town so they could pass the whole thing off as locally sourced."

"They were from the Summer Springs souvenir shop," she admitted.

"We're saving these, and I'm making you a proper cup of hot chocolate."

"Can a top chef make chocolate out of ten-cent ramen? Cause that's all I have."

I had ingredients in my trunk. And the furnished apartment Celeste rented also came with the dishes we needed for our mini cooking session.

"Hot chocolate is supposed to be thick, rich, and luxurious," I informed her when I returned.

Her eyes twinkled. "You like your hot chocolate like you like your men?"

"If I'm going to be with a man, he better be rich."

"Don't forget thick."

"Necessary to keep up with what I've got."

Okay, the banter had officially gone too far. Celeste smirked, but her blush betrayed her nonchalance. The way she bit her lip reminded me of her expression during our encounter last year, when she took my hard length out.

My pants got tighter, and I focused on getting the plastic off the gift box of chocolates. I wanted to pull her close, so she could feel the effect she had on me. Instead, I gave myself a mental slap across the face. Get it together, man.

Because of what happened last time I spontaneously kissed her, I would keep my hands to myself, unless expressly asked otherwise.

I opened the box of chocolates and pulled out the pure chocolate pieces. Celeste nabbed a piece of nougat and popped it between her full pink lips. I busied myself by emptying my tote of the ingredients from the restaurant kitchen. I took out a bottle of whole milk from the local dairy farmer.

Celeste exclaimed in delight when I pulled out the pineapple.

"Don't get too excited. I'm not putting this in the hot chocolate."

Her mouth curved in the cutest pout I'd ever seen. "Why must you tease me with my favorite fruit?"

"I'll still serve it to you. As a side snack to the hot chocolate. Have you ever had Abacaxi before?" She shook her head. "It's Brazilian grilled pineapple. They coat it with sugar and cinnamon and then baste it with a brown sugar cinnamon butter glaze while grilling it."

"That sounds amazing."

"I'll leave some of the chocolate to drizzle over. It's not the Brazilian way."

"But it's our way now." She grinned. "I didn't realize you cooked Brazilian food. I thought it was all French food."

"French Cuisine is my specialty. But I still eat and learn about all the cuisines I can."

I started heating the milk on low and added a cinnamon stick to imbue some of the spice flavor. The second pot I filled with water, and while I waited for it to boil, I began preparing the pineapple for frying.

"Is French cuisine what you studied in culinary school?"

"No. It became my specialty during the years I worked with Chef Sené."

"So, when you open up your own restaurant, is it going to be French Cuisine?"

I paused from slicing the fruit. "I thought so. But now I'm not so sure."

Celeste waited for me to continue. I organized my thoughts as I finished seasoning the pineapple with sugar and cinnamon.

"I thought I knew who I was. What kind of chef I was. But it all went out the window when Chef Sené died."

She leaned in, but I didn't know what else to say. The butter in the pan was melted and sizzling by that point, so I slipped the pineapple slices in and began melting chocolate in a metal bowl over the simmering water. The only sounds for a few minutes were the sizzling pineapples and the scrape of my spoon against the bowl as I stirred.

"I think you are limiting yourself to the best he could do in the kitchen. But you were always a better chef than him."

I gave her a sideways glance. "You're saying that because I was sober enough to satisfy your munchies last year, while Sené was higher than you were."

"No. I'm saying it because it's true."

I took a deep breath as I turned off the heat on the pineapple and melted chocolate. "Sené built Savoir from the ground up, and I can barely keep the lights on."

"Because he's been sabotaging you. Angus, I tried Savoir's food under Sené. And I've tried it under you. Yours is better. Your chicken soup is better than anything on that pretentious French menu. And you're a better head chef to your crew."

I focused on stirring the chocolate. I couldn't let Celeste see how embarrassed I was to hear all this.

"You're more than ready for your own restaurant," she said with finality when I didn't answer her.

"I can't leave Savoir and Bryson House in the lurch. Not to mention, there aren't good options in town right now for a new restaurant."

"What about the PF Chang's over on 3rd and Clark?"

Locals considered that place cursed. Over the past five years, seven different chain restaurants closed down.

"I thought only locals knew about that damned corner," I said with a smile.

"I hear things. And I'm hoping to be a local soon anyway."

"It's simply a matter of time."

She smiled. "I can scope the place out to see if the so-called curse is bad franchise management, or if there is an upset ghost."

I would like to continue needing Celeste's help beyond Sené. I nearly asked her out on a date to PF Chang's right then and there. Then, I remembered her reaction to my suggestion that we continue seeing each other after sharing that one incredible night last year.

"I'd take any help you can offer," I said neutrally. "And what about your paranormal shop? Have you seen the empty storefront on Main?"

"Every day since I've arrived," she admitted. "I took your advice. I spent a few weeks in Vegas and helped some ghosts haunting the casinos there in exchange for their help cheating at the poker tables. I made it out of town with a tidy sum."

"That's amazing!"

"Thank you."

"Next thing I know, you're going to tell me you opened a bank account."

"That's next year's goal," she said, hand waving away.

"You could also put that money in an investment account."

"Too much financial speak."

"Or at least a high-yield savings account."

"Next year's goal!"

"Alright, okay!"

"But I did take another step recently." She beamed at me. "I talked the crystal shop lady into giving me a job."

"Well done."

"Getting to know the local businesses and potential future clientele. Like you said."

"I'm proud of you." I really was.

I had advised her to find a ghostly clientele that could actually pay her for her work. She came up with the idea for Vegas poker all on her own.

Mixing the melted chocolate into the cinnamon milk, I couldn't help the excited warmth that bubbled up inside. Her dreams aligned so perfectly with mine. We could wake up together, go to our own businesses, and then spend the evenings catching each other up on our days at our dream jobs.

"Is that supposed to be overflowing?" Celeste pointed to the pot of milk.

I took it off the heat and mentally chastised myself for letting it come to a boil.

"Sorry, that's a mess I could have avoided."

Celeste laughed and ran a rag under the faucet. "This is something I can help with instead of sitting around distracting you."

I liked the distraction, though.

By the time she'd finished clearing the mess, I had finished combining the melted chocolate with the spiced cream and had drizzled the rest of the chocolate over the fried pineapple slices.

"Bon appétit."

We took sips from our mugs. The cocoa was thick and chocolatey, like I was used to, but with the added spice from Celeste's suggestion.

"Mmm, that's good," she said, but it wasn't as enthusiastic as I had hoped.

"What's wrong?"

Surprise lit her eyes. "Nothing's wrong."

"I don't buy it."

"Seriously." She laughed. "It just tastes so much like my old foster mom's hot chocolate, I was transported for a second. She was my favorite. The first adult who made a real effort to get to know me."

Celeste's smile faded, and her gaze focused on something far away. There was a sad end to that story. But before I could ask, she reset her eyes on me.

"You know what's wrong? This isn't surprising enough. This is standard Mexican cocoa. I want something more special."

"We could add the marshmallows." I'd forgotten to top our mugs with them.

"Not special enough. I want this hot cocoa served to me," her eyes twinkled mischievously. "On fire!"

"Hot chocolate flambe?" I didn't have the heart to tell her that it had probably been done before, as a seasonal drink in some bar or another. She looked too excited. "Okay, we'll need alcohol to fuel the fire."

"Whiskey!" Celeste said, delighted, as I pulled out the bottle from my gift bag. "Like—"

"We are not putting as much as your irresponsible uncle."

"He wasn't irresponsible. Just an alcoholic."

"Those things are mutually inclusive."

I poured less than a shot into our mugs over the marshmallows, and Celeste pulled a lighter from her pocket.

"There you go," I said as the flames danced happily. The smell of toasted marshmallow filled the room. My internal safety marshal sounded the alarm at the sight of the fire and chided me for not checking first. "You don't happen to have an extinguisher, do you?"

Celeste was already bringing the cup to her lips as if to taste the flames. "What for?"

7

Celeste

THE FIRES IN our drinks burned out quickly, despite Angus's concerns.

"You put a pitiful amount of whiskey in there," I said as the flames died. "My uncle would be ashamed."

"I'll accept that as a compliment, thank you."

We clinked mugs, and the next sip of cocoa took over my senses. The cinnamon and hint of whiskey reminded me of the hot chocolates of my childhood, but really, this belonged to a league of its own. The quality of the chocolate and the milk was far beyond any drink I'd had before. The fire had toasted the marshmallows perfectly, leaving them crispy on the top and melty on the inside. Almost like drinking a s'more. The whiskey also added a hint of smokiness, which increased the cozy campfire vibes.

The bite of pineapple provided a zing that woke my tongue up from the sleepy coziness of the rich cocoa. Pineapple was my favorite fruit, but it had never tasted so good before. The cinnamon sugar coating paired perfectly with the spiced drink.

"That is the face I wanted to see," Angus said proudly.

"Shh, don't distract me." Each bite and sip brought me closer to the edge of a food-gasm. By the time I'd finished, I floated in another dimension of satiated bliss.

"You talk pretty fondly of that uncle." Angus brought me back to earth abruptly. I could have stayed in that post-food heaven a while longer. "I mean, considering that situation didn't work out long term," he finished.

"Yeah, well. He wasn't the one who sent me away. CPS heard about that hot chocolate he served us, and that was the end of that." I wiped my hands, sticky with pineapple syrup, on a napkin. "I tend to look back more fondly on the people who didn't actively reject me."

Angus's blue eyes clouded with anger and sadness. I didn't like getting pity for my less-than-normal upbringing, but Angus's response didn't feel as passive as the *oh, poor you* reactions I was used to. He seemed angry that he didn't have a time machine to go back and change the past.

"It's not fair," he said.

"I don't hold on to grudges," I replied, gently. "It doesn't help anything."

"You were a kid. How could so many people reject a kid?"

Many of them were my blood relatives. But I set that aside, as I'd always done. "I was a weird kid who could talk to ghosts. Most people couldn't deal with that." I shrugged. "I'm an adult now. All my experiences have shaped me into who I am today. Someone who doesn't get excited at the prospect of someone else making a home for me. If I'm to have a home in this town, it'll be because I made it for myself."

His expression held a mix of respect with a hint of something bittersweet.

"What?" I prodded.

He braced himself as if pulling off a Band-Aid. "I would never send you away. I'd do the opposite."

What would that be? "You'd chase me?"

His midnight blue eyes pierced mine. "If you wanted me to, I'd chase you to the ends of the earth."

Warmth spread across my cheeks and down my neck to my toes. The electric heat between us was too much, and I broke away.

Without missing a beat, he casually began to clear the dishes from the counter and put them in the sink.

"Wait! You did the cooking, which means I do the dishes," I said.

"I over-boiled the milk. It's my mistake that's created an extra crusty rim that'll need serious elbow grease to get off."

I hip-checked him to get access to the sink. "Nice try. You sit over there and let me work."

"I'm taking the pot with me."

I tried to snatch it from him, but his ironclad grip wouldn't give in. He took a seat across the counter from me and got to work.

"Has anyone ever told you that you hold onto things too tightly?"

His mouth opened as if to deny it. Instead, he said quietly, "Someone's got to hold things together. Or else everything falls apart."

Everything? "That's a lot of pressure to put on yourself."

"I'm a chef. We thrive under pressure."

"To keep a kitchen together for a busy restaurant. That's more than enough pressure for one person."

"In every relationship, someone's got to be the one holding on."

As if he saw my twitch at the "r" word, he clarified, "My parents were busy with my younger brother. So, I needed to be the one to make them notice me. Sené was busy with his kitchen, so I was the one who needed to make the appointment with his doctor and make sure that he went." His gaze fell. "And it was on me to realize he was hiding something when he got his diagnosis. But I didn't. And by the time he finally told me, it was too late to do anything about it."

"Why was it on you? None of that was your fault."

He gritted his teeth and focused on the crusty pot with renewed vigor.

I put my hand over his. I always avoided his penetrating blue eyes; they seemed to be able to look too deeply into what I would rather keep hidden. But now it was I who was able to see through to his soft side.

I knew about his younger brother, but I didn't understand before how that turned into a fear of letting go. His steadfastness and reliability terrified me, but when he focused his attention on something else, I loved to see it. His loyalty made him vulnerable. And I was falling in love with this vulnerable man.

Wait.

What?

That sweet feeling, as if gentle music played in the background, came to a record-scratching halt. The cocoa-induced warmth in my belly turned cold, and a shadow passed over the room.

Angus also reacted to the vibe shift.

"Are you okay?" he asked.

Sure, I was okay. Why wouldn't I be okay? The air was simply getting really thin, like I'd been transported to a mountaintop.

"I'm fine." It came out relatively normal, despite my lack of eye contact.

I'm not in love with him. I'm not in love with anyone. I'm safe. I'm strong. I can stand on my own, like I've always done.

After swallowing, breathing came easier, and I was able to lift my head again. Angus's night sky eyes emanated worry. His perfect lips pursed in such a way that drew more attention to his carved jawline.

"Are you sure?" he asked.

How could concern look so sexy?

He moved as if to reach for me, and I jumped up from my seat before he could feel how hot I was getting, like I would burst into flames at his touch. "I'm good. Just don't want to sit still. Ever feel like that?"

He tilted his head. "Sometimes. Like when I can't sleep and end up spending the night cooking in my kitchen."

I didn't want to cook. I wanted to run. It was the same urge that propelled me after our kiss. But I had already handled that. And I wasn't going to run from my own apartment simply because Angus was looking at me all sweet and heart-throbby.

"I'm antsy, like I want to run away." At his startled expression, I joked, "Maybe I should do laps around the kitchen island."

"Would that help?"

"Nah. That's not running away. That's cardio." I made a blegh face to express my disdain for exercise.

"I could chase you."

To the end of the earth?

My heart sped up as the electricity between us returned.

No, no. Why do I need to make this so serious? He's simply proposing a chase around my apartment. A little tag to help release my pent-up energy.

That could be fun.

I didn't say anything, but my feet inched into position. And when he lunged for me, they were ready.

However, I wasn't ready for the gleeful squeal that burst out. I sounded like a kid running down the stairs on Christmas morning. Redirecting my nervous adrenaline into this game filled me with a pleasure I couldn't articulate.

Angus's long strides were no match for how quickly I could pivot around the corners of the square counter. I kept him on the far side of the island, modulating my speed so he couldn't spin around and have a shorter distance to cover to get me. I got my laughter under control, though barely.

Angus's breath got heavy, and he paused, observing me over the counter, adjusting his strategy. He grinned as impressed with me as I was with myself that I could outlast him.

Then he arranged the counter chairs to create some obstacles for me before bursting back into a sprint.

The time it took me to navigate the chairs gave him enough of an edge. My panting laughter took on a manic edge as I tried to get the distance between us back, but he was gaining. His hand reached out. In another second, he'd have me.

"No!" I squealed, not ready for the game to end. "Stop it!"

He halted in his tracks, and before I knew it, I was on the opposite side of the counter from him again. We both stared at each other, chests heaving. And I realized in my desperation for the chase to continue, I had stopped our game.

"I—" I glanced down, embarrassed. "I didn't mean it."

His lips quirked into a crooked smile. "Okay. If we're gonna play like this, we need a word for when you do mean it."

A safe word. A grin spread across my face as the implications set in.

My early freak-out was at the thought I might be in love. It wasn't love. I was simply horny. And now this game between us could be more than a bit of tag. I clenched my thighs together at the thought of how far I wanted this to go. But we did need a safe word.

"Okay. Anthropocene."

He blinked in surprise but didn't question me. "Alright."

The game was back on. But instead of continuing to chase me in laps around the kitchen, he climbed onto the counter. I yelped and clamored to get away, but outmaneuvering him around corners was my winning strategy, and there were no more circular paths in my studio that I could lead him through. I ended up in the farthest corner from him I could get, which happened to be my bed. I burrowed under the mountain of clothes and blankets piled up on it.

I squirmed around as he pulled item after item off.

"Good god, woman, how many blankets does one person need?"

He slowed down as if he wanted to relish the act of unwrapping a present, instead of tearing away the entire pile in one motion. The extra minute was all I needed to slither out of my dress. When he unveiled my head, I let one bare shoulder out.

He pulled back for a second. Surprised, but the want in his eyes made a wave of heat gush between my legs.

I sat up enough to expose my second shoulder and let the covers slip past my nipples. Then waited for his next move.

Eventually, he pulled his gaze back up to mine. An insatiable hunger pulsed between us. With a slow grin, he undid the front of his button-up shirt and slid it off. My mouth watered at the sight of his chest, his biceps. I followed the lines of his abdomen down, but his hands made no moves to unbutton his pants and show off the hard bulge beneath.

I raised an eyebrow at him, and his lifted in return. A silent you go first.

Oh no. That's not how this was going to go.

I ducked back under the covers, slithering onto my stomach.

"Hey!"

I shivered with delight as his weight pressed into the mattress, his hands running over me with only a sheet between us. He uncovered my head and ran kisses over my shoulders and down my back. His hard dick ground against my ass, and when I looked back, his eyes shone like a predator about to devour his prey.

It was so fucking hot.

He turned me, and his mouth went down to my exposed breasts, kissing and lightly biting my nipples. His hands grazed my purple bikini briefs, the last piece of clothing I left on, and he began moving down my stomach, but I pulled him back up.

I loved getting eaten out as much as the next girl, and I knew he was good at it. I stored the memories of last year's encounter in 8K resolution in my spank bank. But right now, I needed him inside me. I hoped my grip on his cock, still frustratingly encased in his jeans, made that clear.

With heavy breaths, he got up to finally take them off.

"There are condoms in the hamper," I said in a voice that was a little too excited to be sultry.

He straightened the overturned laundry basket, revealing the fresh box. A courtesy move-in gift from Sadie. That sneaky minx always knew.

He got out a condom and slipped it on as soon as he was fully naked.

Fuck, I wanted him.

But remember what happened last time? A small, frustrating voice piped up, accompanied by another rush of adrenaline telling me to run.

I remember what happened last time. I got my brains pounded out of me better than I'd ever had before or since, and I would really like another go at that, thank you very much.

But with the safe word still in play, I let myself give in to the rush of the moment and twisted around, scrambling toward the edge of the bed. It would be very Greek myth for our game of tag to continue with us naked as nymphs.

For better or worse, it didn't get that far.

"Oh no, you don't!" His grip on my ankle was gentle but firm.

I squeaked as he pulled me back across the bed like I weighed nothing. Trapped under his body, I kept squirming, now from my need for him. My last scrap of clothing shifted lower with my wriggling before his hands pulled them off completely.

I stilled, dripping wet and ready, breathless with anticipation.

He gripped my chin and turned my head to scan my eyes. I hadn't said the word, but he needed that one more bit of confirmation that I wanted this.

I kissed his open mouth, and he kissed back hard, then thrust into me harder.

I moaned in pure bliss and met him each time. We fucked in perfect rhythm with each other, moving to new positions driven by the overwhelming urge to get closer, go deeper. His grunts propelled my climax forward, pushing me toward a cliff. I squeezed around him until I tipped over the edge, and every tightened muscle released.

I was back in that place his first kiss sent me, between floating and falling, but magnified by a thousand. Wave after wave of pleasure pulsed through me. When I thought it was ebbing, the shaking grunt of his release sent more shuddering bouts of ecstasy through me.

He held me tight, and I didn't feel trapped or overcome with the need to run.

Maybe my body was too exhausted by all the chasing and fucking, but for once, I was content to lie, secure and at ease, in Angus's strong, protective embrace.

8

Angus

THE SUN STREAMING through the window woke me, and for a second I couldn't tell where I was. I'd hung blackout curtains on my windows specifically so that my rare sleep-in days wouldn't be interrupted like this.

Celeste's blond hair, shimmering in the light of her apartment, oriented me. I lay quietly on the pillow, observing how her long tresses fell over the edge of the bed, picturesque as a Renaissance painting.

She stirred and turned over, facing me.

"How long have you been watching me sleep, you creeper?" she asked with a wry smile.

"I woke up less than a minute ago. You have excellent timing." Or we're perfectly in sync.

Like last night.

A slight shiver went through me, and my mind started racing, disrupting the unusual peace I woke up with.

Was it as good for her as it was for me?

Did she really want that to happen?

Did I push her?

Did I take things too far?

The questions paused at Celeste's yawn. Her body stretched languidly as a cat.

"Why'd you choose Anthropocene for the stop word?" I asked.

She laughed. "It refers to humans' impact on the climate. It was the least sexy thing I could think of in the moment."

A relieved chuckle escaped me, and I relaxed back into the pillow. She wanted sex when she chose the word. We were on the same page. And despite what my anxiety wanted me to believe, I knew it had been good for her. I felt her pulsing climax around me. Fuck, I was getting hard again.

But one loud fear kept me from initiating round two: What if she leaves again?

It wasn't a possibility I could easily dismiss. She left the last time we had sex. My body tensed at the sudden stabbing ache blooming between my ribs. I couldn't let go of that lingering pain from when I learned she'd left town.

"Is something wrong?" she asked.

I blew a long breath out. "Nothing." I propped up on my elbow to face her. "I want you to know that this is cool. It was fun, but it doesn't have to be more than this." You don't need to be afraid of me. You don't need to run away.

She smiled. "Nothing serious."

"Totally casual."

"Just between friends." She seemed happy with that, at least on the surface. But underneath, I sensed discontent in her body language. Maybe that was wishful thinking.

Or did she want to be more than friends?

I wanted to be more than friends.

She picked up her stuffed hippo and fiddled with its ear. "I don't have a lot of friends. Who are living at least."

"You have Sadie."

"Yes. She's the best."

"Did she give you that?" I touched the toy in her hands.

"Oh, no. My foster mom gave me this. The one who put cinnamon in her hot chocolate." She stroked its worn fabric face. I let the silence grow, waiting for her to continue. "She was the only foster parent to try to get to know me. They found a new cousin during my placement with her, but she had mentioned wanting to adopt me, and my cousin was like, 'I don't need an extra mouth to feed.' But then she died a couple of weeks before Christmas. The rest of the family didn't like it when I said I could still speak with her. The social worker came to pick me up on Christmas Eve."

I put my lips against her hair, thinking of little Celeste, so hopeful to have a true family for Christmas, only to be whisked away again to start another new school mid-year in a new town.

I couldn't hold back. "They could've dealt with their discomfort long enough not to send a little girl away on Christmas Eve."

She hugged the hippo to her chest. "They were grieving. I wasn't making it easier. And at least they gave me the present she bought for me before she passed. I unwrapped it on Christmas day, but I wish I had unwrapped it right there on their doorstep, where her ghost could see how much I appreciated it. She might have sung it with me one last time."

'I Want a Hippopotamus for Christmas'—her favorite carol. I made fun of her for keeping such a childish song as her favorite in adulthood.

A smile bloomed over my face. She did hold on to things after all. She didn't drop everything. Celeste held onto the things that were truly important to her. The hippo she took with her everywhere. And Sadie, whom she kept returning to.

Hope sparked that I could be on that short list, too.

"I'd like to get you something for Christmas," I blurted out.

Her eyes widened with nervousness. "You don't have to do that."

I messed up. I might as well have been totally honest and told her that I was falling for her. It would have gotten a similar response.

She glanced at the window, jumped out of bed, and all too quickly, tossed a dress over her naked body. Then she opened the window and leaned out. After a moment, she shouted, "I'll be right there." Shut it, then turned to me. "I'm needed at the hotel. You've got to go."

Was this a show to get out? An excuse? I had to trust that Celeste wouldn't feel the need to lie to me to get me out of her apartment.

"Sure," I said, trying for an easy-going tone. I got dressed. "Maybe I'll see you again at the hotel then?" So much for easy-going.

"Maybe," she replied lightly, but an undeniable distance emanated from her.

I did my best not to take it personally when she hurried me out of her place.

"I can give you a ride up to the hotel," I offered.

"No!" she said, then blushed. "I like taking the funicular."

And she needed space from me. At least she wasn't running, merely walking away really fast.

I sighed and got to work getting the snow off my car. A plow had come through already to clear the road.

I could continue home. Unwind and cook in my own kitchen on my day off. But in our haste to leave Celeste's apartment, I'd left the ingredients in her fridge. That was okay. At least she now had some real food in her home.

I could drive up to the hotel. Help my crew out with breakfast or try some experimenting in the old kitchen. But that risked running into Celeste when I wasn't sure she was ready.

I drove to the town's farmers' market. In the summertime, it opened daily, offering new produce and goods for sale, along with bustling crowds of tourists and locals. In the winter, they held it weekly, and the same farmers selling their hardier produce were outnumbered by the local artisans with non-perishable pieces to sell.

Many chefs extol the virtues of farmers' markets as a source of inspiration. The different local ingredients helped conjure ideas of seasonal dishes, but nothing inspired me like Celeste's wild palette. Last year, she challenged me to make chicken that would prompt people to respond, "Tastes like crocodile."

Yesterday's hot chocolate paired surprisingly well with the tropical fruit side dish. Another thing I wouldn't have thought up without Celeste. Last night, I dreamed of more desserts that paired an after-dinner, decadent drink with a sweet, tangy bite to offset the richness.

Celeste unlocked a creative side to my cooking that I hadn't had since I was a child. I wanted to meet more of her crazy requests. I wanted to hear her moan with each bite. And then chase her down and make her moan even louder in bed.

I zipped up my coat, grateful that it was long enough to cover my stiffening parts, as I recalled last night. That was the best sex of my life. Even better than last year.

But was it worth the sting of rejection afterward? Was it worth risking Celeste's ability to stay in this town and pursue her dream?

Thinking of Celeste's future paranormal shop, I backtracked a couple of steps instead of passing the crystal shop booth.

Rocks and stones of all colors and sizes stood artfully arranged on the table.

"Let me know if there is anything I can help you with," the woman behind the booth said, barely looking up from her romance novel.

Celeste said she got a job with this shop. Would she run this booth sometimes? I imagined coming by under the pretense of getting some local ingredients, stopping at her booth to chat. Convince her to come up to Savoir to grab a quick bite.

The shopkeeper regarded me. How long had I been standing here, taking in the view of the rest of the market? I focused on the rocks. Pretended I was here to check them out. And after a minute or so of establishing I was normal, I would leave.

"I can usually peg crystal people. Which helps identify my customers." She winked. "But I didn't peg you."

I returned a hesitant laugh. "I'm shopping for someone else." I picked up a shiny stone.

"Friend or girlfriend?"

"She's just a friend." I don't know why I spoke so quickly. Celeste couldn't hear me.

The shopkeeper raised her eyebrows like she didn't believe me.

"And you want it to be something more?"

"I can't—she can't be in a relationship."

"Why not?"

"She needs space."

"Hmm. Whereas you like to hold on to things as tight as you can?"

How did she know?

She tossed a pointed glance at my fist, clenching the crystal from the table. White knuckles betrayed the intensity of my grip.

Apologetically, I put it back on the table. "I don't think we should be in a relationship anyway. I've been burned by her before."

"And you're hanging onto that too."

"Well, I've learned my lesson. Isn't that better than making the same mistake twice?"

The shopkeeper shrugged. "You might not be a crystal person, but can I interest you in a salt lamp? It absorbs negative energy and can improve your mood."

Alright, thanks for calling me a negative grouch.

I turned to walk away. "That's okay, thank you."

"Something else about rock crystals," her tone stopped me. "They go through a process called efflorescence, where they flake off their outer layers. This removes impurities and helps the crystal grow." She blinked. "You've heard this before?"

"I've never heard of efflorescence."

"No. I'm talking about a snake shedding its skin. A bird mottling its feathers. Letting go of what no longer serves you so that you can grow."

They did talk about that in the grief counseling I attended briefly after Sené died. My old boss was a dick, but his sudden passing left a pit in my stomach. The sessions didn't really help fill it, though. I stopped going when they talked at length about releasing our loved ones. As if it were my fault, Sené haunted the kitchen. Not to mention this casual way they discussed letting go, like it was so easy to drop the pain of losing someone.

Like you would even want to. That's the equivalent of saying they didn't matter.

But maybe that wasn't what they meant by letting go.

"I hadn't heard it like that."

It wasn't about letting go of everything. You hold on to what's important. But you let go of what's holding you back. It seemed so obvious now. Something so natural even rocks did it.

"Thanks," I told her. The rock salt lamp had a pleasant, warm glow. I didn't believe in energies, but I bought it to remind me of efflorescence.

9

Celeste

ADELIA WAS SO worried about Sadie that she sent a message to me through Terrance, who passed it along to Main Street Maggie, the town crier for the paranormal side of Summer Springs.

I hated that Sadie was going through a depressive spell, but I did appreciate the excellent excuse to jump out of bed and get some space from Angus. The sex was awesome, but the morning talk was getting to be a little too claustrophobic.

Seeing Sadie, pale, smelling of booze, and buried under blankets triggered a focused surge of protectiveness. All the distractions in my personal life fell away as I talked my best friend off the ledge of her own relationship drama. And now, with hands deep in soil, at home in the greenhouse, the color returned to her cheeks. Sadie was coming back to life more and more.

"Thanks, Celeste," she said. "I think that's the best way I could tell Clive about my auras."

"I still don't know why you're so worried," I said. "Being honest with him isn't going to kill the sparks in your auras. If it did, then there wouldn't have been sparks to begin with."

"Those sparks are already dead."

"Then I would see the ghost of them, wouldn't I?"

She flicked dirt at me.

"Hey, that's for your roses. I don't need the nutrition."

She had developed the most beautiful deep-purple Christmas roses that could withstand the bitter winter snow. I was helping her pot them to donate to the park.

"I've talked enough about Clive and sparks for today," Sadie said. "How have you and Angus been?"

"Angus? He's been fine. I think Sené is finally giving the kitchen crew some space. Hopefully, they don't need my help in the kitchen anymore. Everything's great. And normal. And fine."

I avoided eye contact, focusing instead on a particularly clumpy patch of soil. If I looked at Sadie, she would be able to read my mind.

"You guys fucked didn't you?" she asked.

Goddammit. "Did my aura give it away?"

"Oh yeah. You've got finally-fucked-him aura."

"Finally? We already slept together once before."

"A year ago. I mean, finally, since you got back."

"You say that like it was bound to happen."

"Cause it was. You're welcome for that box of condoms by the way."

I ignored her wink. "Alright, it happened. And we aren't going to let it get in the way of our friendship."

"Friendship." Sadie held out two dirt-covered hands and made air quotes around the word.

"Stop that."

"Was it as good as last time? Did you have fun?"

I still got goosebumps thinking about how hard I had cum. "It was even better than last time."

"Aww. I'm happy for you."

"It's not serious."

"Sounds not serious."

"You know I don't do long-term relationships."

"I don't know that, actually."

I stared at her. "Name one person."

"Me. It's been twenty years since we met. If that's not long-term, what is?"

"You're different," I mumbled.

"Why can't Angus be different, too?"

I blew a wisp of hair from my face. "He takes things too personally. Like if I run off in the middle of the night, it'd hurt his feelings. You wouldn't care."

She scoffed. "Yeah, right, I don't care."

For the first time, Sadie's weaponized sarcasm was directed at me. "Wait, do you care when I leave?"

"I mean, I'm used to it. I understand you're dealing with a lot when you need to go suddenly. But it still hurts to be dropped without so much as a goodbye. Most times, I don't even know why you left. And I can't get a hold of you. So yeah, it hurts."

My stomach sank. "I didn't realize."

She shrugged. "It would be nice to get a call."

Sadie had already put up with so much, and to top it off, she got me for a shitty friend.

"I will," I promised. I would do better.

"Or you won't need to. Cause you'll stay here for good and never want to leave," Sadie said lightly.

I laughed, but my gut sank even lower. Why? That was the plan after all. "I mean, you know me. I'm an air-spirit. I go where the wind takes me."

She narrowed her eyes. "And where does starting a shop fit into that?"

"Well, I can have other employees." But that wasn't in my dreams. I imagined being the one behind the desk, not starting a business and flitting off like some franchise owner.

Sadie regarded me patiently until I finally admitted, "I'm scared. I've never stayed in one place before. How do I know this is the right place for me?"

"You know, some plants grow these specialized stems called runners. They grow horizontally from the base and establish roots in the new soil. Strawberries are like this. Also, wisteria." Sadie gestured to the beautiful purple flowers hanging off the trellis behind us. "Just because you put down roots somewhere doesn't prevent you from putting new roots down somewhere else. But you need a strong foundation to grow from."

"If the plant is in the wrong soil to begin with, it will be too weak to grow a runner and embed itself somewhere else." I frowned up at the wisteria. Did Sadie forget what she told me about this plant last year?

Its beautiful blooms make people forget they are an invasive species. Climbing up trees and sucking the life from them.

Mistletoe was the same, despite the kissing traditions associated with it.

Kissing Angus was becoming a bit of a holiday tradition, too. Was it as harmful to the hotel's ecosystem? Would I be if I planted myself here?

"Was that the last rose?" I asked, brushing my hands together to dislodge the soil and my spiraling thoughts.

"Yeah. Do you want to get lunch?"

"Celeste!" A voice hissed at me from the door. Sené waved me over.

"Sorry, there's a dead chef who needs me."

"You've got all the chefs in this place in the palm of your hand," Sadie joked.

I blew her a kiss with said dirty palm and went over to Sené.

"It's nice to see you outside the kitchen," I greeted him. "Enjoying the rest of the grounds?"

"They're fine. George has been introducing me to the other ghosts."

I smiled, thinking of the kindly grandfather ghost in the library. "I'm glad you're making friends."

"Well, they won't get off my back. I tell one story about cooking for the Pope in '87, and it's all 'Oh, tell us more about Italy! Where else have you been? Who else have you cooked for?' It's tedious entertaining les plèbes."

I rolled my eyes at his pompous air. But I could tell he faked this put-upon attitude. He was loving being the center of attention.

"Well, as long as it's keeping you out of the kitchen." And out of Angus's hair. I guess they didn't need me for the case of the haunted chef anymore. I mentally pulled my stomach back up and stapled it into place. Enough with this random ache. Interpreting for Sené had gone on long enough.

"I actually have one last message I need you to give Angus," Sené said.

"What? Is the pâté en croûte not symmetrical enough?"

He waved dismissively. "It will never be as symmetrical as I could make it. But that's the point. I want you to tell Angus that it's time he moved on."

"What do you mean, moved on? Like to another restaurant?"

"He wants to start his own right?"

"What are you going to do if he doesn't want to leave? Are you going to try to haunt him out of your kitchen?" Oh god, were we back at square one? Was Sené even worse than when I started?

"It's not my kitchen anymore," he replied, knocking me completely for a loop. He gave me a sardonic grin. "What? You're the one who told me that. I needed a few days to process it, but you were right. It's never going to be my kitchen again. Even that week that you were telling them my every word, something wasn't right. It was the lack of me."

Typical self-absorbed Sené. But this time, he was right.

"So, wait." Back up a second. "What exactly do you want me to tell Angus?"

10

THE CREW HAD nearly finished wrapping up lunch service when Celeste entered the kitchen. I struggled to keep a broad smile from taking over my face. I'd just seen her this morning, yet here I was like a dog, ecstatic that its owner returned from getting the mail.

Calm down, Angus, I told my thudding heart, but it was useless.

I zeroed in on Celeste's serious expression. "What's wrong?"

"I'm here with Sené," she said, in full embodiment of a professional medium. "He has a message for you. Can we talk in your office?"

"Uh, sure. Daniel, can you oversee these last orders?"

"I got it, Chef."

With barely concealed trepidation, I followed Celeste into the office. She closed the door behind us.

"So, Sené's had some time to think after the last revelation here."

I blinked at her, not following.

"About you starting your own restaurant."

"Oh." It caught me off guard, but I could catch up quickly. "I don't need to start that anytime soon. I know I'm needed here at Savoir."

"Sené says you should start it now."

That hit me like a punch to the gut, worse than his cajoling of my mistakes through the burners. "He's giving up on me? He wants me out of his restaurant?"

"Angus, this is your dream. Don't put it on hold for something that no longer exists. Sené was focused entirely on himself, but what he wanted was impossible. What you want is possible. I think that's why he left the way he did last week." She glanced to the side. "I'm not armchair therapizing you. I'm calling it like I see it. Alright, alright, fine! No more commentating." Turning back to me, she continued, "I'm going to repeat Sené's words verbatim now."

"Sené, I'm sorry I've been such a disappointment," I cut in. "But I thought the week with Celeste really helped. We were doing things right. You didn't have any feedback for us in the last few days."

"I'm not disappointed in you, Angus. Not really. You've been a convenient punching bag. I'm disappointed I'm dead. That Savoir will never be the same without me. That means Savoir is dead."

"I can keep it alive. Please, give me another chance."

"Angus, let go of Savoir. I finally have."

I stared at the ground, angry tears burning the back of my eyes. "So that's it then? You want me out of here." I couldn't believe a ghost was firing me. Through the woman I slept with, no less.

"I want you to stay." Celeste's words were gentle. Sené was never gentle, yet for some reason, I didn't doubt she was staying true to her promise to interpret only. "Savoir is mine, and it dies with me. But the kitchen and the restaurant are yours. You can make it into whatever you want."

"What if I want to keep it Savoir?"

Celeste cocked her head. "You want to be some try-hard copycat version of me for the rest of your career? I thought you were more ambitious than that."

"I mean, not for the rest of my career," I mumbled. I never intended to throw away my own future restaurant. Merely put it on hold. But on hold till when?

"You want your own restaurant. Why wait? Why not start right now?"

"Well, the holiday season is ramping up. Not a good time to change a whole menu—"

Celeste threw her hands up in a signature Sené move. "A burnt soufflé has more give than you, obstinate oaf!" A twinkle of amusement lit her eyes, but she straightened her smile. "In the new year, then. Why not start implementing your own menu after the holidays?"

Why not? This obstinate oaf had no retort.

"I'm excited to see what you come up with," Celeste said for Sené.

"You might be ready to let go of Savoir. But what if I'm not? Why can't I do this on my own time?"

"Why can't you let go of Savoir? It was never even really yours."

"Because it's yours!" My voice grew dangerously close to cracking. "It's yours, and if I let it go, that would be like letting you go. And I'm not ready to do that yet."

Sené hadn't only made my life hell by haunting me. Learning under him was like being in military training. But that rigor made me who I was. I treasured every rare moment of prideful affection he showed me. One drop of validation could get me through a desert. Sené was dead now, but I still had a chance to make him proud while he was haunting the kitchen. That would be gone if he moved on.

I am an excellent chef because of Sené, but I'm not sure what I am without him.

"I don't ever want to forget you."

"P'tit gars." Celeste's French accent was terrible, but Sené's endearment came through anyway. "You have to let go and move on from me and Savoir. That's not disregarding my memory. It's honoring my memory. I'm proud of you. Of the chef you're becoming. Of the master chef I know you can be."

My vision blurred. "I miss you, Sené."

"I miss you too."

I reached across the counter. Celeste didn't move. But goosebumps dotted my arm as Sené's unseen presence lay his hand on top of mine.

11

Celeste

I HAD NEVER seen Angus so happy. His shoulders shook, yet the tears streaming down his face were those of a man finally set free.

"Thank you, Celeste."

I couldn't help but laugh as he picked me up and swirled me in a jubilant twirl. "I feel light. I feel—I feel like planning my own menu."

He put me down and began wiping the French recipes off his office whiteboard. "If this is really happening so soon, I need a fresh concept. We don't need to stay tied to Sené's French recipes. Do you have any crazy suggestions for me?"

I didn't. But when I opened my mouth to say so, he held up a hand.

"No, don't tell me. I don't need to rely on you for inspiration as I did with Sené. I have to feel it."

Energy poured off him in waves. I couldn't guess his next move. His quick kiss caught me off guard.

"I felt like doing that." He paused. "And now I feel like a fusion restaurant would be cool. Something that takes inspiration from cuisines around the world but recreates them using ingredients local to these mountains."

I giggled as he brushed another kiss on my cheek while reaching around me to scrawl the idea on the whiteboard.

"I'm going to try out my new recipes with the Bryson employees at the Christmas Eve party. Will you be my date?"

"Okay," I answered, caught up in his joyful mood.

"The menu should reference the earth," he said suddenly. "The source of all our food. I need to experiment." He moved to the fridge.

I laughed again. I couldn't stop laughing. Angus inhabited a world of creativity. I stepped outside to give him space. Sené stopped me on my way to the funicular.

"Thank you," he said simply, but the words held more gratitude than I had ever heard from him before. He didn't meet my eyes, as though embarrassed by his own vulnerability. "I'm sure Angus and I would have come to some kind of resolution eventually."

"Maybe," I conceded. "But I'm glad it could happen sooner." I smiled over my shoulder back at the kitchen. "I love seeing Angus like this."

Sené grunted, but I knew he felt the same.

"Don't change your mind now!" I warned him. "I'd better not hear of any more ghostly shenanigans in the kitchen."

"It was my idea for Angus to make Savoir into his own place," Sené responded, affronted. "It's his to do what he wants with it. If it fails, it won't be because of me."

"It won't fail." It couldn't. Not with sturdy, steadfast Angus behind it.

I took the funicular down the mountain and practically floated back to my apartment, high on thoughts of Angus. I thought he needed to leave Bryson House to find his dream, but I was wrong. And somehow, now that Angus had tethered himself even more to that place than ever before, I'd never seen someone so free.

He was going to be busy with the holiday season plus planning his new menu, but I hoped he'd still have some time to hang out with me. I didn't want to wait until the Christmas Eve party to see him again.

My smile slipped from my face as I caught up to my own train of thought and how needy I sounded. What was happening?

He asked me to be his date to the Christmas party.

And I said yes. And now all I could think about was him.

My key froze in the lock of my door.

I loved him.

The sudden and extreme shift from happiness to fear overwhelmed me. I couldn't process it.

I needed to turn the knob. Enter my apartment and get into bed. Hope this anxiety would subside if I held onto my pillow tight enough. But my muscles refused to cooperate. The only thing they wanted to do was run. My feet remained planted, but with significant effort.

Why was this so hard? Why could I barely hear my own thoughts?

There was nothing but the impending pain of getting my heart crushed, my dream life ripped out from under me.

I never got into my apartment. Didn't even pack my bag. My brain entered full panic mode, so my body did what it always did to protect me. Less than an hour later, I rode the bus out of town.

The screaming in my head subsided when I reached the highway, leaving me feeling cold and unbelievably stupid.

I was back where I was a year ago, as if I hadn't made any progress at all. If I could leave Yelp reviews for ghost therapists, Dr. Waltz would get one star. At least I could do one thing differently this time.

My phone didn't have much charge left, but I'd use it to do right by Sadie.

"Speak of the devil," she answered cheerily. "We were just talking about you—"

"Sadie, I don't have much battery, but I wanted to let you know I'm okay."

"What?"

"I'm leaving."

"Leaving? Wait—"

"I mean left." I took a steadying inhale. "I left."

A quiet voice said, "Give me the phone." Then Angus's baritone was right there. "Celeste? Are you okay?"

I jolted at his sudden voice, heart racing all over again. I focused on the evergreens passing my window. "I'm okay."

"You had to run?"

He spoke with such understanding. Like I had to go to the doctor's office, and his worrying about it wouldn't help the situation. "Yes."

"Do you want me to chase you?"

"No—"

"Wait. Anthropocene. Do you want me to chase you?"

"Anthropocene." The word came out choked. "No."

"Okay."

"I'm sorry for doing this. Again. You need to forget me. Focus on your restaurant. You need to spend time with people who can help you reach your goals. Not hanging around with a flight risk like me."

"I want to hang out with you," he said simply. "I want to play poker with you, even though you will always win every hand. I want to hear you moan when you eat something delicious. I like how you can ease the tension in a room simply with your presence. Like, even the ghosts are glad you're there."

"Angus—"

"I love that your favorite carol is 'I Want a Hippopotamus for Christmas.' I love how that is no one's favorite carol except for you. I love your paranormal shop dream. This town needs a paranormal shop. The crystal lady can't meet the demand on her own."

He took a breath. I needed to stop him, but if I opened my mouth, I'd be dealing with full-fledged sobs instead of silent tears.

"Maybe this is the worst possible thing to say at the worst possible time, but Celeste, I love you. And that's not going to stop, no matter how far away you run. I love y—"

I ended the call. The hand I pressed against my mouth sufficiently muffled my cries.

My battery completely drained, and the phone screen went dark in my hands.

12

Angus

I DISTRACTED MYSELF from how much I missed Celeste by working late in my office, including tonight. By the time I got home most nights, all I could do was toss and turn in bed, thinking of Celeste's lithe body next to mine. Some nights, I slept at my desk, the salt lamp acting like a nightlight, chasing away negative energies.

My lips twisted. I was now a full-blown crystal person.

West rapped on the doorframe of my office.

"Hey, sorry this was the only time we could meet," he apologized. "You know the holiday season craziness."

"You don't need to apologize. I completely get it."

"Still, hate that you had to stay back here so late."

I waved my hand. "Honestly, I would have been here anyway."

West took a seat. "So how have you been?"

"Fine. Good. Fine."

He regarded me skeptically but thankfully didn't ask anymore. I charged ahead with a change of subject.

"I'm planning some major changes to the menu. Would you like to take a look?"

"Sure. Happy to." After reading over the sheet, his eyebrows went up. "Wow, this is all new. Sounds delicious."

"It's not all French anymore. Do you think the board will have a problem with that?"

"Hey, man, you're the head chef. You have full control of the menu. I'm excited to see you really making it your own. Letting go of Sené's old stuff. I mean, he was good, but I think these changes are great."

I smiled, relieved at the positive feedback. "Thanks, man."

West held back a yawn, his eyes watering.

"You should go to bed," I said. "Sorry to keep you up if this meeting could have been an email."

"Hey, this isn't a meeting. I want to catch up with you." West blinked but couldn't clear the sleepiness from his gaze.

"It's okay. We'll catch up later. Get back to Nic."

He blushed, clearly wanting to curl up, not only in his bed, but with her in his arms.

I turned to my salt lamp so West wouldn't catch any jealous flare in my eyes. Those two had been circling each other for years. Everyone at Bryson House was glad to see them finally together and happy. Celeste and I had known each other for a fraction of the time, but I wanted what they had. And I wasn't going to get it.

"That's cool. Is it new?" West asked, attention drawn to the orange glow of the lamp.

"Yeah. I got it to remind myself of efflorescence. Letting go of things that don't serve me. Focusing on what I can control."

Like this restaurant. And not on a woman who skipped town at a moment's notice. The thought of her made my heart race, and not in a good way. In an I've-spent-the-night-with-her-in-my-arms-and-will–never-sleep-again-without-her kind of way. But I had to let her go. And if she really was meant to set down roots here in Summer Springs, then she'd be back. One day. And the only hope of us rekindling something again was if I used efflorescence on the anxiety and ache her departure left me with.

West paused thoughtfully. "That's a good philosophy. God knows I've been working on that myself."

"It's been a lot harder than I thought."

West laughed. "Preaching to the choir. Something that helps me is this thing my mom said." He pressed his lips together. "Do I sound like a total dweeb, referencing my mom?"

I chuckled and shook my head. It was nice that West's family was close. Not only proximately. I can't remember the last time I felt close enough to my mom to have a vulnerable conversation.

"She told me about how much pressure she felt to hang on to me, protect me, especially after what happened to my dad. But eventually she had to learn to let go. To accept she couldn't control everything and trust that things would be okay."

I nodded. "That makes a lot of sense. Your mom is a wise woman."

"Don't tell her that. I'll never hear the end of it."

I walked West out. I could head home, too. Fall into bed. Try not to let the stress of everything keep me up. "Thanks for talking to me. Now I need to ensure that I can source the ingredients for the new menu and train the staff on it, so we're ready for the New Year launch. I've got a ton to prepare."

"Don't stress. It'll work out."

"Not without me working at it, though."

"Of course. But you can't force things. Do your best and trust that what is meant to work out, will."

Thoughts of Celeste plagued me on the drive down the mountain. Worries about where she slept. What she wore. Sadie told me that she left all her stuff at her apartment. Was that a good sign? Did it mean she would be back soon? And if she did return, what did that mean for us?

I let out a long breath and recalled the glow of the lamp. The words of West's mom.

By the time I got home, my mind had quieted enough that the moment my head hit the pillow, I was out like a light.

13

Celeste

THE SUN HAD risen a good hour ago, yet the lights on Reno's "The Biggest Little City in the World" sign still flashed. The ghost walking along the street swung his pocket watch with each step of his spat-covered boots. He didn't notice I could see him and so didn't acknowledge me. I took it as a good omen. Summer Springs was too small. Everyone knew everyone. Everyone knew me. Reno was a good-sized town. I knew some people. Okay ghosts. They were excellent clients, haunting the busier casinos on South Virginia Street. They usually had low-stakes requests, and in exchange for my help, they'd assist me in collecting a tidy sum at the poker tables.

I walked over from my hotel in Midtown. That was my neighborhood, rife with psychics and crystal shops. No spaces available to lease yet, but it was only a matter of time. Then I could add my own paranormal shop in with the bunch.

A tweed-vested ghost, Taylor Bowers, waved from the door of the Silver Legacy Resort Casino. I braced myself before approaching.

"Is Jessie around?" I asked him.

"I wanted to talk to you alone."

Jessie and Taylor had an ongoing bet about the Soul of Reno, and had tasked me with surveying the living to determine the answer: Should Reno embrace its Wild West roots and lean into its vices, as free-spirited lady of the evening Jessie believes? Or should it let go of its history and lean into its potential of becoming a center of progress, arts, and growth, as the buttoned-up Taylor argued?

I felt very dumb asking tourists and locals alike. More than one person asked me where the camera was. Why else would I be conducting these street interviews if not for internet content?

I didn't even know when I could call the request completed. I wasn't delivering a personal message to a living relative. I was settling a long-standing argument between two bored ghosts. The only reason I agreed was that they both haunted a casino with arguably the best poker tables in town. And having two ghosts owe me meant double the chips I could sweep from suckers.

"Sorry, Taylor. According to the votes, Reno is a place for fun."

"That's what I thought you might say. But it's been bad timing," he insisted. "The Santa Crawl just finished. Most of the people you talked to were probably here for that. Of course, those drunkards are going to prefer the more debaucherous side of this beautiful city. If you were asking people during the StartUp Reno Convention, your results would align with my argument."

So, what was I supposed to do about it?

"When does the StartUp Reno convention happen?" I could give it another week in exchange for more table time with Taylor.

"Usually in September."

"No way! I'm not doing a year-long ongoing survey. I've done enough for you guys already. Take your answer and let's get to those poker tables."

He stopped me with a pleading expression before I blew past him. "Did you at least ask the people in South Reno? People who moved to that newly developed area will tell you how the city's growth and potential are what brought them here." He clasped his hands in front of him. "Please."

"Fine. I'll take the bus down and ask people today. Then this job is done." This stupid job that doesn't even make any real difference to anyone anyway. Whatever. Remember the paycheck.

"Taylor? What are you doing hanging out the door?" Jessie called from inside.

Taylor shooed me away before Jessie discovered us conspiring against her.

I boarded the next bus to South Reno and took a seat closer to the back. There were a handful of people on board, which dwindled to me and an older gentleman after a few stops. I glanced over at him sitting across the aisle. Didn't seem like a tourist. Also, not someone new to the city.

"Excuse me?" I asked.

He flinched then gaped at me with wide eyes.

"Do you mind if I ask you a kinda random question?" When he shook his head, I went on. "What do you think about Reno? Like at its core. Is it a product of its history and all those wild west vices? Or is Reno about the future? Innovation and progress?"

He blinked at me. "What is this about exactly?"

"I have two friends arguing about the soul of Reno." This was so dumb. It was one thing to interview random drunk tourists on the street, but I shouldn't be bothering this poor man on his commute. "Never mind."

"Well, wait, let me think about it for a minute."

The bus stopped. A couple got on and sat a few rows in front of us. It wasn't until the bus began moving forward that the man continued.

"Well. It's both, isn't it? Reno can't let go of its history, like none of us can let go of our history. But we shouldn't let history define our potential. Especially if what we want is to grow past what our history makes us think is our limit. We aren't limited. Not until we are dead anyway."

"That's true." Leave it to an old man on a bus to impart his words of wisdom. Maybe I could convince Taylor and Jessie to drop this silly debate.

"What's true?" the guy in the couple turned around.

"What he said. About the soul of Reno being both its history and its future."

The young man glanced around and smirked at me while his female companion pushed the "stop" button on the pole.

"And what's that?" he continued with the air of a scientist observing an insect.

I blinked at him, putting together the pieces, but before I could respond, his girlfriend pulled at his arm until he stood, practically dragging the guy to the doors as the bus slowed down.

"Babe, relax. Have you never ridden the bus before? She's harmless."

Then they left, and the bus moved on with only the driver and me.

I turned to the old man. "You're a ghost."

He nodded with a sad smile. "And a ghost's future is very much determined by their past. Much more than for the living." He gestured to the surrounding empty seats. "We are bound to our haunting grounds. I had never wanted to set down roots, so I moved from place to place during my life. One heart attack later, here I am. I got what I wanted, I guess. I'm constantly on the move."

"Riding the same route over and over?"

He cringed. "Picking one place felt too much like giving up my freedom. But in the end, my place of rest was chosen for me."

The bus halted, and the driver called back, "Last stop."

"Go on now," the ghost said. "Don't stay stuck on this bus like me."

On uneasy legs, I disembarked and sat at the bus stop bench to steady myself. This feeling was more than the usual unsettled and annoyed sting I got when I talked to a ghost, thinking they were a living person. I kicked at the fluff of a dandelion sprouting out of a crack between the bench leg and the pavement. Its seeds scattered on the breeze.

Deep breaths did little to ease the deepening pit in my stomach as I imagined being trapped in Reno forever. My little paranormal shop would fit in just fine, but it would be one of many. No one would care about yet another medium on the block. Here, a few people might know me, but I wasn't special to anyone.

I'd tried to convince myself over the past few days that this was the place for me. Now I couldn't escape the truth. It stood as solid as the wooden seat beneath me. I didn't want to set down roots in Reno. I didn't want to keep flitting from place to place until death chose my haunting grounds for me. Like a seed dropped wherever the wind stopped.

I pulled out my phone and stared at the last texts between me and Sadie. We hadn't spoken since our call. I kept meaning to text her my plans to settle in Reno, but something kept stopping me. I think I finally knew what it was.

I wanted to choose Summer Springs as my ground. That was where Sadie was. It was where my favorite ghosts in the country were.

It was where Angus was.

Angus didn't only make me feel good; he listened to my stories about growing up and gave back something more than pity. More than outrage. He saw me. And accepted me.

And loved me.

So, of course, I fucking panicked. What else could I do in the face of that stupid, perfect man I loved back?

I was so scared to try to build something real with him, just to have it inevitably blow up. But that wasn't the worst-case scenario. I was living the worst-case scenario right now.

I didn't want to be afraid of trying. If things didn't work out with us, it didn't have to drive me out of town. If Summer Springs was my true home, then I didn't have to put so much pressure on any single relationship. It wasn't like when I was a kid, and a falling out with a family meant leaving for another part of the country. I was an adult, and I chose what to let destabilize my whole life.

The bus to Downtown approached from the other side of the street. I hurriedly got up and crossed to the northbound stop. I didn't have anything important at the hotel. I needed to get on the next bus out of this town. Because as fun as Reno was, full of potential, growth, and psychic businesses, it wasn't Summer Springs.

I'd finally had enough of traveling.

It was time to go home.

14

Celeste

Bryson House glowed especially bright with holiday spirit. The stands outside the hotel tempted me with their dispensers of mulled wine. But I needed complete control more than I needed liquid courage.

The hotel brimmed with guests and ghosts alike, milling in and out of the common areas. I spotted George near his usual haunt by the library.

"I'm glad to see you back," he said. "I still owe you for your help with my granddaughter."

"Continue keeping Sené out of the kitchen, and you can consider us square."

He smiled. "I think I can manage that for at least the next fifty years. No promises after that, though."

"That'll do."

A closed sign hung on the door of the restaurant. I could hear the muffled sounds of the staff party. Not all the employees were present, though. The rest of the hotel had to run, so West manned the front desk. He greeted me with a smile.

"Hey, Celeste. They're all in the restaurant. Go on ahead."

He said it casually, like there was never a question that I would make it.

I wasn't staff. He must have assumed I was Sadie's plus one. Angus wouldn't have kept me as his invite after our last call. Would he?

"Hey, West. You don't get to attend the party?"

"I'm switching out with Hunter at nine. And Nic is bringing me plates in the meantime."

Nic came up the hallway with a dish piled high with bites from a cheese platter.

"You're a Christmas Angel!" he said, taking the plate off her hands and giving her a peck. She blushed at the PDA and glanced at me. "Hi, Celeste."

"Hey. Merry Christmas." But I didn't stay to chit-chat. The couple clearly wanted a bit of time alone, and I had stalled long enough.

Sadie saw me first as I walked into the room, her smile wide and beaming. She left Clive's side to hug me. At least one of us had figured out their Christmas romance.

"I knew you'd come back soon," she said.

"You didn't think I'd take another year before returning with my tail between my legs?"

"You can't stay away that long. Not anymore."

She glanced over my shoulder, and I turned. Angus had come out of the kitchen and placed a fresh platter of food on the buffet table.

He stared in our direction.

This was my chance to explain myself. I needed to walk forward. Go on foot, take at least one step.

Angus went back into the kitchen.

Was he running from me?

I stomped after him. Was he trying to give me a taste of my own medicine?

"Hey, I don't run away to hurt you," I said. "And I know that it's hurtful. But you running just to stick it to me is childish."

He regarded me over his shoulder with an amused expression. "I wasn't running from you." He shifted so I could see past him. "I only had a minute before I had to be back to stir this sauce. Or it would burn. You, on the other hand, I figured could wait." He took the sauce off the burner. "Only fair considering how long you made me wait."

I blushed. "Okay, so I would have been back sooner, but there was a bus delay."

"I'm not talking about these last two weeks."

"It was closer to ten days," I murmured.

"I'm talking about the last year." His steely eyes held mine. He'd been waiting for me for so long.

But I was ready now.

"I'm sorry I ran. I don't want to. I want to stay. I want to plant roots and grow here. With you." I fidgeted through my vulnerability. "I understand if you are done waiting. My tendency to flee requires an unreasonable amount of patience, and I don't blame you if you don't want to be with someone like me."

"I want to be with you," he said. "You may not see it, but you give more in this relationship than you take. I know I can cook without you next to me, but you inspire me. You take everything on so fearlessly, and I need more of that in my life. More taking on the unknown and less clinging to what feels safe."

"I'm only like this because nothing has ever felt safe enough to cling to." I pushed through the discomfort of going full honest. It felt as if I was removing not only my clothes but my skin and bones. Letting him see to the very core of who I was.

He stepped forward and cupped my face. "If you have to run again, I won't take it personally. I only hope to be the person you can feel safe returning to."

I blinked away tears. "You didn't let me finish. I'd never felt anything was safe to cling to until you." I wrapped my arms around his waist and buried my face in his chest. "You are the strongest, most steadfast person I've ever met. You're organized and methodical in a way I can only dream of being. I know I need that if I'm ever going to open my own shop. But I do not doubt that you'll be able to succeed. You'll open a whole chain of restaurants and be a world-renowned top-class chef."

He laughed and hugged me like he would never let go, and I didn't feel trapped by the embrace. I was solid. Grounded.

"You'll open that shop," he said. "You can do even more than that. Whatever you want, you can achieve."

He spoke with such assurance and strength; I couldn't help but believe him. Even though the voice at the back of my head still whispered that this could all easily fall apart, right now, we were here together, and running was the last thing on my mind.

This man. This town. These ghosts. It was all so right.

Almost as right as Angus's fingers grazing my throat. Cupping the back of my head. Our kiss, deep and certain.

I didn't want a hippopotamus for Christmas this year. This year, I wanted Angus.

And by some miracle, I got him.

About the Authors

Chanel Schwartz writes small-town, character-centric contemporary romance with a focus on mental health.

chanelschwartz.com

Jessica Krueger is a scientist of hearts and molecules, who writes genre-blending romance where fantasy meets danger and desire.

authorjessicakrueger.com

Emelia Stonefield writes fantasy romance for people whose love of adventures didn't end at twenty-five.

emeliastonefield.com

Cassandra Trevelle, inspired by the stories that shaped musical theatre, writes contemporary romance and romance suspense retellings of those classic tales.

cassandratrevelle.com

Published by Kissing Booth Books
kissingboothbooks.com